DOCTOR MALLORY

ALAN HART (1890-1962), assigned female at birth, was born in Hall's Summit, Kansas, the only child of Albert and Edna Hart. After his father died when Hart was two, Hart and his mother moved to Albany, Oregon, where his mother remarried. As a child, Hart dressed and regarded himself as a boy. He attended Albany College (now Lewis & Clark), transferred to Stanford, then returned to Albany and graduated in 1912. He graduated from the University of Oregon Medical School (now Oregon Health & Science University) in 1917 with the highest honors. In medical school, Hart wore the required skirts for women but masculinized his appearance by wearing men's coats and collars. After graduating, he persuaded a doctor to perform a full hysterectomy on him, making Hart the first trans person in the United States to receive gender-affirmative surgery. Afterward, Hart cut his hair short, wore only men's clothing, and changed his name to Alan L. Hart. While living in Washington state during the Depression, Hart published four socially-conscious novels (*Doctor Mallory, The Undaunted, In The Lives of Men*, and *Dr. Finlay Sees It Through*), all medical dramas set in the Pacific Northwest. In 1948, he and his wife, Edna Ruddick, moved to Hartford, Connecticut, where Hart earned a master's degree in public health from Yale. Hart dedicated the rest of his professional life to tuberculosis research and was one of the first doctors to document how tuberculosis was transmitted and how it could be slowed by detection. Hart and his wife lived together in Connecticut until Hart's death from heart failure in 1962.

ALEXANDER HOUSTON (they/he) is a writer, educator, and community organizer in Portland, Oregon. Their work focuses on literature, queer/trans studies, and youth empowerment. Alongside his academic and literary work, they direct programs for LGBTQ+ youth that center belonging, creativity, and care.

DOCTOR MALLORY

ALAN HART

Foreword by
ALEXANDER HOUSTON

NORTHWEST
COLLECTION
Portland, Oregon

ABOUT THE RESTORATION

An existing pdf of *Doctor Mallory* was photographed and scanned to create a new digital manuscript. Errors created in the scanning process, as well as flaws in the original pdf (missing, damaged, or blurred passages) were checked against an archival copy of *Doctor Mallory* held in the Watzek Library at Lewis & Clark College. The restoration is the original published version of the novel, including orthography and punctuation of the era, except for a small number of typographical errors in the original that have been corrected.

Restoration supervisor: Dan DeWeese
Rights and permissions coordinator: Madison Rogers
Digitization process: Madeline DeWeese
Proofreading and process correction: Sean Gentry

SPECIAL THANKS

Special Collections, Aubrey R. Watzek Library, Lewis & Clark College; Steve Duckworth, Manager, Historical Collections, Oregon Health & Science University.

THIS IS A NORTHWEST COLLECTION TITLE
PUBLISHED BY PROPELLER BOOKS
4325 NORTHEAST DAVIS STREET, PORTLAND, OR 97213
www.propellerbooks.com

Photo credits:
"Historic District of Gardiner from Steamboat Island" and "Boathouses on the Lower Smith" by Aëron Blackman. Full license: https://creativecommons.org/licenses/by/3.0/
"USA Oregon Dunes" by Rebecca Kennison. Full license: https://creativecommons.org/licenses/by/3.0/
Photo of Alan Hart courtesy Dr. Alan L. Hart collection, Lewis & Clark College Special Collections and Archives, Portland, Oregon.

Cover and interior design by Dan DeWeese

ISBN 978-1-955593-12-0

THE NORTHWEST COLLECTION is a series of titles that represent the rich literary history of the Pacific Northwest, published in editions featuring introductions and insights from contemporary writers.

FOREWORD

Alan Hart's *Doctor Mallory* first appeared in 1935, quickly becoming a bestseller for W.W. Norton. At once a small-town novel and a study of gender, medicine, and belonging, it also carries traces of its author's own complex navigation of identity and profession. Hart—a physician and novelist we might now call a transgender man—had spent years establishing himself in medical practice while living under constant scrutiny of his gender presentation and professional competence. This lived experience of performing masculinity in high-stakes environments profoundly shapes *Doctor Mallory*, creating a novel that examines how men are made, sustained, and sometimes transformed by the pressures they face.

From the beginning, Hart stages masculinity as something both rehearsed and urgently chosen. The novel opens with Robert Mallory at ten years old: stocky, competent with horses, and spitting into the dust like hired men. But his bravado collapses into vulnerability when he asks a local doctor, "How long does it take to get to be a doctor?" Young Robert's insistence that he already knows a doctor is what he wants to be ("I don't think so. I know it!") is not only the declaration of a future career, but an early performance of manhood itself, rooted in work, certainty, and a desire to be recognized. That blend of posturing and longing haunts the novel. For Hart—who the University of Oregon Medical School listed in its graduation file as "Hart, Lucille (aka Robert L.)" before he established his practice in Gardiner, Oregon, as Dr. Alan L. Hart—the performance of professional masculinity was both essential and exhausting. His protagonist inherits that double vision: masculinity here is never secure, always something to be proved.

As Robert grows, the costs of that performance come into sharp relief. In a harrowing night at the Rescue Home, he witnesses a sixteen-year-old girl nearly die in childbirth. Hart's medical background shows in the clinical precision of the scene, yet Robert's response explodes beyond professional detachment: "A baby illegitimate! Why not rivers and floods and winds and mountains, too?" The question shatters the logic of the sexual codes around him. For Robert, the work of being a man means siding with the vulnerable and refusing to let cruelty masquerade as morality. Hart does not sentimentalize him—Robert's indignation often coexists with pride and stubbornness—but he insists that another kind of masculinity is possible, one that stakes itself on care, protest against injustice, and the refusal to look away.

Hart proves equally penetrating about the contradictions men carry. Robert's friend Norman Reilly praises his devotion to medicine as "not a way to make a living, but a way to live." Yet Norman diagnoses Robert just as sharply: "half of him is caveman." This duality captures the novel's central tension—between the civilizing force of medical vocation and the primitive pull toward control and dominance. In one scene with Katherine, Mallory's physicality slips into a kind of blunt, domineering masculinity. Katherine reflects that his hand is "hard and thick and it made hers seem weak and useless," and although she doesn't resent that helplessness in the moment, it marks the relationship's imbalance. Later, during a movie date, his arm slacks and he simply falls asleep on her—his presence heavy, unrefined, almost oblivious. That tension between vocation and control, compassion and rigidity, threads through Robert's relationships, revealing masculinity not as a fixed identity, but as an ongoing negotiation between competing impulses.

Practicing small-town medicine, Mallory discovers, means navigating an intricate web of obligations and expectations where these internal struggles become public performance. In Glenwood, the fictional town on the Siltcoos River (rendered *Silticoos* in the novel) where Robert establishes his practice, everyone is watching: the "Sunshine Club" gossiping about the morals of teachers and doctors, patients weighing his competence against his youth, and friends ribbing him for his lack of polish. Drawing on his own experience practicing medicine in small Oregon towns during the 1910s and 1920s, Hart understands how characters contend with the demands of propriety, the pressures of public reputation, and the tension between private desires and communal norms. While the novel contains sharply observed portraits of women negotiating these constraints, Hart's most sustained attention falls on his male characters as they wrestle not only with illness, injury, and economic uncertainty, but with the constant, exhausting work of proving themselves as men. In moments when that performance falters—through vulnerability, moral doubt, or unmet ambition—the fragility of traditional masculine ideals become starkly visible.

Relationships between men become the primary stage for these tensions. Hart's characters do not abandon masculinity; instead, they inhabit it with an awareness of its constructed nature. This is masculinity seen both from within and at a critical distance, shaped by lived experience and conscious choice. Hart writes with deep affection for his characters but proves unflinching in showing the toll exacted by a model of manhood rooted in dominance, competition, and emotional restriction. Yet in the cracks of that rigid system, Hart allows other possibilities to surface. A knife fight defused without violence; grief carried openly rather than swallowed in shame;

tenderness at a dying woman's beside—these moments are fleeting and fragile, but they reveal masculinity otherwise. Robert dreams, finally, of building a hospital named The Haven, a name that encapsulates Hart's broader vision: strength not as a fortress but as refuge. The alternatives that surface in *Doctor Mallory*—whether fleeting acts of care, unexpected intimacy, or quiet refusals to escalate conflict—invite readers to imagine ways of being that rely on connection rather than control, and on strength that does not diminish others.

This Northwest Collection reissue arrives at a moment when such questions feel newly urgent. In our age of the "manosphere"—a sprawling network of online communities ranging from self-styled "men's rights activists" to more extreme "incel" forums—public conversations about masculinity often collapse into panic, grievance, and zero-sum thinking. These communities fixate on a perceived crisis: that traditional male roles are eroding, that women's gains necessarily come at men's expense, and that masculinity must be constantly reasserted through increasingly exaggerated performance. Beneath their rhetoric lies a deep insecurity about identity and worth—an anxiety remarkably similar to what Hart's male characters quietly endure.

Hart reminds us that this sense of masculine crisis is not new. Writing during the 1930s, when economic upheaval and changing gender roles challenged traditional masculine authority, Hart reveals masculinity as a shifting, contested terrain rather than a fixed inheritance. In the novel's world, the very pressures to perform manhood create the vulnerabilities men fear most. Robert's struggle to balance professional authority with emotional openness, his desire to protect without controlling, and his need to prove himself while remaining authentic—these conflicts mirror the impossible double-binds that fuel contemporary masculine anxiety. And yet, within these same conditions, Hart makes visible other possibilities: solidarities among men that resist hierarchy, moments of tenderness that do not read as weakness, and forms of resilience that thrive without constant performance.

These are not utopian answers. Hart does not present a perfected masculinity, but rather sketches experiments in living: partial, imperfect, and deeply human. What emerges is a vision of gender as something that can hold contradiction without breaking, and of strength as something expansive enough to include care, vulnerability, and mutual dependence. Where today's manosphere often retreats into rigid hierarchies and defensive posturing, Hart's characters model something different: ways of inhabiting masculinity that find their power not in what they exclude, but in what they dare to embrace.

In our current political moment—when discussions of gender are polarized, when transgender lives are under increasing attack, and when "the future of masculinity" is debated in bad-faith soundbites—*Doctor Mallory* offers a reminder that these conversations are neither new nor resolved. Hart's work calls on us to dismantle the conditions that make masculinity feel like a performance to be defended at all costs, and to imagine what abundance—emotional, relational, and communal—might look like if we refused that premise altogether. The result is a novel that speaks across nearly a century: a story from the past that still has the power to shape how we think about the future.

—Alexander Houston

DOCTOR MALLORY

CONTENTS

DOCTOR MALLORY

FORECAST

Down the long dusty path to the horse barn ran Robert Mallory, aged ten and a half, as fast as his short legs would allow him. Bursting into the stable where Dr. Farrar's driving horse was munching hay in the manger, the boy dragged up an old backless chair, climbed upon it, and retrieved a bridle from its peg high on the back wall of the barn.

"If I hitch up for him I'll have a good chance to ask him." Robert's lips moved as though he were reiterating to himself his determination to speak to the doctor. "I ain't scared of him. He ain't like the old doctor. He don't look cross. I'll just say to him…"

Being too short to reach the horse's head, the boy mounted the old chair again and slipped on the bridle with quick, accustomed fingers.

When Dr. Farrar reached the gate between the garden and barnyard, he was surprised to see his horse and red-wheeled buggy waiting for him. At the animal's head stood the small boy he had noticed a little earlier in the house. The lad drew in a deep breath and said, "He's ready for you, doctor."

Something about the eager attention in the bright blue eyes made Farrar look with interest at the small figure in front of him. His first impression was of solidity. He found attractive both the boy's compact stocky body with its straight square shoulders and his round red-cheeked face with very blue and very earnest eyes.

"Thank you, young man." Farrar looked from the youngster to the horse. "You see, I'm not very handy at harnessing and hitching up. In town I keep Captain in the livery stable and the men there take care of him and bring him around when I need him. But I suppose you know all about this sort of thing, don't you?"

"Sure," answered Robert. "Sure I do." His manner was entirely matter-of-fact. "I harness the teams every morning for the field and take care of 'em at noon and curry and feed and bed 'em down at night. That's my job. I get ten cents a week for doing that and pumping the water at the barn."

Then, recalling that perhaps the doctor had never enjoyed such excellent opportunities to learn the mysteries of harnessing and hitching up, young Mallory went on politely, "But I expect, livin' in town, you don't get much chance at horses."

"No," replied Farrar, "I don't. That's a fact. But aren't you pretty young to be doing this sort of work?"

The boy drew his body up to every inch of its possible height.

"I'm not so young," he protested. "I'm ten, goin' on eleven now." Robert spat into the dust at his feet just as he had seen the hired men do. "Last spring, at school, I licked Johnny Shier and he's prit near two years older 'n me." He stole a sidelong glance at the doctor. Of course he didn't know Johnny and that might account for the fact that his face remained unimpressed after this recital of achievement. But Robert decided to change the subject. He was anxious to lead up to the question he wanted to ask.

"That's a nice horse you got here," he observed in his most adult voice.

Farrar smiled genially at the lad, more entertained than ever.

"I'm glad you approve of Captain. He's a lazy bugger but when he feels like it, he can put the road behind him at a pretty clip. You're keen about horses, aren't you?"

"You bet! Aren't you?" The burning sincerity in the boy's manner left no doubt in the doctor's mind that he would think there was something terribly wrong with anyone who did not like horses.

"Yes. The longer I practice medicine among people, the better I like horses." Farrar laughed and held out his hand for the reins. "Well, I'll have to be getting along. There are sick people in town, too, you know. And I'm much obliged to you for hitching up for me."

But Robert Mallory did not surrender the reins. Instead he stared up at the doctor with the same concentrated attention that had attracted the man's notice at first.

"Can I ask you something?" he blurted out.

Dr. Farrar took his foot down off the buggy step and turned around.

"Of course. What do you want to know? I'll tell you if I can."

Sudden embarrassment flooded the boy's face with crimson. He realized that he had been talking in a way his mother would not approve: he had boasted of whipping an older boy, he had said "prit near" and "ain't" to a grown-up stranger, and he had not once said "sir" to him. And now he was about to ask a question that might well be considered impertinent.

Digging a bare toe into the sun-baked earth, young Mallory stole a hasty glance about him but the familiar scene that he saw— the big red barn, the pump-house and watering trough beside it, the long row of chicken houses and the orchard beyond them—gave him no inspiration for a substitute inquiry. With an effort he raised his eyes to the kindly face above him and plunged.

"How long does it take to get to be a doctor?"

With the question out at last, the boy continued to watch Farrar's face. For a moment the man smiled broadly but under the grave scrutiny of those bright blue eyes he quickly became serious again.

"Do you want to be a doctor, young man?"

"Yes, sir. I do. I *got* to be one!"

"Got to be one? I'm afraid I don't quite understand you."

"Well." The boy paused to gather his thoughts together. "Well, it's like this. All my life, ever since I can remember, I've wanted to be a doctor. I don't think mother'd like me to be one: she says it's a dog's life. So I never said anything to her about it. But I can't ever be anything else."

Robert marshaled his most convincing argument; he had found the adult mind extraordinarily obtuse in many things. "Every time I get a cold or have to stay in the house, I play hospital and operations. Pretend operations, I mean. And so I want to know how long it takes to learn to be a doctor and how you start."

Farrar sat down on the horse block and said, "Tie Captain up, young fellow, and come over here a minute. I want to know more about this. How old did you say you are?"

"Past ten, goin' on eleven. But I'm strong. Just feel my muscle."

The boy doubled up his arm and offered it for Farrar's inspection.

"That's the biceps, ain't it, doctor? I read about it in the physiology at school."

Farrar's fingers rested on the arm for an instant.

"Um-m-m. Yes, that's the biceps all right. You're getting a start on anatomy, I see. . . . What's your name? I can always talk to a man better when I know his name."

"Robert Truscott Mallory…sir." He had almost forgotten the "sir" again. "But I don't use the Truscott. I don't like it."

"And you think you want to be a doctor?"

"I don't think so. I know it!"

The passion that rang out in that answer startled Farrar. His memory flickered back to a classmate of his who had had that sort of sureness about his choice of a profession. Through terrible hardships and poverty that man had persisted in studying medicine and now he was professor of surgery in Pittsburgh. But men who had seen him recently said he was old, worn out before his time.

"…and I've learned the physiology book by heart…almost."

"That's more than most of the doctors could say." Farrar sighed. "But what was it you said a while ago about playing hospital and operations?"

"Well, I fix the chairs in rows for beds and then I tie the cats onto them as far as they'll go. I use the dogs too when Mother'll let me bring 'em into the house. When I was little a long time ago, I had some dolls and I used to operate on them until all the sawdust leaked out and they're no good." Robert wondered why grown people always had to know so many irrelevant things. "If I was a girl I could get some more dolls and that would be handier than the cats."

"I see. And do you cut up the cats too, may I ask?" Farrar's voice held astonishment as well as amusement.

"Oh, no. Mother won't let me." The boy shuffled his feet in the hot dust. "I just cut off their hair in patches and pretend it's been an operation. That's the best I can do."

Farrar looked at the boy with the memory of that classmate, who had been so sure of his calling strong within him. He had had a fearful struggle and had finally reached the top. But suppose this boy were to have only the struggle without the reward. If he studied medicine he would be in perpetual bondage to people and to sickness. And yet…

"Well, Robert, I'll tell you about this business. Getting to be a doctor isn't easy any more. You'll have to finish the school here first and then come to town and go through high school. After that you'll have to take a year or two in college before you can enter medical school. It takes four years to go through medical school and the chances are that by the time you graduate you'll have to put in a year in a hospital before they'll let you practice. You're past ten now. By the time you're a full-fledged doctor ready to start out for yourself, you'll be about twenty-seven years old."

Into the boy's eyes came a look of astonishment but they did not waver.

"Gee whiz, that's a long time. Seventeen years from now! Why that's longer 'n I've lived yet, in my whole life!"

"I know," nodded Farrar gravely. "But you'll need every minute of it if you're going to be a real doctor."

"How old are you?" There was not the least trace of impudence in the query.

"Thirty-nine. I graduated when I was twenty-one. But that was in '79 and the course is longer now and a lot harder."

Robert Mallory, thinking hard, leaned against the hitching rack. With a searching look at him, the doctor got up, untied his horse, and climbed into the buggy.

"Better think over what I've told you, young fellow, and don't be in a hurry to make up your mind. You've got lots of time. When I come out the last of the week to call on my patient in the house, I'll bring along my old physiology for you to look through. How would you like that?"

The boy looked up eagerly. "I'd be much obliged," he answered.

Farrar settled the lap robe about him and tightened the reins over the horse's back.

"Climb in and ride down to the gate with me, won't you? Get up, Captain. Show the young man here how you can travel when you want to."

When he drove out of the lane into the road, the doctor leaned back in his seat and called out, "Goodbye, Robert. Glad to have had a talk with you."

"Good-by, sir." Young Mallory, having closed the gate, climbed up on the cross-piece and hung over the top. "You won't forget the book, will you, when you come again? The physiology, I mean."

"No. I won't forget." Farrar touched Captain lightly with the whip and drove briskly away.

The boy, left behind, clung to the gate and stared down the road after the doctor. Seventeen years! That was a long, long time. He would be a man grown then, almost thirty years old.

For an instant his old dread that he would never be tall returned. But not for a moment did his courage quail. If it was going to take that long, the sooner he started the better.

With purpose in his stride he went back to the barn and a few minutes later was calling "Kitty, kitty, kitty" in his most beguiling tones.

PART ONE

CHAPTER I

On a warm day in the spring of his junior year in medical school, Robert Mallory, clad in a dirty surgical gown, was sitting before a long wooden tray on which rested an object which the experienced student of anatomy would have recognized as part of a human body. To his left lay a battered copy of Cunningham's manual of dissection and at his right a doughnut from which he had just taken a bite was stuck on the end of an upright, sharpened stick fastened to the side of the tray.

Another young man whose curly blond hair was brushed straight back from his forehead without a parting leaned against the wall nearby. His face was softer in outline than Mallory's, his features less rugged, his eyes less interested; he regarded his companion with the respect due a brilliant student. Both men were finishing their third year in medicine but the numerous carefree hours Norman Reilly had spent during the past winter in the company of Gerty Mannering, dancer, rather than in study, had driven him to seek tutoring in surgical anatomy from his more studious classmate.

In front of them stretched tiers of doors from floor to ceiling. Behind these doors, in cold storage, lay the bodies left over from the year's work in the dissecting room. Robert Mallory, student assistant in the department of anatomy, was at this moment demonstrating the floor of the female pelvis for Reilly's benefit.

"Better get down here a little closer, Norman, if you want to see anything," grumbled Mallory in a deep, rumbling baritone. "You've got to get your nose into it to work out the layers of the pelvic floor. It's complicated as hell."

Reilly kicked a stool toward the tray, squatted down on it, and tucked his gown carefully about his legs.

"Getting my nose into it is just what I don't like," he objected. "Mary's pelvis doesn't smell as good as it did two or three years ago when she was fresher."

"Old Prof. Acheson won't give a damn about the smell, Norman. And he's sure to put at least one long question about the pelvic floor in the final. It's only two weeks until the examination, remember."

"Oh, very well then, wiseacre. Lead on. And where you lead me I will follow. What are you digging at now? Where's the book? Here goes. 'The perineal body is a pyramidal structure composed of fat and…'"

For fifteen minutes Reilly droned on, looking up from the text now and then to follow Mallory's dissection; then he laid the book down.

"Good God, Bob, how can you eat that damned doughnut down here? I'm not what you'd call squeamish but I couldn't swallow a bite of that sinker to save my soul."

Mallory laughed and laid down his forceps and seeker.

"Don't forget that I've been tinkering with these stiffs down here all year, to say nothing of my three regular semesters of dissecting. I've got used to them, Norman. Whew, my back aches! Been humped up here on this stool too long." He got up and stretched his stocky body to its full height and threw his arms about. "But let me tell you, boy, I didn't feel that way about corpses when I started in here. I'd never seen a dead man in my life except in a coffin dressed up for his own funeral until that morning we went up to the dissecting room in our Freshman year. Remember that day, Norman?"

"Do I?" answered Reilly. "Here's one fellow that won't forget that morning if he lives a thousand years! Twenty stiffs, stark naked, all lying on nice soft warm stone tables. Talk about a shock to the nervous system. That was a whole charge of dynamite to mine. It was three months before I really felt easy up there and I don't think I'd enjoy it after dark even now. I know I had a hell of a time holding my breakfast, especially after the guy across the table lost his. It was a relief when Old Man Acheson passed around the vaseline and got us busy greasing up the bodies."

Having first impaled another doughnut on the upright stick Mallory sat down to work again.

"Well, it's a good thing you've got plenty of money so you don't have to get one of these jobs like mine to pay your tuition. I've got to be pretty intimate with the dead down here but, even when a fellow's used to it, it is spooky at night injecting blood vessels and shifting stiffs around in the icebox to get out new ones for the classes upstairs. . . . Begin with the pudendal artery, will you? I had the blasted thing out here once but now I've lost it again. If I don't get the relations of the pelvic floor pounded into my head pretty soon, I'll be flunking Acheson's exam myself."

"Like hell you will!" grunted Reilly. "If you don't know the layers of the pelvic floor, that's the only thing in anatomy you don't know. If I knew half as much as you do…I should worry! Now pin back your ears, Bob, and listen to the fascinating tale of the pudendal artery. Once upon a time there was a little blood vessel that got lost in the female pelvis."

"Lay off the foolishness, Norman. Go straight through that section. And when you've finished that you might stick up another doughnut for me. Your hands are cleaner than mine."

"Didn't you have breakfast this morning, Bob?"

"No," replied Mallory in what Reilly called his none-of-your-business-manner. "Didn't have time."

At four o'clock Reilly threw down the manual and his notebook and stretched his legs.

"How about knocking off for the day, Bob? I'm stiff as a poker, squatting here on this cock-eyed stool since half past eleven. And God knows what time you got here this morning. Besides, I've got a date with Gerty to-night—a party after the show. We're going to play roulette and take money away from some fellows that think they're wise guys. Come on, boy. Let's put Mary back on the ice till to-morrow."

Mallory rose slowly and opened the refrigerator door.

"Well, I think you ought to know the pelvic floor well enough now to get by." The barest trace of doubt lingered in his voice. "You'll be all right if you don't get mixed up about the origin of the levator ani. But if you want to, it's O.K. with me to quit. I wouldn't mind going and getting something to eat. I'm fed up on these damn doughnuts."

Reilly helped push the tray into the icebox.

"It's been a mystery to me for three years now why you don't die on this diet of yours. One meal a day and doughnuts. That's enough to kill even you."

The two young men began peeling out of their dirty gowns and washing up.

Mallory was stocky and thick-chested, short of his hoped-for six feet by three inches. The incipient burliness of his figure was relieved by his bold rugged features and crisp, straight chestnut brown hair, and the heaviness of his face was redeemed by the bright blueness of his eyes. Reilly was shorter and slighter and, whereas Mallory's clothes were always nondescript and baggy, Reilly wore his expensive tailored suits with an air of accustomed awareness.

When they came out the basement door of the medical school building, Reilly swung himself into the low seat of a Stutz Bearcat, parked by the curb.

"Better climb in, Bob, and let me take you wherever you're going."

"Would you mind dropping me at Thirteenth and Pine? I can catch a car there that'll take me straight down town. I'm bound for the Bee Line Cafeteria and I'm going to put away sixty cents' worth of meat and potatoes and gravy so fast it'd make you dizzy. You're not the only fellow that can have a night out, Norman."

Mallory paused in packing the bowl of his bent-stem pipe and grinned.

"That makes me think," said Reilly, pulling a bill fold out of his pocket. "What do I owe you this far? To-day finished the first week's cramming. I want to pay you now before I lose all the money I've got on that roulette wheel of Gerty's. Speak up. How much?"

"Oh, I don't know," muttered Mallory. "I don't like to take pay from you. I don't think I'm really teaching you anything."

"The hell you're not!" exclaimed Reilly. "Now don't get my Irish riled up, Bob. This last week down in the basement with you I've learned more anatomy than I did in three semesters upstairs. You not only know the stuff yourself but you tell it to me in words of one syllable so I can understand it. I'll flunk the exam if you don't go on with me, and I won't accept tutoring from you for nothing. So that's the end of this argument. How much, I repeat. How much?"

Mallory squirmed in his seat and fumbled with a match.

"Oh, three and a half, I guess. . . . Thanks, Norman."

"Now go on a splurge, Bob. Get ten cents' worth of ice cream to top off the potatoes and gravy, or go to a movie. That Pickford girl with the long curls ought to be about your speed. At the Columbia."

When Reilly let him out on the corner of his choice Mallory watched the roadster out of sight with a questioning face. Soon after undertaking to tutor Norman, doubt had assailed him. Was Reilly getting anything out of this cramming? Did he, as a matter of fact, need it as badly as he pretended? Or was he using it as a pretext to get money into his friend's pockets?

Mallory shrugged his shoulders and thrust his hands deep into those sagging and almost empty pockets.

"I should worry," he said to himself. "Cash runs through Reilly's fingers as though they were sieves. And what he gives me Gerty Mannering won't get."

CHAPTER II

"Hell's bells! What a night!"

Robert Mallory ran his fingers through his tumbled shock of thick, straight, brown hair and in unusual weariness stretched his arms full length above his wide, square shoulders.

"What'd you expect in a dump like this? You can't always have easy cases."

"Chuck" Brantner held out a packet of cigarettes. Mallory reached eagerly to help himself. The flaring match showed two tired young faces.

Side by side the men leaned against the porch railing, facing the east where a faint radiance was just beginning to border the upper rim of the valley. Mallory looked up presently at the taller, slimmer figure beside him.

"I don't expect to have easy cases always, Chuck. But a mess like this one to-night doesn't make me any keener about obstetrics. That girl had five minutes' fun, three months' vomiting, and then this! In a Rescue Home, of all places. Shrieking, blood, uproar, all of us fogging around like mad all night!" His eyes turned toward the vaguely outlined shrubbery on the lawn below them.

Brantner exhaled a cloud of smoke with a sigh so deep that it was almost a grunt.

"It could've been a God damn sight worse, though. She might've died. And I haven't lost a mother out here all year."

"That would have spoiled your record," said Mallory dryly. "And you're so proud of it. What gets me is that I'm in for this job next year—eight months of it."

"Well, you're a damn sight better prepared for it than most Junior medics. Let me tell you that," retorted Brantner. "You've been out here with me on every case I've had and I let you do more than Stockton ever let me when I was his assistant. I counted up a while ago. We've done forty-one deliveries in the Home since October and there are two more due before I graduate. And so far not one of them lost! That's what tickles me. Some record for my Senior year, eh boy? And a damn good nest-egg for you to start with, even though you don't appreciate it."

"Yes, if you feel that way about it." Mallory flicked off the ash and looked at the glowing end of his cigarette. "But I still think the whole thing is a God-forsaken, hellacious, damned job for everybody concerned, and especially for that washed-out rag of a girl in there! I'm not crazy over the prospect of this work next year."

"Oh hell, you'll get used to it." Brantner tossed away his stub. "Guess I'll have a look at our patient and then take a snooze. We can't get a car into town until six o'clock anyhow."

Except for the double windows to the right of the entrance, the Anne Morrison Memorial Rescue Home was in darkness. Before it stretched the soft, smooth sward that extended outward fifty feet to the highway. Mallory walked softly down the steps and on to the lawn; the thick cushion of grass was pleasant underfoot. He looked back at the building, saw a shadow move briskly across the lighted windows of the maternity room, and smiled; even Miss Jackson's silhouette on the window-blind managed somehow to seem angular and severe.

In spite of the fact that their patient had not died, Mallory was still depressed. True that they had been forced to send into the city for help and that, while they waited for the arrival of the professor of obstetrics, Brantner's self-confidence had cracked, but that wretched sixteen-year-old who had been down to the gates of death was alive. And her baby had lived too. A squalling lump of unwanted, red humanity. What was ahead of them, or—for that matter—of any of the twenty-five girls upstairs whose time had not yet come? Through the open casements of the upper floor Mallory thought he could hear the faint sounds they made in their sleep.

He shook himself and retraced his steps toward the building. Life seemed such a mess when he was out here at the Rescue Home. Two years ago, he remembered, he hadn't known such places existed.

Brantner was just coming out of the maternity.

"She's in pretty good shape, Bob, considering what she's been through. Her pulse is better and she's not flowing so much. I'm going to lie down awhile. There's still an hour and a half before the first car."

The two young men walked back along the corridor, through a door marked "Doctor," into a small room furnished with a smooth leather couch, three chairs of the Mission variety, and one ancient tattered upholstered armchair. On the wall was an old-fashioned telephone with a crank, beyond it the door into a washroom through which Brantner promptly disappeared.

Mallory flung himself into the decrepit armchair and pulled out a brown briar pipe. His shirt hung open at the neck and his sleeves were rolled high over thick muscular forearms.

"Yes, I think she's going to pull through," said Brantner, standing in the doorway wiping his hands. "I admit I thought it was all up with her for a while. Even Robinson, you noticed, looked down his nose when he first saw her. Nobody can sneeze at eclampsia. This is going to look good on the records." A smile broke over the thin hawk face. "Twenty-two convulsions, and alive and O.K. Besides, it was good for you to be in on a case like this, Bob. You might've gone for a long time before you saw another like it."

Mallory scratched a match loudly.

"Oh, shut up, Chuck! You make me sick! All you ever think about is that damned record of yours. And you talk as though you'd arranged the whole thing for my benefit. Bah! You were scared as bad as I was, and you know it. How's your underwear this morning?"

"None of your damn business!" Brantner threw himself down on the couch. "Gimme a cigarette, will you? You'll admit, I suppose, that I never let on in there that I had the wind up. Out here a fellow has to remember to keep up a front. The girls don't know we're not full fledged doctors yet, and if they knew we were scared the nurses would go to pieces too. They can't realize like we do that it's perfectly safe, with the profs. on call for emergencies."

From the depths of the aged armchair in which he rested on the small of his back Mallory looked ironically at Brantner.

"You don't say so, Chuck! Now ain't that something? Everything perfectly safe! Well, well! . . . But it's that kid in there, that girl, that I can't get out of my head."

"Aw, pipe down, Bob. The girl was just obeying the laws of biology. What she did and what happened to her were perfectly natural." Slowly Brantner's face lost its look of interest; his words began to blur and run together; his lips sagged apart.

"I didn't say it wasn't natural," whispered Mallory as he bent forward, picked the smouldering cigarette out of Brantner's mouth, threw it on the floor and set his foot on it. Then he tiptoed across the floor, threw open the back window, and leaned out. He had been too close to death that night to relax as Brantner had done.

The air was cool and sweet on his warm skin, the morning stillness grateful to his ears that all night had been ringing with the tense sounds of travail. Across the garden he could see a grove of trees stark against the lightening sky. The world outside was beautiful; only inside were there pain and harshness and injustice. People, that was the trouble; people, with their worn-out notions of right and wrong. Building Rescue Homes in a fine glow of philanthropy so that the shame of girls might be ostentatiously covered with the cloak of blatant charity.

Robert Mallory might have said truthfully, like the cinema star of a later day, "I'm no angel," but in him there was a desire for something better. Now it flickered down and now it flamed high, but it never died out. With the secrecy of the young male about things spiritual, he concealed it from his fellows, partly from shyness and partly from an impulse to conformity. But this morning that fire burned brightly. He hated the injustice that made this Rescue Home necessary, that had brought into it a sixteen-year-old girl, that would brand her baby illegitimate. A baby illegitimate! Why not rivers and floods and winds and mountains, too?

It was not fair. Often the boy Mallory had resented with his fists whatever had seemed to him unfair whether it had been expedient to do so or not. The man Mallory felt the same impulse. Many emotions flooded over him as he stood by the window. Inarticulate, hazy emotions, but stirring, for all that. Somehow he meant to do something about all this injustice. He would stand for life against death, for light against darkness, for the weak against the brutal. He had helped to win that night; he would win in the nights to come. He would beat back death from his patients. Some one must always stand between life and death, keeping back the dark invader so that life could develop and find the good and the beautiful. He would be that someone. He would help make progress possible. He would be a defender of the gates of life behind which evolution might go on unhindered.

Mallory straightened himself. He was tired and his back ached. He was even vaguely aware that he was hungry. But he was too vibrant with aspiration, too full of wonder at the promise of his calling, too sure of his own election to the company of the defenders of life to think of sleeping or eating. Leaving the window open so that the early morning breeze might sweep across Brantner's thin, tired face, he stole quietly out of the room.

In the maternity he found Miss Jackson working over the new-born and engrossed in her task. Mallory went to lean on the foot of the mother's bed. Lying on her back without a movement except the slow heaving of her chest as she breathed, the girl was so thin and pale that he was almost ashamed of his own thick-chested robustness. Her mouth was a little open, her sallow face held not one fleck of color. Mallory counted her respirations, then went to the side of the bed and laid his square-tipped fingers gently on her wrist. Pulse almost normal. She was better, not a doubt of it, much better. She turned her head a trifle and her bluish lips puffed out with every labored expiration.

To Mallory she still seemed half dead. And she was too young to be there. When children got caught in belts and flywheels, somebody stopped the machinery and got them out, but no one did that sort of thing for these girls. And yet it was the same sort of situation. They were caught by a biological urge that was too strong for them to control; they were little girls, most of them, but they had to pay the price. Little girls, women's penalties!

Miss Jackson's brisk voice startled him. "Come and look at the baby, Dr. Mallory. Isn't he fine? Seven pounds, twelve ounces."

The nurse beamed upon the infant as though part of the credit for his excellent condition belonged by right to her.

Gravely Mallory looked down at the red wrinkled face with its closed eyes and barely parted lips; he slid his hand inside the blanket. The baby closed a fist on one thick finger. Liking for the firm softness of a baby's flesh flashed out in the man's quick smile.

"He's certainly a fine boy." The nurse repeated her pronouncement.

"Yes, he's a good-looking youngster." Mallory's voice was deep, quiet. "But what's going to become of him, Miss Jackson? What chance will he have in the world? I may be all wrong but I was just thinking that there's seven pounds, twelve ounces too much of him. It might've been better for him and his mother too if he'd been born dead."

"Why, Dr. Mallory, how can you talk that way? I'm surprised at you. We very seldom lose a baby in the Home. I'd have been broken-hearted if we hadn't pulled this case through. I'm sure we'll be able to find a good home for such a nice looking baby. Don't forget that he's in God's care. He'll have his chance."

"I hope so," answered Mallory. "I hope so. Because nobody else is going to give a damn about him, I'm afraid."

In his way of speaking there was doubtfulness as to the dependability of Providence in these matters, but in his eyes was the look of the tolerant adult who hesitates to spoil a child's faith in Santa Claus. If Miss Jackson really felt that way about it, it was better not to disturb her.

From the door Mallory looked back again. The bare whiteness of the room was repellent; life ought to begin in peace and beauty, not in a barren place like this. But of course Brantner's record for never losing a mother and the Home's record for seldom losing a baby were more important than what happened to either.

Save the mother. What for? To go back home and be whispered about and pointed at on the streets? Save the baby. What for? Only God knew. For one blinding instant Mallory saw the chamber of existence with walls pierced by many archways but by only two that led anywhere—birth and death. Through these there was one-way traffic. About this girl and her infant there was just one thing certain: having both been born, they must both die. There was no escape from that finality. True, he had helped to defeat death that night, had held the gates of life against him, had beat back the black destroyer. But it was not for long. Like fire, life is a triumphant, beautiful thing; but it is finally extinguished. Why? Mallory asked himself. Extinguished here only to spring up again somewhere else, and repeat the performance?

For his ignorance Mallory shrugged his shoulders and stole softly back into the doctors' room.

CHAPTER III

I

Reilly paused in the act of tying a white bow to shout "Come in."

Promptly the apartment door opened to admit Mallory. He wriggled out of his overcoat, tossed it on the table, and walked into Reilly's bedroom. In the doorway he paused and glanced uneasily down at his stiff shirt bosom which bulged alarmingly on the right. Having finally achieved a marvelous bow, Reilly turned around and looked his friend up and down. Dismay spread over his face.

"Good Lord, Bob, where did you get those clothes?"

"I rented 'em. I thought they looked pretty good but this damn shirt keeps flying open all the time. The buttonholes…"

"Bob, you look like a picture of what the well-dressed man will not wear. The seat of your pants hangs down a foot below the coat."

Bewildered by this onslaught Mallory looked down at his

shirt bosom and then craned his neck in a vain attempt to examine his posterior.

"I don't see anything much wrong except the shirt," he protested.

"Shut up. You don't know anything about clothes. Squat! Have a chair. *Sitzen Sie sich*. D'you understand? Gerty'd have a fit if I dragged in anything that looked like you do. Don't you even know enough not to wear a canned tie? I'll have to rustle you some duds, that's all."

Reilly went to the 'phone with that last withering remark and Mallory, much embarrassed, sat down stiffly on the edge of a straight chair. As he did so, his shirt front gaped open and discharged a button which hit the wall beside Reilly's head.

"Easy on the machine gun fire, there! . . . Hello. That you, Joe? Norman Reilly talking. Listen. I want you to bring a dress suit to my apartment. . . . Yes, that's what I said. Clawhammer. . . . Thirty-two waist. Forty. And thirty-four trouser length. That right, Bob? Yeah, thirty-four, Joe. . . . You do like I say and get these things up here right away. I'm a good customer of yours and I always pay your damn bills just as you send them, robber that you are. . . . And say, Joe, bring up a shirt too. One with a solid, one-piece bosom. Fifteen and a half. . . . All right, I'll be expecting you."

A trim, well groomed figure in black trousers and dress shirt, Reilly turned toward his friend, sitting dejectedly on the edge of a chair.

"God, wouldn't you be a sight for Gerty and her gang? One of those buttons would probably fly out the first thing and hit her in the eye. You don't want to destroy the lady's eyesight, do you? And when they were all out and your noble emphysematous chest showed through, think what a strain on the girls' maidenly virtue. Now, peel, Bob. Everything but your shoes and B.V.Ds. Hear me?"

Reilly rattled on, going back and forth between his living room and bedroom while Mallory stripped to shoes, socks and underwear and sat down again uncertainly on his straight chair.

"Maybe I'd better not go," he began uneasily.

"*Halten Sie den Mund*," retorted Norman. "All I want is for you not to disgrace the profession. The girls think medics are wild men who carry detached ears and pieces of fingers about in their pockets to drop in the soup and on card-trays. I insist that you look civilized, whether you are or not. That's all."

The buzzer interrupted him in the act of buttoning his white waistcoat.

"There's Joe now with your things."

Exactly fifteen minutes later Reilly gave a last tug at Mallory's coat tails.

"It's a little snug around the shoulders and it wrinkles a bit in the back. But it'll do. The only trouble with you is that you bulge over the chest and shoulders. If you only had a better reach, I'd advise you to drop medicine and go in for fighting. Grab your overcoat and let's beat it. We're late already. . . . Here, give me that hat. You'll be knocking your front teeth out with it. It opens this way."

Reilly handed the opera hat back to Mallory, settled his own on his beautifully brushed blond head, and pushed his friend out of the apartment ahead of him.

II

Having little fund of small talk, Robert Mallory found himself quite lost in the babble of strident voices and loud alcoholic laughter about the supper table. At the head of the board sat the hostess, Gerty Mannering, lean, brown, hardbitten but with an air of romance about her. Reilly was beside her. Mallory looked wistfully at the pair: they never ceased talking for a moment. What he himself had managed to say to the young person with carmine lips who sat on his left had bored her so much that she had turned to her other more entertaining neighbor with whom she was now having a champagne consumption race. On Mallory's other hand was a haughty brunette from Gerty's company who said she was interested in modern art and, having found that he did not even know what Imagists were, dropped him as unworthy of any further effort.

Thus Mallory sat, an island of comparative sobriety, and watched a social spectacle unfamiliar to him.

Gerty Mannering had engaged the Hotel Bancroft's Gold Room for her supper party. It was the farewell that climaxed a long engagement in the city, the length of which had indeed compelled Reilly to turn to Mallory for tutoring. The bragging that Norman had done about his friend's brilliancy had aroused Gerty's curiosity to the point where she had insisted that Reilly bring him to her last party in Mannewaque. Now, between bantering replies to her male neighbors, her glance wandered down the long table with its flowers and silver and wine bottles to the flushed, uncomfortable face of the prodigy of learning. The very fact that Mallory was so obviously ill at ease made her wonder about him and once or twice she lagged perceptibly in her retorts to Reilly.

Before he left the table Mallory drank more "bubbly" and Burgundy than he had intended and he felt curiously detached from his surroundings as though he were floating two or three feet above the floor. He was really surprised to find himself in a secluded corner behind a cluster of potted palms and ferns telling a dissecting room story to a blonde who leaned distractingly on his slightly bent shirt-front.

"Honestly, I had no notion of pulling anything on them. The poor girls were just peddling Milk Fund tickets, and some dirty bugger put them up to coming to the medical school. Junior Leaguers, I guess. Looked like it, anyhow. But we all said absolutely no cash unless they came inside and looked at the stiffs. Then I started to unwrap mine—I was on head and neck—and when the last cloth came loose, the old bird's skull-cap fell off and rolled down the floor toward the two dames. I'd forgotten all about the thing being loose, honestly I had. Well, the last we saw of the girls they were hightailing it down Milford Street, ten seconds flat."

The blonde, saucer-eyed, gazed up into Mallory's face and purred.

"Oh, you awful man! You ought to be ashamed of yourself! Tell me some more. I always knew medical students were terrible. Did you ever rob a grave?"

But before he could collect himself and think of another tale satisfactorily lurid, Gerty Mannering caught sight of them in their corner. The lean, slender dancer came around the palms and stood with her hands on her hips staring coldly at the scene before her. Hastily the blonde removed her pale curls from Mallory's bosom and somewhat unsteadily rose to her feet. More slowly Robert pulled himself up from the settee.

"So here you are?" said Gerty in her low husky voice. "Your time's up, Cutey. Well, don't stand there with your face hanging open! Can't you see I'm waiting? You heard what I said in the first place. Clear out!"

The blonde fled without looking back, and Gerty sank down on the seat and motioned Mallory to sit beside her.

"Norman has told me everything about you except how many fillings there are in your back teeth. It's probably all lies, of course. I don't always believe Reilly's tales, you know. Well, sit down. Sit down! I won't bite you! Sit down, doctor, and talk to me. You aren't one of those he-vampires are you, that dog us poor woiking goils of the stage?"

Afterwards Mallory could never remember what he had said to her or she to him, but he had a spotty picture of many faces floating past their corner and peering in through the palms and ferns and laughing, and he never forgot the steel-like smoothness and hardness of Gerty's arms or the queer hoarseness of her voice. And he distinctly heard her say, "I don't open in Fort Manton until Wednesday and maybe we could fix up a week-end."

III

Robert Mallory tossed about in his tumbled bed, opened a pair of dark-rimmed blue eyes, and yawned and stuck out his tongue. His mouth tasted rotten. Finally he swung his legs out of the bed and sat up, propping his head on his hands.

The room was in disorder. Both chairs were heaped with socks, shirts, and vests jumbled together. On the study table by the window, among his thick text books, were strewn collars and ties and keys. On top of the wall 'phone, lying rakishly on its side, was a cloth-of-gold evening slipper.

Mallory stared at these things and rubbed his aching head. His watch had stopped; he did not know what time it was or what day. The distempered, bilious brown walls of his cheap room looked unhelpfully down on the amateur follower of Bacchus.

He gagged and tottered into the bathroom where, presently, he sat down on one of the three steps that led upward from the floor to the tiny dressing room and closet built above the cubby hole into which his bed was pushed during the day. Nothing was clear after the hotel Friday night. He could recall snatches of music—Caruso, the Banjo Song—a jumble of many sounds and voices meaning nothing. And, before drunkenness had completely engulfed him, he had etched on his brain forever the lines of Gerty's lean, brown body so firm and yet so soft under his hands.

Mallory ran his fingers through his hair and leaned against the wall. Not only had he made a damned fool of himself but he had gone off somewhere with Reilly's girl. No matter what else a fellow did, it was up to him to keep off his friends' preserves. He was an ass. He had had no business to fall for the woman in the first place. God, what a headache! And what a taste in his mouth! Then he was violently sick again.

Reilly banged loudly on the door of the room three times before Mallory heard him. Miserably Robert looked at him, clear-eyed and pink-cheeked, very spruce in brown home-spun.

"I suppose you've come to…to…" Mallory ran his fingers helplessly through his rumpled hair trying to think what a man could say at a moment like this.

"Sure, I've come, you poor sap! Come to snake you out to a Turkish bath and get you boiled out. A fellow like you that hardly ever takes a drink is out of luck on a party. Now with me a few extra over the week-end don't matter. But, Bob, I give you my word you looked like the heroine of 'Ten Nights in the Barroom' when I dragged you home last night."

"Did you bring me home? I can't remember…"

"That doesn't surprise me," grinned Reilly. "You were in no state to remember anything, and, if I hadn't rescued you, you'd have suffered the fate of the male spider by now. Gerty was pretty hot under the collar, having her week-end fizzling out on her like that."

Mallory lifted his head and faced his friend.

"But, Norman, you don't understand. I…you see…I…well, Gerty and I…"

Reilly laughed and swept a pile of shirts and socks off a chair and sat down on it.

"Oh, I don't understand, don't I? Well, that's just where you're wrong, my lad. It's you that don't understand. I saw Gerty giving you the once-over on Friday night and hiding out in the corner with you, behind the palms and what-not. I've had several rounds with the lady and I know her technique. And I know, too, that she's a man-eater and you didn't have the ghost of a chance against her. I had a damned good idea of where she'd take you but I certainly was surprised when she called me up yesterday and asked me for God's sake to come and get you. It was too much for Gerty to be treated like a lady because, forsooth, you thought she belonged to me. Virtue triumphant though intoxicated—that was your line, Bob. I thought I'd die laughing when I saw the two of you." Reilly's eyes roved about the room. "I see you parked that cock-eyed slipper of hers on the 'phone. I hope that's the only thing you brought home with you besides your jag."

"But, Norman, I hadn't any business to do it. It was just as much my fault, our going off like that, as it was hers."

"Your fault, my eye! Don't make me laugh. I got a sore lip. I just told you, didn't I, that Gerty is a man-eater. Don't you suppose I know? I've had my day, several of 'em in fact, with Gerty. Now get up and stick your head in a bowl of cold water. You've got to get sobered up. You have to run that demonstration on intracranial circulation tomorrow for the visiting big-wigs

from Boston. Don't tell me you forgot that. Why, the honor of
the school depends on you, as they say in football. It's a cinch
nobody else around here knows anything about it."

Without another word of protest Mallory dragged his
body wearily back into the bathroom. If he in his drunken
sentimentality had played a hoax on biology over Saturday and
Sunday, biology was having its little joke on him this morning.

CHAPTER IV

I

Reilly stretched his neck in his collar and looked to right and left along the line of black-gowned young men in academic caps and green velvet-lined hoods. Here they all were at last, at the end of the road or perhaps at the beginning of a new one. The bald-headed chap in the circular collar evidently thought it the finest road in the world that lay before them; Reilly gathered this opinion from the man's remarks addressed to God. He felt sure that the Latin prayer book with which he had once been much more familiar than he now was contained many better petitions to the Almighty.

Besides, this was no time to be praying over them. Half the class ought to have been pitched out of medical school three years before and started into ditch-digging as an occupation more suited to their talents. Praying over them thirty minutes or so before their medical degrees were to be conferred Reilly considered a perfect example of love's labor lost.

Mallory, standing on his left, shifted his feet a little. Reilly looked over at him with affection and approval. There was a chap who would be a good doctor. His thick, crisp, brown hair and the set of his neck in the folds of the absurd green-rimmed hood spelled vitality. His eyes were staring straight out over the audience toward the great stained glass windows of the chapel. Reilly knew he was far away. A scrubbed, hard jawed, stocky fellow, firm on his feet. A chap with plenty of steam to drive him through any sort of fight. Reilly smiled dreamily to himself.

The clergyman droned on about the "preparation of thy servants, O Lord, for the work in thy vineyard." Reilly heard a faint snicker from the man on his right. He stood with his eyes closed, swaying a little. Norman was sure he had just thought of a dirty story and was, unreasonably, annoyed by this idea. The fellow was another high-binder like that buzzard, Brantner, who had graduated last year and gone west. He was always writing about the great opportunities in Pacific City which, according to Brantner, was to be the metropolis of the west coast. Well, both he and this bird next in line were the sort that would find opportunity wherever they went—opportunity to make money and have swanky offices and carry on with the office nurses when their wives went away. They were the kind one could count on to watch for the main chance and butter their own bread plentifully. Reilly had a sudden desire to hit the fellow's blue-shaven jaw. What a commotion that would make! He laughed silently. At least it would stop this endless invocation.

Then suddenly the preacher said "Amen" and every one rustled about and sat down. In the scuffling for chairs Reilly found it possible to fetch a sidelong kick at his neighbor's ankle and was purged of his evil impulses by the look that came into the man's face. Then he settled down comfortably, facing the speaker of the evening. Thank God, this chap wasn't a preacher and wouldn't be likely to talk about the Lord's servants in his vineyard.

II

Robert Mallory was, all the while, far away from the brightly lighted, crowded chapel. Somewhere in the audience was his mother but he could not see her and did not even think of her. He was conscious only of himself. His mind was questing back over the score of years that measured the span of his memory.

The farm, the big red barn with the running horse on the cupola, the great barnyard with the brook at the bottom of the slope and big green maple trees here and there, the white and gray barred chickens pecking in the dirt, the horses drowsing in the shade with their legs relaxed and their hoofs tilted off the ground, the watering trough and the pump house, the winding path between fruit trees and garden that led back to the gable-roofed farmhouse in another grove of maples.

There was himself, running breathlessly to harness Dr. Farrar's horse so that he might have an opportunity to ask how one went about studying to be a doctor. Himself hurrying to open the big gate for the team and double buggy bringing the family home from town. Himself walking slowly down the road toward the country school, a mile away. The schoolhouse, white with green shutters, standing beside the white steepled church on a rounded hilltop crowned with oak trees. Himself, home once more, stalking one of the cats, intent on proving or disproving what the teacher had said in physiology class about the length of a cat's intestine. Himself in a shirt that was ragged and none too clean, watching Dr. Farrar's skillful fingers folding powders and tapping grandmother's chest when she had pneumonia.

Himself again, a little older now, peering into his own mouth with a mirror in search of "Koplik spots," a sure sign that one really had measles. Himself, high school age, sitting on the chest of a terrified younger boy who had fallen into the creek and run a fishhook through his eyelid so that the barb was inside next the eyeball, and cutting out the hook with his pocket knife.

The day he had told his mother he was going to be a doctor. Her gravity of manner as she said, "It's a hard life, my boy, and not what I would have chosen for you. But if you have a call to it, I won't oppose you." That was it—"a call to it." Longer ago than he could remember, when he was only a scrubby kid, he had had that call. It had always seemed to him impossible that he should be anything except a doctor. There was something in the Bible about "he that loseth his life shall find it." That was the way he had always felt about being a doctor.

The fellows in school talked a lot of rot about making money and the young doctors in practice told tales of fee-splitting and trumped-up operations. But that sort of thing was unprofessional, it was the exception. He would follow the old Greek oath of Hippocrates to the letter; he would be honest. There seethed within him an inchoate jumble of ambition and aspiration and desire to do right. Behind him he swept all the shady episodes of medical school, all the experiences with Gerty and her kind of women, all the physical urges of young manhood. Before him he saw only the narrow path of his profession, "shining more and more unto the perfect day."

III

"Snap out of it," whispered Reilly out of the side of his mouth. He cracked Mallory's ankle with his foot. "Come to, you idiot. Can't you see Dean Winkley getting set to pin the medal on you?"

Somehow Mallory stumbled across the platform to stand before the kind-faced, white-haired, old dean. Distantly he heard a voice talking, talking.

"Each year since 1885, the trustees have conferred the Seeman prize upon the member of the graduating class who has achieved the highest academic standing throughout the course. This reward is not given for preeminence in any one subject, but for excellence in all. It marks the man from whom we expect a real achievement. It marks the man upon whom the eyes of the school rest and its reputation depends. Those who have won this medal in the past have—some of them—done notable work and some even now are carrying the torch of knowledge into the far places of the earth. We are proud of them.

"Robert Truscott Mallory, in the name of the trustees and faculty of Mannewaque University, I present you this medal in token of your high scholastic attainments and with the hope that this may be only the prelude to greater accomplishments and greater honors in the days to come."

Applause thundered up from the crowded hall. Mallory's legs went weak beneath him. The old dean fumbled with stiff, arthritic fingers, trying to pin the medal on the front of his gown. The Seeman prize! Then it was true that he had gotten this coveted award. Last night when they had first told him about it, he had only half believed them.

The dean's rheumatic fingers at last pushed the pin of the medal through Mallory's gown and suit into his skin underneath. But even that rude reminder of the present did not bring Mallory down to earth. Back in his seat he rubbed the pricked spot on his breast and waited, still incredulous, for that magic moment when the chairman's voice would confer the degrees.

He had been twenty years getting ready for this. Twenty years in school. And now the goal was at hand, the first goal in a long series. M.D.—doctor, doctor of medicine! Doctor Mallory from now on, as long as he lived! There rose a sudden tightness in his throat. Doctor Mallory!

CHAPTER V

I

Dr. Mallory opened the door from the dingy hallway and entered his own quarters. The bare floor of the room was still damp from its weekly scrubbing. A certain dankness and unwholesomeness permeated the whole of the internes' rooms in the Pacific City Hospital.

Quickly he pulled off his crumpled white uniform, tossed it on the floor, and pulled on a bathrobe. He was relieved that Reilly wasn't in; that would give him a chance to pack his things without interruption.

"This place is not so swell," he muttered, "but I bet what I draw over at Contagious will be worse."

He looked about him. In opposite corners, at one end of the room, were two high narrow beds with white cotton coverlets. Beside each stood a small stand with a house 'phone. Near the foot of Reilly's bed a single window opened out into the open space between the internes' quarters and the main hospital building. Across the end of the room opposite the beds were two built-in closets with drawers underneath, and between them a lavatory with towels and a huge chunk of pink soap. A mirror hanging above the bowl reflected an imitation oak study table in the middle of the floor and two wooden rockers with imitation leather seats.

"Not so swell. I'm surprised Reilly hasn't cleared out before now and got an apartment somewhere." Mallory reached for the box of cigarettes on the table.

On the wall over Reilly's bed was a swinging shelf of books that were a surprise to Mallory whenever he looked at them, for they were—none of them—medical texts. Some were novels by Conrad and Hardy, some were poetry, a few were biographies. He always felt he ought to read some of them. "They must be pretty good, from what Norman says. I'll get at them as soon as I finish Kolmer's new book on serums." But he never had done so yet. Through the cigarette smoke he regarded these frivolous volumes for the thousandth time. "Chance." That was an interesting title. He really must read that one anyhow.

At the head of Reilly's bed hung a quadruple group of photographs of Gerty Mannering, all bearing fervent inscriptions to Norman. Mallory's eyes, resting on them for a moment, went on to the print of the "Anatomy Lesson" that dangled on a long wire from a nail above his own bed. When he had first unpacked he had come upon a girl's photograph in his trunk and had been half of a mind to put it up as an offset to Gerty. But, upon studying it carefully, he saw that it looked strange and old-fashioned; after all, he hadn't seen the girl for four years and she had married some fellow he didn't even know, the previous spring. So he had hung up, instead, the anatomical print someone had given him as a graduation present. Now there it was, dangling above his bed, staring at him.

Vaguely aware that something was lacking in his existence, he flung away the stub of his cigarette and began to lay out his shaving things. "I'll have to shake a leg to get away from here right after supper," he thought.

Through the open window came the faint sound of far away chimes playing "O'er the tumult of our lives' tempestuous sea."

Some wealthy man, so Mallory had been told, had installed them in a downtown church supposing that their melodies would turn the thoughts of hustling business men toward the next world. Mallory stopped lathering his face to listen.

Already he had learned that a doctor's life was always tempestuous and likely to become more so rather than less. Even now he was bound in chains of professional obligation to those five hundred beds full of sick people in the dingy red-brick building across the courtyard. From now on he would always be tied in that way to some group of human creatures. He found himself wondering why they all clung so desperately to life, even when it was bleak and hopeless. Those miserable old women in his ward, for instance.

Without warning the door opened and Reilly and Brantner walked in. Reilly's uniform was as near perfection as any white suit can be after a man sits down in it.

"Hello, Bob," he said, beaming at sight of Mallory. "Sit down, if you can find a chair, Chuck."

Unabashed, Brantner peered over Mallory's shoulder into the mirror and adjusted his red-and-blue-striped tie. "So you scrape the face twice a day, eh? Getting particular, aren't you, since you came to Pacific City?"

"Is it my fault that my whiskers grow fast?" growled Mallory.

Brantner was as sleek as ever; his blue suit was handsome and becoming. He annoyed Mallory excessively. Even the fact that he had helped him and Reilly get interneships in Pacific City did not mitigate that instinctive dislike.

In the act of removing his trousers Reilly paused and sniffed. He went to the window and sniffed again. Three floors below the internes' dinner was being cooked. There was no mistake possible: they were going to have kidney stew again. "Thank God, I'm going out to eat." He pulled his head in and banged down the window. "Why in the name of all that's holy can't they wash the damned kidneys before they put them on to boil?"

"Ask me another one," said Mallory. "Another one I can't answer."

Brantner sat sidewise in one of the rockers and swung his legs over the arm.

"Aren't you going to offer me a drink?" he inquired. "Or have both of you gone prohibition?"

Reilly looked up from putting cuff links in a clean shirt.

"Open the drawer in the corner, Chuck, and you'll find a bottle of Gordon Dry. It's all I've got here. Help yourself—but not to all of it." Norman glanced at Mallory. "What's eating you, Bob? Whenever you begin slicing your neck that way I know something's wrong."

"Oh, the Sup. just told me I've got to go over to Contagious right after dinner. Daniels is down with diphtheria."

Brantner whistled. "God! That makes the third interne to get it this fall. Must be some bugs they got over there. All the boys still there?"

"Yes, they're all in bed still. I'll have them to look after besides the patients."

Brantner gulped his second tall drink of gin. Reilly looked at him sharply.

"I say, Chuck, didn't I tell you not to lap up all the liquor I had? Leave a snort for Bob and me, will you? What's wrong with you anyhow? Ever since you've been in with that gang of abortionists you're working for you've been drinking like a gold fish. Judging by that suit you've got on, you could afford to buy hooch for yourself once in a while instead of sponging it off me all the time."

Brantner's sallow face seemed to go even paler.

"Oh, all right, all right. You don't need to get sore about it. Here's your damn bottle! Take it."

"I will," said Reilly. He measured out three fingers into each of two tumblers, slopped in water, and handed one glass to Mallory.

"Here's hoping that none of the cunning little diphtheria bacilli set up housekeeping in your throat, Bob." He drank off the gin quickly. "But if I were you I wouldn't cry over leaving that women's chronic ward you've had. A batch of old girls like that would drive me nuts. Nothing but bum hearts and worn-out kidneys and blood vessels that have gone bad and can't ever be fixed. Now over at the Contagious your patients will either die or get well. Every few days you'll have a new bunch. Here's to you. Better have another drink, Bob. You might not have another chance for quite a while."

"No, thanks, Norman. I've got to get down and eat the minute the bell rings and I'm not packed yet. . . . You may not think much of my ward here but I was counting on helping Wolf with that ganglion injection in the morning and I don't like to miss it."

Brantner laughed loudly. "Can you imagine that? Grieving because he won't be there for that crab to cuss at. Everybody hates Wolf. . . . Say, let me have that drink if Bob isn't going to take it."

"Sure. Here it is." Reilly looked curiously at Brantner's long nervous fingers clutching the glass. "Go on and drink till your liver's hob-nailed if you want to, and see if I care."

Mallory reverted to his disappointment. "That's all right for you to say, Chuck, but I've never seen a ganglion injected."

Brantner tossed down his third glass of gin.

"Well, I have, boy. And it'll be all right with me if I never see another one. Jabbing around in a guy's head trying to hit a nerve the size of a twine string with a hypo needle, shooting in the alcohol when the fellow yells the loudest. It's a little too thick even for a hard boiled egg like me."

"But they'll work out a better way to do it before long, I bet," insisted Mallory.

"Will you two pipe down? You give me the willies." Reilly glared at Brantner. "You, drinking like a fish and shaking like you had exophthalmic goiter. And Bob, yapping his head off about the wonders of modern surgery. Every night he sits here and bones on Cabot's case records. He lugs home books on X-rays and radium. He sits and draws pictures of something to make good X-ray plates of fat people's insides. In between times he's in the morgue dabbling in liver abscesses and helping do the post mortems. No wonder I've been driven to drink— more drink."

Brantner leered up at Mallory who was tossing shirts and socks into a suitcase.

"How about the squab probationer I hear is chasing you?"

A vivid blush swept over Robert's face and neck. He had kissed the girl several times when they were alone in the accident room at night and held her on his lap, but...

"Oh, that's all washed up, Chuck. Hadn't you heard? Bob's going to take the veil. Remember what the noble poet says? 'His strength is as the strength of ten because his heart is pure.'" Reilly dodged the slipper Mallory threw at him and went on, "Honestly if I knew a hard boiled woman around this town that I could trust I'd get her to educate Bob."

The supper gong burst into noisy clamor.

"Got to run, Bob? Wait a second. Put these books in your bag." Reilly handed over "Almayer's Folly" and "Chance." "They're grand yarns and they'll be a change from Kolmer on specific therapy. But disinfect them before you come back. Cheer up, fellow. If you catch diphtheria I'll come over and peek in at you and make faces through the glass."

Reilly followed Mallory into the hall.

"Take care of yourself, boy. I'll call up every day and find out if you're O.K. Let me know when you have your half-day off so we can get together. So long. I'll be seeing you later."

II

Still aglow from Norman Reilly's staunch though well camouflaged comradeship, Mallory presented himself cheerfully at the Contagious Hospital at seven-thirty that evening. A middle-aged nurse in uniform looked up from behind her desk.

"Oh, so you're the new resident? Yes, this is where you report. What did you say the name was? ... Dr. Mallory? Just sign the register here, please, doctor. I'll ring for the maid to show you your room. There probably won't be anything for you to do this evening. Dr. Long, the chief physician, made rounds just before he went out and he said he wouldn't be later than ten getting back."

Presently Mallory found himself inside the door of a narrow closet of a room containing, besides the ever-present cot and house 'phone, only a small rocking chair and a tall, slim chest of drawers surmounted by a little mirror of wavy glass. Beyond the foot of the cot was a small window and two doors down the hall, the maid assured him, there was a bathroom.

"I knew it," he thought. "I knew it would be like this. If it was any smaller I'd have to come in sideways. That chair will break down the first time I sit in it. Back of this rag I guess is the only place to hang up anything." Mallory lifted a multicolored cotton curtain near the chest of drawers and peered at the hooks behind it. "Well, thank the Lord, I won't be here forever."

At eight o'clock there came a knock at his door. The nurse who had met him in the office suggested that he accompany her on her regular hourly rounds in order to familiarize himself with the layout of the hospital. Accordingly Mallory followed her into a sort of rotunda from which wings extended in four directions. The nurse turned to the right, through a pair of heavy swinging doors. After slipping into sterile gowns and tying masks over their nose and mouths, she and Mallory went through another set of doors, past a service room, and into the diphtheria ward.

Along both side walls were cubicles separated from each other by partitions of wainscoting and glass and opening into the central corridor of the ward with glass doors. The supervisor asked Mallory to look at a child with "serum sickness" and suggested that he speak to his three predecessors who were all in bed at the far end of the ward. Most of the patients Mallory could see were children; they lay curled up on their sides in their little glass cells, breathing jerkily in their sleep.

In three adjacent cubicles at the end of the ward were the three sick internes. Two of them were sitting up in bed playing solitaire but the third was sprawled out with his face close to the wall.

"You're the new guy, eh? Mallory? Glad to see you. My name's Walker and that hunk of rubbish next door is Benny Butler. He got these damned bugs first and gave them to me the first time I swabbed his throat. I woke up sick the fifth morning I was over here. We're both O.K. but they can't get negative cultures on either of us and the Lord knows how long we'll be shut up in here."

Butler said he was unfortunate enough to have a whole colony of diphtheria bacilli thriving in his nose eighteen days after his illness began.

"It'll be just my luck to be one of these damned carriers who go about scattering bugs among their friends. I was always an unlucky fellow." He lowered his voice. "But Daniels was mighty sick, no foolin'. A lot worse than Walker or I've been. He had to have 30,000 units of antitoxin intravenously, all in one shot. Looks like he's going to be all right now, though. You haven't got a package of cigarettes on you that you could leave, have you?" Butler peered up through thick-lensed glasses. "Oh, thanks. I've been smoking like a furnace all day. Thought maybe the bugs wouldn't care for cigarette smoke. Well, see you in the morning when you take our cultures."

Mallory slipped into Daniels' cubicle. The flushed, feverish face on the pillow and the restless movements of the young man's body gave evidence that he was very sick. Gently Mallory counted his pulse, pulled open his gown and listened to his heart.

"That boy was very ill," said the supervisor when he had rejoined her. "Here's his chart. Temperature was over 104 last night but it's down this evening. He seems to be coming along nicely now. . . . Suppose we go to the Scarlet Fever ward next, doctor. There's a child over there who worries me."

While they were taking off their gowns and masks in the dressing room, a loud clanging burst upon their ears.

"The ambulance," explained the supervisor.

"It's the police wagon." A white-capped head was poked through the doors. "Maybe they've got a gun-man."

Mallory found two policemen in the rotunda, one of them with a small bundle in his arms, from which came wheezing, gurgling sounds.

"It's a Jap kid," said the officer with the bundle. "And damn near dead, too. I think it's got diphtheria. Two of my kids had it last year and I know the signs."

"We found the kid in back of a store," explained the other officer. "Some of the neighbors got scared and squealed on 'em. The Japs were afraid of quarantine and we had quite a time gettin' in after it."

The small patient's face was a curious dark color, a combination of racial sallowness and the purple of asphyxiation. At every breath his whole lower chest heaved and his little ribs stood out like pickets on a fence.

"It's wicked to let youngsters go like this until you have to intubate," exclaimed the supervisor indignantly.

"Intubate!" Mallory's voice was curiously muffled.

"What else can you do? The child will die before antitoxin can take effect even if you give it in the vein." The supervisor hurried away after the nurse who had taken the child. "Get him prepared as quickly as you can, Miss Fremont. And have two intubation sets ready."

Mallory stood alone in the rotunda, staring after the nurses. Intubate that kid? He couldn't do it! He'd seen only one intubation, had never done one. There were very few cases these days allowed to go so far as to demand intubation. Intubate? Impossible! And yet there wasn't any one else to call. The chief physician would not be back before ten o'clock, too late to do any good. Walker and Butler were both in bed and, besides, they probably didn't know any more than he did. Intubate? Sweat ran down the little gutter along his backbone and the palms of his hands were wet.

A nurse put her head through the doors.

"Are you ready to scrub up, doctor?" she asked.

Like an automaton Mallory followed her, mechanically took off his shirt and began to scour his hands and arms with soap and brush and hot water. What did Stewart's Manual of Surgery say about intubation? He could remember a picture of the "introducer"; there was a trigger on it and you tied a silk ligature around the tube and to your little finger. Beyond that, intubation was a complete blank so far as Mallory was concerned.

He put on a sterile gown and bent down for the nurse to tie on his mask, then he walked into the treatment room. It would have been as easy, he thought, to go up to the muzzle of a double-barreled shotgun.

The sterile nurse hovered over an instrument tray, the supervisor stood beside the table with her fingers on the child's wrist.

"No time to spare," she said. "Pulse is about 170 and respirations 50. The intubation set is ready, doctor. Shall I hold the child?"

Mallory took a long breath and swallowed hard.

"No. I'm not going to intubate. I think tracheotomy would be better. Here, let's get this pillow under the kid's shoulders. That's better. Now the skin. Get prepared as fast as you can."

The nurse who ran for instruments looked questioningly at the supervisor who in turn glanced quickly at Mallory's face; then she nodded and the nurse did as she had been told.

Mallory put his forefinger on the child's throat. There was the thyroid cartilage under the fingertip, and here the cricoid. The incision must be in the mid-line, and an inch and a half long; not too deep, just through the skin and fascia. Like that. Handle of the knife separating the muscle fibers. Gently, gently. Pushing down the thyroid gland out of harm's way. Yes, he could feel the cartilaginous rings of the trachea under his fingers. Steady now, a firm grip on that trachea. The tip of the knife must go just below the fourth ring, with its cutting edge up toward the child's chin. Cartilage cuts easily. One, two, three rings.

"Hemostat, Miss Fremont. Spread the jaws a little. That's right. Now the tube."

He was surprised at the ease with which it dropped into place.

"Sutures. . . . Gauze to slip under the flange. . . . There we are."

Mallory stepped back from the table. Drops of sweat stood

on his lips and beside his nose. They dripped off. But the queer weakness in his knees had gone.

"Let me have antitoxin now and I'll shoot it into a vein while the kid's on the table. Ten thousand units, please. Better to use plenty the first time. Too much won't do any harm, but not enough is almost as bad as none."

III

The next morning when Mallory finished taking cultures from Benny Butler's nose and throat, that young man looked up at him with quizzical, curious eyes.

"We hear you did a neat job last night, the very first crack out of the box. The girls are all hepped up about it, they think you're pretty foxy. The kid, they told me, is fine as frog's hair this morning. Well, some guys are lucky. But you were a wise bird to pull off something spectacular like that right to start with: it'll make people know you're around. And Long likes big doses of antitoxin too, big doses and only one of 'em."

All the while Butler rattled on, it trembled on Mallory's tongue to confess the ignorance that had forced him to do a tracheotomy rather than intubation, but some instinct made him think better of putting it into words.

"Well, Butler, I'll do all I can to make these cultures come out negative to-day if I have to sit and scowl at the incubator all afternoon. You must be sick and tired of sitting here in this glass box. Here's hoping!"

"Yeah, it does get pretty thin after nineteen days of it," agreed Butler. "And then, remember, in another three or four days you'll be needing the bed yourself." He followed Mallory down the corridor with shrewd, near-sighted eyes. "That's a smart boy, John," he said to the occupant of the neighboring cubicle.

CHAPTER VI

I

Mallory, followed by Norman Reilly, stepped briskly out of the elevator on the fourth floor of the central police station and hurried into the Emergency Hospital. For the moment the whiteness of the woodwork, chairs, and ceiling in the waiting room made them both blink.

"Good evening, Dr. Mallory." From behind a small desk a uniformed nurse turned a wise well-seasoned eye upon the two young men.

"Mrs. Hathaway, this is my friend, Dr. Reilly. He's going to help us to-night."

"How do you do, Mrs. Hathaway. I hope your New Year's Eve celebration comes up to Bob's ballyhoo about it. He's spent two weeks talking me into coming here instead of going to the Benton Hotel."

Mrs. Hathaway smiled at this banter.

"I think you can expect a stirring time but quite different from anything you'd have found at the Benton, Dr. Reilly. New Year's Eve sees many sorts of people in the police station."

"Just what Bob told me." Reilly grinned at the nurse in his most attractive Irish gamin fashion. It was no wonder, he thought, that Bob liked her; he liked her himself, at first sight. Thirty-eight or forty, he estimated, a widow, natural or artificial, comfortably plump but not fat, with quick eyes that appraised one accurately but kindly. There should be more women like that in the world.

But though he often had serious thoughts Reilly seldom spoke seriously.

"You know, Mrs. Hathaway, I'm not used to the sort of rough drunken men you and Bob deal with. So I thought I'd ask you to send me down to the women's division. I'm sure I'd do well there."

The nurse laughed outright.

"I'm sure you would, too. I know you're timid, Dr. Reilly, but we need you up here so badly that we'll just have to see to it that you're properly protected from our less cultured patients."

"And we can arrange for Norman to take care of any spe- cial lady friends of his that come in, can't we, Mrs. H.?" Mallory dodged a kick from Reilly.

"I hear the elevator again," observed Mrs. Hathaway. "This is probably Dr. Daniels."

Almost before she had finished speaking Benny Butler and John Daniels came in, young Butler peering about him in the sharp way characteristic of the very near-sighted.

"Well, just look who's come now," jeered Reilly. "None other than Benjamin R. Butler, Jr., himself, in person, spectacles and all. How come, Benny? How come?"

"Oh, the family are throwing a party at the Benton to-night— one of those damned duty parties where you ask all the dumb eggs. Mother's working off her social obligations. To get out of a smear like that I'd do anything—even work."

"It's seven-thirty, fellows," said Mallory. "Time to strip for action. The avalanche will be upon us any time now."

Flinging ribald remarks back and forth, the other young doctors trooped after him into the dressing room to get into their uniforms.

Outside, in the bare white anteroom, Mrs. Hathaway listened and smiled. It was good to hear laughter in this sordid place. After six years in the police Emergency Hospital she felt soiled even after her hot tub at night. And she worried over what it did to the internes who worked there. So often they became callous, indifferent to pain, cynical. Even Mallory had lost his illusions.

Mrs. Hathaway remembered the first night he had worked with her. They had both been busy and when they were tired from their long session they had come upon a man hanging dead in the toilet with a sheet twisted about his neck. She had watched horror, pity, comprehension follow each other across Mallory's face as he read the note the man had left, penciled on a scrap of paper toweling. "I've come to the end of my rope. Let me go out as John Smith. I don't want my people to know." Yes, Mallory was different from the other internes she had worked with during her six years in the police hospital; his disillusionment had not made him harsh. He had the same code she had to care for the human derelicts they worked with as well as they possibly could, and to disregard the fact that they were derelicts.

II

Mrs. Hathaway, Reilly, and Mallory walked down the corridor that led off from the waiting room. On one side were two padded cells, on the other, two treatment rooms, and between them a small recovery room designed for patients sleeping off an anesthetic. At the end of the corridor the three emerged into a large ward.

Down one side wall was a long row of single beds pushed close together. Along the other walls were large bundles of gray blankets lying at intervals on the floor.

"This is a good idea, Mrs. H. We can stow the fellows that are badly hurt in the beds and put the drunks on the floor. With all these blankets, they ought to be considerably more comfortable than in a flop house."

"I have learned from experience, Dr. Mallory, that one must dispense with niceties on New Year's Eve down here. The first year I had the horrors for a week after the holidays, but now I'm used to it."

Suddenly, from the direction of the anteroom, came a long wild howl like that of a coyote. Reilly jumped.

"Good Lord," he cried. "What's that?"

"Probably the first patient," replied the nurse calmly.

Through the doors at the far end of the corridor rushed two policemen dragging between them a man who howled and kicked furiously. Behind the group Daniels and Butler ran in, buttoning their fresh white uniforms.

"D.T.," shouted Mallory. "Hang onto him. Reilly, roll up his sleeve. There's alcohol to swab his skin with right behind you on the shelf." He darted into one of the treatment rooms and ran out with a hypodermic syringe in his hand. "Hold him still, just a second. . . . There you are. All right, officer, shove him into the first cell there."

The policemen pulled open the cell door and pushed the man inside. As soon as they released their hold of him, the alcoholic fell down and began to claw the floor and emit maniacal wails.

"He'll pipe down pretty soon," observed Mallory in the tone of experience. "Nothing like H.M.C. hypos for these birds. Anyhow, he can't do any harm to himself in there."

"No," grumbled one of the policemen. "But he done plenty to me while we was bringin' him up here. Put some iodine on my hand, will you, doc, where he bit me? God, I'd rather try to hold a wild cat than a guy like that."

The other officer tucked down his torn collar and pulled his tie back to the front of his shirt.

"Aw, come on, Hogan. You're always bellyachin' about something. By mornin' you won't take no notice of a little thing like a guy bitin' you. What's a bite more or less on New Year's Eve, I'd like to know."

The policemen went out. The man in the padded cell gave a

hair-raising yell, banged his head against the wall, and finally subsided in a heap on the floor.

"We won't hear anything more from him to-night," prophesied Mallory. "There's the elevator again. Let's divide up here. You and Benny take the first room, John. How's that suit you? Reilly and I will do plain and fancy sewing in here, then. Now, Mrs. H., be impartial in distributing the cases. Have they sent up those fellows from downstairs to help you keep the obstreperous ones in bed?"

"Yes, they're here. Don't worry about me, Dr. Mallory. I've got plenty of help."

A policeman came through the swinging doors with a sobbing, cursing man whose jaw gushed a stream of red.

"This bird's got his jaw laid wide open, clean to the bone," said the officer. "Where d' you want him, doc? He's bleedin' like a geyser."

"In here. On the table," ordered Mallory. "That's O.K. Now run along and bring us some more. We're all set for a big rush."

The injured man struggled to sit up; his jaw dripped blood into a pool beside the table.

"Here, you. Lie down again. You don't want to bleed to death, do you? Then lie down and let us sew up this hole in your neck. Come on, Norman. Give me chromic for the ties, Mrs. H."

Half-sobered by the sight of his own blood, the man collapsed on the table, and Mallory and Reilly set to work on him.

III

Not until four o'clock in the morning did a lull come to the Emergency Hospital. By that time all the beds in the ward were full, and on the floor, wrapped in gray blankets, were two long rows of drunken and slightly injured men. Standing in the doorway, Mrs. Hathaway surveyed them. In the dim light their bandaged arms and heads made indistinct splotches of white. The nurse shook her head. 'What a mess,' she thought, 'what an incredible mess people make out of living.' Slowly she went back down the corridor.

For the first time since eight o'clock the previous evening there was no one waiting his turn and no cursing patient was struggling with the doctors. The four internes had knocked off work; their uniform coats were gone, their sleeves were rolled up nearly to their shoulders, and blood-stained operating gowns dangled about their legs. Butler's eyeglasses were dotted with small red spots, and Reilly's curly blond hair fell about his face in waving locks. All four lighted cigarettes before speaking.

"*Gott im Himmel!*" exclaimed Reilly after inhaling deeply. "What a way to spend New Year's Eve!" He strolled out into the corridor.

Returning, he grimaced at Mallory.

"This is a nice refined joint you got here! Why don't you put up umbrellas over those fellows in the ward or else turn them over on their stomachs, each man in his own vomit?"

"Good Lord," cried Daniels. "Did you go in there? Just a whiff when the door opens makes me sick at my stomach. And I'm used to alcohol, too, first hand and second hand."

Mrs. Hathaway approached the group.

"I wish I could learn to smoke," she said. "You all look so comfortable. But I've tried and tried, and it always makes me ill."

"Try Bull Durham," suggested Benny Butler.

"Shut up!" snapped Mallory. "Mrs. H. is tired. She's been on the run all night just as much as we have." He turned toward the nurse. "And I owe you a vote of thanks. If you hadn't thought to requisition more catgut and silkworm yesterday, we'd have been tying up jugulars with shoe strings before now."

"If you were to ask my opinion," growled Reilly, blowing out a huge cloud of smoke, "that would've been plenty good enough for some of these fellows."

"Experience has taught me to lay in plenty of sutures for New Year's Eve," answered the nurse. "I believe I'll lie down for a few minutes. Things seem so quiet just now."

Mallory opened the door into the recovery room.

"Go in here, Mrs. H. It's the cleanest place around here."

Mrs. Hathaway smiled up at him.

"Thank you, Dr. Mallory. Call me when anything comes in."

Four minutes later the elevator doors clanged. The internes sprang to their feet, as two officers carried in a man on a stretcher. He lay motionless.

"The ambulance just brought this fellow in," explained one of the policemen. "They were on the way back from a false suicide alarm, and a guy ran out of a hotel and stopped them. Said this bird had just shot himself. He looks to me like he's done for."

"Put him on the table over there," ordered Mallory, "until we can give him the once-over." He laid his fingers on the unconscious man's wrist. There was no pulsation there. He whipped out his stethoscope, pulled back the man's shirt, listened intently.

"Stone dead," he said, and straightened up.

The patient's head fell over to one side, turning into the light a narrow white face with long dark hair hanging on each side.

"Good God, Norman!" cried Mallory. "Look! It's Chuck!" Reilly ran to the table and looked down at the body.

"Are you sure he's dead, Bob?"

"Listen yourself. Here's my stethoscope. He must've been dead before they got him to the station."

A little blood had run down over Brantner's right temple and cheek from the wounds in his scalp; above his temple the tissues were puffed and swollen. On the side of his neck there was a dried trickle of clotted blood. His chin had begun to sag. Brantner's thin, hawk face, chalk-white in death, was haunted, hag-ridden.

"He shot himself," murmured Reilly in a horrified voice. "Right here, on the right side." He peered sharply at the wounds above Brantner's temple but did not touch them.

Mallory shook himself and looked up. Even though a leaden weight seemed to have taken the place of his heart, there was something must be done.

"We can't keep Chuck up here. Call the morgue, Benny, on the house 'phone and ask them to send for him. Then let's go through his pockets and see if we can find anything to explain why he did it."

Their search revealed besides the loose change and trinkets

usually found in a man's pockets a sealed envelope addressed to
"Dr. Robert Mallory, Pacific City Hospital." The letter inside
had been typed, according to its date line, on the previous day.
Into it were folded several laboratory blanks and a smaller
envelope with Reilly's name on it.

"Dear Bob:

"This time I'm in a mess there's only one way out of. Not a
girl. I've laid off that sort of thing since my last year in medical
school. But something so damned ironical I have to laugh
whenever I think of it myself.

"Just before I went down to the Clinic to work last spring,
I examined a woman in the hospital. She had a chancre, and
after I'd finished with her the nurse found a hole in one of my
gloves. Right on time to the day, a chancre showed up on my
index finger. This is where you stop reading and laugh. The bad
boy is being punished just as he is in books.

"I've been nearly crazy since then. Gilman's shot me full of
606 and mercury and iodides and gray oil, but my Wassermann
shot right up to four plus and there she sticks. If you think I'm
exaggerating, look at the enclosed laboratory reports. Gilman
says that doesn't mean a thing, that it may take three or four
years to get a negative Wassermann and still a fellow can be
cured. But I know what's going to happen to me. I'm not the
ordinary case of syphilis. I haven't had any secondaries worth
mentioning, but I know the bugs are in my brain and spinal
cord and thirty years from now I'll hear from them.

"I'll lose my legs in bed and fall down in the dark and have
lightning pains. I know. I'll think I'm Napoleon and Julius
Cæsar, and ride in a wheelchair, and wet myself. I've seen too
many of these vegetables in sawdust bins in the nuthouses
messing on themselves not to know what I'll be like. At nights
I can lie and see myself like that. Lately I haven't slept much or
done very good work; mostly I've been drinking. That's why I
always drank so much of Reilly's gin and whisky when I came
up to your room.

"I went to work for the clinic down on Canal street because

they offered me a good salary and I wanted the money. They may be a gang of abortionists, but they do clean work and they don't have women dying of infections. Of course when they get hold of a dame with money they make her pay through the nose, but they do lots of work for women who can't afford high-priced 'ethical' abortions. That just by way of self-defense, I guess. I hadn't meant to say that sort of thing.

"There's something I want to ask you to do for me. I've got a family in the east. They don't know what a rotter their brat has turned into. Will you try to keep it from them that I killed myself? It would save them a lot of pain. I'll put my dad's name and address at the bottom of this page. You can see that he lives far enough away for you to tell him almost anything without being found out. If you'll do this I'll be grateful (in hell, I wonder?). But a fellow's father and mother never know him as he is.

"In the small envelope enclosed there's some money for Reilly. He helped me out of a scrape the last year in school. I'm sorry I can't pay him for all the liquor of his I've consumed this year.

"I don't expect you to mourn because I've passed out of the picture: I've been no ornament to the profession. But you and Reilly are square shooters and I wanted to tell you I know it.

"There's some money coming to me from the Clinic—enough to bury me and send a little home to the folks. If it's all the same to you boys, I'd prefer cremation.

"And now, as they say in books, farewell. From the next world, which I sincerely hope will be different if not better, I wish you both 'good hunting.'

"CHUCK."

Beside the signature there were two spots on the paper.

"Tears," thought Mallory. "He was crying when he wrote it."

Reilly's face was wiped bare of all levity; his gray eyes were softer than Mallory had ever seen them.

"The best thing Chuck ever did," he said softly, "dying. He went out without a squeal. I hope I can do as well when my time comes."

IV

By seven o'clock in the morning the day staff was ready to take over the Emergency. Reilly had taken Mrs. Hathaway home in his roadster, and young Butler had driven off with John Daniels. But Mallory in his street clothes went for one last look at his patients.

From one of the padded cells came disjointed strains of "Shall We Gather at the River?"; from the ward arose an overpowering stench of vomitus and stale whisky and urine, Mallory stood in the doorway looking at the rows of men, listening to their harsh breathing, thinking of Brantrier.

Life was so different from what he had expected it to be. Once in all sincerity Mallory had thought that right was pure white and wrong dead black, that the path of righteousness was a plainly labeled though stony trail and the way of evil a broad paved highway marked "To Destruction." But everything was gray, nothing was white and nothing black. For destroying unwanted babies Brantner had been paid a good salary; but in examining a charity patient he contracted syphilis, from terror of which he killed himself. Life became more and more complicated as one went on with it; the practice of medicine would probably be full of situations like this one or worse.

One of the patients near Mallory rolled over and moaned in his sleep. He was young and had a scant blond stubble on his cheeks; about his head was a blood-soaked bandage. In the next bed was an old man with both eyes swollen shut and dried blood crusted on his loose puffy lips. Mallory bent over him. Pulse 64, full, bounding. The fellow was all right. Mallory walked on, down between the long rows of unconscious or sleep-drugged men.

They were derelicts, all of them. He remembered a Great Lakes harbor where he had once seen old ships that had been abandoned. Good vessels they had been in their time, but that day was over. These men were like that. Life was hard for men as for ships; there were winds and storms and wrecks. He recalled the Rescue Home. Those girls and these men—all derelicts, shunted out of the main current of life. This was a strange world he lived in: sleeping drunken men, police officers, illegitimate babies, Brantner and his gang of abortionists, murderers and suicides, Reilly and Mrs. Hathaway. Every one of them was part of his life.

As Mallory came near the end of the long ward he lifted his eyes to the high windows. Across the low buildings nearby he could see the mountains east of Pacific City. Along the upper border of the dark range there was a narrow rim of gold and crimson. Thick clouds overhead forecast a dull day, but through this crevice in the sky the sun sent his New Year's greetings to these derelicts. A Happy New Year to all!

CHAPTER VII

I

Mallory turned over in bed and looked across the room at Reilly.

"But, Norman, I don't care anything about going to this shindig. I've no desire to become a social light."

"I've heard that line of yours so often, Bob, that it doesn't register any more. I know perfectly well that you'd rather sit here absorbing Osler on Malta Fever or go down and cut up stiffs in the morgue. But, good Lord, man, you can't spend all your life that way. You'll forget that there are girls in the world whose conversation includes anything beyond 'Yes, doctor,' and 'No, doctor.' The first thing you know that probationer that's got her eye glued to you will have you sewed up in the bag. She's the man-eating kind, too."

"Oh, now, Norman, that's not fair. She has trouble with her back. Lifting patients is hard for short girls; the beds are so high. But nobody ever seems to realize that. I've X-rayed her back several times, and I think I've found the trouble. Her fifth lumbar..."

Reilly sat up and glared at Mallory.

"Oh, my God! Her fifth lumbar! That girl never knew she had one until you hugged her the first time. Miss Huff says she's never done enough work since she's been here to strain a mosquito's spine."

"No, that's just it. All the supervisors are down on the kid. They pick on her and report mistakes the other girls make against her."

"Tra, la, tra la! And so our old friend Galahad rushes to the rescue. Or is it Don Quixote this time? With his nice pure heart. Pure apple sauce! Thank God, your brains are not in the same compartment as your emotions, Bob."

"But I tell you you don't understand."

"Oh, yes, I do. A damn sight better than you will if you live to the year 2000!" Reilly flopped down in his bed and stared at the ceiling. "You haven't sense enough to know a streak of luck when you run into it. Here's Benny Butler laid up in Contagious for nearly three weeks with a mess of diph. bugs in his nose, and you go over there and get him cleaned up and out of the place. And then it turns out that he lives here in town and that his old man is wealthy and the family knows everybody. They throw a party and invite you because you were kind to Benny and invite me because I'm your side-kick. And you want to stay home with your rotten livers! Sometimes, my dear young doctor, you make me sick—sick da bell, as the dagoes say."

Before this outburst Mallory sank back into bed and pulled the covers up over his head. When Reilly began an angry tirade, he could never think of a retort to make.

After two or three minutes of stark silence Norman snorted loudly, reached up over his head to his book shelf for a volume which he proceeded to prop open on his chest and read. The alarm clock above the lavatory ticked busily from 10:30 to 10:40 before Mallory capitulated.

"I'll go," he said, raising his head. "You win."

But there was only another long silence.

"You'd better turn off the light, Norman, and go to sleep. You're on second call to-night and you ought to get in a few winks before they start ringing you."

Another silence. Mallory tried again.

"What's the book?"

"Conrad. 'Heart of Darkness.'"

"Oh!"

"No 'Oh' about it! It's just as sensible for me to read it as it is for you to spend your life trying to figure out the forty-seven differences between parenchymatous and interstitial nephritis when there isn't any difference. They're both Bright's disease and they both kill you.... Oh, hell, there's that damned 'phone now!"

Three minutes later Reilly was padding down the hospital corridor fastening his belt as he went, and Mallory had shoved his head as deeply into the pillow furnished him by the Pacific City Hospital as its scrawny proportions would permit and was thinking how he could get the money for a dress suit without borrowing it from Norman.

II

On the following Thursday evening Benny Butler looked across his mother's drawing room at the group of well-groomed people who clustered about Katherine Harper. Benny had played with Katherine when they were both children, had fallen in love with her when she was thirteen, and now he was watching her welcome back to Pacific City.

Most of the guests, old and young, had known the girl all her life. They had seen her leave home for an eastern finishing school, a slender gawky seventeen-year-old who tried to cover both shyness and aspirations with a mask of assumed sophistication. In the seven years since then they had had only casual glimpses of her in the few summer weeks she had spent with her parents in alternate years. Some of them had been amused and some had approved when after leaving school she had refused to come home and enter society and had, instead, gone to Boston to study music. And all of them were interested in the exquisitely graceful young woman who had finally returned to Pacific City for an indefinite stay.

The sight of Katherine's ivory-skinned face, with its full curving red lips and soft brown eyes flecked with amber, had stirred Benny's adolescent passion again. More than a little dazed by the charm of her manner, he watched her this evening. Whenever she moved, her gold-colored frock clung to the graceful lines of her tall, slender figure. Her dark hair was massed high on her head; her voice was low and sweet-toned. Now and then Benny could hear her soft, rippling laughter. He was almost sure that sooner or later he would relapse into his old sentimentality over her. Then he caught sight of Mrs. Harper's proud face and grinned to himself as he recalled her old exasperation with Katherine because the girl was absorbed in music and took little interest in juvenile parties.

'The old dame finds it something else again to show off her only child now that she's done something out of the ordinary,' he thought. 'I wouldn't put it past her to call the meeting to order and read aloud that letter she had from the Conservatory about Katherine being the most promising young pianist they've turned out since 1900.'

It was not until just before dinner that Benny saw Norman Reilly come in alone. Hastily he made his way to the new arrival.

"Hello, Norman," he exclaimed, looking with approval at Reilly's faultless white waistcoat. "How come you're late? And where's Bob?"

"Oh, I've been waiting for that bird. He got tied up in the accident room at the last minute. They just hauled in a whole bunch of men that got blown up in a boiler explosion. Bob promised he'd come along as soon as he can, but that won't be for an hour or two anyhow. . . . Well, where's Exhibit A? I must meet this feminine wonder, Benny, before I die of curiosity about her."

Young Butler shrugged his shoulders. "I was going to put you down for Katherine's dinner partner. I thought you'd be more like the eastern fellows she's used to than the rest of us western hicks. But mother put her with the new symphony conductor;

she said they'd have something in common to talk about. So I had to pick another girl for you, Norman. You don't need to worry, she's a good looker. Come along and I'll find her for you."

"Benny," said Reilly, "you're a double crosser. Here I went and got a new tie and had a haircut, on account of this Katherine Harper, and when I get here all I can do is hover around the edges. I ask you, is that fair?" Suddenly Benny heard him stop talking and, following his eyes, saw that he was looking at Katherine.

"Who's that girl?" asked Norman, flicking at the dark red flower in his lapel. "The one in the gold dress, over there with all those fellows."

Benny grinned. "That's Katherine," he said.

"Good Lord," said Reilly. "And I supposed she'd be a blue stocking. Why didn't you put a danger signal on her, my boy? It's not right to turn a girl who looks like that loose among unsuspecting males." With a backward glance that held a tinge of regret, he followed Butler away, in search of his own dinner partner.

After the guests left the dining room they were shepherded by Mrs. Butler and Benny into the music room. At one side an open fire glowed softly in the grate. All the lights were turned off except one tall lamp beside the piano; it threw a pool of radiance over Katherine's figure when she sat down before the instrument. As she lifted her hands to the keyboard there came a polite hush, but scarcely had she begun to play when the stillness of courtesy gave place to the spell wrought by the sorcery of music.

Katherine's thin white hands sped over the keys with swift assurance. In her playing there was none of that lack of power sometimes felt in women pianists. Her slim body lost the hint of aloofness it had had during dinner, became suddenly taut with feeling. Music flowed from her flying fingers in a torrent of passion, then in tranquillity, then in flamboyant gayety. The men sat up straighter, watching her with eager eyes; the women's faces grew softer and less self-conscious.

With short pauses between, she went from the sonorous

beauty of Beethoven to the sad sweetness of Grieg and the florid charm of Brahms. In her golden gown the girl sat in the center of the pool of light that shone over the gleaming grand piano and played away her hearers' petty cares and worries, beckoned them into that world of beautiful sounds in which she lived.

Her listeners scarcely stirred. When at last she stopped to rest a little, there were none of the usual banal compliments. Katherine herself went to stand by the fire for a moment; but her mantle of self-possession did not at once enfold her again. In the curves of her body under the clinging gold-colored frock, emotion seemed to linger. Her corsage of violets and yellow rosebuds rose and fell with her rapid breathing, and when, after a few minutes, she returned to the piano it seemed that she was glad to play again.

Not until ten o'clock did Mallory, flushed and ill at ease, hurry up the steps of the Butler home. In the dressing room to which a maid showed him, he inspected himself anxiously. Upon the few other occasions when he had gone out in evening clothes, Reilly had been there to look him over, but to-night he had struggled alone with the white bow that defied all his attempts to keep it straight. As he surveyed himself in the mirror on the door, he succumbed to envy of Norman's faultlessly brushed hair, trim slender body, and impeccable ties. He was sure he could never master the art of sitting down without crumpling his stiff bosomed shirt or learn to refrain from stuffing his hands into his trousers pockets. In a last effort to achieve sleekness he sopped water on his hair and combed the whole brown mass of it back off his forehead, then in a sort of bewildered resignation gave up the attempt.

Had it not been for his promise to Reilly, he would have fled before the attack of stagefright he felt at the prospect of meeting a group of strangers who belonged to that mysterious entity called "society." He wiped off his patent leather shoes, brushed his coat collar, fiddled with his cuff links, and rubbed his freshly shaved jaw while he staved off that moment when he must face these people; but when he had done all these things two or three times over he found he had used up only ten minutes. At last, feeling like the football player who runs up and down before being sent into the game, he opened the door and walked downstairs, his clammy hands clenched at his sides. The maid was waiting for him.

"If you'll come with me, sir, I'll show you to the music room."

Wondering why she had to walk so fast, Mallory followed her. Just around a corner in the hall she stopped and pointed to a pair of doors partly open, through which faint light fell.

"Just wait here," she whispered. "Miss Harper is still playing."

Mallory nodded and stood still. Here was another ordeal; he hated waiting, it was harder than doing things, than doing anything. But there was no help for it. He was late and he could not charge into the room, among strangers, interrupting...

Then, for the first time, he became really aware of the music that filled his ears. His knowledge of music was slight. He had enjoyed Victor Herbert's band and "The Chocolate Soldier" and "Madame Sherry," but at college he had detested piano recitals of classical music. So, now, he did not know that he was listening to Schumann's "Whims," that it, like everything beautiful, had been born in wretchedness and pain, that it embodied poetry and loveliness and courage. He only felt that the very air about him was changing, that this was different from any other music he had ever heard, although he did not know how. These sounds seemed to laugh, to play together, to grow serious, to hint at bravery, and then to laugh again.

A queer unquiet crept over him—the same sort of vague restlessness and sense of something lacking in his life that always came when he looked from Norman's photographs of Gerty to his own print of the "Anatomy Lesson." Slowly he stole down the corridor until he could see through the half-open doors.

In the dusk that bordered the music room were the pale oblongs of the men's white shirt fronts, the larger pale blurs that were the women's light gowns. But in the circle of soft radiance at the end of the room there was a shining, golden figure before a gleaming piano; it glowed with life, it shone like a torch. Outside the doors, Mallory stood motionless, staring. The music died away, rose again, became impetuous and gay, ended in a flurry of sheer joyous beauty. The girl dropped her hands from the keyboard, swung about toward her audience, laughed in a soft, throaty voice. To Mallory came a faint fragrance of flowers and perfume, always hereafter to be associated with her laughter.

"I'm sure you must all have had enough of me by this time," she said. "I know I have."

Mallory, his hand on the doors, still gazed at her. She was beautiful, everything about her was beautiful. And she was utterly different from any other woman he had ever seen. The girls he had known in high school and college had been mostly country town products, healthily fond of the outdoors, and in medical school he had been too poor for more than casual acquaintances with women. Gerty Mannering and the probationer who had been flirting with him at the hospital flitted through his mind without lingering there. This girl was not like any of them: she wouldn't play tennis or hockey, or walk cross country in divided skirts, climbing gates and fences, or speak stage argot, or talk about her spine. Her profile stood out against the light like a cameo cut in ivory. Her gown was a blur of gold in his eyes.

Benny, opening the doors to lead the way back to the drawing room, stumbled into Mallory standing in the dimly lighted hall.

"Good Lord, when did you show up?" he cried. "How long have you been out here? Don't you want something to eat? Been working all evening, I suppose."

"Yes. No. That is…No, I don't want anything to eat."

"Too bad you couldn't get here in time to hear Katherine play," went on young Butler.

"I did hear her," said Mallory, gathering his wits together. "A little, that is. I waited out here. I didn't want to interrupt."

Benny seized Mallory's arm.

"Come along with me, Bob. Mother's been wanting to thank you for getting me out of Contagious. She's sure I'd've been there yet if you hadn't got busy on me. And then I'll introduce you to Katherine so you can get a dance with her."

Ignoring Mallory's protestation that he was the rottenest dancer alive, Butler dragged him off across the room.

Late in the evening Mallory came to his turn with Katherine, but she told him she was too tired to dance with anyone, however expert he might be. Benny, who was pushing manfully at a plump, middle-aged friend of his mother's who considered herself still light on her feet, waved at them as they left the dance floor.

"Benny is never going to grow up," said Katherine in her low-pitched voice. "I've known him for years and years and I simply can't think of him as a doctor."

Mallory looked down at the slim white hand lying on his black sleeved arm. It was incredible that two thin hands like that could make the music he had heard that evening. He wished he dared tell this girl how wonderful he thought she was. Once, he remembered, he had heard someone quote a line about beauty being its own excuse for being that, it seemed to him, was precisely the right comment on Katherine Harper. Silently, only half aware of what he did, he walked beside her.

Surprised that he did not reply to her remark, Katherine glanced up. He looked into her brown eyes, so near the level of his own; deep down in them were shining flecks of amber. He felt himself sinking into their soft liquid brownness. Nothing else seemed real to him.

Katherine smiled. Instinct told her that this young man was rugged, direct, dangerous perhaps. But his open admiration was as incense in her nostrils. She left her hand on his arm.

"I think Benny told me you haven't been in Pacific City long, Dr. Mallory," she said.

"No, Miss Harper, I haven't. I came out to the west coast last summer from Mannewaque."

"I should not have taken you for a middle westerner. You haven't the flat voice I associate with the corn belt."

From Mallory's legs, all the way up through his body, there flashed a strange sensation: his arm quivered ever so slightly under Katherine's hand. Feeling this, the girl looked at him again. She liked the ruggedness of his face, the way his neck came up straight out of his shoulders; she liked the instinctive knowledge that she could make him do what she wished.

"My mother came from New England," answered Mallory after a pause. "When I was a kid she kept after me about pronunciation and using the right words and all that sort of thing. I guess that's why you didn't spot me."

"Isn't that interesting? I've just come from New England, you know. I went to school near Boston and the last four years I've been in the Conservatory there. I've been home only about two weeks and I know I'm going to miss Boston awfully."

They had been walking slowly along the hallway, Mallory with no idea where he was going, but now, turning a corner, he saw the music room ahead of them.

"Why can't we go in here and sit down?" he asked. "You're awfully tired, I know, and no one will find us here."

There was an intensity in his rumbling baritone voice and an eagerness in the way he looked at her that pleased Katherine afresh.

"I'm simply worn out," she said. "It takes a lot of energy to play as long as I did this evening. It's really the equivalent of a concert so far as exertion goes."

When Mallory pulled up chairs before the grate, the fire was still flickering. At first he kept his eyes resolutely on the flames, but something he could not control kept pulling them across to the girl. She leaned back in her chair with her face in the shadow, but the firelight played on her frock, on the yellow rosebuds at her breast, on her hands, on her cloth-of-gold slippers. And in the air of the room there seemed to linger the spirit of beauty that her fingers had called from the piano.

Mallory pictured himself a courtier of an earlier century, kneeling before her, kissing her hand, being made her knight. Those ceremonies, ridiculous as they had seemed when he read about them in history, really had meant something after all.

"Are you fond of music, Dr. Mallory?"

At the sound of her voice he started and, before his brain

could frame an answer to her question, his larynx said, "Yes, Miss Harper, I love music."

The instant the words were out he was abashed. She would think he knew more than he did, she wouldn't understand that until to-night the music he liked best had been the waltz from *The Merry Widow* and "Every Little Movement" and things like that. A flush crept up his brown cheeks.

"I don't know if I can make you see what I mean, Miss Harper. I never had much chance to hear good music, I never had any lessons, I don't really know anything about it. But to-night I stood outside in the hall there and listened to you playing that last piece—I don't know what it's called. And it made me feel queer all over—glad and sorry and afraid and brave, all at once. I can't explain it any better than that because I don't understand it myself. But music never made me feel like that before, and I know it was real music to-night—different from the sort I've always liked. I want to learn about it, learn to listen to music and know what it means."

There was something in his voice and in the way he leaned toward her when he spoke that made Katherine's eyes soften. So few people cared for the thing that was the center of her life. By his own confession this man knew nothing about music, but he had felt something when she played. He had no idea how difficult that Schumann composition was, and he did not know what it had meant to her, but he had heard in it gayety and courage and poetic beauty. Suddenly she knew that she wanted to see more of Mallory, that she wanted to play for him other things she loved.

CHAPTER VIII

On a bleak late-winter Sunday Reilly, sauntering along Mallison street, saw Mallory crossing the street ahead of him. He hastened his steps and barely managed to achieve the safety of the opposite curb before an avalanche of motors swept by. He had seen very little of Bob in the two weeks since Mallory had gone on emergency room duty in the main hospital; the internes on emergency slept in a sort of kennel back of the accident room and had almost no free time.

Reilly drew up rapidly behind his friend.

"Hey," he called out. "What's your hurry?"

Mallory looked around and stopped.

"Oh, hello, Norman. Long time no see. What you doing?"

"Looking for a drink. Hard job to find a decent drink on Sunday. But I know a place up here on Sumner a couple of blocks that's pretty good. Come along, Bob?"

"What time is it?" asked Mallory looking about in search of a side-walk clock. "This blasted cheap watch of mine only runs when I do. One-thirty. Well, I don't mind if I do. I can spare a half hour and still be on time."

"On time where?" asked Reilly, idly.

"For the symphony."

"Oh," Reilly's voice was sardonic. "I see."

When they sat at their table in the Clermont with gin fizzes before them, Norman looked uneasily at his friend.

"Going in for music pretty strong lately, aren't you?"

"Oh, I don't know. I never had a chance to hear any good music until I went to college, and what I heard at recitals then I didn't like. I thought classical music was the bunk. But everybody that knows anything thinks that kind of music is the best, so I got to learn to like it, too. I guess the trouble's with me and not with the music, but it's a hard job. That man, Bach, now."

Reilly laughed.

"Well, I'd say Johann Sebastian is quite a way along the road of musical appreciation. Why don't you try something not quite so tough to start with? Schubert perhaps, or that Russian, Rachmaninoff. Every one is torturing that Prelude of his to death and there's a million records of it. I bet he wishes he'd never written it. It's mysterious, ends up on a minor chord, makes you wonder what happens next."

Mallory shook his head and finished his drink.

"No, this isn't foolishness with me, Norman. I'm really getting something out of it. The last symphony I heard they played somebody's overture to…to…Oh, well, it doesn't matter whose. Anyhow there was a storm and you could hear the thunder and the rain, and afterward it cleared up and the sun shone and you could hear the birds sing. Before they got through I was covered with gooseflesh. You wouldn't think music would do things like that to a fellow, would you?"

Reilly spun his empty glass round and round in his fingers.

"Oh, I don't know about that. I'd say you represented the protoplasmic school of musical appreciation, Bob. Your head doesn't know a thing about it, but your emotions get all stirred up and they stimulate the nerve-ends in your skin and give you gooseflesh. Perhaps it was a compliment to Rossini that you had gooseflesh over his music. Certainly that ought to be as legitimate a way to enjoy music as to thrill with the elderly virgins when their favorite conductor prances out on the stage and flutters their suppressed sexual desires. Have another drink?"

"No, thanks. One gin fizz is O.K. Two loosen my bearings, and three make me begin to babble."

"I take it, then, that there is to be someone with you to whom you do not wish to babble."

"Yes." Mallory's brown face turned pink.

"Miss Harper?" There was a dangerous silkiness in Reilly's voice.

"Yes," defiantly. "What of it?"

"Nothing," said Reilly softly. "You're at perfect liberty to make a fool of yourself if you want to."

"I'm not making a fool of myself over Katherine Harper," cried Mallory, pushing back his chair. "She's one of the finest girls in the town. Why shouldn't I go to symphonies with her if she'll let me? Isn't that better than lying around the internes' quarters telling smutty stories and shooting craps? I'd like to learn something so I won't always be a sap from a country town."

"You're not a sap now, but you soon will be," retorted Reilly, leaning across the table. "Do you think I don't know what's the matter with you? Why, if Katherine Harper didn't go in for music, you wouldn't know but that Bach was the name of a new brand of beer. And if she wasn't so refined and artistic you'd never have developed this sudden aversion to dirty stories."

Mallory jumped to his feet and glared down savagely at Reilly.

"That will be enough out of you," he snarled. "Don't lay your dirty tongue on a girl like Katherine. You mess around with a woman like Gerty Mannering and then criticize Katherine Harper. I'd like to knock your damned head off!"

He grabbed his hat and started for the door. Reilly threw a silver dollar on the table and hurried after him.

"Wait a minute, Bob," he cried. "Don't be sore! I didn't mean to say anything off color about Katherine Harper. It's just that I hate to…see you getting into an affair with her. You can't afford it, you haven't got the money, you never will have. You…"

By this time both men had reached the entrance.

"What's money got to do with it? I don't care anything about her money and neither does she. Money means less to her than to any girl I ever knew before. You think it's the most important thing in the world, you're always paying up things and getting out of scrapes by coughing up wads of money. But Katherine's not like that."

Reilly made a desperate effort to speak calmly. "I know that, Bob. But why does she care so little about money? Because she's always had plenty of it. No one ever disregards money so blandly as the folks who've never known what it is to have none. Nobody preaches the simple life as loudly as the people with forty-seven servants to simplify their lives for them. The Harper girl has plenty of money now, she always has had. You've never had any and I doubt if you ever will have. Silk and satin are as matter-of-course to her as ragged underwear is to you. Don't you see what I mean?" Reilly peered into Mallory's darkening face and disregarded it. "She's geared to a twenty-five thousand dollar income and you've never had over fifty dollars a month in your life, Bob. The thing's bound to break up, so why start it in the first place? It's not that I object to girls. Hell, no, I like 'em. There's lots of girls in Pacific City, and swell girls, too. Why, there's even one or two among the flat-foots at the hospital that aren't bad when they're dressed up to go out."

Mallory snorted, but Reilly rushed on.

"Ever since you met that girl at Benny's party you've been going around in a daze. For a girl, when the world is full of other girls. A dozen good lookers have walked past us while we've been standing here. Then why must you pick out one that's absolutely poison for you? It's not that there's anything wrong with Katherine Harper herself, but she's not the girl for you, Bob."

All the time Reilly had talked Mallory's face had been growing harder and more stubborn.

"Have you finished? Said everything that's on your chest?" he demanded. "Because, if you haven't, you'll never say the rest of it. Not to me. It's time for the concert. Just let me tell you something, for a change. There are people on earth who don't think money's the whole show, and Katherine Harper is one of them. And I'm another. But of course you can't see that. What would you be without your money?"

Reilly's face turned an angry red.

"Why, you dirty son of a sea-cook! For that crack I ought to hand you one in the jaw! Where would you have been a dozen times in the last five years if it hadn't been for my money?"

"Oh, go to hell!" cried Mallory. "Go to hell and stew there!"

He rushed off toward the Heilman Theatre where the symphony concerts were held.

"Well," said a voice behind Reilly, "that's that."

Norman spun around and saw Benny Butler leaning against the wall of the building near the entrance to the restaurant.

"Where'd you spring from?" he growled.

"Out of the Clermont, right behind you two. You're not the only fellow in Pacific City who knows where to get a drink on Sunday. I was just going to speak to you when you started on your big speech, so then I kinda stuck around to pick up the pieces if Bob hit you. You ought to be careful with that boy. If he ever landed on your chin with that fist of his, it would be just too bad for you. What's eating you anyhow?" Benny peered curiously at Reilly through his thick eye-glasses. He had never seen that young man so serious before except over Brantner's body. "Come on back into the Clermont, Norman, and have another drink or something to eat. It'll make you feel better."

"All right, Benny, I will. I need a drink."

Over a whisky and soda young Butler asked, "What's wrong with Bob having a girl? And why not Katherine Harper if he likes her?"

"There's nothing wrong with Katherine Harper, and I don't object to Bob having a girl, Benny. But he hasn't any sense about women. He believes all they tell him, whether it's how they suffer or how hard they work or how good their intentions are. He's always giving me a wild tale handed him by some hard-boiled wench up in the hospital about some man who took advantage of her innocence. And now he's convinced that Katherine Harper is going to live with him in a garret somewhere, on nothing a week, all for love. She's a musician: ergo, thinks Bob, she lives on art and beauty. He can't see that money is as necessary to her as the air she breathes, precisely because she's always had plenty of it."

Reilly stared blackly at his half-empty glass and drummed the table with his nervous finger tips before he went on, "Nobody can disregard money quite as well as those of us who've never known what it's like not to have plenty."

Benny shook his head.

"It's too bad," he said, "but what could you expect? Everyone falls for Katherine—always has—except a few wiseacres like you. Why, when I was in high school there were weeks I couldn't eat or sleep because of her. And, if I thought I stood a chance, I could fall in love with her all over again now. She's a swell girl; none of us fellows she's turned down ever stay sore at her. I think Bob would be lucky if she'd take him."

Reilly made an impatient movement toward the soda bottle.

"No, no, Benny, you don't see what I'm driving at. Bob is different from you and me. He thinks about medicine like missionaries are supposed to think about their work: it's not a way to make a living, but a way to live. There's a difference, Benny, a big difference. He loves medicine. Once he told me he'd had a 'call' to it, just as preachers used to think they were 'called' to the pulpit." Reilly squirted more charged water into his glass.

"You and I will be pill peddlers, saw-bones, to the end of our days. But Bob could do more than that…if he had a chance. Well, I want him to have that chance, Benny, do you see? And if he goes off and gets married, it'll spoil everything. He'd have to settle down somewhere to make a living—probably in some jerkwater place only big enough for one doctor.

"And besides that, getting married would be a serious business for Bob, right now. He won't make a good husband for a modern girl, Benny. Half of him is caveman; he'll absorb the woman he marries without giving it a thought. His instincts are primitive: he'll want a home and a fireside and a flock of kids, and he'll be insulted and injured if the girl thinks she wants a little something more than that out of life. Then the whole thing will go to smash. No, Bob needs to be aged—in the wood, like this whisky—before he gets married."

Butler looked at Reilly with a puzzled expression as though he felt it strange that Norman took so serious a view of a love affair. "Well," he said doubtfully, "I never thought of it that way. But maybe you could talk to Bob and kinda reason it out with him."

Reilly snorted. "Reason! With that bird? I might as well try moral suasion on a grizzly! You heard him a while ago, didn't you? Telling me that I'm a rotter and don't understand his feelings about Katherine Harper because I go around with Gerty Mannering and her gang, that all I care about is money! God knows what else he thinks about me. Sometimes I think he's just an egotistical prig." Reilly regarded the remnants of his whisky and soda gloomily. "But I know better than that. And I wish to the Lord I could think up some way to get that one-track mind of his out of the clutches of biology and its urges."

Benny snapped open his flat, gold-lined cigarette case and extended it toward Norman.

"If you're asking my opinion," he said, "I think you're going off half-cocked. There's nothing wrong with Katherine. I've known her all my life and I like her. I wish to God she'd fall for me. What if she is good to look at? What if men do like her? What if she has got money? Is it her fault that she was born with 'come hither' instead of a hare-lip? The girl's got brains, and instead of sitting around here at home playing the society game as her mother wanted her to do she's been making something out of herself. She studied music in spite of her family and now they're proud as punch of her, just like the rest of us."

Young Butler looked hard at Reilly's worried face.

"Now, listen, Norman. That girl is going places. She's got ambition. If she's in love with Bob she'll marry him and push him along and make a big man out of him, don't you worry. She can do it. And I happen to know that she's got some money of her own too, some that her grandmother left her; she told me once that she had enough to go to Boston and finish up abroad without asking her father for any help."

Butler smoked thoughtfully for a moment, then thumped the table cheerfully.

"Cheer up, Norman, old boy. Katherine won't ruin Bob's career if she marries him. I'll bet you, two to one, that she'll have the fellow in the east studying before they've been married a year—if they get married—or in Europe, if the war's over by then. You're just imagining things, Reilly. Why, Katherine's got more ambition than Bob has and, with her back of him, he'd probably shoot ahead like a rocket. Honestly, I can't see any reason why you should object to her, especially when you say you want Bob to do something out of the ordinary. It looks to me as though Katherine and her money would be the very way to keep him from settling down in a one-horse country town."

Reilly's eyes were still serious and unconvinced, but he forced a laugh in response to Butler's arguments.

"I guess I object because I'm a fool, Benny. The first time I ever saw those two together, the night of your party, I had a hunch that they were going to smash, trying to love each other. It's not that I think there's anything wrong with Katherine Harper. But I'm afraid of her. She's like one of those things chemists call catalysts: they don't do anything they shouldn't, but when you put them into a mixture the other things in it begin raising Hell. That's why I'm afraid of her, Benny."

CHAPTER IX

Dr. Drake, roentgenologist to the Pacific City Hospital, put his head into the dark room of the X-ray laboratory.

"Mallory," he said, "can you step into the office before I leave the hospital? I want to talk with you for a minute."

"Wait a minute, please, doctor," cried Mallory. "Will you look at this and tell me if you see a fracture across the neck of the femur?" He held up an X-ray plate, fresh from the fixing bath, before the viewing box.

Drake came in and studied it intently.

"Uh…yes, I think there's a fracture line right here." He pointed to a very faint dark line across the bone. "Another fat old lady fallen down on a rug on a polished floor, eh? This is the sort of case your diaphragm ought to help us with."

Mallory grinned broadly.

"Just what I thought, Dr. Drake. So I made an exposure with it." He fished another plate out of the tank and held it up beside the first one. "There's a difference, isn't there?" Pride spoke in his voice. "I made myself look at the plain plate first and I thought there was a fracture. But see how sharp it looks on the plate made with the diaphragm."

Mallory was not exaggerating. On the one plate the bones of the hip were barely visible against a foggy gray background while on the other they shone out startlingly white, with the fracture a distinct black line across the bone.

Drake nodded his approval.

"That's fine, boy. Fine. You've got something worthwhile in that piece of apparatus. Is there anything special you want me to do to-day?"

"There are the plates on that stomach case. I looked at him with the fluoroscope this morning and then made a bunch of exposures afterward."

"What's the matter with him?"

"Ulcer, I think, Dr. Drake. The history suggests it and the duodenal cap is irregular in outline on most of the plates."

"Have the girl bring them into the office and I'll look at them before I go. And don't forget to come in yourself."

Drake walked slowly through the examining room into the private office. He had liked Mallory from the moment the boy appeared in his department; he thought him the best interne they'd ever had in the X-ray laboratory—honest, frank, ready to admit mistakes and take criticism, never bellyaching about accident cases that had to be examined at night. Drake was proud of all the boy had learned: he could make an excellent stomach examination and handle acceptably the routine work of the department. It would be a big thing for him to go east to study. Then there was this diaphragm he had designed; that might turn out to be something of real value.

Drake tilted back his desk chair, cut a tiny chimney in the end of a cigar, and began to smoke while he pondered the situation that confronted him. He agreed with Reilly that Mallory, having had one brilliant idea, would probably have more, that he must be sent east to study radiation and then to Europe. Almost any means to gain these ends, they both felt, would be justified. Drake was not exactly sure how Reilly meant to sustain the "fellowship" illusion, but no doubt he could arrange to remit the money in such a way that Mallory's suspicions would not be aroused.

Drake found himself envying that young man's prospects. Once he got the ratio of curves and distances exactly right, his diaphragm would lose the one drawback it now had: there would then be no lines on the plates. He recalled his own surprise at the first picture of a hip that Mallory had made with this instrument of his invention: the bones had been so plain that it seemed almost indecent to exhibit the plates of the poor old lady's pelvis. Since then the boy had improved upon his first rough model, eliminated this part and changed that. That diaphragm might be the making of the fellow. Ten years from now he might be one of the big X-ray men in the country.

There was a sharp knock at the door.

"Come in. Sit down, Mallory. I want to talk to you."

Drake fidgeted in his chair and played with a stack of requisition slips on his desk. He was obsessed with the feeling of guilt he always felt when he was about to put something over on a friend. Mallory leaned against the door jamb, waiting, with his hands stuffed into his trousers pockets and his blue eyes resting on Drake in mild puzzlement.

"Neeley, the head of the educational department of the Torvac X-ray Company, has been in town this week and I took the liberty of showing him this diaphragm of yours. He thinks it might prove to be a fine thing if it was perfected. I could see that he was impressed with it. But this is what I really wanted to tell you, Mallory. Neeley says the Torvac people have a few fellowships in this country and abroad that they give to promising young fellows who are interested in X-ray work. There's not much in them, just enough for a man to live on if he's careful. Neeley thinks he can get you one of them on the strength of this diaphragm you've built. You'd start off with a year in Boston or Philadelphia and then go to Europe if things quiet down over there."

Drake looked sidewise at Mallory and then quickly away. He pulled out a handkerchief and mopped his face. By Jove, he believed he had actually pulled it off without the boy suspecting anything! But his relief was shattered by the grave, troubled face that Mallory turned toward him.

"Dr. Drake, I'm awfully sorry, but I can't do that."

"Can't do it! Why, what do you mean?" Drake's tone was blank with surprise.

"Just that. It's impossible. I'm sorry, really awfully sorry. But it is impossible."

The young man's mouth and shoulders looked very square and decided.

"But, Mallory, you don't realize what you're doing! Two or three years' work with no cost to you. Holmes in Boston, Pancoast and Pfahler in Philadelphia, Regaud and Mme. Curie in Paris, Åkerlund in Stockholm. Why, when you came home, you'd be the best trained young radiologist in the country!"

"I realize that, Dr. Drake. And a few months ago I'd've jumped at the chance. But now I can't."

"What's happened in the last few months to change things? See here, boy." Drake looked squarely into Mallory's eyes. "If you're afraid of charity, forget it. The Torvac people never do anything altruistic. If they offer you anything, you may be sure they think they see a way to get their money back." That was a neat touch, he congratulated himself, about the Torvac Company not being in business for generosity.

For a minute or two Mallory did not speak; then he straightened up and looked over at Drake with eyes that seemed to the older man the bluest and frankest eyes he had ever seen.

"It isn't anything like that, doctor. I'm not worrying over charity. But you see…" A flood of red began to creep over the tanned face. "I'm going to be married…that is, I expect to be."

Drake was dumfounded at this announcement; Mallory had always seemed too interested in his work to have much time for women.

"You see, Dr. Drake, I'm in debt now for my education. I've got to get to work earning something as soon as I'm through here at the hospital. When I get squared away and have some money saved up, I'll try to get some post-graduate work. But

I've decided that the thing for me to do just now is to go into general practice for a while."

"So you're going to try that game? Have you found a location?"

"Oh, yes." Mallory's voice stumbled for eagerness. "Two weeks ago, when I had that time off, I went down and looked the place over. Glenwood, on the Silticoos River, right near the mouth. It's just north of the Candon Bay country. Glenwood is a fishing town but there's a good-sized sawmill, too, and the railroad built in there last year."

Through the smoke of his cigar Drake watched Mallory. He knew from experience what a general country practice was like.

"Is there any business down there? You know it's hard to get anywhere in these little towns. All the people that have enough money to pay their bills go away to larger places."

"Well, the man who's leaving made enough in eight years to take a trip abroad. I know because I saw his books." Mallory spoke slowly but very definitely. "The lumber business will probably increase now that they've got rail transportation as well as water. Then a big salmon cannery is going in at Westport, just across the river from Glenwood, this summer."

Through Drake's mind flashed the thought that the physician who was leaving probably wanted to get away before he spent all he had made off the railroad construction in the last year or two.

"Where's the nearest hospital, Mallory? You can't do any surgery without some sort of hospital."

But Mallory had an answer for this practical question.

"There's a hospital right there, in Glenwood. I'm going to take it over and run it myself. I don't think I would have considered the proposition if there hadn't been a hospital."

"Why, I didn't know there was a hospital in that whole section outside Baypoint down on Candon Bay."

"Well," Mallory's voice became a little uncertain for the first time during the conversation. "Well, it mightn't seem like much of a hospital to you, Dr. Drake, but it's a start."

"How big is it?" persisted Drake.

"Eight beds. That's all," admitted Mallory. "But there's a small surgery that Peters has used for ordinary stuff, and an X-ray machine. Of course, it's an old-fashioned static with gas tubes, but it works. I made some pictures with it when I was down there."

"I see," said Drake thoughtfully. "And you are going to take over this…institution?"

"Yes. I expect to. The terms Dr. Peters made me are very liberal. Five years and the contract can be renewed after that if I like."

Drake thought to himself, "Now I'm sure the fellow, Peters, is unloading the thing on a young chap he's picked for a sucker."

"And the hospital building—what sort of shape is it in?" Drake probed softly but persistently while he watched Mallory's exuberance slowly dying under this fire of questions.

"Well, you see, doctor, there isn't any hospital building by itself. It's upstairs, over some stores and the barber shop. Right on the water-front, close to the wharves. It's in a good location." Mallory spoke now with a bare trace of the apologetic in his manner.

"And how big is the field? How many people?"

"Glenwood has a population of about four hundred and fifty, and there are as many more in Southport, just across the river. Then there are the people living along the valley for twenty miles, up as far as Blackberg at the head of the tide—at least another four hundred of them. The cannery and logging camps bring in still more. The saw mill's going to run full blast this summer, they say. There'll be more than twelve hundred people, you see."

Mallory looked anxiously at Drake, but the older man sat buried in thought; his brain was full of logical arguments against Glenwood but instinct told him that Mallory, having made his decision, would not give up the plan easily. Drake found himself hesitating to advise the boy to stay in the city with its office buildings already overfull of doctors. And, now that there were telephones and electric lights and highways and automobiles, the country would be very different from the western Nebraska territory where he had practiced in the

90's. He tossed away his cigar and clapped a hearty hand on Mallory's shoulder.

"Well, lots of doctors have made a living with no more than twelve hundred people to draw from. As a matter of fact, I did myself, twenty-five years ago in Nebraska. You're all right, boy. I've got faith in you. . . . While you're still at the hospital, come in often and I'll give you a lot of good advice free: pointers on how to deal with women who want you to do abortions for them, fee-splitting with the other medicos, collecting in advance for venereal disease."

Mallory's eyes brightened.

"You needn't worry about those things, Dr. Drake. There isn't any other doctor on the Silticoos, none nearer than Candon Bay. And I'm not going to get into any jams on this illegal stuff, not on your life! I've learned a thing or two, this last year, in the police hospital."

In his own mind Drake doubted that the thirty-five or forty miles between Candon Bay and Mallory's valley would prevent professional competition and fee-splitting, but since he did not know the local situation he said no more about the matter.

"Well, don't forget I'll always be glad to help you any way I can, Mallory. . . . Oh, by the way, are you making your matrimonial intentions public around the hospital?"

Once more Mallory's face turned dark red.

"No, Dr. Drake, I'm not. They don't like married internes here, you know. So we'd planned not to let any one know until June, when I've finished here. Just as soon as I get my diploma from the hospital, of course…"

"All right. I only asked because I didn't want to spill the beans for you by accident. After all, it's your own business. Go ahead and do what you want to, and good luck to you."

"Thank you, doctor. I…I appreciate this. You see, I kind of counted on you understanding how it was, but a fellow can't ever be sure."

"Don't worry, boy. I won't give you away." From his desk, Drake watched Mallory's stocky figure swing away down the corridor. His white uniform was rumpled and his thick hair bristled over the crown on the back of his head, but he walked like a conqueror. Drake drew a long breath. He remembered his own enthusiasm over the practice of medicine, his creeping disillusionment in the Nebraska of the 90's, the mounting debt he could never pay off, his escape into a specialty through an unexpected legacy.

He could picture Mallory plodding through the rain and wind of an Oregon winter, on backwoods trails and the teetering sidewalks of a fishing village. Certainly the professional experience at first would do him good, give him confidence in himself, but he might easily get so entangled financially that he could never get away. It was possible, Drake admitted to himself, that Mallory would be a good businessman, but he didn't look like a good collector or the sort that would make money.

Then, he was too idealistic—not about his patients; the police hospital had seen to that—but about his own standards. He was the kind of doctor to sink money into a hospital regardless of the returns he could expect, to spare neither effort nor expense for his patients. Drake shook his head. He could see Mallory getting older and less energetic, tired and shabby. It was too bad. He had been the only interne in Heaven knew how long who had made medicine his vocation, lived it and worked it and dreamed it.

But would he be any better off if he stayed in town? A man had to do so many unpleasant things, even dishonorable things, if he was to get good staff appointments and build up a practice. That old notion that a physician needed only ability and good training was poppy-cock, but it was a damned shame that a doctor couldn't put his mind on the work he knew how to do and pass up the boot-licking and kow-towing and sharp practice. Drake looked down at his beautifully creased, expensive trousers; he hadn't had hundred-dollar suits in Nebraska in the 90's. But did having them now make him any happier? He ran his hand over his forehead lingeringly. He was suddenly tired, appalled at the contrast between Mallory's youthful zeal and his own cynicism.

Then he reached for the stack of reports on the desk beside

him. He might as well scrawl his name on the damned things and get it over with.

Not until two hours later, as he was unlocking the door of his private office downtown, did Drake remember that Mallory had not said when he was to be married or to whom.

'My brain must be softening. . . . I must get in touch with Reilly right away, too. There's no use wrangling with Mallory about this "fellowship" business. His mind is made up and it's going to stay that way.'

He pushed the button for his secretary.

"Will you get Dr. Reilly at the City Hospital on the wire for me?"

PART TWO

CHAPTER I

I

Restlessly, Robert Mallory paced up and down the open platform that clung to the side of the railroad embankment along the north fork of the Silticoos River, and peered northward along the track through the slanting autumn sunshine. The train in which Katherine was coming to Glenwood was late. As he walked back and forth he whistled "Tipperary" and snatches of "My Little Dream Girl," and once he tried to push his untrained baritone to the high notes of Chauncey Olcott's "Little Bit of Heaven." Then he lit a cigarette, sat down, threw the cigarette away half-smoked, got up again, and resumed his nervous pacing to and fro.

Somehow, in the midst of a forenoon spent in struggling with a fractured wrist, a case of itch, a baby with a huge boil on one buttock, and a logger with a deep ax-cut in his foot, Mallory had snatched time to visit the barber and the little cleaning shop. His crisp chestnut brown hair was brushed back in a shining mass, his dark cordovan shoes twinkled in the sunlight, his gray tweed trousers hung for once in knife-edge creases. And in his heart was a blurred mixture of happiness at Katherine's approach and vague pleasure in the beauty about him.

North, west, and east loomed the green, fir-covered mountains of Oregon, made mysterious by the soft haze of early autumn. Into Mallory's mind flashed a phrase from a half-remembered poem: "The blue beyondness of the hills."

These mountains, so different from the jagged half-bare Rockies, seemed to sprawl against the sky with an arrogant assurance of perpetual youth; tier after tier they rose over the Silticoos until they blotted a massive profile against the pale blue of the horizon. Below, at their feet, flowed the great mile-wide river. Now and then a salmon, jumping, arched a bow of silver in the cool September air. Screeching gulls swept down out of the sky to rest on the piles along the river bank. And over the distance there hovered a half-veiling curtain of grape-blue haze.

From the railway platform a wavering line of corduroy road angled off southwest toward the stream and five hundred yards away disappeared around the sharp point of land which intervened between the embankment and Glenwood. At this turn in the road Mallory soon saw the stage appear—a Ford touring car with flapping curtains and a trailer lurching along behind. It bounded up beside the platform and stopped. From it clambered a tall loose-jointed flaxen-haired Swede who wiped his face on the sleeve of his blue jumper and peered up cheerfully at the doctor.

"Well, doc, I expect ya got worked up a sweat, walkin' down here, didn't ya? I knew ya was scared I'd never get here on time, and I didn't blame ya. When that lizard dies on me like she done to-day I always have the heck of a time startin' her again. She like to kicked the arm off'n me this afternoon. I ain't goin' to turn off the ignition now."

Mallory grinned down at the stage-driver who was biting off the corner of a gnawed plug of tobacco.

"That's what I told you, Hansen. One of these days you'll have a Ford fracture, and they're nasty breaks, let me tell you."

"No, doc, I won't have no arm broke. Not with no Ford. I always ketch hold of the crank with my thumb up, so's not to get caught when it kicks."

Hansen propelled a mouthful of saliva and tobacco juice from his lips in a long arc like the purposeful curve of a pitched ball. 'Just like the stage trick of a country hick in vaudeville,' thought Mallory, 'but Olaf 's no hick.'

"Bathroom workin' all right now, doc?" continued the stage-driver. "I reckon Mrs. Hathaway told ya I had to put in new taps. Them old ones never was no good. Doc Peters was always havin' trouble with 'em."

"I'm glad you put in new ones, Hansen. And I'm grateful to have things fixed up on such short notice, too."

"Oh, that's all right, doc. Ya got to have things workin' right with your wife comin' and all. Besides, I wasn't busy nohow. With a train down to the Bay every day, folks don't bring me their watches to fix like they used to." Hansen selected a long splinter from a nearby plank and sat down to whittle. "The train's late, ennyhow. I reckoned it would be. They got a lot of stuff to unload for the new store up to Lakeview. I expect we'll have to wait quite a spell, ya and me."

At which Mallory and Hansen settled into a friendly silence, punctuated irregularly by the coughing of the idling engine of the Ford.

II

For the thousandth time that day, the doctor reminded himself that it was his wife who was coming on this train: it seemed impossible but it was true. At the memory of the short ceremony that had made them legally husband and wife, his skin tingled again just as it had done five months before on the beautiful April day when they had stolen away to a shabby parsonage on the outskirts of Pacific City to pledge themselves to each other.

Mallory even then had known it was a risky business for an interne, getting ten dollars a month and his board, to marry: he had realized that there was neither family influence nor money behind him. But he could not control the passion Katherine had roused in him. His very lack of experience with women made him helpless before it. She was slim and graceful, her eyes were soft and brown, her voice was low, her lips responded to his kisses, her body intoxicated his senses, her love for music and her flair for evoking moving poems of sounds from the piano invested her with a sort of other-worldly charm. As he sat waiting for her, little shivers of delight ran over him: he had never known before all a woman could mean to a man. She was coming, she would be with him to-night. His wife!

Mallory stared at the fir-clad hillside in front of him. For weeks he had been building jumbled air-castles of the hospital he meant to build on the Silticoos and the home he wanted to make for Katherine. With such passionate intentness did he hold before him the vision of the future as he desired it that the actuality of things as they were seemed unimportant. Even though the dingy hospital, full of the discarded belongings of his predecessor, had seemed forbidding to him when he arrived in Glenwood in June to begin practice, he had put the disagreeable part of the situation out of his mind while he worked. When his own energy and the labor of Dr. Peters' maid-of-all-work, Sairy Paine, had not changed the hospital as quickly as he wished, he had written to Rachel Hathaway in Pacific City to ask if she knew of a nurse who might be persuaded to go to the backwoods.

When her reply came saying that she herself might leave the police Emergency Hospital and come to Glenwood, he felt that the battle was almost won. And, indeed, the two months since Mrs. Hathaway had arrived had seen many changes. No longer did Mallory live on Sairy's diet of fish, boiled potatoes, and coffee stew. No longer was he forced to carry trays from the hotel dining room for his patients to whom he dared not offer Sairy's menu, and no longer did he bathe and nurse his patients and make their beds and wait on them. That first month when he had been doctor and nurse and hospital orderly had already become a vague memory.

Mrs. Hathaway had galvanized Sairy into astonishing activity, and fresh paint had followed hot water and soap and scouring paste. Mallory felt that the hospital had been revolutionized and he had written Katherine many glowing letters in which the present situation and the future were so intermingled as not to be distinguished from each other.

Only that morning at breakfast he had spoken to Mrs. Hathaway of all she had accomplished.

"What you've done around here, Mrs. H., is wonderful. The hospital isn't the same place it was when I came last June. I won't be ashamed to have Katherine come now. And I want you to know that I appreciate it all."

Mrs. Hathaway smiled at the young face that looked so straight at her. Her eyes—soft blue-gray—were full of understanding; they seemed to say that a woman, especially a middle-aged nurse like herself, would have been disillusioned before this by the Silticoos valley but that she was glad Mallory still had confidence in Glenwood.

"It's been a pleasure to do it, doctor. And since I have to stay here too, it wasn't altogether altruism on my part."

Before she finished her sentence, Mrs. Hathaway realized that Mallory did not hear what she was saying, that he took no notice of the bright autumn sunshine spilling through the window on the spoons and syrup pitcher. Her face sobered as her thoughts too turned to the girl who was now on her way to Glenwood. Did she know what sort of place it was? Or had her husband's enthusiasm for the future painted too bright a picture of the actual present? An abrupt movement of Mallory's recalled Mrs. Hathaway's attention to the breakfast table.

"Sairy," she called pleasantly.

At this summons there appeared in the doorway between kitchen and dining room the apparition of a woman of indeterminate age and no visible charms, whose scanty mouse-colored hair was drawn back tightly from a bulging forehead and the neck of whose faded cotton frock displayed a well-developed goiter.

"What d'you want?" she demanded.

"Will you bring some fresh hot cakes, Sairy?"

The servant nodded sullenly and dived back into the kitchen.

"May I give you some hot coffee, doctor?" continued the nurse.

Mechanically the young man held out his cup. His face, usually so alert, was abstracted and distant and, when Sairy put down a plate of hot pancakes before him, he glanced at them as though he wondered what they were for.

"It seems a long time since you saw your wife, doesn't it?" asked Mrs. Hathaway quietly.

Mallory started and looked up at her.

"Ages, Mrs. H. Ages! I came down here the first week in June and this is the fourteenth of September. I'd no idea three months could be so long. But Katherine thought it was only fair for her to spend the summer with her father and mother. They were pretty decent about our getting married so suddenly. But it's been a long time since June."

Mrs. Hathaway smiled to herself, recalling the stir made in Pacific City when Mr. and Mrs. Harper had announced their daughter's marriage as a deed already accomplished. Then, watching Mallory's rugged face, she became suddenly full of nostalgia for her own youth and the enchanted days of her early marriage, the sort of thing she always told her friends no middle-aged widow had any business to think about.

After Dr. Mallory left the table she lingered, drinking a third cup of coffee and considering the day before them. She had grown very fond of Mallory in the months she had worked with him. She had watched him learn to face emergencies alone, she knew he looked at each patient as an individual and not a case number. She had seen him keep his professional standards intact in the police hospital and, in spite of his ineptness at expressing his ideals, she had divined much that he hoped to do for the Silticoos valley. She knew that he believed a physician should take a significant part in community life, that he was determined to improve the environment and make the children better than their parents, that he had a vision of a hospital that should be everything most small town hospitals are not. She seemed to hear again what Mallory had said to her the day she arrived in Glenwood: "Mrs. H., they need you and me here. They need us and the things we can do." She knew how this sense of being needed filled Mallory's heart so that, in its glow, the sordid present faded before the splendid future.

But, suddenly disquieted, she found herself wondering if the doctor's wife would have that same comforting feeling that she was needed. What would this girl, accustomed to luxury, think of the bare floors and walls, the wood stoves, the bathroom whose taps were so often out of order? And of Sairy and her illegitimate child who spent much of her time in the hospital kitchen? How would she adapt herself to living in the institution, using the waiting room or the doctor's office as her sitting room in the evenings?

Then, annoyed by these uncomfortable thoughts, Mrs. Hathaway told herself that, after all, this was neither her business nor her responsibility. The doctor and his wife must solve their own problems. Finishing the last swallow of coffee and resisting the temptation to ask Sairy for more, she put aside speculation and rose to go about her morning's work.

III

When Katherine Mallory, her husband's hand under her elbow, stepped down from the train to the Glenwood station platform, she did not know how entirely new a phase of life she was entering. For one thing, she was still feeling Mallory's arms tighten around her as he rushed into the car to meet her, and, for another, she was still savoring the satisfying odor of soap and tobacco that emanated from his rough tweed coat when she put her face against it. 'It's been so long,' she thought. 'So long!"

But very quickly she caught sight of the porter's knowing smirk and thereupon gathered about her like a cloak her accustomed self-possession. Swiftly she looked at the great green hills above them and at the silver river.

"Bob," she said softly, putting a gloved hand on his arm, "it's lovely."

Mallory looked at her proudly. To him she seemed more beautiful than ever this afternoon. She wore a suit of reddish-tile cloth that flared about the hips and above the ankles, and around her neck and wrists there were bands of beaver fur. Her hat tilted up sharply on the side toward him so that her profile stood out against the warm brick-red color of the opposite side of the brim. Mallory was proud of her, even proud that she was dressed more appropriately for the city than for Glenwood. He caught at her hand as it lay on his arm and tucked it into his own thick warm palm.

"Better ya get in, doc," admonished Hansen as he dragged past them the last of Katherine's three trunks. "We'll be goin' as soon's I get the mail sack. I guess one of the trunks 'll have to wait, though. They ain't room in the trailer for all of 'em and the mail too. But I'll have it up to ya before supper, don't ya worry."

"Wait a minute, Olaf. I want you to meet my wife. Katherine dear, this is Mr. Hansen, one of my best friends in Glenwood."

The tall Swede, acutely bashful, blushed as he bobbed his head at her.

"Pleased to meet ya, Mrs. Mallory." He held out a big dirty hand, then snatched it back before Katherine could touch it. He bobbed at her again. "Better ya get in," he insisted. "We'll go just as soon as I get that mail sack up there."

Mallory helped Katherine into the Ford and, turning a broad back on the solitary brakeman looking their way, bent over and kissed her mouth swiftly. But when Olaf returned, he found the doctor saying commonplace things to her.

"You see, dear, this is the only machine in the valley. There's just this short stretch of corduroy road between Glenwood and the railway. Not another road in the Silticoos. We go around on the river, in gas boats."

"I think I'd like that, Bob. Motor boats are such fun. Father has one at home, you know."

Mallory flushed: he remembered seeing John Harper's sleek, brass-trimmed yacht on the Willapoor.

"Well, these boats down here aren't much like your father's, dear. . . . They're just round-bottomed fish boats with mail-order engines in the middle of them. There's neither looks nor speed to them."

Before Katherine could answer this, Hansen climbed into the car, opened the throttle, and let in the clutch. The Ford bounded off over the loose planks with a deafening roar.

The girl looked about in bewilderment as they flew down the road. She had never seen anything remotely like this country before. The highway angled across the tide-flats obliquely and approached the stream. Across the river she could see a huddle of unpainted gray buildings which her husband shouted in her ear was Southport, Glenwood's rival town. She was sure that the road along which they were bouncing was the roughest she had ever ridden on, until the Ford jolted even more violently after the highway entered a slit blasted out of the rocky cliff along the bank of the stream. She caught the words "gill net" and "first drift" and "a poor run this fall" in Mallory's conversation but did not know what they meant. Here and there on the river she saw ungainly open boats moving slowly.

Then suddenly the road flung itself around a sharp point of land and debouched into a half-circle of level ground between the mountain and the stream. Here houses were perched thickly, like seagulls on a flat rock. The road soon became Main Street and, to her surprise, Katherine saw that it was elevated on heavy timbers several feet above the low ground of the waterfront. Down it clattered the Ford, shattering the late-afternoon stillness and dragging behind it a streamer of dust. In the front windows of the houses Katherine saw observant white faces and realized with a sudden shock that they were peering at her, that she would be an intruder, an object of curiosity, in Glenwood.

On the landward side of the street she saw a sidewalk on the same level as the roadway and also elevated on wooden stilts above the low ground. From it narrow walks led back to small cottages or meandered up the hillside toward more distant houses. The waterfront, on the other side of the elevated road, was cluttered with wharves and landings and boat houses with steep ramps.

Katherine caught sight of a brown wooden structure with the word 'Hotel' painted in big black letters, of men sprawling in chairs before its front windows, of stores opening directly off the sidewalk. Then the car slid to an abrupt jerky stop in front of three sets of many-paned windows at which the girl peered, feeling like Alice arrived at last at the bottom of the shaft down which she had so strangely fallen. The windows were covered with words advertising the presence behind them of the Silticoos River Meat Co., Brown's Barber Shop, and the Burton Drug Co.

Mallory got out and turned to help Katherine. Once on the sidewalk she looked up to see that the three stores occupied the ground floor of a two-and-a-half-story building that looked like a loaf of bread standing on end. Then her memory stirred and she recalled that Bob had told her the hospital was upstairs over the drugstore.

"Well," boomed Hansen cheerily, clambering over the front door of the Ford, "here we all are, home and no bones broke either."

Katherine started: there were only the stores behind her and, across the street, on the waterfront, a sprawling white building with 'Mill Store' in tall black letters—nothing else. Then she smiled. Bob had brought her to see his precious hospital before taking her to their house. Well, it would be rather a bore just now but, after all, she was a doctor's wife and she must get used to things like that.

"Better I help ya with them trunks, doc," Hansen was saying. "They'll be pretty heavy even for a fellow as big as ya."

Katherine looked at her trunks in the trailer, saw Olaf approaching them.

"But, Bob dear, I won't want my things here, in the hospital. Hadn't we better go straight on home with them and come back here later?"

Mallory turned a blank, astonished face toward her.

"Home? Why, this is home! We live in the hospital, didn't I tell you? . . . Just a second, Olaf, and I'll help you with the things."

Even while Katherine clutched at her poise and composed herself again, she felt depression engulfing her. Dully she wondered how she could have misunderstood or forgotten such a bit of information about living in the hospital. There would be sick people about, and the penetrating odor of antiseptics and ether; there would be groans and people dying. Remembering a rubber-tired cart with its sheet-covered sinister load that she had seen pass her door one evening when she was recovering from a tonsillectomy in a hospital, she shivered. And she was going to live among things like that.

Every step she took up the bare slate-colored stairs that led from the street to the hospital deepened her depression. Half blinded by the change from sunlight to the dimness of the waiting room with its solitary tall narrow window, she turned toward her husband.

"Bob," she began. But Hansen, cheerfully oblivious to the tension in the air, interrupted her.

"Ya want I should take these here bags down to the end room too, doc?"

Katherine watched Mallory nod an affirmative to this query and turn his troubled face back to her. Then she saw a large tousle-headed young man with one arm in a sling who was getting up from a straight chair beside the large heating stove. He was staring at the two of them with curious, puzzled eyes.

"Oh, hello, Luarn. I didn't see you," said Mallory uneasily. "Been waiting for me?"

"Yeah, quite a spell, doc. The nurse said you'd went to the train to meet...somebody."

Mallory glanced hastily at his wife, then back to his patient.

"I ought to take a look at that arm of yours with the X-rays to-day, Luarn. Just to make sure it hasn't slipped out of position, you know."

Then Katherine heard relief replace the perturbation in his voice.

"Oh, Mrs. H., come here, will you?"

Looking to the right at the muffled sound of rubber-soled shoes, the girl saw a white-clad, middle-aged woman entering the room, heard her say, "I'm sorry not to have met you downstairs, doctor, but I've been busy with the typhoid case." Katherine felt at once something comforting in that quiet voice.

"My dear, this is Mrs. Hathaway, familiarly known as Mrs. H. She's by far the most important person around here."

The nurse's face crinkled into a pleasant smile.

"That's your side of the story, doctor. The rest of us have our own opinions." Then her warm hands closed firmly over Katherine's. "My dear Mrs. Mallory, I'm glad you've come. We've both been waiting for you a long time."

"Go on into the office, Luarn, and sit down. I'll be with you in a jiffy." Mallory looked anxiously at Katherine. "I'm sorry but I'll have to look at this man's arm right away so he can start back up-river before dark. You understand how it is, don't you?"

Out of the strange sights and sounds that had assailed her in the last half hour, Katherine now saw her husband's troubled eyes imploring comprehension. Taking her self-control firmly in hand, she smiled at him reassuringly.

"Certainly, I understand, Bob. Your patients must always come first."

"Then," said Mrs. Hathaway gently, "perhaps you'll let me take you to your room while the doctor looks after Mr. Luarn."

With something uncertain in his face Mallory stood watching the two women until they had passed out of sight into the room at the end of the north corridor; then, drawing a deep breath, he went into his private office and closed the door behind him.

The bedroom into which Mrs. Hathaway ushered Katherine contained two high narrow hospital beds covered with white cotton spreads, a bird's-eye maple bureau, three small pale pink rag rugs, two wooden chairs, and a dark-stained chest of drawers surmounted by a small square mirror of wavy glass. From under the chest Katherine could see protruding the toes of a pair of men's tan shoes and on it a blue tin of tobacco and a brown briar pipe. Her mind flashed back to her old room at home with its polished floor and four-poster bed and gleaming walnut furniture. It seemed already to have receded far into the past.

"This door," explained Mrs. Hathaway, "leads into your bathroom."

The sight of the small enamel tub scrubbed to spotlessness and the rack of towels above it made Katherine sure that the only possible alternative to hysterical weeping was a warm bath.

"Is there hot water…at this time of day?" she inquired in a voice which she struggled to keep level and calm.

"Yes, I'm almost sure there is, but I'll go and make certain of it."

Katherine turned her face half away from the nurse to conceal the dismay she feared Mrs. Hathaway's understanding eyes would see.

"Thank you. Then I think I'll bathe and change before dinner time. The train was extraordinarily dirty."

The older woman hesitated as though she wanted to say something more, then, instead, laid her hand gently on one of Katherine's for an instant, and went out closing the door softly after her.

Alone, the girl dropped into the small rocker that teetered on the pink rug in front of the bird's-eye maple dresser. What a grotesque place! That wretched dark waiting room with its bare floors, these two hard-looking beds, the three tiny rugs on the gray painted floor, the walls without pictures. Looking up, Katherine caught sight of her own face in the cheap mirror over the chest of drawers; the distorted features seemed to grimace at her. She propped her head wearily on one hand and tried to think why it was she had not realized from Bob's letters that they were to live in the hospital and not in a house of their own.

But before long she got up resolutely, opened a bag, and searched out a dressing gown. After all, Bob had been down here all summer without once emitting a word of complaint about living conditions. The cheerful sound of water running into the tub bolstered her determination to make the best of things. Now that she was here she would set to work to help her husband rescue them both from this morass of the commonplace and unlovely. She had been convinced long before that he had in him the making of a great man and now she decided that it was part of her business as his wife to take an active hand in building up the career that would take them out of this sordid place. But to-night she would be beautiful for him and satisfy her own longing for his admiration and love. To-morrow was soon enough to begin planning.

IV

Dinner that evening was another unprecedented experience for Katherine, marking both her first meeting with Sairy and her entrance into the routine hospital life.

She was, at the outset, amused by Sairy's appearance. It was plain that the cook had made an effort to dress for the occasion. Her face had been powdered and her straggling back hair pinned up, but no artistry could conceal the bony angularity of her figure or the vacant stare of her pale, wandering eyes. Later, Katherine was to marvel that at twenty Sairy had already lost every vestige of youthfulness and become simply a female with mousy hair and the usual number of arms and legs, but to-night she was engrossed by the outlandish appearance the woman presented.

Sairy wore a clean, stiffly starched, cotton dress of green and white stripes, made with a low neck and short sleeves, and her bony forearms and bulging goiter were excellently displayed. Over her face was spread a thick layer of dead white powder that stopped abruptly just below her chin and in front of her ears. Katherine was amused to see how she hovered over the doctor with extra helpings of meat, asking if he liked the salad, confiding to him that there was apple pie for dessert, but her amusement was soon interrupted by whining cries from the kitchen.

At this Sairy scuttled off, and almost at once there came the sound of a smart slap on flesh, followed by strident wailing. Startled, Katherine looked from her husband to Mrs. Hathaway and back again.

Mallory flushed darkly.

"It's Sairy's child," he explained in a low voice. "Juanita. She's in the kitchen."

"But why..." began Katherine, then at sight of Mrs. Hathaway's expression stopped. Here was something she knew nothing about, and this was not the time to investigate. For the remainder of the meal, ignoring both the intermittent shrieking from the next room and Sairy's distraction, she talked to Mrs. Hathaway of the places she had been and the things she had seen that summer.

When dinner was over, Mallory led his wife into the waiting room and on into the surgery. This was one of the two rooms that occupied the street side of the hospital floor. It had two broad windows looking southward across the river. Sunset was just fading and the tips of the firs on the mountain tops were shining in the glow like gilded spears brushing against the darkening sky. Above the leaden flow of the water and the great dark band of the hills, heavy clouds were turning from flame and gold to lavender and gray. Reflecting them the river became a flood of burnished silver, splashing softly at the feet of the sprawling mountains.

Mallory had found that whenever he watched the sunset from those windows something peaceful and serene came to build in his heart such defense as was possible against the dirt and ignorance and disease he confronted in his work. He wanted Katherine to feel as he did. She was standing now within the curve of his arm, with her head against his shoulder. He drew her closer to him and put his lips on her soft, dark hair.

The disquietude he had felt earlier fled away. After all they were both young, just starting out; all things were possible. He gathered the girl into his arms, swept her up off her feet, began to kiss her throat and lips. He felt her body go limp against him, her mouth grow soft and moist; he heard her whisper, "I love you, Bob, and it's been so long since you kissed me like this."

After a little Mallory began to speak of his hopes and plans.

"It isn't as if we'd have to live like this always, dearest. When I stop to think I know you're not used to living the way I've always had to. But I've got things planned out, I know just what I want to do. I'm going to build a new hospital and a house for us right beside it, up on the hill where we can see all up and down the river. Ever since I came down here I've been thinking about it. I want a house with wide halls and fireplaces and porches and polished floors, one that's fit for a girl like you. I can see you in it, dear, with the firelight on your hair. A home, Katherine, that's what I want…a home with you in it… and our children."

So deep in the girl's heart that she barely noticed it there stirred a momentary revolt, but in another instant it was swept away by the passion her husband's kisses aroused in her.

On the waterfront below them Glenwood was staging its most picturesque activity but neither of them took any notice of it. The engines of the fish boats going out on the drift putt-putted sharply and the red signal lanterns flashing back and forth answered their reflections in the water. Men's voices rose and fell rhythmically as they steered out across the stream. But none of all this entered the consciousness of the lovers; even the harsh summons of the telephone did not disturb them.

"Dr. Mallory." Mrs. Hathaway, standing in the doorway, managed to convey by the tone of her voice both apology for interruption and complete unawareness of the scene upon which she had intruded. "I'm sorry, but you're wanted on the 'phone. I can't get the man who's calling to give me the message."

"Hello. Dr. Mallory speaking." Rapidly his words took on their professional cast. "Yes. . . . I see. . . . Why didn't you bring your father down this morning? . . . No, I wouldn't think of advising you to move him now. . . . No, I'll bring everything we'll need. But you get a washboiler scrubbed out and plenty of pans for hot water and have a good fire built. .. I'll start as soon as I can get a boat. . . . Yes, right away. . . . Good-by."

Mallory turned from the 'phone to Mrs. Hathaway.

"That's the hell of practicing medicine. Old man Simmons has a strangulated hernia. A month ago I told his good-for-nothing son this would happen one day. But they think I'm a kid and don't know anything." There was a fleeting tinge of bitterness in these words. "So now they're up against it and so are we. We'll have to go up there and operate on the old chap."

From where she stood in the surgery door, Katherine watched the nurse hurry into the sterilizing room and her husband bring from his office two huge black cases. His face was preoccupied and serious; she wondered how he could so swiftly divorce himself from her.

"Must you go now?" she asked. "Can't you put it off?"

To herself she was thinking 'I am jealous of Bob's work. I don't want it to come between us to-night, like this.'

Mallory threw out his hands in a gesture of helplessness.

"No, dear, I can't put it off. The old man may die before I get there now. I wanted to be with you to-night more than I ever wanted anything before, but I've got to go. There isn't any other doctor they can get until to-morrow's train up from the Bay. This is part of a doctor's job. It's my work. Tell me you understand, please, dearest."

His deep soft voice was pleading with her for comprehension. Quickly Katherine gathered her self-possession and smiled into her husband's serious blue eyes. 'Here,' she told herself, 'I'm funking my very first opportunity to spur him on.' Determinedly she went on smiling at him.

"Of course, Bob. I know you must go. It's only..." She glanced over her shoulder at the darkening windows. "It's only that I'm afraid something may happen. It's dark and the boat might upset or...something."

In spite of her best efforts, the smile faded away. But Mallory laughed aloud in relief.

"Oh, no, it won't. Boats down here don't upset. They're not that sort." He put his fingers gently under Katherine's chin and tilted her face up. "I'll try to get back before morning, but don't wait up for me too long. There are magazines and some books on the shelves in the office if you want to read. But don't sit up all night." He bent down and kissed her mouth lingeringly.

But another terrifying thought had come to Katherine.

"Aren't there some patients ill here in the hospital? Must I look after them while you're away? Or isn't Mrs. Hathaway going with you? I don't know a thing about nursing or what to do if anything goes wrong."

"Listen, blessedness," said Mallory, "you don't have to do a thing. Mrs. H. has already called Mrs. Blake and she's coming up to sit with you and look after the patients. She'll be here in twenty minutes at the outside. She used to be a nurse in Pacific City and she's a grand woman. You'll like her."

Mrs. Hathaway, having finished packing the big kit bags, brought two thick dark coats from the hall closet.

"It's cold on the river at night," she explained, "and the doctor never takes a coat unless I remind him of it. Everything's ready now. And Mrs. Blake is coming right over."

When they had gone Katherine stood alone in the shabby waiting room. The unknown Mrs. Blake who was to come in twenty minutes had not yet arrived and the big room seemed even more barren and forbidding than before. Katherine shivered a little as she looked about her. Before her, in the east wall, was the one tall narrow window, now an oblong of blackness. In the angle between the stairwell and the south wall stood a big black heating stove and beside it a box piled high with chunks of firewood. Opposite the stove was a high, old-fashioned secretary bulging with papers. The painted floor bore the patterned depressions worn by the passing of many feet.

More oppressed than ever by the stillness of the room, Katherine went back into the surgery, thinking she might see Mallory starting off, but it was too dark outside. She pressed the light switch and looked around her. Once or twice she had been in operating rooms with sick relatives and this surgery struck her as a nightmare. The lower part of the wall was covered with white oilcloth smoothly tacked to the wood underneath; the ceiling and upper wall were painted white, but stains here and there bespoke a leaky roof. At one end of the room an enameled sink and drainboard did duty as a surgeon's lavatory, and beside the door an unpainted wooden rack held two dark violet X-ray tubes. Along the side wall there was a cupboard whose half-open doors disclosed jars of gauze and dressings and rolls of adhesive and bandages. In the middle of the floor stood a steel operating table peeling part of its paint, and at its head was a tall iron stand with a glass jar dangling from a hook at the top. The glass-doored cabinet at the other end of the room filled with mysterious shining instruments made Katherine break out into gooseflesh. It all seemed so unreal, so grotesque.

She went to the doorway and stood looking out into the waiting room determined not to break into hysterical laughter. 'I suppose,' she thought, 'that this awful cabinet over here with those huge wheels inside it and the wires dangling is the X-ray machine Bob wrote so much about. Oh, the whole place is horrible!'

Then she saw the door leading into the kitchen corridor open and Sairy appear, dragging by one arm a wizened child with a big top-heavy head. Juanita sniveled desolately and pulled back from her mother's grasp. Over her small face, so grotesquely like an old woman's, rose a high, domed forehead and from beneath the overhanging brows peered out two shallow pale blue eyes.

"Is the doctor here?" asked Sairy in a voice half whine and half drawl. "I wisht he'd look at Juanita a minute. She ain't a mite like herself to-night. Seems like she musta caught a cold… or somethin'."

Trying to conceal her instinctive repulsion, Katherine said, "Dr. Mallory and Mrs. Hathaway were called away just a few minutes ago, but Mrs. Blake will be here in a little while, Perhaps she can help you…if the child is ill." She looked doubtfully at the little girl.

"Oh, it don't make no difference," answered Sairy with the volatility of the feeble-minded. "The kid can wait, I guess. She's kinda puny-like, but she never gets very sick." Then a new idea struck the woman. "Would you like to hear Juanita talk, Mrs. Mallory?" she exclaimed. "You know folks here on the river always said I couldn't never learn the kid nothin'. Well, I'll show 'em. Right now I got her learned to say 'Thank you, Sairy,' and she's only three. Say it for the lady, Juanita. Say it now like I tell you, or I'll spank you. 'Thank you, Sairy.'"

With difficulty the little imbecile slowly whined, "Hank oo, Hairy! Hank oo, Hairy!"

In spite of the disgust she felt, Katherine found herself pitying the child: she was pale and thin, and perhaps she was ill besides.

"Why don't you put her to bed?" she suggested, "and I'll ask Mrs. Blake to look at her as soon as she gets here."

But pride in Juanita's linguistic achievements still animated Sairy's face.

"No, it ain't bedtime yet. I guess I'll take the kid and go over to see Ma for a while. She'll be surprised when she hears Juanita talkin' like that."

Seizing her unfortunate child by the arm again, Sairy dragged her off sniveling and crying. Katherine shivered at the desolate sounds made by the little girl. Suddenly the room seemed more repellent than ever, and she realized that it was cold.

She contemplated the heating stove. She had never used a wood stove. How did one manage the fire in it? Did one open the top or the door in the end to put in fuel? She lifted the lid, but clearly none of the huge chunks of wood in the box would go in that way. Then she opened the door in the end, and small blazing brands rolled onto the zinc-covered shield that protected the floor. Nervously she brushed them up with her hands and blistered her palms and fingers before she got them all back into the stove.

It was here—rocking back and forth in pain on a creaking little chair—that Mrs. Blake five minutes later found her. "You're Mrs. Mallory, aren't you? I'm Alice Blake… Why, my dear, whatever have you done to yourself?" White-clad, soft-spoken Mrs. Blake took Katherine's burned hands gently in hers. "Come and let me bandage you up at once. Nothing hurts more than burns like these."

With her hands in cool moist dressings, Katherine sat by the replenished fire while Mrs. Blake attended to the patients in the house and went to see if Sairy had gone out with her ailing child. Try as she might, the girl could not overcome her dismay at the situation. She smiled wryly when she remembered how she had told her friends that her husband was superintendent of a hospital, how she had pictured herself living in a rambling cottage with wide porches and window boxes full of bright flowers. Now that she was shaken out of her daydreams, she realized how closely it had resembled the Cape Cod cottages of her well-to-do Boston friends. It was not Bob's fault, she knew, that he had been called out on her first evening in Glenwood, but it was most disagreeable. Her hands stung and Juanita's face haunted her. Over and over she could hear that whining voice: "Hank oo, Hairy. Hank oo, Hairy."

When Mrs. Blake finally returned to the waiting room, her work completed, Katherine found it hard to maintain a conversation: she was by nature reserved and did not make friends of other women readily. She had never known any nurses personally and, had she been asked point-blank, would probably have admitted thinking them in a social class below her own. Besides this, she was distracted by her new experiences and the unrest they had stirred in her. But she tried to be courteous to Mrs. Blake and about nine o'clock consented to go with her for a cold drink.

The two women went down the street a block and a half to the pool hall, where there was a small side-room with a soda fountain. While she sipped her lemonade Katherine could hear the click of billiard balls next door and men's rough voices calling out the count. The proprietor, Otto Schmidt, informed quietly by Mrs. Blake of Katherine's identity, became expansive.

"And so Doc had to go up-river the very first night you got here! Ain't that a shame, now? But it goes like that with doctors—no sleep nor time for their wives. When bad weather comes I bet you it gets a lot worse, too. Doc won't be home then at all. You'll see. Tch, tch!" The friendly Schmidt clicked his tongue against his teeth in deprecation. "So you're from Pacific City, Mrs. Mallory. I like to go there. It's a swell place. That's where they cut my leg off." Schmidt slapped his artificial thigh and wrinkled up his rosy cheeks in laughter. "They done me a swell job, too. Some fellers used to say it was awful, me losin' my leg that way in an accident, but the leg I got now never aches nor gets tired. And I walk so good with it that I bet you couldn't tell I got a wooden leg just lookin' at me."

He beamed at Katherine so genially that she was compelled to smile back at him, even while it occurred to her that a stranger's wooden leg was not really an object of merriment.

From the billiard room next door came a shout. "Otto, you got any more of them two-for-a-nickel stogies? . . . Well, I can't find 'em nowhere."

"Excuse me, ladies. These here fellers I got workin' for me can't do nothin' without I watch 'em, seems like. Glad to've met you, Mrs. Mallory. No, no, you put back your thirty cents, Mrs. Blake. I guess we can stand Doc Mallory's wife a treat to-night, seein' as he's gone off and left her. . . . All right, Oscar, all right. I'm comin'. Keep your shirt on!" Cheerily Otto Schmidt creaked away on his artificial leg.

When they stepped out into the damp salt air to go back to the hospital, Katherine wrapped her fur collar close about her throat and stole a glance of envy at Mrs. Blake who marched vigorously along with her coat open, breathing in great lungfuls of the chilly air.

"Have you lived in Glenwood long?" inquired Katherine.

"Nearly three years. And very happy years, too."

"Then you like it here." Katherine's tone was a mixture of wistfulness and doubt.

"Yes, I do now. But I didn't at first. It was so different from anything I'd ever known before. You see, I was born and brought up in the Middle West and then I worked in Pacific City, in St. Mary's Hospital. When I first came to Pacific Glenwood, I was lonely. You will be, too. You'll think the people very queer. But there are many worse places. My husband has lived here almost all his life and there isn't a finer man alive." For the first time pride tinged Mrs. Blake's voice when she spoke of her husband.

Katherine looked sidewise at her. The air of simple health and kindliness about Alice Blake was attractive.

"Glenwood does seem queer to me, Mrs. Blake. I've always lived in cities and recently most of the time in the East. I can't picture to myself what it will be like with no clubs or theaters or concerts or dances."

Alice laughed softly.

"No dances! You'll be surprised, Mrs. Mallory. The last Saturday of this month is the annual Fishermen's Ball and the whole valley will be here. I suppose the doctor dances."

"Oh, yes. And surprisingly well for a man who's had so little time for frivolity."

Katherine smiled to herself in the darkness, remembering the dogged persistence with which he had counted time and stepped the square to phonograph records because she wanted him to learn to dance well. There was something appealing in the memory of his determination to master the waltz, in the picture she had of him going to concerts, listening to music he didn't yet appreciate because she told him it was good. She had found out that, when he made up his mind about a thing, he was irresistible, just as he was when he swept her along as they danced together. Now and then she had been startled to realize that he dominated her as no one else had ever done, but most of the time she found it pleasant to let him carry her along without effort of her own. Only occasionally did she find it faintly annoying.

Slowly the two women climbed the hospital stairs. There was no sign that the doctor and Mrs. Hathaway had returned.

"I suppose Dr. Mallory has drawn one of these all-night cases," said Mrs. Blake regretfully. She threw her coat over a chair. "I must look at the patients and make sure they're all right. Then I shall lie down in Mrs. Hathaway's room. It seems to me that you'd better not wait up any longer. You must be tired after your trip."

Katherine stifled a yawn.

"I am tired," she admitted. "And I suppose there's no sense sitting up all night waiting for Bob to get back. Since I married a doctor I might as well get used to this sort of thing. Good night, Mrs. Blake. I am ever so grateful to you for giving up your evening to me."

But when she went into her room, it seemed to be full of the people she had encountered that day and, when she crept into her solitary bed, she thought she could see in the dark the pink rag rugs and the bird's-eye maple dresser and Hansen's rickety Ford and the wobbly operating table and Sairy's foolish face, and hear Otto Schmidt laughing and Juanita's whining, "Hank oo, Hairy! Hank oo, Hairy!" It was not until she dreamed that Mallory's arms were close about her, holding her, that she fell into a restful sleep.

V

As they neared the Mill Store dock, Mrs. Hathaway and Dr. Mallory met the stalwart Henry Blake.

"I have to go up-river to see Old Man Simmons, Blake. Can you take us? Not using your boat on the drift to-night, are you?"

"No, the fish boat's busted and I was just goin' down to the pool hall. Sure I'll take you. How're you, Mrs. Hathaway? Here, give me that bag you're carryin'. We'll take the cabin launch. It's right down here, by the slip. Now watch your step, Mrs. Hathaway. I don't want a drownded nurse around here."

Blake's launch—the Greyhound—was the speediest boat on the Silticoos. Henry himself, sunburned, broad-shouldered, self-reliant, took the wheel. Mallory stacked the big black cases of medical supplies against the rack of life preservers, and Mrs. Hathaway ensconced herself where she could lean comfortably back against the cabin wall.

After he had maneuvered clear of the wharves and fish boats near the north bank, Blake eyed Mallory speculatively. He was fumbling for pipe and tobacco with an abstracted air.

"Hell of a note, doc, havin' to go out like this the first night your wife's here! Good thing Alice could go up and keep her company. 'S not easy, a life like a doctor's. But it always seemed to me a man'd feel like he'd done something real when he pulled a hard case through."

"You bet that's so, Blake. There's not another thrill on earth like it."

Blake shifted his cigar across his mouth to the opposite corner.

"The other day I was in the drugstore, doc, and I heard Burton shootin' off his face about Simmons. Seems the son said they wouldn't have no doctor for the old man unless they got one to come up from the Bay. Now, if I was you, I'd make them pay me to-night, right while I was there. If you don't you're liable never to get a cent out of them."

Discomfited and perplexed Mallory watched the smoke curling up from his pipe bowl.

"Damn it all, I just can't seem to get the hang of collecting. That's my weakest spot and I don't know what to do about it."

"Maybe your wife could help you out with it. Lots of women are good at that sort of thing."

Mrs. Hathaway, listening, smiled at the picture of Katherine Mallory collecting her husband's bills.

"No, Blake, she couldn't do that." Mallory spoke decisively. "She's not the collecting kind any more than I am. I wish I never had to ask any one for money. I hate it!"

"I don't see no reason to be ashamed of askin' for money you've earned," said Blake in surprise, but Mallory did not answer. He got up and went back to the stern where he could look out at the river behind them.

The moon had not yet risen over the mountain rim of the valley but it was perceptibly lighter than when they left Glenwood.

Realizing that the doctor was in no mood for general conversation, Mrs. Hathaway began to talk to Henry Blake.

"Do you know, I believe I shan't ever get used to going around this way in boats, having no roads, seeing the houses built along the river with wharves where their front gates ought to be."

Blake nodded good-naturedly.

"Yes, I guess it looks right odd to somebody that's not used to it. But there ain't either enough money or enough people to build roads down here, not when there's nothin' but a narrow strip of good land along the river. Them forest-service trails is a big help, I can tell you, when it comes to gettin' into the back-country. Why, when I can first remember, nothin' but a snake could get through the underbrush, and now a feller can get around on horseback easy." Blake paused for a moment and then went on. "It always seemed to me it was the people here that was funny."

"I don't understand just what you mean."

"Why, I mean the folks themselves. Some of 'em ain't so much, you know. Ever since the railroad come in, I been hopin' that some new people would show up down here and kinda run out part of the old-timers. You can't make a gas engine out of a bale of cotton handkerchiefs and you can't make decent people without havin' decent stuff to start with. Now doc insists on messin' around, tinkerin' them that are already here, in spite of them bein' more than half ruined before they was born. Take Sairy and Juanita, for instance. Now what can he do with them? Nice prospects, ain't they? Sairy's mother and grandmother had fits, and they was six brothers and sisters in the family to start with, and only one of 'em knows enough to come in out of the rain."

Blake wagged his head and squinted at the nurse.

"This valley was settled by a kind of backwash from the California gold rush. The wagon freight for the mines in southern Oregon all come up from 'Frisco in schooners and was hauled overland with teams from the head o' tide. Well, when these here mines shut down after 'while, the early settlers got marooned in here, and they been here ever since—marryin' back and forth, raisin' kids, and burying one another. Why, Mrs. Hathaway, the folks down here is so related that a fellow daren't say nothin' about any one for fear he's talkin' to some of their relations."

"But how are you sure you can lay all their shortcomings to the door of inbreeding?" objected the nurse.

"I ain't sure. But I've set out on this river a lot of nights, thinkin' and fishin'. It's a better place for thinkin' than it is for fishin'. And I've watched these folks for a long time too. I'm thirty-five years old and I've lived down here nearly all my life, remember. I come to the conclusion that most people is ruined before they're ever born. And mighty few of 'em improve any after they're born. The pioneers gone to seed—that's what these folks down here are. And some of the pioneers wasn't nothin' to brag of. I guess likely the places a good many of 'em come from was glad to see the last of 'em.

"Now, doc's goin' to make over the new generation by feedin' 'em cod liver oil and green vegetables and doin' intelligence tests on 'em and findin' out if they're smart enough to work in the sawmill or will they just have to do nothin' but fish all their lives. He's thinkin' that they'll be a big improvement on the older folks. Maybe they will. Maybe he's right. But I always wonder how Sairy and the like of her can be the mothers of anything very much better than they are."

"I think there's a lot in what you say," said Mrs. Hathaway thoughtfully. "But I don't feel sure of the truth, either way."

Henry Blake grinned.

"Neither do I feel sure. That's the trouble with thinkin'. When you get done you don't know what you think. . . But anyhow I said a lot of things that's been on my chest and I feel better even though doc didn't hear a word of it. We been arguin' this thing back and forth ever since I begun to haul him around the river and we ain't never agreed on nothin' yet. He always begins talkin' too, instead of listenin' to me, and then we can't ever get anywhere."

Blake cast a rapid glance at Mallory who leaned against the back door of the cabin staring at the wake of the boat in the water. There was a slump to his wide shoulders and his back looked dejected. The nurse's eyes followed Henry's. Then silence fell between them.

An hour later Blake peered at the dark river bank where a tiny point of light could be seen in the distance.

"This is Simmons' place right now. Hey, doc, snap out of it! Now, watch your step, both of you. Simmons never patches the holes in his landin', and I'd hate to have to haul you outa the river. . . . Hold the painter, doc, and kinda steady her while I hand out these bags. Gosh, they're heavy enough to be full of lead. Good luck, doc. I hope the old man squeaks through, but he ain't worth a plugged nickel to nobody. They got a 'phone here, so you call me up when you're ready to come home and I can come after you."

On the bank above a door opened and a broad band of radiance shone out into the darkness.

"That the doctor?" called a man's gruff voice.

"Yes. How do we get up there? Where's your gangplank?"

"Wait a minute and I'll get a lantern."

"No, don't bother. We've got a flashlight. But you might come down and carry the nurse's bag."

Grumbling, Simmons led the way to the cabin.

"I thought you was never comin'."

"Well, we started as soon as we could pack up and Blake said he'd made an unusually fast trip. You can't fly in a boat, you know."

The cabin was stifling hot. On a tumbled bed near the front door two dirty youngsters were asleep. In the kitchen beyond, Mallory could see a red-hot range with a wash boiler on it; evidently Simmons had followed his orders about hot water. To the left was the third room of the shack and from it came the stertorous breathing of a comatose person. Mrs. Hathaway went at once to the kitchen while the doctor rolled up his sleeves, opened the bags, and took out his stethoscope and blood pressure apparatus.

The patient was an old man with straggling chin whiskers and a bald head. His foxlike face was bluish gray and there was a fetid odor to his breath. Mallory laid his stethoscope gently on the bony chest. His intelligently searching fingers felt the old man's pulse, went over his rigid distended abdomen. Half-aroused from his stupor, the patient flinched and then gagged violently. Gently Mallory pressed on the mass he found in the old man's groin.

"Let me have some hot towels," he said when the nurse came in from the kitchen. "The old chap's pretty rotten. I don't like the idea of operating on him. God, why don't they bring people to the hospital before they get so bad?"

After a time Mallory got up and pulled the covers back over the patient.

"It's no use, Mrs. H. The thing simply won't go back. It's probably gangrenous by now, or soon will be. The only thing I can do is to operate right now. We'd better get things squared away as fast as we can."

The younger Simmons stood in the doorway staring at Mallory.

"What's the matter?" he asked sullenly.

"Plenty," answered the doctor. "How your father's managed to get by all these years with that rupture I don't know, but now a piece of intestine has got out into the sac. It's right there under the skin in that lump you can feel in his groin. Gangrene will soon set in if it hasn't already. When did you say he got sick?"

"Yestiddy mornin'. Pap always pushed it back hisself till then. But yestiddy it wouldn't go."

"You ought to have sent for me then or brought him down to the hospital."

"Pap never did hold much with doctors and cuttin'. And I ain't aimin' to take him to no hospital to be butchered, neither." There was a sneer on Simmons' long yellow face.

"It would kill him to move him to the hospital now, but if you'd done as I told you a month ago this wouldn't have happened," said Mallory sternly. "Of course you know more about such things than I do, and so you wait. And yesterday you waited again, wasted nearly forty-eight hours before you sent for me. Now we'll have to operate here, in your dirty shack, because I don't dare move him. Your foolishness has cut your father's chances more than in half."

A look of suspicion came into Simmons' small, pig eyes.

"You must be a hell of a doctor if you can't get it back where it belongs. Doc Peters always shoved it in. I guess you just figure on scarin' me and runnin' up a big bill by stayin' all night and operatin' and everything. Well, if you do, I won't pay you for it."

Mallory's patience snapped.

"Let me tell you something, Simmons. If I operate on your

father you'll pay me for it if I have to wring your filthy neck. Do you hear me?" The doctor's voice rumbled ominously. "But I'll tell you something else. If you want to take the responsibility, I'll pack up and go home. Before twenty-four hours you'll have a corpse on your hands and a funeral to pay for. Do you want me to go or stay? Make up your mind quick! There's no time to stand here and argue about it."

Simmons peered over Mallory's shoulder at the old man on the bed; even he could see the signs of death approaching.

"Well, I don't know, doc." He weakened and the bluster went out of him.

"I know. That's my business—to know. If I don't operate at once, your father will be dead by noon to-morrow. Maybe he'll die anyhow, in spite of anything I can do. But if he does, that will be your fault—not mine. You wait until he's two-thirds dead before you send for me." Mallory's face was full of disgust. "Well, make up your mind, if you've got one!"

Simmons was cowed. No doctor had ever spoken like this to him before.

"Well...I ... I guess you'd better go ahead, doc. I didn't mean nothin'. I..."

"All right. Then get out of the way and stay out!"

Mallory strode into the kitchen, pulled off his shirt, and began to scrub his hands and arms. Mrs. Hathaway was at the stove lifting instruments out of the wash boiler to a tray.

"The surgical supervisor at St. Mary's would have a spasm if she could see our technique! A wash boiler! Imagine it!"

"What's wrong with the wash boiler?" asked Mallory. "We haven't had an infection in any case we've operated on in the home. It's unhandy as hell, and hard work, but it can be done safely when it's necessary.... How many sterile sheets did you bring? ... Good.... You go on in. I'll be there in a jiffy."

"Local anesthesia, doctor?"

"Yes. The old man's too shaky for a general."

Mrs. Hathaway pressed a half-grown girl into service and between them they covered the floor of the bedroom with clean newspapers, carried in the kitchen table and sewing machine, pieced them together to make an operating table of sufficient length, padded it with quilts, and spread over all a clean sheet. On this improvised table lay the old man with sterile sheets across his chest and upper abdomen and thighs. The narrow zone of visible skin was painted with iodine.

Swiftly Mallory checked the details of the procedure in his mind.

"He's had his hypo, Mrs. H.? O.K. You watch his color and let me know if he begins to slip. I'll work just as fast as I can. Syringe, please. And be sure to have plenty of solution ready. There's no use being economical with the anesthetic."

Welts began to appear as he injected novocaine into the skin around the site of operation.

Mallory recalled his terror over the tracheotomy at the Contagious Hospital a year ago. It was strange how rapidly one got accustomed to the feel of tissue under one's fingers. The police Emergency Hospital, if it had done nothing else, had taught him skill with his hands. The steps of this operation were as clear in his mind as the scenes in a movie. He felt no hesitation whatever.

"Look, Mrs. H., there's the sac of the hernia. That bluish thing right there. . . . Yes, it's got fluid in it, all right. . . . Just as I suspected. . . . Let me have those blunt-pointed scissors."

The blade of the scissors slid in along his left forefinger. Snip. The constricting band was cut.

"Ties, Mrs. H. Quick! I got a bleeder this time."

The catgut was swiftly tied, tight about the blood vessel.

Tissue slipped easily through his rubber-gloved fingers. Dark, bluish-red tissue whose normal luster was almost absent. But after a pinch the muscle moved sluggishly.

"Hot towels, Mrs. H. I believe gangrene hasn't actually set in yet. There's a chance that it hasn't, anyhow. . . . How is he? . . . Pulse fair? I can't stop now, no matter what happens."

Mallory peeped under the corner of his hot pack. Yes, the color was better. The red was coming back, slowly. The tissue getting brighter.

"More hot towels, lady. Here, you hold these while I look

up a little higher. I've got to be sure there's nothing wrong up above, you know."

It was remarkable, Mallory thought, how an old man nearly eighty could stand all this messing about so well. And it was remarkable, too, that a fellow like himself could learn what to do for cases like this, and then go out and do it on a kitchen table by the light of two kerosene lamps without getting into a funk. As a matter of fact he found a thrill in it, a sense of mastery and power.

"Well, Mrs. H., I guess I'd better stop now. The old chap won't stand a hell of a lot more. If he gets along all right, we can sew him up solid later on, but the main thing now is to close this incision and get him back into bed. . . . Chromic down here. And silkworm for the skin stitches."

Carefully Mallory lifted the thin old body into the bed, felt the pulse. One hundred and sixty. Pupil reflexes normal. Heart sounds fair. The doctor's mood of exaltation persisted. It was over, he had done a good job—one he wouldn't mind the men in Pacific City seeing.

The younger Simmons had suffered a change of heart. He hovered between the kitchen where his daughter was helping Mrs. Hathaway wash instruments and his father's bedroom, full of questions and comments.

"Now, Simmons, I'll give my orders to your daughter. I don't know where she got them, but she has brains. She tended the lamps, fetched and carried for us, helped all through the operation. How she came to be your child is beyond me! . . . I'll be back up here, to-morrow. . . . What time is it anyhow? . . . I'll come in the afternoon, before four o'clock. And the Lord help you if everything hasn't been done exactly as I've ordered between now and then."

Mrs. Hathaway and Mallory were the only passengers on the down-river mail boat that morning. Wearily the nurse propped herself in a corner and leaned against the mail sacks, but Mallory was too deeply stirred to know that he was sleepy.

He stood on the small rear deck with one arm thrown on the

cabin roof, watching the sunlight spill over the tops of the great green hills to the east and cascade downward to the gleaming silvery river. The sun! It was the symbol of life. That night again he had stood with light, had beaten back the darkness, had won back a life. He was filled with exhilaration. He remembered that he had thought once of going into research and he was suddenly sure that the laboratory could offer a man no thrill to compare with this. His patient was alive, he was going to get well! That was all that mattered.

Mallory straightened his body and stretched his arms full length above his shoulders in the same gesture he had used on that summer morning at the Rescue Home after his first hand-to-hand battle with death. Silhouetted against the sky, his figure was that of an ancient sun-worshipper. For the time being he had no thought of Katherine, for his heart was in the keeping of his older love—medicine.

VI

Conscience-stricken, Katherine was thinking how tired her husband looked. It was sweet of him, she thought, to bring her down to Baypoint so they could be alone but she was appalled when she found that he had not been in bed the night before she arrived in Glenwood. Two sleepless nights separated by two busy days—that was the way he lived. Then she saw him looking at her bandaged fingers.

"Bob, dear," she protested, "will you please not pay any more attention to my silly burns? Really they don't hurt me at all now and I'm sure they will be well in a day or two."

"It was the devil of a thing to have happen to you, though, on your very first night." Mallory leaned over the table toward her. "I love your hands."

Katherine smiled into his rueful face.

"This is a poor place to make love, my dear—in a public dining room. The consequences might surprise you. But don't let's talk any more about my blisters. Do I dare smoke a cigarette here? Or is smoking taboo for women in Baypoint?"

"I'm afraid it is, dear. I don't mind, of course, but Glenwood is only forty miles away and some one would be sure to run and tell on you. The Silticoos emphatically does not approve of women smoking."

"Oh, well, it doesn't matter. I only thought it would be nice to smoke with you." She watched her husband snip off the end of a cigar and light it, then glanced idly about her. "I'm surprised to find such a nice little hotel in a small town like Baypoint. Our room is very comfortable and downstairs here everything is quite good looking."

Mallory made a little grimace at her.

"Don't let the natives hear you calling Baypoint a small town. It is the metropolis of the Candon Bay country and people don't like to have it spoken of as a small town. And the Grand Hotel is advertised far and wide as having the best beds to be found west of the Coast Range. The Crystal Palace where we're going to-night to see William Farnum is the pride of Candon Bay, let me tell you. They just installed one of these big new organs—the kind that comes up out of the floor—and imported a fellow from San Francisco to play it." He looked at his watch. "I don't want to hurry you, but we'll have to go if we want to get in at the beginning of the picture."

On the street Katherine saw in the window of a furniture store a display of bedroom pieces—a low oak bed with bureau, dressing table, and chest to match. She stopped short to look wistfully at them. What fun it would be to buy them and throw away the bird's-eye maple atrocity and the pink rag rugs in their room at the hospital!

"The mattress on your bed is the same as that one there," said Mallory proudly. "The best make on the market, everyone told me. I looked at every mattress in Baypoint before I bought it."

Katherine slipped her hand through his arm. She knew that his own mattress was a relief map of a mountain system and she loved the care with which he had selected a new one for her. She must not say anything to hurt his feelings or let him guess how horrible she thought their room. With this resolution, she tore her eyes off the oak dressing table only to see facing her in the opposite window a shining rosewood baby grand piano.

"Oh, Bob," she cried softly. "Isn't it beautiful?"

Looking at her face full of admiration and hunger, Mallory said firmly, "You shall have that piano or one just like it, Katherine. I'd've had one waiting when you came…only things didn't break just right."

But the girl hardly heard him. She was sick with longing to get her hands on the keyboard of a piano. Suddenly it seemed to her she could not live without one.

"Dearest, we must hurry or we won't be in time for the first picture," coaxed Mallory. And when she still did not move, he went on, "If you don't come along now, I'll kiss you right here on the street in full view of Baypoint."

Katherine started.

"Oh, Bob, you wouldn't!"

"I will if you stand here any longer, I swear I will. And no man with eyes in his head would blame me. You're gorgeous in that dress with the collar sticking up behind your head. Red is your color, dear, there's no doubt of it. And I'm so proud of you I want everybody to see you. I know they'll all wonder how on earth you came to marry a clodhopping fellow like me, but I don't care as long as they know you're mine."

Katherine forgot the piano in the window and looked up at his eager face.

"When I remember how tongue-tied and funny you were when you first made love to me, I'm amazed to hear you say things like that."

"It's just your influence, that's all. One look at you to-night would limber up the tongue of a wooden man. Now come along, dear."

They had barely seated themselves in a tiny corner loge for two when the lights went out in the theater and the fifth episode of "The Exploits of Elaine" flickered on the screen. Mallory fumbled in the dark for Katherine's hand. She leaned back in the hollow of his arm with her cheek against the rough cloth of his coat and sniffed happily at the tweed-tobacco-soap odor she associated with him.

"I never liked this Pearl White any too well," rumbled Mallory deep in his throat. "She's too blonde. I prefer brunettes."

"What does it matter," thought Katherine, "about furniture or even a piano when we feel like this, when just being together is sheer joy?"

She explored his hand with her fingers; it was hard and thick and it made hers seem weak and useless. But, curiously, she did not resent that feeling of helplessness. "I wish we hadn't come to this show," she thought. "I wish we had stayed at the hotel."

Neither of them ever had the least idea of what happened to Elaine that night or saw a single scene of the feature picture, "The Spoilers." It was not long before Katherine became aware that Mallory's arm was gradually slackening its hold about her. Then his fingers dropped apart, his head sagged against the back of the seat, his body slumped down, and he was asleep.

Sitting there in the dark beside this man she had married, feeling his slow deep breathing and the weight of his limp arm against her shoulder, Katherine listened to the organ and tried to orient herself in the experiences of the last twenty-eight hours. Did all women feel helpless with their husbands? Why did this particular man stir her to passion? Why did she feel, when she was in his arms, that nothing else mattered, that she wanted no more than that from life, that even music was of no real importance to her? Why had she been willing to go away and marry him without telling her father and mother what she was doing? Why was she willing now to go back to Glenwood with him to-morrow and live there in that squalid bedroom? It was not, she realized, because she—like her husband—had had a dream of a home together with children shouting on the stairs. At the thought of children she felt a flicker of distaste, but when Mallory stirred in his sleep and touched her that flicker was swallowed up in a flood of feeling.

There was no use thinking about it, she reflected, no use asking herself why she loved this man. Love came when it would and it was no respecter of persons. Her sense of humor was so submerged that she could not even smile at the realization that a year ago she would not have tolerated for an instant any man who went to sleep beside her in a theater.

The next morning she woke before he did, and found him lying with his arm thrown across her and his face tucked down between her neck and shoulder. Cautiously she twisted her body about until she could see him more plainly.

During the night, it seemed to her, his face for all its rugged features had lost its adult look. Lying there now, he looked a defenseless boy. His thick brown hair was rumpled and a faint dark stubble dotted his chin and jaw. His pajamas were open at the neck and she could see the line where the coat of dark tan stopped short; below that line his skin was surprisingly smooth and white. Under the sheet she could trace the outline of his body: the wide shoulders, big chest, tapering flanks.

Passionate desire flamed up in her again. This man was hers, all of him. She loved his body, she was proud of her power to make him love her. Her skin tingled when she remembered his voice saying "Katherine! Katherine!" She put her arm around his head and laid her cheek down on his face and rubbed it back and forth. It was good to feel that scrubby contact with his stubbly beard.

She wanted him to wake up, she wanted to see the bright blueness of his eyes, she wanted to see the look that would come into them when he kissed her. Very gently she put her lips on his eyelids, then she kissed his forehead and his hair softly. But he did not move.

"Poor Bob," she thought. "I ought to leave him alone and let him rest. He's tired. He works so hard."

But she did not stop caressing him. Instead she kissed his mouth, pressing her lips down hard against his.

He opened his eyes and looked up at her, into her brown eyes full of bright golden flecks. He saw there unashamed desire. Instantly the boyishness that had touched her when she first awoke vanished from his face. He raised himself in bed and, turning, gathered her roughly into his arms, pushed back her head, and put his mouth against her throat.

"Katherine, I love you! Do you hear me? I love you! You're the only woman I've ever loved this way, the only one I want to love this way. But I'm going to make you more mine than you've ever been before, and I'm going to keep you always. Always!"

To the breathless passion in his voice her quivering flesh made the only answer of which she was capable.

CHAPTER II

I

In the small shed behind the building which housed the hospital Dr. Mallory was splitting wood, swinging his ax in the crisp air of morning with an extravagant display of energy. At the moment his mind was concerned with his maid-of-all-work. Soon after Katherine's arrival he had noticed that she had an instinctive aversion for Juanita which she found it impossible to conceal, and he was on the verge of discharging Sairy.

Looking up from the chopping-block, he saw Burton, the druggist, standing in the back door of his shop. Burton was a short, thick-set man of thirty-five with a waving lock of oily black hair that drooped over his forehead. It always seemed to Mallory that his small dark beady eyes were ferreting out stray nickels and dimes in people's pockets.

"Sairy sure sees to it that she don't split the wood any more, don't she, doc? Well, I expect that's as good a way as any to spend the time while you're waitin' for practice to pick up."

Mallory selected a new block of wood and swung his ax overhead before he answered.

"Sairy has never mentioned the woodpile to me. But I don't like to see women doing this sort of thing."

"It depends on the woman, don't you think? Not your wife, of course. Or mine. But with Sairy it's different." Burton grinned maliciously. "I always wondered why Doc Peters kept her around when he knew what he did about her. But then maybe Sairy had something on him. You know, the womenfolks don't think much of her kind bein' in the hospital. It might make a hit with the female population of the valley if you was to get rid of her."

Mallory rested the ax-head on the ground and looked coldly at the bright-eyed man leaning against the door jamb.

"And suppose I fired her, Burton, what would she do then? She's got to make a living for herself and the child, and apparently Juanita's father doesn't help her at all."

The druggist's yellowish teeth flashed in wide-mouthed laughter.

"Ha, ha! That's good, doc! That's good! Juanita's father. Why, nobody knows who he is, not even Sairy! Ha, ha!"

"What difference does that make?" Mallory's voice was all the icier because he had just been thinking of discharging the woman. "The kid's on her hands just the same. She's got to look after her. And what other sort of job could she ever hold down?"

"Well, it's nothin' to me what you do about her." Burton's manner was distinctly aggrieved. "Or about anything else, for that matter. I just thought I'd drop a hint how people felt about her. Take it or leave it. It's nothin' to me."

Mallory's temper subsided a little. Was it possible that this man was actually trying to be helpful rather than offensive?

"I'm sorry if I seem pig-headed, Burton," he said more quietly. "But I don't see how I can turn Sairy out. At least not now."

After a minute of silence Burton cleared his throat and began another approach. "Heard anything about Mrs. Lane up-river bein' sick?" he inquired eagerly.

"Lane? No, I haven't seen any one by that name that I can recall."

"They tell me she's right sick, but I expect she won't have a doctor unless they get Bentley or Kronheit up from Baypoint. She used to have Doc Peters, of course, right often, but now…" Burton paused expectantly.

Mallory said nothing.

"Too bad, doc, but maybe you'll have better luck after while when people get more used to you. Right now lots of folks are goin' down to the Bay. Mrs. Spaulding was in the store yesterday. She'd been down to see Dr. Kronheit. She said he was goin' to operate on her next week. Down in Baypoint, I guess. She used to be one of Doc Peters' standbys; there's always something wrong with her."

Mallory split a huge knotty chunk into two cleanly riven pieces with one blow of his ax, as though it had been the druggist's head. Burton watched him a moment longer, chuckling in the enjoyment of tormenting him.

"Well, I got to get busy, doc. Three or four prescriptions of Dr. Kronheit's come in yesterday and there's a couple of Doc Peters' old ones to refill. Any time you have a chance come down and chin a while in the store. I'm always glad to see you. So long."

Mallory glared after the tubby little man. He hated the familiar "doc" from Burton. He wondered if the druggist thought he could be browbeaten into discharging Sairy and instantly resolved to keep her on. He asked himself if Burton could actually think him so stupid as not to recognize the unprofessional attitude of certain physicians in Baypoint. Then he realized that, two years before, he would not have believed such chicanery as Bentley and Kronheit practiced possible in the medical profession.

Heavy-hearted, he walked around the woodshed to a point from which he could look up at the great fir-clad hill back of the hospital. It was beginning to dawn on him that many of a doctor's troubles arise within the ranks of his fellow prac-titioners. He planted his feet wide apart and stood staring up at the forest defiantly, as though challenging his rivals to defeat him if they could.

II

The door at the foot of the hospital stairs opened and Olaf Hansen's booming cheerful voice floated upward.

"Now, take 'er easy, Mr. Morgan. We got all forenoon to get up these steps if need be, and they ain't a mite of use of ya hurryin' thisa way and gettin' yourself all tired out. Mornin', Mrs. Hathaway. Mornin', doc. I'm bringin' your patient again. Seems like since ya been doctorin' him he's gettin' mighty spry. He comes up these here stairs like a two-year old."

The broad-shouldered Hansen topped the last step supporting a cadaverous white-faced man whose shrunken blue lips were twisted into a determined smile. He tottered to the nearest chair and wiped the sweat from his forehead.

"You're a little stronger than you were last week, aren't you, Mr. Morgan?" asked Mrs. Hathaway.

Morgan took several deep breaths before he answered.

"Well, some days I feel pretty good and some days I don't. It just depends. To-day I ain't so good, seems like."

Mallory turned on the motor of the X-ray machine. "I'll be ready for you just as soon as I test my tube."

"Oh, that's all right. Take your time, doc," said the sick man. "I ain't in no hurry. Took two years to find somebody that knows what's the matter with me, and I don't mind waitin'. You know, Olaf, this X-ray is a great thing. At first the sparks and the noise like to scairt me stiff but now they don't bother me at all. X-rays don't hurt and they don't taste bad either, but that's more'n I can say for doc's medicine. Benzol he calls it, but it's just gasoline with a fancy name. My mouth tastes like a carburetor all the time. Burton fixes it in capsules that is supposed to skate through my stomach without meltin', but I reckon if I was to belch real hard clost to the fire I'd blow up all right."

Hansen scratched his head and shifted from one foot to the other in embarrassment; he looked at the nurse and saw in her eyes admiration for a man who could jest on the brink of his own grave. The X-ray machine at the other end of the room settled down into a steady roar and the tube flashed and glowed.

"Ready now, Mr. Morgan," said Mallory.

The patient pushed himself up out of his chair.

"I think I can make it to the table on my own legs to-day," he said, waving aside Hansen's help. A staggering gait carried him across the room to a wooden bench beneath the lighted X-ray tube. "Let 'er go, doc," he panted. "I'm all set."

Mallory's hands spread protective lead gently over the sick man's chest; his face was very grave.

At the luncheon table an hour later he was still thoughtful.

"That chap, Morgan, gets me," he confessed. "He knows he can't get well but he won't admit it. And he knows that I know it, too. I've written to every man in the country who's made a study of leukemia and none of them give me any hope. There's something rotten about knowing you can't do anything for a patient."

"Has he been ill long, Bob?" asked Katherine with interest.

"Over two years. First he went down to Baypoint and the bright surgical lights there took out his appendix and then his gall bladder. Last year they operated on his stomach, sewed it up to his diaphragm or backbone or something equally foolish. I saw him the first week I was here, found him all doubled up with pains in his legs. I didn't know what the devil was wrong with him, but on general principles I took a blood count anyhow, and in five minutes I had my diagnosis. It makes me sick when I think that a simple blood count two years ago would have saved Morgan all these unnecessary operations. But now it's too late and in spite of everything I can do the old fellow's going to pass out on me."

"Why didn't the doctors in Baypoint do a blood count if it's such a simple thing?"

"For the same reason they don't do a lot of other things. Because they're in such a hurry to operate and collect a surgical fee that they can't be bothered to find out what ails their patients. Here's Kronheit, Burton tells me, going to operate on Mrs. Spaulding next week. You remember her, don't you, Mrs. H.?"

The nurse nodded.

"Well, it's just three weeks since I examined her thoroughly. There's nothing wrong with her body except that almost everything she can exist without has already been taken out of her by aspiring surgeons. The trouble is primarily in her mind. And now she's been to Kronheit and he's going to operate again."

"But why didn't you explain things to her, Bob, so she'd understand?"

Mrs. Hathaway smiled and the doctor snorted.

"Explain! Good God, I talked to the woman for two hours and the more I talked the sorer she got and the less she believed what I said."

Katherine looked so bewildered that Mrs. Hathaway leaned forward toward her.

"Your husband, Mrs. Mallory, is likely to speak too bluntly to these neurotic women when they consult him. That's the trouble. They must be handled with tact and diplomacy, and the doctor doesn't always take the trouble to do that."

"Tact! Diplomacy! I suppose you call it tact and diplomacy for Kronheit to argue that woman into a useless operation and for Bentley to go to church and prayer meeting and be superintendent of the Sunday school in the biggest church in Baypoint. Because I won't split fees and send my cases to Baypoint for those two to operate on, they're going to steal every patient from me they can."

"Dear, I don't understand what you mean."

Mallory with an effort lowered his voice and turned to his wife.

"It's this way, Katherine. Bentley offered to give me forty per cent of the fee on every operative case I sent down to him. Kronheit offered to come up here and operate on my surgical patients and let me keep thirty per cent of the fee. Three or four other doctors in Baypoint made me propositions of the same sort. The idea is for me to go out into the woods, get the patient down here, make the diagnosis, decide what ought to be done, and then stand by while some one else does it. I'd have the after care of the patient and most of the responsibility, but I'd hand over nearly all the fee to the surgeon. Sometimes, of course, I'd be allowed to assist him but mostly I'd be a salesman selling operations on commission.

"But I've had good surgical training and I want to do my own ordinary cases. I can handle them just as well as these fellows at Baypoint. But they're diplomatic and tactful, they hold the women's hands and work the religious game, and people fall for it. People want to get stung, they ask for it. What's the use of being honest, trying to tell the truth? Nobody believes you. Everybody runs back to Bentley and Kronheit and their kind, over and over, for useless surgery. And I'll be damned if I'll do that sort of thing, try to beat them at their own game. It just isn't in me to do it."

When Mallory had left the room, Katherine looked questioningly at Mrs. Hathaway.

"Is this all really true? I never knew such things went on among doctors."

"Oh, it's true, Mrs. Mallory. Quite true. The doctors in Baypoint who do most of the surgery are bitterly opposed to the younger men in the small towns taking care of their own operative cases, and they split fees and do unnecessary surgery just as the doctor said. A few of them have even gone so far as to subsidize Mr. Burton downstairs and give him a commission on every case he sends down to them."

"But, Mrs. Hathaway, doctors aren't like that! Surely they aren't."

Katherine's face was horrified.

"No, of course most of them aren't. Most of the doctors in Baypoint are honest decent men. But unfortunately the few who aren't are the prominent ones and the ones who do the most surgery."

Katherine was pale with concern and now the concern began to turn into anger.

"Well, isn't there anything we can do about it, Mrs. Hathaway?"

The nurse smiled so whole-heartedly at the girl that she felt her determination mounting.

"In the long run, Mrs. Mallory, your husband will win out, even here. He is so capable and so kind-hearted and so interested in his cases that when people have once been his patients they stick to him afterwards. But he's too outspoken, too blunt with a certain type of nervous woman, and he thinks tact is the same thing as dishonesty. If you could make him see that it isn't, help him to be a little more diplomatic, it would help him a lot."

"I'll try, Mrs. Hathaway. And I think that once Bob sees what we mean he'll be all right. His bluntness is a surface thing built up because he detests everything that isn't absolutely straightforward."

"I know that," assented the nurse, rising from the table. "Tact is a foreign language to men like Dr. Mallory, and personally I like him all the better for it. One always knows exactly where one stands with a man of that sort. It's only that it makes things harder for him than they need to be. We must talk this over again, but just now I must run. We've got the first clinic for pre-school children this afternoon and there are a few things I must do before they get here."

Katherine looked after the energetic figure in its crisp white uniform.

"I shall make it a point to be on hand and watch this clinic myself," she decided. "Something must be done about things and Mrs. Hathaway or I will have to do it."

III

Mallory went straight from the luncheon table to the bank in the yellow frame building next door to the hospital. He strode past the teller's window where Otto Schmidt, the good-natured proprietor of the pool hall, stood in conference with Mrs. Doan. Mrs. Doan, wife of the manager and cashier of the Glenwood State Bank, was a shrill-voiced, red-haired termagant who ruled her husband and their two cowering little girls with a heavy hand. She was careful to consult the doctor by telephone whenever possible so that he would not send her a bill for professional services.

The memory of Mrs. Hathaway's remarks about tact made Mallory speak politely to Mrs. Doan in spite of his acute dislike for her, but he hurried on past her wicket toward the railed-in space in the rear of the room where Doan had his desk.

Samuel Doan was a slender subdued-looking man with brown eyes and smooth gray hair; his face harbored a certain scared shrewdness. As befitted the guardian of Glenwood's bank accounts, he dressed with scrupulous neatness. He was the superintendent of the Sunday school and commonly reputed to be a man of God. Certainly he attended prayer meeting regularly on Wednesday evenings with his wife and went to church every Sunday, and it was reported that at Mrs. Doan's behest he swept and dusted the house of worship early Sunday mornings.

This afternoon the banker was sitting at work in the railed-off corner of the room behind the cages. He looked up from his desk and smiled hesitantly at Mallory.

"How do you do, doctor? What can I do for you to-day?"

"I dropped in to see if I could arrange for another small loan. There are some repairs that can't be put off much longer. The hospital plumbing has broken down again and the sterilizer must be replaced. I'm just beginning to realize how badly run down the whole place is."

"H-m," said Mr. Doan. "Yes, I'm sure that Dr. Peters spent practically nothing for new equipment or building repairs the last few years he was here." Then with a shade less cordiality, "How much did you have in mind, doctor? And can you give me some idea how much you have outstanding and who owes you the larger accounts? Just a matter of form, of course, but…"

"I think I've got all the data you want here." Mallory pulled from his pocket several sheets of paper. "You'll see that there is about eleven hundred dollars coming to me."

Doan scanned the rows of figures.

"Yes, doctor, but will it ever get to you? That's the question.

Dr. Peters always found collections very slow until the railroad began building. And here on your list I see several of his oldest debtors. This fellow, Simmons, for instance. He never pays any bill voluntarily."

"I'm not surprised to hear that," said Mallory grimly, recalling the night in the Simmons' cabin. He harbored a dull anger at that long-chinned, yellow-visaged individual.

"And how much do you estimate that you need, doctor?"

A slow flush crept into Mallory's cheeks. He found borrowing money disagreeable and the knowledge that he was about to try to mislead the banker made him even more ill at ease. The lowest deposit the Baypoint Furniture Company would accept on the Steinway piano was two hundred and fifty dollars and this sum must be added to that required for repairs at the hospital.

"About four hundred dollars," he answered in a muffled voice.

Doan's eyebrows lifted perceptibly. He did a little sum on the blotter on his desk.

"That will make $750 you owe us," he said with a hint of sternness. "We shall expect some payment when the fish checks begin to come in. You should collect the major portion of the accounts on your books between now and Thanksgiving."

When Mallory had put his memorandum of credit for four hundred dollars into his pocket, he hurried away from the disquieting eyes of the little banker and tried to slip out without attracting Mrs. Doan's attention. But her sharp eyes noticed him as he passed her wicket.

"Dr. Mallory, your account is overdrawn nine dollars and forty-seven cents. Will you please attend to it before the bank closes this afternoon?"

This remark in Mrs. Doan's piercing voice dropped among the half-dozen customers in the room like a stone into a pool of water. An inaudible titter seemed to form just beneath the surface of the quiet that followed.

His face scarlet, Mallory turned toward the woman. As he did so he caught sight of Mr. Doan who was standing inside his little enclosure beside his desk; he was sure he saw shame in the man's brown eyes. Then he heard his own voice saying, "If you'll take the trouble to look it up, Mrs. Doan, you'll find that I've already looked after the overdraft."

But, despite this neat retort, Mallory carried out of the bank a depression he had not had when he went in.

Later, in a lull of business, Mrs. Doan went back to her husband's desk.

"Well, how much did he get this time?" she asked pointedly.

Mr. Doan looked up from a letter file with assumed absent-mindedness.

"Who do you mean, my dear? I don't understand you."

"You know perfectly well what I'm talking about, Samuel. How much did the doctor get this time?"

"Oh, not much. Just a small amount for some repairs at the hospital."

Doan's hands, busy with the file, seemed to flutter ineffectively and hopelessly among the papers. His wife stood silently beside the desk and watched him.

"Four hundred."

"Huh!" snorted the woman. "Huh! It's that girl. She'll be the ruin of him. You'll see."

Doan looked up at her in surprise.

"I don't know what you're talking about, my dear. The money is for plumbing repairs and some new apparatus in the hospital."

"That's what he told you, Samuel. But that was just a blind. He got it for that young wife of his. I just found out about her yesterday. Her father is John Harper of the Columbia Insurance Company. She's a high-stepper, used to lots of money. That ought to open your eyes, Samuel Doan. She's always had money and since her husband can't earn enough for her, he borrows it from you."

"Almira, you shouldn't say such things when you don't know whether they are true," expostulated Doan weakly.

"But I do know," insisted his wife. "I do know. Haven't I been right time and again about things like this? I can tell from the way a man acts when he comes in to borrow money whether he's telling the truth about it or not. I knew that young man was trying to put something over on you this afternoon, Samuel. Probably he is going to have the roof patched and the plumbing fixed, but at least half that money is for that wife of his to spend on foolishness. I'm sure of it."

Haughtily Mrs. Doan turned her back and stalked back into the teller's cage. But Doan propped his chin on one hand and stared apprehensively after her. Suppose she was right! He had known her to be right just as she had said in other similar affairs in the past. And he had loaned that man Mallory $750 in less than four months. A strip of gooseflesh prickled out along Samuel Doan's backbone. Suppose Almira was right!

IV

At nine o'clock that evening Katherine sat in front of the stove in the waiting room alone. Mrs. Hathaway and the doctor had just been called out on a fracture case and Sairy had taken Juanita and gone to spend the evening with her brother and his wife. The last hospital patient had been discharged that morning and no one admitted during the day. The very air smelled solitary.

Katherine was facing actuality, trying to think things through. The situation in which she found herself was not even remotely like that which she had once pictured for herself as a doctor's wife. She had taken her conception of physicians from those middle-aged or elderly medical men her parents had called in; they had ample incomes, their wives and children had always been well dressed. She had been brought up to obey their orders without question and in her limited experience with hospitals it had always seemed to her that doctors were autocrats whose least wish must be anticipated.

She had thought of Mallory, before she came to Glenwood, as the wise young medical patron of the valley who would lead the people in the ways of health and command their respect and deference. Because she had never known what it was to lack money, she had taken it for granted that she would have a comfortable home if not an elaborate one. It had never occurred to her that she would have to live in a hall bedroom, that a man like Burton would dare criticize her husband, or his fellow physicians meet him with unfair competition and dishonesty.

But these last weeks in the hospital had shown her many things and now the free clinic for pre-school children had finished her disillusionment. Mallory had taken up the project to examine the children with enthusiasm, sure that this innovation in public health would find a ready response among parents and that they would appreciate his giving time and services without charge. Less sanguine, Mrs. Hathaway said that they would probably get a tonsil operation or two out of the afternoon.

At a few minutes before two o'clock the first boatload of children had arrived from up-river. Katherine was sure she had never seen so wretched a group of youngsters and from what she heard her husband and the nurse say she knew that even they were startled by these underweight, crooked-backed, flat-footed children who were bowlegged and pigeon-breasted from rickets and open-mouthed from enlarged tonsils and adenoids. Many of them complained of "growing pains" and several had already developed rheumatic heart disease; some of them had tuberculosis of bone and a few dripped pus from tuberculous sinuses.

An ill-mannered mob, they had overflowed the waiting room, swarmed into the surgery and sterilizing room, clambered over the X-ray machine, and finally invaded the kitchen whence the irate Sairy drove them forth again. The mothers moved bovinely among them, impotent to control them, gossiping avidly with each other. When Mallory tried to talk to them about their children, they gaped blankly at him. Katherine remembered their faces—like fish that had only just been pulled out of the water.

Fifty of them had been examined that afternoon. Katherine had helped Mrs. Hathaway record the findings on Children's Bureau blanks. Over and over she had checked such items as "underweight," "anemic," "rachitic," "knock-kneed," "enlarged adenoids," "infected tonsils," "carious teeth," "defective hearing," "mitral valve lesion," "poor posture," "pot belly," "pigeon-breasted," "suspected TB," "should have eyes examined and glasses fitted." And while she wrote up these records, she watched her husband's enthusiasm beat vainly against a wall of ignorance and indifference which no scientific information could shake. The mothers were convinced that none of this was of any importance. All their lives they had lived on salt fish and potatoes, and what had been good enough for them was good enough for their children. Their menfolks wouldn't spend money for oranges or green vegetables like spinach, and the women themselves had no desire to work in the hot sun making gardens just because this new young doctor said the kids ought to have greens and lettuce and carrots. Doc Peters had never talked about newfangled things like vitamins. Everybody had growing pains more or less, just as everybody had to have whooping cough and mumps and measles. Besides, snake oil was a specific for leg ache and rheumatism in children was nothing to be afraid of. What possible connection could there be between the joints and the heart? The new doctor was just trying to drum up business. And anyhow there was too much "cutting" nowadays, especially tonsils and adenoids.

When the crowd trooped off Katherine saw one woman with a skinny little boy lagging behind to ask how much it cost to have tonsils taken out. But when Mallory, anxious to encourage this feeble flicker of interest, slashed the fee schedule adopted by the County Medical Society and said fifteen dollars, she cried out that her "old man" wouldn't "hear to no such a bill" and rushed downstairs protesting that the new doctor "charged too high."

So not even one child was to be better off for this carefully planned clinic and Mallory was to glean not even a single tonsillectomy from it.

Katherine's head ached: the shrieking children and their shrill-voiced mothers had worn her nerves threadbare. All she could remember was that her husband had been misjudged, his motives misunderstood, his ability underestimated. As she sat brooding, her resentment mounted steadily. Bob was a fine doctor and he was wasted in the Silticoos valley. So far as he was concerned it was a blind alley: he could never achieve a reputation or acquire a competence there. And even that was not all. It was a miserable place to live.

Oftener than not she was quite alone in the evenings. Aside from the Blakes and Mrs. Hathaway there was no one she cared for. There was not even a movie nearer than Baypoint. There was no music, no art, no concerts, nothing to do but work and sit at home, nowhere to go but to bed. Katherine could feel her fingers stiffening for want of a piano. She could see Mallory and herself degenerating into a pair of villagers whose greatest dissipation was an annual trip to Pacific City. They would never have any money for clothes or books or pictures or music. And suppose they were to have a child one day? It would grow up among little savages like those who had swarmed through the hospital that afternoon. Katherine shuddered at the idea.

She rose and walked into the surgery to close the windows against the sea breeze that swept into the rooms. With her hand on the sash she paused. From the sidewalk below came the disagreeable twang of Burton, the druggist.

"Glad you dropped in, Mike. It's kinda lonesome in the store around this time of an evening. . . . Yeah, I guess to-day'll spike Doc Mallory's guns aplenty. I like to died laughin' him examinin' all them kids for nothin' and not drawin' a single job outa the whole bunch! Several of the women was in the store after they come down from the hospital and they figured they'd go down to Bentley if they had to have anything done to the kids. Now there's a real surgeon, let me tell you. But upstarts like this man Mallory always get it in the neck. Just takes a little time, that's all." The key rasped in the drug store door. "Well, goo' night, Mike. Come in again."

Then footsteps hurried away along the dimly lighted sidewalk.

But Katherine, her face transfigured by fury, stood motionless at the window. Burton had laughed at Bob, had called him an upstart, had said the women at the clinic had played him for a fool. This ignoramus who said "goo' night" had made fun of the man who was hers. The whole valley made sport of him, thought him an easy mark. He worked for them at all hours and they ignored his bills because they knew he would come again if they sent for him. But when in their own opinion they were dangerously ill or required surgery, they went to Baypoint to Mallory's unscrupulous competitors. Such things were not to be borne. The spirit that had made Katherine defy her parents to study at the Conservatory bestirred itself again.

From the first she had disliked Glenwood; now she hated it. The people were stupid. There was no reason why Bob should sacrifice himself for them; they were not worth it. Let some doctor who didn't know much come to the Silticoos; the natives would probably like a physician who was stupid like themselves. But Bob was too good for them, they did not appreciate him, they would never know how good a doctor he was. Even though he were to stay on, working for them all his life, collecting just enough to maintain existence, they would never recognize that he was a great man buried alive among them.

And what of herself? She had not meant to think of the career she had abandoned to marry Mallory, but to-night the old hunger for music swept through her and the old ambition reasserted itself. Was she to live here on the Silticoos all the rest of her life, be nobody in her own right, only the doctor's wife? Was she never to feel again the sense of power that came when she brought an audience under the spell of music? Was she never to have again the feeling of being made clean and fresh by the release of her emotions when she played? Was she to have children and watch them grow up, little barbarians, in Glenwood? Bob took it for granted that she wanted babies but she was not sure that motherhood attracted her. She loved her husband but she could not discover in her heart any longing for children. Why should all women want babies? As a matter of fact she felt she did not want them and now she resolved that she would bring no child into the world so long as she lived in Glenwood.

She struck her hand against the window sill. She had not flinched at giving up her career to marry the man she loved, but it was not fair that she should have to give up everything that made life worth living. Bob must get away, he must study and fit himself for city practice or teaching, he must begin soon to build a career in medicine that would be the goal of both their lives. Only in making him a great man could she find recompense for giving up her own work.

Katherine pulled down the window with a bang. She would not sacrifice herself and she would not permit her husband to sacrifice himself and all his possibilities for the stupid people of the Silticoos valley.

CHAPTER III

I

It was the night of the annual Fishermen's Ball. Main Street was crowded. Every inhabitant of Glenwood except the minister and his wife and the bedridden invalids was on parade, and gas boats from up-river constantly discharged more pleasure seekers. The men gathered in knots along the wharves to discuss the run of salmon and the women clustered on the sidewalks to gossip in high-pitched voices. The children raced up and down the street calling to one another and making belligerent gestures at any one who ventured to remonstrate with them.

No one saw the sun sink behind the great bulk of the mountains and no one noticed the evening star glowing above the rim of the horizon. The firs caught the fiery gleam of the afterglow and the river flowed softly on its silvered way but, as darkness fell, the human hubbub grew ever louder and more strident.

Otto Schmidt, the rosy-faced confectioner, hustled his extra help back and forth between the ice-cream parlor and the pool room with trays of sundaes and ice-cream sodas. His wooden leg creaked cheerily as he hurried among his customers and his cash register sang a song of sixpence.

Next door to the confectionery, the Odd Fellows' Hall stood open-doored and a stream of light poured out upon the sidewalk. Even though it was still an hour until dancing would begin, a handful of women straggled inside and sat down in groups on the row of straight chairs that encircled the room. That afternoon the floor had been freshly waxed and polished but it still exhibited the scars of other balls. Windows high above arm's length lined the hall and in the back of the room a stairway slanted up to the second floor.

In the upper room women in white aprons were sorting and spreading upon tables the delicacies destined for the dancers' refreshment: cold fried chicken, pressed veal, salmon loaf, rolls and cookies, doughnuts, pickles, jelly, and spiced fruits. In one corner four ice-cream freezers leaked dismal streams of brine along the unpainted floor.

At eight-thirty four musicians came into the Hall and clambered upon a platform under the stairs where there was a battered square piano, veteran of many similar balls. The pianist strummed A while the fiddler squeaked up and down in pursuit of the proper pitch; the tall man with the clarinet adjusted the mouthpiece of his instrument and tasted of it as though it were a forbidden fruit; the drummer loosened his cuffs, turned them up over tattooed forearms and began to practice the roll.

At the sound of the drum merrymakers began to swarm in from the street in a kaleidoscope of ages and sizes. On the Silticoos everyone went to the Fishermen's Ball: grandparents to look on, the middle generation and the young people to dance, infants to gaze on the scene with wide solemn eyes. As soon as they were inside, the sexes divided. The masculine elements remained milling about near the entrance, ostensibly talking among themselves but covertly engaged in sizing up the women and girls who sought chairs along the wall, the married women together at the far end of the hall, the marketable girls in a group somewhat nearer the doors. This segregation was traditional in the valley.

At ten minutes of nine the Mallorys arrived and, not knowing that they were breaking a taboo, walked together down the floor and sat beside Mrs. Blake. A titter followed them and broke into giggling when the doctor helped his wife remove her wrap.

Mrs. Hathaway had advised Katherine not to wear an evening gown and, when the girl looked about her, she was glad she had left her elaborate dancing frock at home. Alice Blake wore a princess dress of hunter's green with a long panel down the front, but there were girls from the upper valley in white wash dresses with bright ribbons at neck and waist, there were others in middy blouses and blue skirts, there were some in figured percale house dresses. The middle-aged and elderly women wore their Sunday skirts and white waists. For a time it seemed that Mrs. Blake's costume and Katherine's frock with its long transparent sleeves, flaring lace collar, and spreading skirt would be the chief topic of discussion among the women, but suddenly everyone's attention was drawn to the violinist who was flourishing his bow and shouting orders for the Grand March.

At the head of the column were Mr. and Mrs. Burton. It was but seldom that the druggist left his soda fountain and pill-tile for an evening of frivolity and, having enticed him to do so on this occasion, his wife wore an air of coquetry as self-consciously as she did her elaborately puffed curls. Burton himself was resplendent in a dark suit with the padded shoulders and peg-top trousers that had been fashionable when he was in the school of pharmacy. Immediately behind the leaders came a lanky man in a collarless shirt and lavender arm-bands whom Mallory recognized as the younger Simmons and his partner, a girl from the hills whose dress gaped between buttons in the back. Farther down the line was Sairy, powdered into a chalky pallor and clad in a stiffly starched white uniform filched from Mrs. Hathaway, promenading proudly on the arm of a man in blue overalls.

Behind the long line of couples came a squabbling, pushing

mass of small girls who hoped to attract attention from the adolescent lads huddled by the door. From the marching throng rose a discordant sound of tapping slipper heels, slapping house shoes, and clumping boots. Now and then some ribald comment was tossed by the marchers at the spectators along the walls.

After four rounds of the hall, the orchestra stopped the march abruptly and, with a few preliminary scrapings, burst into the newly popular Missouri Waltz. When Mallory put his arm around her and swept her away over the floor, Katherine smiled up at him. She loved to dance, she found something sensuously appealing in the music, and she knew her husband was thrilled to be dancing with her again. He held her very close and brushed his cheek gently against her hair.

"You're the best dancer in the place," he said softly. "And you're gorgeous in that dress. When the light shines on it, it's exactly the color of the flecks in your eyes. Like dull gold."

"That's why I bought it, Bob. Did you think the color was an accident? But I'm glad you noticed it. It would be ghastly to have a husband who never knew what I had on. You look very nice yourself, Dr. Mallory." She looked at the Persian pattern of his scarf. "I like that tie with a dark blue suit. But you're at your best, dear, in dress clothes with a broad white bosom and a standing collar."

Mallory laughed.

"Just imagine what a hit I'd've made to-night if I had appeared in a Tuxedo and a boiled shirt! Probably I'd 've been mobbed."

"Yes, you probably would have been." Katherine sobered. "In this beastly little place! I don't suppose there is any one in Glenwood except the Blakes and Mrs. Hathaway and possibly the Doans who know what dinner clothes are."

Mallory shook his head at her.

"Now, now. Don't be too hard on these people. Good Lord, honey, how can you expect them to know any better? They've never had a chance."

At this rebuke, gentle though it was, Katherine stiffened in resentment and drew back a little from her husband. But in another moment the waltz was over and he dropped his arms from about her and began to clap for the encore. In a mood of irritation she walked beside him. After all it was even more on his account than her own that she disliked Glenwood.

Mallory returned Katherine to her place next Mrs. Blake and, observing now the conventions of the Silticoos, went with Henry who had been dancing with Alice toward the group of men and boys near the door. On the edge of the knot, two youths were threatening each other with violence. The older belligerent, a low-browed, dark-skinned boy, dared the other to fight.

"Yeah, you reckon I stole your girl. Come on and see if you can lick me. You're scared, that's what you are! Nobody takes my girl away from me, but you you got no guts. You can't keep a girl nohow."

"You shut up, damn you! Who says I'm afraid of you? Why I could cut you up and feed you to the fishes. Come on now, come on you ——— ——— ———!"

Both lads broke from the hands of their friends and rushed each other. Fists smacked hard on bare flesh, feet scuffled as the boys fenced for openings. The sound of their breathing rose above the music. Then the larger youth drew a great gush of blood from the other's nose. The bleeding one snarled like an animal and suddenly rushed his enemy with an open knife in his hand.

Henry Blake and Mallory had shouldered their way through the group until they were in the inner ring, and now they ran in and pulled the combatants apart.

"Boys, boys," shouted Blake. "Lay off this fightin'! This is no way to do in here, before the womenfolks."

The youths stood with lowered heads glaring at each other. Henry twisted the right arm of the lad he had seized and the knife fell on the floor.

"You're tryin' that stuff again, are you? If you two had a scrap to settle, why didn't you go outside and do it decent? What's the matter anyhow?"

The boy screamed fiercely, "Let go of me! Let go of me! He got my girl away from me and they been dancin' together. Let me at him!" Furiously the scarlet-faced lad lunged forward but Blake's hand jerked him back.

"Stop it! You're not goin' to fight in here. Why didn't you watch your girl and dance with her yourself instead of sneakin' off drinkin'? You smell like a whisky barrel. I wouldn't blame a girl for ditchin' you. Got any more knives on you? Frisk him, doc, and be sure, will you? Now, get on outa here and stay out! Beat it, and don't come back around here or I'll put the toe of my shoe to you."

Blake dragged the sullen youth to the door and shoved him outside. A murmur of approval rose from the men and boys about him. Henry picked the knife off the floor and put it in his own pocket.

"I didn't realize he had a knife," said Mallory, "until you shook it out of his hand."

"Oh, that Painter kid is a bad actor. I wish he wouldn't come down to the dances here in town. Last time he was here he knifed another boy for dancin' with his girl. Tom Painter's a good-for-nothing and the boy's goin' to be worse than his dad, I believe."

The two men went outside and leaned side by side against the railing along the sidewalk in front of the hall. Mallory lit a cigarette and watched the match in its incandescent flight and listened for the little hiss with which it struck the water below. Silently he and Blake smoked and looked at the people going in and out the open doors. At last Henry peered thoughtfully into the younger man's face and said, "You know, doc, I been kinda envyin' you to-night. I used to think I wanted to be a doctor."

Blake transferred his gaze from Mallory's face to the clear dark sky.

"I was sixteen when my father died, and there were three kids younger than me, so I inherited dad's responsibility for 'em. By the time I got all them educated my own pep had kinda run down. One brother teaches chemistry in a college in Iowa and the other one's a lawyer down in California. My sister married a fellow in a bank in Pacific City and he's worked up to be cashier now. . . . And here I am, runnin' a launch and a fish boat on the Silticoos. Beats hell, don't it?"

Mallory studied the end of his cigarette. "How can a man ever tell what's going to happen to him?" he said at last.

"Well, anyhow, I'm glad Alice happened to me. And that was a funny thing, too, doc. I got hurt in a street car smash in Pacific City better'n three years ago, and she took care of me in the hospital. Nursin' was just about to get the best of her then, she was pale and thin and tired. So after while we got married. When she come down here she kinda stirred me up again, got me readin' books and magazines like I used to. She even tried to make me talk proper. And, all in all, we're not doin' so bad: there's the ranch up-river and a boat fishin' and the passenger launch. I guess there ain't much for me to kick about, but I always wish I could've been educated like the rest of the family."

Blake's voice was softly tinged with melancholy.

"And there's something I been wantin' to tell you, doc. You got a lot of plans for health work and a new hospital in Glenwood and all. Well, you saw how the kid clinic turned out. Now if you go on all enthusiastic workin' at these things, you're goin' to get hurt for nothin'. These folks are dumb, they don't understand what you're after. Lots of the old pioneers was fine men but some of 'em was none too particular about what they handed down to their kids. Some of the people in the hall yonder are just simple and some of 'em have taints in their blood and some of 'em are plain stupid. But you can't make 'em over, doc, and if you keep on tryin' to, you're goin' to get bumped—and bumped hard." Blake wiped his forehead on his coat sleeve. "Just think it over," he concluded. "What I say's the truth."

Presently Mallory went to the door and stood there watching the crowd. These, as Blake had said, were the people of the valley. Many among them had stupid faces with lax mouths and vapid eyes. It was a motley throng of bent-backed, stoop-shouldered, scrawny-necked, flat-footed human creatures hopping gracelessly about to ragtime and jazz. Foolish laughter echoed about him as he studied them.

It might be, as Henry said, too late to do anything for these people. But to admit this was to deny the concepts of modern social science. Changing the environment should bring corresponding changes in them and their children. It was not fair to condemn them for being stupid when they had never had a chance to be otherwise. Mallory shook himself free from the gloomy thoughts aroused by Henry's talk. If these people, he told himself, were only approached properly, they would respond and raise themselves to a higher plane of living.

Looking about the room, he noticed Katherine coming from the dancing floor with Blake, and his mouth relaxed and his eyes softened. Surely no man had ever married a more wonderful woman. She was the spark of light, the bit of loveliness that made life thrilling. And to-morrow the Blakes—co-conspirators with him—were to take her in their launch up the North Fork while he and Olaf Hansen got the piano she had admired in Baypoint upstairs into the corner room opposite their bedroom which Mrs. Hathaway had cleaned and refurbished. Katherine had no idea that such a plan was under way; her surprise would be complete. Mallory laughed softly, picturing her face when she first saw what he had for her.

He was overtaken by a sensation of being watched and, glancing to his right, saw Sairy standing partnerless, in her rumpled hospital uniform, with her eyes fixed on him. Even to a man more unsophisticated than Mallory it would have been apparent that Sairy longed to dance with him. Somewhat ruefully he made his way to her.

Sairy danced as poorly as she cooked; there was no rhythm in her strange jerky movements. A mingled odor of carnation perfume, Bandoline, and scented powder floated up from her head. Physical repugnance struggled against the queer compassion he felt for the girl, but when he saw the joy that irradiated her unattractive face as she looked up at him from her haven within his arm the repulsion died away. Once, catching the look in her groping vacant eyes, it seemed to him that Sairy realized her own stupidity and the doom it sealed for her. He was careful to take the encore with her and to bow and thank her for the dance with scrupulous courtesy before he rejoined his wife and Mrs. Blake.

Katherine had been dancing with the principal of the High School and seemed not to have noticed his adventure with Sairy, but Alice Blake, who had seen it all, looked at him with warm approval. She was a woman to whom maturity had brought added charm; her smooth black hair, pale skin, and clear blue eyes were more attractive at thirty than they had been at twenty. She talked so entertainingly to Mallory, and laughed so gaily at his jokes that he felt as though something special was being done for his pleasure, but as she said nothing of his dance with Sairy he did not know exactly why he stood so high in Mrs. Blake's graces.

II

It was almost midnight when a messenger with a note from Mrs. Morgan found Mallory. He seized his hat and, with a word to Katherine, slipped away from the dance and climbed the hill to the Morgans' white cottage.

The sick man was propped up in bed on many pillows, gasping for breath, and a ghastly slate color was creeping over his lips and ears. When Mallory came in and paused an instant at the foot of the bed, the dying man raised one bony hand and pointed at him.

"You've done for me," gasped Morgan. "Killed me, that's what you have with that gasoline I been takin'."

"No, no, George. Hush!" crooned the tear-bleared woman beside the bed. "The doctor's done everything he could for you. Lie still, George. Don't talk. It makes you so short of breath. I'll fan you again. There! Ain't that better?" She looked at Mallory with a terrified question in her eyes.

The doctor leaned over the lean figure in the bed, put his fingers on the pulse, then went out to the kitchen to prepare a hypodermic. The woman who was there tending the fire went to sit with Morgan and the dying man's wife came out to sink into a chair beside the range and pleat and unpleat her gingham apron with restless fingers. Her eyes were full of tears.

"Is…he…goin' soon?" she whispered.

Mallory nodded.

"Yes, Mrs. Morgan. His heart has simply worn out. I'm going to make it as easy for him as I can, so he won't suffer. That's all any one can do now." He put a hand on the woman's shoulder. "Stay out here a few minutes, until you get hold of yourself. I'll call you if there's any change."

As he gave the hypodermic injection Mallory looked down at the man in bed with pitying eyes; this was the shame of a chronic wasting disease. It had left Morgan a big-boned skeleton with a glistening yellow skin and a deep wide chest that heaved spasmodically for air. His big knobbly hands lay limp on the coverlet. Morgan, knowing his doom, had gallantly ignored it for months, had joked about the taste of benzol in his mouth, had insisted he was constantly improving. During his whole illness he had furnished stamina for both himself and his wife; he had showed true courage. The sordidness of the Silticoos had not tarnished his spirit. But now…

Suddenly Morgan's eyes, far back underneath his bristling brows, popped open and looked upon the dimly seen, receding objects of the familiar world. For the first time there was horror in them.

"I'm goin' to die, I tell you! I'm goin' to die! And I ain't ready, I ain't ready!"

It was the scream of an animal in terror, of a man who had been made a coward by the treachery of his dying brain. Mrs. Morgan came running from the kitchen and fell on her knees beside the bed.

"Oh, George, don't! Please don't," she moaned, clutching at her husband's struggling hands. "Always you been a good man, a good husband. God knows that better than we do, and He'll take care of you. Of course He'll take care of you."

She buried her face in the quilt. The neighbor woman resumed the vigorous fanning that Morgan's outburst had interrupted.

Only the soft swish of the paper through the air and the gasping respiration of the man in the bed could be heard.

Mallory kept his eyes on Morgan's face, his fingers on the pulse. Mrs. Morgan still kneeled, tears streaming over her sunken pale cheeks, watching her husband's gray-blue lips.

Abruptly the patient unclosed his eyes again. His huge, bony hand angled upward uncertainly to point at Mallory. A hoarse gurgling issued from his throat.

"That…man…there…that…man…killed…"

His arm dropped, his head sagged sharply to one side, the gurgling ceased. The neighbor looked at Mallory, stopped fanning, and fled. Still the widow knelt beside the bed clinging to her husband's arm.

"Come, Mrs. Morgan. There's no more we can do for him now."

Having arranged for the undertaker to come and having sent Mrs. Morgan to stay with the neighbor for the night, Mallory left the little cottage. At the gate he paused to look down from the hillside at the scattered buildings of the village below. The dance hall was still lighted and faint music echoed about him—"Poor Butterfly." He shivered.

Morgan was gone—his patient for whom he had worked in vain, whom he had treated for months without avail, whose cheery heroism he had admired so much. He had gone shrieking with terror, into the outer darkness—alone, just as he had once come into the world. Such an end was not fair for so gallant a man. The poisoned, dying cells of Morgan's brain had betrayed him into final cowardice. That was the last revenge the man's body could take on the spirit that had lived in it and made it a servant for so many years.

His patient was gone and Mallory was suddenly lonely for him. Lonely, because that strange impalpable tie between physician and patient had been broken and a bit of himself had gone with Morgan on his great adventure into the unknown.

Again Mallory's eyes fell on the lighted dance hall. Those people down there, ignorant and crude, were his people. He had made them his when he came to the Silticoos; he would keep them his so long as he lived. They had but little concern for life and they ignored death, but yet it stalked all of them—as it had stalked Morgan—from the day of birth, certain of overcoming. He must help them get more out of living, lead them into a broader way of life. There under the bowl of the dark night sky he brooded, deeply moved, over his people and their valley. For the time he had forgotten Katherine.

CHAPTER IV

I

When she came into the waiting room from the side corridor leading to the kitchen Mrs. Hathaway saw Dr. Mallory sitting on the top step of the stairs with his arms wrapped about his knees and his calling bag at his feet. He was smoking a bent-stem pipe with obvious pleasure.

"Life insurance examination in Southport, Mrs. H. Katherine's changing her clothes to go with me. Mrs. Blake will probably get here before we do but Henry's taking us over and I'm sure he'll get us home in plenty of time for dinner. So have Sairy go ahead. Henry enjoys his food."

Mrs. Hathaway smiled.

"Of course you don't enjoy yours," she retorted. "Especially not string beans and radishes."

"String beans and radishes and roast beef are my idea of good food," asserted Mallory, grinning at the nurse. "And I shouldn't think you'd begrudge me food when you know I've been entertaining Mrs. Dickson for an hour and a half."

"Just to cheer you up, doctor, I'll tell you that I have my eye on Sairy and that there will be beans and roast beef both for dinner."

"Hurrah for our side!" cried Mallory, puffing out a great cloud of smoke. "But seriously, Mrs. H., that Dickson outfit is driving me nuts! Have you heard the latest?"

"No, I don't think so. But nothing you could tell me about them would surprise me. Mrs. Dickson is a genius. Only a genius could live on this valley for fifteen years and raise eight children while she was doing it."

"Well, listen to this, Mrs. H. The old girl comes tearing into the office to-day to tell me that I'm a bum doctor and don't know the first thing about setting broken bones. Her precious Ned—you remember him; the one we've had in here off and on all summer—got into a fight up at the Southport school house yesterday noon and broke his arm again. The same one he broke before, mind you, but down close to the wrist this time instead of up by the elbow. Ma, being sure he couldn't have broken that arm under any circumstances if only I'd set it properly the first time, takes her offspring down to Baypoint yesterday afternoon. To Bentley, of course. She got home on the train this morning and promptly rushes over here to bawl me out for Ned's bad luck. Oh, I tell you, Mrs. H., the practice of medicine is an inspiring occupation at times."

Grimacing, Mallory tamped down the partly burned tobacco in his pipe and held a match to it. But what he had told her made the nurse's habitual cheerfulness evaporate.

"That makes me furious. Think of all the trouble you took with that boy's arm so the elbow wouldn't be stiff. And they've never paid you a cent, have they?"

"Why should a genius pay a doctor's bill? Especially when she can get all the medical attention she wants for nothing. All I hope is that she stings Bentley good and hard. Oh, there's that damned 'phone! It's done nothing but ring all afternoon."

The nurse took down the receiver.

"Glenwood Hospital, Mrs. Hathaway speaking. . . . Yes, he's here. . . . No, he's just starting over to Southport. . . . Just a moment." Mrs. Hathaway turned toward Mallory. "It's your friend, Mrs. Dickson. She wants you to come over right away. Sis is ill." The gray-blue eyes twinkled.

Mallory jumped to his feet.

"I'm sick of that gang. Tell her to jump in the river or take Sis down to Baypoint or…"

Mrs. Hathaway removed her covering hand from the mouthpiece.

"Hello, Mrs. Dickson. The doctor will be in to see you before he comes home. . . . Good-by."

"Now, see here! What did you tell her that for? I haven't the least intention of going near that woman!"

"I know you haven't, doctor. Not now. But you'll change your mind about it before you're halfway across the river. So I thought it best to tell Mrs. Dickson at once that you'd be there."

Mallory muttered something unintelligible, sat down again on the step, and scratched a match noisily on the floor. Presently he looked up sheepishly at the nurse with the little cross-hatched wrinkles at the outer corners of his eyes puckered up, and both of them began to laugh.

"I give up, Mrs. H. I've got no chance against you. You're too clever for me by far."

When Katherine appeared, wearing a brilliant red sweater and tam, her husband was smoking quietly and Mrs. Hathaway was rolling bandages.

On the Mill Store dock Henry Blake was waiting. At sight of Katherine his eyes brightened.

"Well, well, Mrs. Mallory. I'm glad to see you. You don't often ride with us."

"It's so gorgeous to-day I couldn't bear to stay indoors. I was out all morning on the hill back of the hospital trying to make some sketches. But I didn't succeed very well." She looked up at the blue October sky in which a few large white clouds were drifting. "I think I've forgotten how to draw."

"Well, after dinner to-night, Henry will find out that you haven't forgotten how to play the piano and sing."

"Bob, dear, every one doesn't enjoy listening to me as much as you do."

"Oh, Alice and I are both right anxious to hear you. I guess you've got the only grand piano on the Silticoos. I expect it sounds quite a lot better than the ordinary ones."

Something in Blake's manner suggested to Mallory that Henry had private qualms over the prospect of an entire evening devoted to music, but he did not suspect that it was the fact that Katherine was playing and not the beauty of the music itself that made him sit for hours listening dreamily to Beethoven and Brahms.

"How much you got to do in Southport, doc?"

"Not much. One life insurance examination and a call on your friend, Mrs. Dickson."

"My friend? How come? I heard her ravin' about you to-day, in the drug store."

"If you'd been in my office you'd 've heard her rave more."

Blake grinned: he had known the Dickson family for a long time.

"Well, while you're workin', I'll show your wife the great city of Southport. I know she'll think it's great." Blake pointed toward the middle of the stream. "That's the best way of all to live, Mrs. Mallory. Handy to move whenever you take a notion."

Going slowly up-stream was a house perched on two large logs, fore and aft, and propelled by a fishboat with a spitting engine mounted amidships. On the meager shelf that served as a porch sat a row of children, their feet dangling over the water. Blake raised an arm in salutation to the man in the boat.

"You mean that a whole family lives in that...shanty?" asked Katherine incredulously.

"Sure. Lots of 'em live like that. Many a man around here's been born and lived most of his life in a floatin' house."

"And most of the floating houses haven't had a window open since they were built," observed Mallory. "They're the slums of the Silticoos. Another thing we've got to get rid of."

Henry Blake cocked a skeptical eye at the doctor, but said nothing.

As they approached Southport, Katherine saw a long row of floating houses perched on logs and tied by ropes to trees on the bank. From shore to porch, on each, ran a teetering gangplank. There were neither curtains nor open windows to be seen and all the houses had rusty stove pipes protruding from their unpainted roofs and vomiting blue wood smoke into the still air of late afternoon.

Along the waterfront a little farther on were wharves and behind them a line of unpainted one-story buildings with towering false fronts bearing the name of Southport's business men. Among them was a branch of the Burton Drug Company.

While Mallory went about his calls, Katherine and Henry walked back, along narrow elevated walks made of two parallel planks, among the double rows of shacks that comprised the residential quarter. Underneath these houses the water sloshed back and forth continually. The windows in the unpainted walls were small and curtainless and there were various obscene words and occasional smutty drawings penciled on the siding. Through open doors here and there they could see up-ended boxes used as chairs, rusty stoves and tumbled beds. To Katherine it seemed impossible that human beings could live in these hovels.

"It's a great town to smell, Southport is," chuckled Blake as a puff of wind brought them the odor of the fish cannery on the lower waterfront. "But it ain't much to look at, for a fact." He swept a hand around the tide flats and the huddle of shacks. "Not much to look at."

"It's awful," exclaimed Katherine. "Much worse than Glenwood. I don't see how people can bear it."

"Oh, they don't know any different, Mrs. Mallory. Now, if you'd lived like this all your life, it would look all right to you. And after a bit you'll get used to it, you and doc both."

"No," said Katherine firmly. "I shan't get used to it. And neither shall Bob."

Something in her voice made Blake turn and look at her.

When he did so, he saw a sort of determined hardness in her face that startled him. 'I wonder if she's goin' to be as easy to handle as I figured she would be,' he thought. 'Still and all, in time she'd ought to settle down. Alice did.'

Through the straggling town curved the railroad on a high embankment toward a tiny yellow station built on a fill near the foot of the hills back of Southport. (It was a grievance to the residents of Glenwood that the rival village should have a depot while they had to use an open platform.) Above the station a short distance stood a dull-red box car.

"I believe that's doc now," said Blake. "Up there, comin' down along the track."

He put two fingers in his mouth and blew a piercing whistle. The distant figure waved an arm in answer and Katherine and Henry changed their course to intercept his. When Mallory came up to them, his face was troubled.

"What's the matter, Bob? What's happened, dear?"

"Something gone wrong, doc?"

"Plenty. It's that Dickson outfit again. They're always sick or hurt and they're always broke. Don't any of them ever work at anything, Henry?"

"Oh, the old man used to get a job now and then for a few days at a time before he died. But he spent most of his life drinkin' cheap whisky, and I guess some of the boys are startin' off to be like him."

"Well, it's not the boys this time. It's Sis, the ten-year-old girl. She's got typhoid. In spite of all I could do that fellow up Squaw Creek spread the germs around last summer; there 've been three or four cases over here since August. And now the Dickson girl's got it and her mother has moved her into that box car up above the station. The agent says he won't kick her out as long as nobody complains. I ought to take her over to the hospital, but the old lady says she won't go anywhere but to Baypoint and I can't unload them on the hospital down there without a cent. Meanwhile they'll probably spread typhoid all over Southport."

The doctor shrugged his shoulders hopelessly.

"It sounds like a nice mess, all right," said Blake and added philosophically, "but it's just what I'd expect of the Dicksons."

This was one of those autumn evenings when the sun slips down behind the hills unobtrusively, leaving a calm golden glow that fades into rose and lavender and pale green. Low over the mountain rim, when the dark of the upper sky crept downward toward the valley, the evening star appeared. The forested slopes swept upward in saw-toothed tongues of darkness.

Behind the homeward bound launch marsh and hovels sank into the enveloping dusk while lights sprang up in the valley and men's voices, softened by distance, came over the water. Shortly there remained of Southport only the faint glimmer of its lights arched over by the bowl of the sky. But there was in Katherine's face a sharp, persistent purpose.

II

After dinner Mallory led the way to the music room Mrs. Hathaway and he had contrived in a corner of the hospital. The baby grand Steinway he had bought for Katherine was now to be exhibited to Alice and Henry for the first time.

Since the room was small there was space in it for little other furniture. Near the piano was a small music cabinet and there were two rockers and three arm chairs. On the piano stood a lamp with a painted parchment shade and on the floor lay several small many-colored rag rugs. Mallory's print of the "Anatomy Lesson" and two tinted photographic landscapes hung, framed, on the wall. In the corner nearest the door was a little stove. Mrs. Hathaway had built a fire before dinner and the room was pleasantly warm.

"The evenings are gettin' nippy enough to make a fire feel good," observed Blake with a look of approval at the heater.

At sight of the gleaming piano with the lamplight reflected in its polished surface Alice Blake's eyes brightened.

"It's lovely," she said softly.

Indeed she found the whole room more attractive than she

had expected. The woodwork was pale yellow, the walls deep cream. The windows, although they were high and narrow, had hangings of yellow and cool blue and the rugs were gaily multicolored. If only there were a fireplace, she thought, instead of the stove. . . . But in Glenwood people regarded fireplaces as old-fashioned. It was not until last year that she had been able to persuade Henry to build one in their own living room. No doubt by next winter Mrs. Mallory would have one, too. It was plain that the doctor intended to make everything as nice for her as he possibly could. If only his practice would grow and people would pay their bills…

These thoughts were interrupted by Katherine's voice saying, "No, I don't like davenports, Mr. Blake. They're uncomfortable, never long enough to stretch out on, and the cushions are always so hard that one can't tuck them in anywhere. Some day I want Bob to get me the sort of settee I've seen in New England, with a back at the proper angle to lean against and cushions that are soft." She touched her husband's hand as he stood looking proudly at her. "I've got a lot of ideas about furnishing our home when we get one."

Suddenly something in Alice Blake's brain said to her, 'That won't be in Glenwood.' Disquieted by this idea sprung from nowhere, she moved over to the little group in front of the stove and said, "Won't you play for us now, Mrs. Mallory? I know I should wait a reasonable time after dinner but music is such a treat to me that I'm impatient."

"I'm afraid I'm not in very good form. You see, I spent most of July and August vacationing with my family and Bob didn't have the piano when I first came down here. But I'll play anyhow." Without pretending unwillingness Katherine sat down at the instrument. "What would you like first, Bob?"

Mrs. Blake saw the quick flush of pleasure that spread over Mallory's cheeks at being thus consulted.

"I liked that thing you were practicing last night, dear. I think you said it was by Chopin. It was so sort of cheerful."

Katherine laughed softly.

"Chopin wrote many things that are cheerful, my dear, and

if you like them we'll go on a spree of his music. This is what you meant, isn't it?"

She lifted her hands to the keyboard.

As soon as Alice Blake had listened to a dozen bars she knew that Katherine was an artist. She leaned back in her chair and abandoned herself to the sheer beauty of sound that poured out around her in a flood of gay melody. There was something splendid about hearing music so skillfully played. Katherine's slender hands, ordinarily so frail looking, flashed over the keys with cool precision and exactness.

Alice found herself watching more than listening. This young woman, she began to see, might have become a concert pianist. There was about her a sort of passionate intentness as though she had forgotten the people in the room and had made contact with some hidden source of vivid life. Her usual air of self-possession fell away, she seemed to burn with energy. The trace of languor which Alice had so often noticed in her movements vanished and her body took on a tautness that seemed to add to her beauty. Surprised, Mrs. Blake thought, 'This girl is capable of passion. She is passion, when she plays.'

There was a final flourish of gayety and caprice and then Katherine dropped her hands to the bench beside her. There was a queer silence in the room. It seemed to Alice Blake that the girl had pulled down between herself and them a curtain of reserve. Mallory gazed at his wife with something very like adoration, Mrs. Hathaway stared at the flames that flickered behind the open slides of the stove, Henry sat far forward on his chair, looking at Katherine in astonishment.

Alice was still too deeply under the spell of her hostess's personality to break the silence. At this instant the door was pushed ajar and Sairy's sullen angular face was thrust into the room.

"Telephone for Mr. Blake," she announced.

Henry jumped. "What on earth! Who's callin' me here? You sure it wasn't doc they wanted?"

"Henry Blake, the feller said," insisted Sairy. "That's you, ain't it?"

Alice laughed a bit uncertainly and glanced at Katherine. "I suspect central heard you calling me this morning, Mrs. Mallory, and so when some one wanted Henry to-night she rang up here instead of our house. You can depend on the girls in the telephone office to know where every one is."

"There certainly is no such thing as privacy in Glenwood."

At the cutting edge in the girl's voice, Mrs. Blake looked up quickly.

After a moment Katherine added, "Of course it's sometimes convenient, I know. But I hate to think they're keeping watch on me."

"I never felt the girls do it to be nosey," said Alice quietly. "But in so small a place people naturally observe their neighbors more than they do in a city where there are so many other things to take their attention."

"I think you're right," agreed Mrs. Hathaway, "but that doesn't make one feel any less exposed. It's practically impossible to go anywhere without central finding it out and spreading the news."

"I got to leave." Henry reappeared in the doorway. "The fishboat's gone haywire. The engine's been actin' up for a week and now it's gone completely on the blink. Mike was just callin' me from his brother's shack across the river to come and tow him in."

"Oh, Mr. Blake, I'm sorry," cried Katherine.

"Well, you ain't as sorry as I am. I figured on some more playin' and on hearin' you sing too, after your dinner settled down. I never heard any music that sounded like that piece you just played—not on the piano. It was grand, Mrs. Mallory. And I guess it was what you'd call classical music, too."

Katherine laughed but there was not a hint of patronage in her manner.

"Yes, that was classical music, believe it or not, as Bob says to me when he's trying to explain scientific things I don't understand. People imagine good music is hard to listen to, but it isn't. It's grand, just as you said."

"When you play," said Alice. "Not when I play it. That's why

my poor husband and many other people have a horror of
music that is labeled classical. They forget the difference the
performer makes."

"Why not come back after you've rescued your boat?" asked
Katherine. "It won't take very long, will it?"

"Oh, about an hour I guess."

Katherine turned to Mallory.

"Don't you want to go with him, dear, and bring him back?
It wouldn't be much fun for you to sit here with three women,
and besides I want to talk with Mrs. Blake. Run along, Bob,
and get back as soon as you can. While you're away I'll look
out some songs I'm sure you'll both like."

III

When the men had gone off on their errand Alice felt again
in the atmosphere of the room the trace of tenseness that
had followed Katherine's remark about the lack of privacy in
Glenwood. For a time she watched the fire flickering behind
the slides in the stove door, then turned to look at her hostess.
Katherine was rummaging in the music cabinet and it struck
Mrs. Blake that some of the passion so noticeable when she
was playing still clung to her. The older woman's eyes grew even
kinder and more friendly.

Mrs. Hathaway had excused herself on the plea of work to
do.

"Even when there are only three or four patients in the house,
it takes time to fix them up for the night. And there are eight
o'clock temperatures to be taken and charts to be written up."

Left alone with the doctor's wife, Alice Blake did not speak
until Katherine had laid aside her music and come to sit beside
the fire near her guest.

"Henry and I were saying this noon how fortunate Glenwood
is to have a doctor like your husband. And I realize that we
are just as fortunate to have you, too. I can't tell you how much
I enjoyed your playing or how I look forward to hearing you
often this winter."

"Thank you, Mrs. Blake. I won't pretend I don't like hearing you say that, because it wouldn't be true. But I'm much more pleased to have you say what you did about Bob. He is, really, a very clever doctor. He graduated at the head of his class and the staff at the hospital considered him the best interne they'd had in years. But I don't believe Glenwood appreciates him."

Alice saw so plainly the girl's pride in her husband that a glow of approval came into her face.

"You're quite right. Glenwood doesn't see Dr. Mallory as he is. But I'm afraid few doctors are appreciated by the rank and file of people. I used to notice that when I was in hospital work. The patients were provoked at being ill, they were uncomfortable and, part of the time, in pain, and their families were worried over them and annoyed by the expense. So they complained— about the doctors and the nurses and the food and the beds and everything else they could think of—but half the time they didn't mean it seriously. It's the same here. But within a year or two your husband will be accepted as part of the town and most of the trouble with the Baypoint doctors will be over." Then, seeing Katherine's look of surprise, she added, "You must remember that I'm a nurse and that I hear most of the medical scandal in this part of the country."

"That has upset us terribly," confessed Katherine. "I know Bob never expected older doctors to treat him this way. It seems so unprofessional and undignified. I never dreamed such things went on."

"I know, Mrs. Mallory." Alice nodded understandingly. "It is a shock to find that there are such men in the medical profession. But what can you expect when there aren't any moral qualifications, when any one with money to pay his expenses and brains enough to get through two years in college can go to medical school? You see, my father was a country doctor in Illinois and my two brothers both studied medicine, so I know something about this both from their experience and my own observation in hospitals."

Katherine held out a pack of cigarettes.

"No, I don't smoke. But I haven't the least objection to your doing so, Mrs. Mallory. In fact I must confess that I've tried—unsuccessfully—to learn."

Katherine selected a cigarette thoughtfully and studied her guest's face through the smoke rising from it.

"There's something that worries me more than the doctors in Baypoint and their dishonest tactics. I'm afraid Bob is going to settle down here in Glenwood and he's too big a man, Mrs. Blake, to do that. The only two words I can think of to describe this place so far as he is concerned are 'blind alley.' If he stays here he'll always be a country doctor dabbling in everything, over-worked and under-paid. I can't bear to think of him wearing himself out down here."

"I know there's a lot of truth in what you say, Mrs. Mallory, but I can't agree with all of it. If your husband stays here he will, as you say, always be a general practitioner—a G.P. my father used to call himself. And he'll never get rich here. But isn't there another side to it? Don't people in small towns need care—and as good care—as people in cities? Haven't they the same right to competent doctors? And mightn't Dr. Mallory have more chance to live, here, than he would in a larger place—more chance to get outdoors and relax and enjoy himself? Mightn't he be really happier here than in the city?"

Katherine inhaled deeply, looking doubtfully at Alice. Then she leaned forward and spoke rapidly and decisively.

"That doesn't alter the fact that Glenwood is a blind alley for him professionally. Bob can't make a reputation or become a specialist here. And I'm ambitious for him. I want the name 'Robert Mallory' to mean something to people when they hear it. I want my husband to be a famous man, not a kindly, overworked, obscure country doctor." The girl's voice rose from its usual low pitch and became vibrant with feeling. "I love him, Mrs. Blake. I want his life to mean something in the world. Gifted men aren't common. They ought not to be wasted."

Watching Katherine Mallory as she talked Alice Blake began to understand her. She had transferred to her husband all the force of ambition which, had she not loved him so passionately, would have gone into her own work. She meant to realize herself not as a concert pianist, but in Mallory's career. She was determined that he should become a famous doctor. All this was now clear, but regret was mingled with Mrs. Blake's comprehension.

"Most certainly gifted men aren't common and surely they should not be wasted. But are you sure Dr. Mallory's life will mean more to the world in the city than in the country? I've seen something of the struggle doctors must make in Pacific City and something of the wretched nervous strain they're under. Your husband would have to do post-graduate work for two or three years and then start at the bottom again, that much older than he is now and probably in debt for the graduate study. Then he would have to scheme and pull wires to get staff appointments to the right hospitals and find paying patients. Believe me, Mrs. Mallory, the city doctors look just as worn and get gray just as young as the country doctors."

Once more Katherine was thoughtful.

"Bob used to say he wanted to do research some time. And a man I knew who interned with him told me that while he was in the hospital he invented some sort of X-ray apparatus that was really remarkable. How can he go on with anything like that in Glenwood, Mrs. Blake?"

"Do you suppose all research must be done in great laboratories? Wouldn't it be possible for a man in active practice to discover something important? They used to, a generation or two ago. Sometimes it seems to me that the laboratory men are praised too much and the ordinary doctors not enough."

The older woman sensed that she had at least shaken Katherine's confidence in her own opinions.

"I don't know, Mrs. Blake. I can't answer those questions. But I know that I resent having Bob at the beck and call of people like the Simmonses and the Painters and the Dicksons, and I dislike Glenwood, and I hate the thought of settling down to stay here. Bob is dragged out of bed at night and he has to go on the river in bad weather and on Sundays, and whenever we plan to go anywhere or do something special he has a call and can't go. Nobody ever pays him for his work until weeks after it's done, and some people never pay at all. He works hard and gets very little for it, little, even, of thanks."

Alice Blake put her warm, firm, competent hand over Katherine's thin, nervous, interlaced fingers.

"Oh, my dear, I understand how you feel. Indeed I do. But you can't rescue your husband from such things by taking him to the city and making a specialist out of him. As long as he's a doctor he'll be at people's beck and call every day and at all hours. All doctors are. But Dr. Mallory would never give up medicine."

"I know he wouldn't. Even I couldn't make him give up his profession." Katherine spoke with a mixture of pride and ruefulness. "Once, when I first knew him, he told me that he had had a 'call' to medicine just as people used to think they had 'calls' to the ministry. When I married Robert Mallory, I married medicine too."

IV

When Blake and Mallory took the *Greyhound* out that night, there were already many fishboats on the river and their red signal lights were winking briskly back and forth. Henry steered straight downstream past the village before he turned away from the north bank on a slanting course across the river.

"Not much room to get past in," he observed, pointing to the dim lines of bobbing floats that marked the gill nets stretched out into the stream. "That's why so many nets get torn up with propeller blades. Look, there's one now, over there."

Looking along Blake's outstretched arm Mallory saw a launch rolling gently in the trough of the swells. Near its stern was a fishboat. A man was holding a gasoline lantern and in the circle of white light Mallory could see two other men hanging overboard, up to their shoulders in water, struggling to unwind their net from the propeller. There was in the scene something picturesque: the slinky black water undulating in long swells, the two boats rocking together, the sharply limned circle of bright light, the red signal lanterns on both craft, the distorted image of the whole picture on the surface of the stream. Presently the fishboat could be seen drifting away from the launch. Across the intervening water came a burst of profanity as the fishermen worked over their damaged net. Then they drifted out of earshot.

"How's business these days, doc?" asked Blake.

"Just fair. Nothing much but baby cases and mighty little money coming in."

"Well, when the fish checks come in this month, you want to be ready to grab off your share of 'em. Everybody figures on collectin' his bills durin' the fishin' season, and you can get the cash in too if you go after it."

"That's what Doan tells me. But the trouble is, Blake, that I'm a rotten business man. I'm a doctor and I'm interested in practicing medicine, not in gouging money out of people who don't want to pay me."

"Yeah, I know, doc. That sounds all right. I know there's folks that feel that way. But you got to eat and buy clothes to wear just like the rest of us. And if you're goin' to do that, you got to come down to earth and go after your bills. If you don't get your money that's comin' to you, these birds'll just spend it for whisky and cheap jewelry and patent medicine and such like. I know 'em: I been watchin' 'em for a long time. There's no sense of anybody workin' as hard as you do for nothin', and nobody else does."

Blake peered at Mallory as though he hesitated to say more about so disagreeable a subject. In the flare of the match with which he was lighting his pipe, the doctor's face seemed strained and worried. Blake shrugged his shoulders and bit the corner off a plug of tobacco.

As the *Greyhound* approached the south bank of the river Henry began blowing a signal with his whistle. At the second repetition came a hoarse answering squawk.

"Mike never could learn to blow that horn decent," said Blake, grinning. "Sounds like a sheep with a cold in its throat."

Within five minutes the launch was rocking beside the fishboat.

"What's the matter, Mike?"

"Oh, it's the ignition, Henry. Can't get her to fire nohow. I guess the coil's done for."

"Well, let me tie you on behind and I'll pull you across slow, so you can get the net in," said Blake.

A figure in glistening oilskins threw a painter up over the stern of the *Greyhound*.

"Don't you want to ride back with Mike?" asked Blake of Mallory. "He'll be pullin' in the net and you can see the fish come aboard. Here, take this. A tin coat's the only thing that'll keep you dry out here."

Mallory dropped over into the smaller boat and squatted down forward, where a flaring canvas roof projected a little way backward from the bow. In the sheltered cubby-hole this formed there was a jumble of rope and heavy twine and gaff hooks, and tucked snugly on a tiny shelf were a black coffee pot, a sterno heater, a box of cookies, and an extra gasoline lantern.

"Things is kinda messy up there," apologized Mike as he went back past the engine into the stern. "But seems like I never get no time to clean it up. Every afternoon I got to work on the net."

"Ready, Mike?" shouted Blake from the launch.

"O.K. Let 'er go," answered the fisherman, bracing himself in the stern to pull in the net.

Angling obliquely away from the boat toward the opposite shore Mallory could see the dim line of bobbing wooden floats.

The net came aboard wet and dripping. Mike, his oilskin coat glistening with water, piled it skillfully in the rear compartment. There were only a few salmon in the haul—not over fifteen or twenty. They flopped wildly—big shining silver fish—in the slanting gleam of the lantern, until Mike thrust them into the covered fish box built across the boat just back of the engine. There Mallory could hear them slapping their bodies against the unyielding walls of their prison in futile rebellion.

"Like people," he thought. "Trying to get out of the place where they are."

"Poor drift," observed Mike when he had all the net piled

up in its compartment. "Nights like this it ain't hardly worth goin' out on the river."

When Blake and Mallory were walking up the village street toward the hospital, Henry put into halting words the thing that had been in his mind earlier in the evening.

"You know, doc, I don't agree with you about cod liver oil and environment and things like that bein' so God damn important to the next generation. But I like you, yourself. Maybe you're right about this and me wrong. I don't know which way it is. Anyhow, I just wanted to tell you that, when you get around to puttin' up that new hospital you're always talkin' about...I might be able to rustle up some cash for it....It ain't likely that you'll have much yourself if you're always goin' to do business like you are now."

Mallory stopped short, his heavy features shining with delight.

"Why, Henry," he cried. "I never meant you to feel I wanted to get money out of you, but..."

"Oh, Hell, doc, I never thought that. It's just that I'd like to help you...if I could." Blake wiped the perspiration from his embarrassed face with his sleeve. "You see, it might just be that you're right about what this country needs most."

Mallory held out a thick warm hand.

"I'll remember this, Henry, when the time comes...if it ever does."

"Oh, it'll come—some day. I can see that new hospital every time I look at you, doc."

Along the rickety sidewalk the two men tramped on together. Mallory felt irrationally happy; the tide of life was high and strong in him. And he felt that Blake had come into the inner circle of his friends that night.

Looking up, he saw the lighted windows of the hospital. At the sight his happiness surged higher. Light—light in the darkness—that was symbolic of what a hospital ought to be. It ought to be a haven for the sick and the tired and the cheated, with lighted windows that beckoned its patients out of the darkness in which they stumbled along.

"Henry," he said suddenly, "when I build the new hospital, I'm going to have a big light on it somewhere so it'll shine all up and down the river at night and show people that we're here, ready for them. And I'm going to call the hospital 'The Haven.'"

CHAPTER V

I

Early on a brilliant April morning, after a week of rain and squalls from the southwest, when the air held a subtle freshness that was almost fragrant, a small outboard motorboat sputtered its way along the south bank of the Silticoos two or three miles above Southport. A glittering Chinook salmon lay gasping on the floor; a few minutes before it had been a doughty adversary. Katherine, perched on a thwart, watched her husband strike it an expert blow with the gaff hook. Its gasping ceased.

"It'll weigh twenty-five pounds," he observed with satisfaction.

Katherine drew her feet a little further under the seat.

"The sight of that blood sickens me," she said.

"Now, my dear, you're imagining things again. You think this is all a one-sided affair: a big brute of a man torturing and killing a helpless fish. But more fish have got away from me than I've ever caught. Most of the time they're more than a match for me."

Mallory laughed but something in his manner suggested that he was making conversation in order to stave off an unpleasant subject. The tension in his voice was not to be otherwise explained.

"We'll have to stop trolling now if we're to get home for breakfast," he continued, looking at his watch. "But this baby will make Henry open his eyes, so I'm satisfied."

Systematically winding in his line, the doctor stowed it away and put about for Glenwood.

Covertly, from time to time, he eyed his wife. On her face he could detect no trace of sleeplessness but he was sure he himself must look disturbed. It exasperated him to think how many hours he had lain awake last night; he felt it was foolish for a man to be so upset by his wife's desire for his advancement. And yet the persistence with which Katherine had pursued this project of hers since the new year worried him.

"You've been thinking over what we talked about last night, Bob."

At the accuracy with which she had read his mind Mallory started. He tried vainly to achieve nonchalance in his answer.

"Yes. In fact I've been thinking about it ever since you first brought it up last winter."

At this admission Katherine smiled triumphantly.

"I've always been sure you'd see things my way when once you realized that was the only reasonable thing to do."

There was a question in Mallory's silence.

"Now, Bob, don't try to pretend that you think there's a future for you on the Silticoos. Last night you admitted that you know there isn't. Glenwood, so far as you're concerned, is a blind alley, and the fact that you came here last year is no reason why you should stay. Especially when you don't need to."

Mallory flushed. There were overtones in her voice that whispered to him, "I've gone over all this before. Why must I do it again?"

"But, dearest…"

"There is no 'but' about it, Bob. And I beg you, don't spring the old gag about no man being able to accept help from his wife or use her money. You and I are modern."

Mallory forced himself to look straight into his wife's face.

"I wasn't going to say that, Katherine. When we got married we entered a partnership that has risks as well as rewards. If I'd had any money I'd 've considered half of it yours as soon as you were my wife, and I can't see any reason why things shouldn't work the opposite way, too. Of course, if I'd known about this money, it would have made a difference about my asking you to marry me when I did. But I didn't know it, and now that we've been married a year I'm willing to consider that it belongs to both of us."

"Well, dear, to tell the whole truth, I've been thinking about this thing ever since that pre-school clinic last fall. And when I saw you worrying yourself ill over bills you simply can't collect, I decided it was time for me to step in and do something. Grandmother left me twenty-five thousand dollars when she died—that was when I was just a little girl—and I always thought I'd use it when I went abroad to study. 'War babies' have done us a good turn, Bob. I had no idea until I wrote to father that there was as much of it as there is. We shan't have to worry about making a living for a long time."

"I ought never to have let you know how things were with me."

"One of those strong silent men who conceal their troubles?" Katherine laughed. "Don't be silly, Bob. A blind woman could have seen what was wrong. You can't keep me from seeing what bothers you, my dear."

An uneasy sense that this was not at all exaggerated came over Mallory, but he brightened again when the girl leaned toward him and put her hands over his.

"You don't know how happy I am to think you're going to get out of Glenwood. We'll go abroad and you can study X-ray and surgery and I'll get started on my music again. By this time next year we'll have forgotten there is such a place as the Silticoos."

Mallory felt a strange premature homesickness sweeping

over him. To go away from these green Oregon mountains and the great silvery river would not be easy. Then something else occurred to him.

"But we can't go abroad—not now. The war over there…"

"Oh, bother the war! I'd forgotten for a moment."

Katherine was disconcerted. "But surely there must be somewhere we can go in Europe where there isn't a stupid war."

Through Mallory's mind flashed the thought, 'She's made twenty thousand dollars in "war babies" and forgets there's a war going on': he only half heard her recital of possible destinations.

"There's Spain, but neither of us speak the language. And Holland, but that's too close to Germany. What about Sweden, Bob? I'm sure we can get along there with German and English."

"Stockholm is one of the best places in the world to study radiation, dear. But don't you see…"

"Then we'll go to Stockholm. Everyone says it's lovely there."

"But, Katherine, I can't simply walk off and leave the hospital. That wouldn't be decent. And with so many doctors going into the French and British medical service it isn't going to be easy to find a good man to take over right away…even if we were sure we were going abroad."

The girl looked sideways at him with eyes that had become calculating.

"Bob, dear, I must make a confession to you. I was so sure you'd come to see things straight that when I wrote to find out how much my stocks and bonds were worth I asked how one went about to dispose of a hospital, and they gave me the name of a medical broker in Pacific City. So I got in touch with him."

"What in the world are you driving at?" There was a new sharp note in Mallory's voice but Katherine did not seem to notice it.

"Oh, I don't mean that I promised him anything or signed any papers. I just asked for information and suggestions. And yesterday I had a letter from him saying that he had recently had an inquiry about the Glenwood hospital from a possible buyer. Wasn't that a stroke of luck?"

"Nonsense! There hasn't been a soul around to look the place over, and nobody would buy a hospital and practice without investigating it."

"The broker didn't give the doctor's name outright—the one who was making inquiry—but he said it was the president of the Candon Bay Medical Society."

"The president of the Candon Bay...! Why, good God, that's Bentley!" Mallory almost shouted the last word, and sprang to his feet. "Bentley can't buy my hospital—not at any price! Not with all the money in Oregon! That dirty double-crosser has caused me more grief since I came to the Silticoos—he and that long-faced partner of his—than everything else put together."

"Sit down, my dear, or you'll upset the boat."

Mallory sank back to his seat, staring blankly at his wife.

"Now be sensible, Bob, and don't act like a spoiled boy. Why not let Bentley and Kronheit have the place if they want it? They intend to run you out of the valley, because they're afraid of you. They know that, if you stay here, they'll soon get precious little work from the Silticoos. I've talked this over with Mrs. Hathaway more than once, and she feels just as I do: they're afraid of your competition and mean to fight it out with you. But if you sold out to them and left Glenwood, they could put a man of their own in to run the hospital and all this fighting for patients would stop. Wouldn't that be better for every one than the way things are now?"

"Did you say Mrs. H. agreed with you about this, Katherine?"

"She agrees with me that Bentley and Kronheit intend to fight you to a finish because they're afraid of you. She doesn't know about the rest of it—the broker, I mean, and selling the hospital."

"I'm glad of that," said Mallory dully. "If Mrs. H. were to..."

"She would agree with me about all of it, Bob, if she knew. Because she has just as much faith in you and is just as sure of your ability as I am."

"And you want me to give up and sell the hospital to these... these bastards down at Baypoint, be a quitter and run away from a fight I started?" asked Mallory bitterly.

"No, dearest, I don't want you to do any of these things. I want you to get out of a blind alley. I want you to go now, while you're young, and study surgery and X-ray. I want you to be a great doctor. I want your name to mean something to people when they hear it. If there was anything in Glenwood worth fighting for, I'd want you to stay. But there isn't. You can't make a career here and you know it. You'd simply waste your whole life trying to scrape together enough money for that wretched little hospital, running up and down this river day and night as you've done all this winter, taking care of people who aren't worth your little finger. Oh, Bob, can't you understand? Can't you put yourself in my place? I love you, I married you. I simply cannot bear to see you throw yourself away!"

The brown eyes Mallory was staring into suddenly filled with tears. Katherine, who so seldom wept, was crying over him. He felt a queer clutching in his breast. She cared that way about it! As though hypnotized he watched the tears slide down her pale cheeks. There was no mistake about the distress in her face. Her lips quivered a little and reminded him of the way they often trembled when he kissed her passionately at night.

Baffled, swept this way and that by his passion for her and his resentment at her arbitrary desire to sell the hospital to his enemies, he turned half away from her and began fiddling with the outboard motor. Katherine, he could see, was more desperately in earnest than ever. Could it be that she was right about this?

There was no doubt that Bentley and Kronheit were fighting him every day and taking so much work away from him that the best he could do was to break even. He had not reduced the notes at the bank by a dollar. Katherine had lived all winter at the hospital, in their bedroom and the tiny music room across the hall. He could not give her an allowance and he had not been able to send her home for Christmas. But she had never complained about not having money to spend and never hinted that he was a failure because he could not collect his accounts. Even when he was out at night and gone all day on Sunday she had been cheerful. She had endured Sairy and Juanita whom she heartily disliked and put up with the dingy hospital during the long dreary months of wind and rain. She read to some of the patients and played and sang for others, and as Mrs. Hathaway said had the good sense to keep out of the way the rest of the time. There was much to be said for her point of view.

Lately Mallory had come to realize that, without intending to do so, he had misled her about the hospital before she came to Glenwood. His letters, he knew, had been enthusiastic because his mind was full of hopes and plans for the future. The drab actuality—the bare painted floors, the dirty wood stoves, the chill dampness of the building, the drudgery that must be done week days and Sunday alike—and the grinding poverty must have surprised her horribly. He could not even take her to Baypoint to a movie and spend the night there without counting the extra dollars carefully. He was glad there was no prospect of the baby they had thought last fall might be coming.

It was true that his work had increased during the winter but that might be because bad weather made it inconvenient for people to go down to Candon Bay. If things went on as they were, it would be another year or perhaps two before they could afford to live away from the hospital and he might never be able to build The Haven.

Mallory did not enjoy the long night trips on the river and the hard rides on forest trails into the backcountry, and he was by no means devoid of ambition. The prospects Katherine's money made possible were very attractive. He could have two or three years of post-graduate training and then set himself up in a city as a specialist in surgery and radiation. Did he, perhaps, owe it to her to do as she wished? It was not as though he would always live off her money. In his own heart he was perfectly sure he could make a name for himself in his profession. His confidence in his ability to make money was considerably less, but surely he could make a living once he was in practice again, and fame seemed to be the thing Katherine wanted above everything else. Many men would not hesitate a second. Why should he? Was he a fool not to jump at the opportunity?

And yet there was the other side, to which he could not blind himself. To give up a fight well started, to go away from the village he had chosen, to leave the hospital and give up his plans for The Haven—that was bad enough. But to desert people who—ignorant and stupid though many of them certainly were—needed him! He choked at the thought.

In the city there were many doctors, many good doctors, and many hospitals. Those people did not need him. They had just as honest and more experienced physicians at their command, and they did not need his little eight-bed hospital. If he went to a city he would have to struggle to make a place for himself in competition with wiser, better-trained, more capable men than he. But on the Silticoos there were only he and his small hospital. If he left, the people would be delivered into the unscrupulous hands of Bentley and Kronheit and their assistants. They would apply the methods of Big Business to medicine, run a branch establishment at Glenwood, send all the major surgery to Baypoint, and install an efficient collection system. His skin crawled when he thought of it.

But he must say something to Katherine now. Her heart was set on leaving the valley. She did not see things as he did. Could he say the words that would make her understand the dilemma that confronted him? He stole a look at her. She sat with drooping shoulders and dejected face. To him she seemed a stricken figure. He wavered. Could he bear to hurt her this way? Should he tell her at once that he would do as she wished? That would end the argument that had dragged its weary length over three months. Why must he have such a decision thrust upon him? Was there any right or any wrong about the whole thing?

Glancing up again toward Katherine he caught sight of a figure beyond her. Through the fog of his own doubt and hesitation Mallory saw a man wig-wagging furiously from the point of land at the mouth of Squaw Creek.

"There must be something wrong at the logging camp,

dear," he shouted above the noise of the accelerating engine. "Somebody's signaling for me."

II

The camp on the point toward which they were racing was a small one operated by the Glenwood Mill Company. All the hillsides next the river had been cut over years before, but further back there was still a small stand of virgin timber on the upper reaches of the creek. Mallory had often been in the camp to see sick men and had seen the skid-road that had been built up the hill and the singing cables running from the donkey engine to hurtle the logs down the mountains to the river bank.

As his boat approached the shore the doctor could hear the man who was waiting for them shouting something but could not understand what he said. When Mallory slipped up beside the little landing, the man grabbed the bow of the boat and tied the painter. He was short and fat; his dirty shirt was open at the neck and his face was covered with a week's growth of stubble. But his eyes were terrified.

"What is it, Mason?" asked Mallory reaching under the bow for his bag. "An accident? Lucky I've taken to carrying my bag along wherever I go."

"Yeah, the cable bust...and hit a feller. Up the creek a ways. He's over here by the engine. They carried him down that far."

Behind his guide Mallory hurried across an open space to the knot of silent men grouped near the donkey engine. They opened a path for him and closed it after him. On the ground in the center of the group lay a tall blond man with rivulets of blood clotting on his neck and cheeks. The upper part of his head was crushed and his yellow hair was covered with dark blood.

Mallory knelt down beside him and felt the man's skull and chest with quick fingers. He shook his head and got up to face the men about him.

"He's dead. Must've been killed instantly. He probably never knew what hit him."

"It throwed him right back against a stump," said one of the lumber jacks. "I was just goin' up the hill and I seen him throwed. I heard his head scrunch when he hit."

A little hissing sound of deep-drawn breath ran through the group.

"It's Olaf Hansen's brother, doc," said Mason. "This is goin' to be hard on Olaf. Him and John was all that was left of the family and they thought a heap of one another."

"I'll have to send up after the body," said Mallory. "I can't take him with me. I've got my wife along. I expect I'd better notify Olaf too."

"Yeah, doc, I think it'd be better if you told him. And mebbe Henry Blake'd come after…it." Mason nodded at the dead man.

"Before I go, let's carry him inside out of the sun," suggested Mallory.

Two men brought a pair of heavy blankets from the bunk house, and they lifted the body on them and bore it inside to the bunk John Hansen had but lately vacated. The clots of blood were still soft enough so that they spread out into dark red splotches on the dirty gray of the blankets.

"What d' we owe you, doc, for comin' over here?" asked Mason.

"Nothing. I couldn't do any good."

When Mallory came back down to the river he found Katherine walking up and down the bank. She looked at him with dark eyes full of surprise.

"Why, Bob, your hands are all bloody and there are even some splotches on your collar. Did some logger cut off a hand or split his foot in two?"

Mallory glanced down at his hands. It was true; they were bloody. He hadn't noticed it before. And there probably was blood on his collar, too. But Katherine needn't have spoken like that. She might have asked what had happened and not taken for granted that there had been only a minor accident. He did not stop to consider that she was already upset over their own situation; he forgot that only a few minutes before she had been crying over him; he ignored the fact that there was no possible way she could know what had happened in the camp. He was both irrationally angry and aggrieved.

When he spoke, his voice was tense and harsh. "This is John Hansen's blood, Katherine. Olaf's brother. He was killed back there on the hill just before Mason signaled me."

He took no notice of the sudden blanching of Katherine's face or the shiver that ran through her body at these words.

III

Mallory's day was full of complaining patients who followed one another in quick succession, but most of them had only minor ailments and only one came prepared to pay for his consultation in cash. None of them presented medical problems of sufficient interest to dispel from the doctor's mind his own dilemma. Three faces haunted him all day: Katherine's, tear-stained; John Hansen's, blood-smeared; and Olaf's, bewildered, stunned.

At one o'clock he ate a sandwich alone in the dining room and went back at once to his office. Late in the afternoon he came in from a visit to find the Luarn family waiting for him. They were a splendid physical pair, big, sturdily built, well proportioned. The woman held their baby in her arms.

"Ya busy, doc? We wanted to see ya a minute if we could."

"No, I just made my last call. Come on in. Well, Mrs. Luarn, I haven't seen you since you took the youngster home from the hospital."

"No, I ain't been to town all winter, doc. Jack he comes down now and then, but I been stickin' close to home with the kid."

Mallory found himself studying this woman. She was big and healthy and wholesome, attractive in her own way. She and her stocky Finnish husband had produced a robust red-cheeked baby. The doctor wondered if he and Katherine could ever do as well.

"All of us been fine all winter, doc," said Jack Luarn. "But we wanted to ask ya about the kid's feed again. Seems like we can't never get him filled up. He gobbles the milk fixed like ya showed us and goes right on hollerin' till he like to worries me and his mother to death. He acts like he was starvin'."

Mallory shook his head.

"That red-faced boy isn't starving, Luarn, or any way near it. I can tell that by looking at him. But he needs more milk at each feeding and it's time to begin giving him cereal and mashed vegetables besides. Have you kept up the orange juice?"

"Sure, doc. Never missed a day all winter," answered Luarn proudly. "But the neighbors is after the woman now. They keep tellin' her it's no use fussin' over him now he's got so big. They all give their kids fish. But I said we'd ask ya first before we begun that. And how about coffee? Would a little likely hurt him?"

Mallory had been running his hands gently over the infant's ankles and wrists, but now he looked sternly at the young parents. He felt once more that solid wall of ignorance he faced so often on the Silticoos. Suddenly he wanted to pound the desk with his fists and yell at these people, to smash them and the hospital and all the other stupid patients he had seen during the day. For a moment he hated Mrs. Luarn and, through her, all women. Why did they bring babies into the world and then feed them on coffee and salt fish? But before he replied to Luarn he reasserted the self-control that was rapidly becoming habitual with him.

"Now, listen to me, both of you. Don't you dare give this youngster coffee or salt fish! If you do, I'll disown you. Haven't I told you these things aren't fit for a baby? Yours is almost the only child I've seen of his age in the valley that hasn't got rickets. His wrists and ribs and ankles are smooth and normal. You should be proud of him. It's the feeding and the orange juice that's done it, and here you are down here yammering at me about coffee and fish. What do your neighbors know about babies? Hasn't every one of them buried more children than she ever raised?"

The Luarns looked sheepishly at each other and grinned.

"I told the woman on the way down that I bet ya balked on the fish business. That's all right by me, doc. We'll do like ya say.

And we're dependin' on ya to tell us what's right for the kid. We want him to get started right. Neither one of us knows nothin' about raising him, and—just like ya said—it ain't sensible that a woman like Mrs. Hughes 'd know a hell of a lot more about it than we do when she's buried most all of her kids."

In her own, words Mrs. Luarn reiterated her husband's promise.

"I'll feed the baby like you tell me. I don't see no use of havin' a good doctor unless you do like he says. I never paid no attention to old Doc Peters, but then he didn't know nothin'. With you it's different, and I aim to raise all the kids we ever have your way."

When they rose to go, a carefully typed diet list in their possession, Jack Luarn pulled a worn billfold from his pocket.

"I guess I can finish up that bill to-day, doc. I hope ya didn't think I was layin' down on it because I been kinda slow. Things hasn't been too good with us this year, but I ain't forgot that there wouldn't be no woman to herd this kid if ya hadn't been there. That was a right bad night, when the kid come, and I ain't apt to forget it no more 'n I am to forget the job ya done on my arm. The way it works you'd never know it 'd been broke."

Mrs. Luarn's face was unimaginative like a peasant's, but it was strong and friendly when she smiled at Mallory.

"Good-by, doc. If there's ever anythin' Jack or me can do for you all you got to do 's say the word. Everybody was nice to me when I was here having the baby and I'm much obliged to you for all you done for us then and since."

They tramped off downstairs with their baby, and Mallory stood looking after them with the little wad of dirty bills Luarn had just given him in his hand. They didn't know what they ought to do for their child, but they admitted it. "I aim to raise all the kids we ever have your way," the woman had said. That was what he had hoped for: if only the children could be started out on life straight, if only he could furnish normal, healthy raw material for the schools, if only he could hold back death and sickness, what might not life accomplish on the Silticoos?

Mallory knew he had made friends in the valley. The Luarns were only one family; there were others, especially among the younger people, who believed in him and his ways. As time went on there would be more. Let the older ones go their own road; they were not important; they would all be gone before long. And their successors would be different and better.

Then the doctor thought of Olaf Hansen when he had told him his terrible news that morning. In the desolation that fell so abruptly upon him the man had turned to Mallory for advice and help as one turns to a friend, sure of his faithfulness. These people, whether they all knew it or not, were his friends; and he was their friend whether they recognized that or not. Something within the man hardened. One does not desert one's friends.

Through the corridor came the sound of Katherine singing to her own accompaniment. The country was flooded those days with war songs—gay, defiant, with an undercurrent of despair in them. The words Mallory heard meant something to him at that particular instant. "Somewhere a voice is calling, calling for me."

While he had talked with the Luarns he had seen how to solve his problem and now, with eyes shining, he swung into the music room to tell his wife.

IV

Katherine's dark brows drew into a puzzled frown.

"I'm not sure I understand just what you mean, Bob. You want to build a hospital here in Glenwood right away and put off the post-graduate work until later. Is that it?"

Mallory knelt beside the low chair on which she sat, throwing one arm about her shoulders. His eyes were very blue, his face very eager.

"Yes, darling, that's it. We can't go abroad with the war going on. Then, after the hospital is finished, I'll get some chap who's through his interneship to come in as my assistant. In a year or two we could get away to study. The war would probably be over by then and everything would work out all around."

Katherine did not answer him at once; her eyes continued

to search his smiling, enthusiastic face. Her hand lay supinely in his.

"Let me explain this city business to you, dear, as I see it," he hurried on. "In a big city I couldn't have my own hospital; I'd have to get a staff appointment and make my way among older doctors who are already well-established. That's hard to do; the old men don't like us young fellows who're on the up-grade. Why, Benny writes me that Pacific City is full of fee-splitting; he says some of the best surgeons there pay commissions for operative cases. I worked in the police hospital, remember, and talk about evil-smelling medical politics, there was plenty of it down there. Fellows have told me how they pulled wires to get clinic jobs part-time and wangled private patients out of them. A man can't build a practice simply sitting in his office waiting for people to hunt him up. You never knew about this sort of thing because, naturally, your father and mother called older doctors of their own generation who were already firmly dug in. But I've heard a lot of things from the fellows I interned with who stayed on in the city."

He took her hand and put it to his lips.

"Down here, Katherine, I can have my own hospital, do my work my own way without having to beat every idea into some bull-headed chief of staff first. After I got a young chap to help me, I could take him into partnership if he panned out all right. I'm making friends here, dear. I know it seems slow, but one of these days we won't have to worry about Bentley and Kronheit any more. We'll have a house up on the hill beside the new hospital where there's a fine view, and every year or two you and I can go away on a trip somewhere. Wouldn't that be better than scratching around in the city?"

Slowly Katherine pulled her hand out of Mallory's and pushed him a little way from her.

"And we would still be in Glenwood, in the blind alley. You can't make an impression on the world from the obscurity of the backwoods."

"Oh, yes, you can. Look at the Mayos. Who'd have thought they could build up a clinic in a small Minnesota town that would be famous all over the world? I don't mean to compare myself to them, you understand, but the minute a handicap's overcome it turns into an asset. Once I get started, the very fact I'm from a small place will be an advertisement. Mallory of Glenwood will mean more just because there aren't a dozen other well-known men here. And, besides, a fellow doesn't have to be such a big frog to make a showing in a small puddle."

But this attempted pleasantry did not amuse Katherine.

"Then I suppose you'd think it wise for a man without hands to go into surgery because—if he were to succeed by some miracle—the lack of hands would be good publicity for him." There was a sharpness in her voice that Mallory had never heard before. "Your whole argument, Bob, is as fantastic as that! Why you want to stay here I can't imagine. The only attractive thing in the valley is the scenery in summer, and surely you're not completely bound up in the beauties of nature. The people are ill-mannered and stupid, and they don't pay you for your work. How do you think you're going to maintain a new hospital, once it's been built, when you can't collect enough money to run this one? Grandmother's legacy won't last forever, and neither will 'war babies.'"

Mallory flushed.

"I only want to use your money to get started, to put up the building and buy equipment. It won't be a big hospital, my dear. And as my practice grows, there'll be more money coming in all the time."

"As your practice grows, Bob, you'll be no better collector than you are now. That's one of the reasons I want you to be in a city where you can work among a better class of people who are in the habit of paying their doctor. Besides, if you're ever to accomplish anything, you need libraries and laboratories that you can't find outside a city. You can't launch a career from an obscure valley on the west coast of Oregon, Bob. This isn't 1876 and you aren't Koch hunting the first tuberculosis germ—or whatever it was he was looking for."

She looked straight into her husband's serious, bewildered, blue eyes.

"I've set my heart on your being a great man. I want people to stop and think when they hear your name. You have the brains, my dear; you have the strength; you can be a success if only you want to. You must go away, get out of here where you'll have a chance, where you can show the world what you can do. You make me wretched because you won't see this."

"Oh, no, darling. Don't say that, please! I want to be more to you than a success. Why, you'll always be the most wonderful woman in the world to me even if something happens so you can't ever play the piano again. I'll always love you and be happy with you."

But Katherine still held him away from her and looked at him very seriously.

"Listen to me, Bob, and try to understand. You've never really tried to do that, you know, and I'm sure you don't see how I feel about this. I was always ambitious, my dear. I always knew I could do things other girls couldn't. From the time I was a tiny child I loved music and when I got older I knew I had to be a pianist…just as you knew you must be a doctor. They told me at the Conservatory I had the talent to be a concert artist. If it hadn't been for the war breaking out, I'd have gone to Europe last year to finish my training.

"Then, dear, you walked into my life that night at Benny's party. I fell in love with you. I'd never really been in love before, I hadn't had time for it, and so nothing else but that seemed to matter. You drove everything else out of my mind, you dominated me as I'd never been dominated before. Because you stirred up in me something I couldn't control, I married you. But since I came down here I've been alone a good deal—you're gone on calls much of the time, you know—and I've had time to think when you weren't with me. This wild romantic love won't last forever. It never does. Sooner or later we'll settle down into ordinary married people, Bob. And when we do, what will we have if we stay on here?

"You'll have your practice, of course, and no time to sleep, or spend with me, and not enough money for us to live decently. And I…what will I have? I'll sit here and play the piano—alone, most of the time. I'll write letters, I'll read. And I'll wait for you, hoping that you'll have an hour for me now and then or that we can go down to Baypoint to a movie once a month. That's all…And, Bob, I'll tell you the truth: that's not enough."

Mallory stared at her, amazed and bewildered.

"But the children, dearest. Won't they make up for these other things?"

Katherine laughed, but there was no gayety in her laughter.

"Men always think children will console women for everything they miss in life, don't they, Bob? I've hinted to you before that I wasn't enthusiastic over babies, but I wasn't emphatic about it because I thought it would shock you. To be perfectly frank, I'm sure I'd hate being swollen up and sick beforehand. I suppose after the baby came I'd get to love it, but the truth is that I'm not the maternal sort. Is there any reason why all women should want children, my dear? No, Bob, I love you, I'm interested in your career, but I'm not greatly concerned over our problematical babies who may never materialize."

"Katherine!" exclaimed Mallory.

"There, didn't I tell you I knew you'd be shocked? But what I've just said is the truth, and you'd have known it yourself without my telling you if you'd ever stopped to think of me as a person. But you haven't. You've taken for granted that I was like all the female characters you've read about in books and seen in the movies. I'm not like that, Bob. Until you came along, music was the center of my life. I gave up my career when I married you, and I must have something in place of it. Not babies, my dear, but your career! Can't you understand?" She put her hands on either side of Mallory's troubled brown face and shook his head gently. "Let's forget all this argument and just remember that we love each other and that our business from now on is to promote the career of one Robert Truscott Mallory, M.D."

Although he knew instinctively that Katherine meant to seduce him into abandoning his own plans by any means she could, Mallory could not resist her charm. The touch of her hands on his cheeks, the fragrance of her perfume, the passion smoldering among the amber flecks in her brown eyes, made him tremble. She had never seemed quite so lovely, quite so tempting. He stood up and pulled her up with him; the softness and limpness of her body made him mad. Suddenly he felt a strange desire to hurt her, to make her cry out in pain of his causing.

When, after a time, he let her go, she looked at him in silence until he saw that she knew he had entirely forgotten her feelings in the violence of his own desires. He was instantly contrite.

"Dearest, forgive me. I'm ashamed to be like this. But sometimes you drive me wild, Katherine. More than you did when we were first married. I never seem to get close to you any more except physically, and I always thought there ought to be more to marriage than that. You stir me up to the highest pitch but, after it's all over, I'm not satisfied. There's something lacking that we used to have. Do you remember the first time we went to Baypoint together?"

Katherine smiled at him with softening eyes and, going close once more, smoothed back his shock of hair with her thin white hands.

"Yes, Bob, I remember. I shan't ever forget. I was so wildly in love that I didn't even mind it when you went to sleep in the movie, so thrilled just to sit there beside you that I thought nothing else in the world mattered. But something else does matter, dear, and that something has come between us. You keep pulling back from the thing I want you to do for us both. I'd give in, Bob, if it was anything else but our whole lives that was at stake. And I'll do anything else you want me to: if you want them, I'll have a dozen babies for you. But I won't let you waste yourself and ruin both our lives by staying here in Glenwood. I can't let you do that. I love you, Bob. Someday you'll understand what I mean."

She reached up and kissed him with lips that retained something of the abandon she had shown a few minutes before, but in her eyes there was a glint of hardness that Mallory had never seen there any other time. He watched her as she went to the door, surprised and dismayed to realize that nothing had been changed, that they were still just where they had been that morning. She couldn't see what he meant, he couldn't make her see it. She thought he was simply pig-headed and obstinate. Then it flashed into his mind that things weren't just as they had been; there was this new hardness in Katherine's eyes.

She paused at the doorway and looked back at him. Why, he wondered dully, was everything she did so provocative to passion?

"I may be a bit late for dinner, my dear," she said. "You've done havoc to my clothes and hair."

Mallory started toward her like an iron filing toward a magnet, but she went out and closed the door after her. Then she opened their bedroom door across the hall and closed it. The sound made him apprehensive: there was something so final about it. Katherine, he saw, did not intend either to stay in Glenwood or to let him stay.

Suddenly fear sprang up in him. He ran to the door she had just passed through but, with his hand on the knob, he paused. At last he knew why he had that sense of something coming between them: there was something, something that pulled her away from him. He could only keep her by going with her, by doing what she wanted, by making a career in medicine that would take the place of the one in music that she had given up. He stood there, staring with blind eyes at the door, but he did not open it.

V

At three o'clock that morning Mallory padded softly down the hall in his bedroom slippers to answer the telephone, then padded back again and wakened Katherine.

"It's long distance for you, dearest...from Pacific City." Still dazed with sleep, the girl listened to the voice that came muffled over the wire.

"It's mother, Bob. She was taken ill three days ago with pneumonia. Father says the doctor told him to-night that she was in great danger. He says she asked for me yesterday. I must go. On the morning train, dear. After all, I'm their only child, and I haven't done many things they wanted me to. . . . Now I must go and help them."

Pale and preoccupied, Katherine preserved her composure before Mrs. Hathaway and the Blakes, who came in after breakfast to say good-by, but when she and Mallory went back to their room for the last time her self-control broke down.

"Darling, I love you so…and I hate to leave you. Promise me you'll look after yourself." She pulled his head down and laid her cheek against his. "I even love to feel the scratchiness of your face. Remember that, won't you? And tell me you'll come, if I need you." She kissed him and buried her face for a moment in the roughness of his coat. "Hold me tight, Bob, once more. I'm afraid…afraid of being afraid…of what's ahead of me. Tell me you love me again, that you'll always love me."

Her tears were still damp on his cheeks when Mallory carried her bags down to Hansen's waiting jitney.

Twenty minutes afterward she was gone and her husband stood alone, on the railway platform, looking after the train. Half of him had been torn away, and the half that was left quivered in pain. He caught the echoes of the locomotive whistling for the first tunnel north of the river, and at this desolate sound a whip lash seemed to fall on the part of him that Katherine had left behind.

Silently he climbed into the front seat of the Ford beside Hansen. In spite of the fact that his brother lay in his coffin in Glenwood, Olaf was carrying the mail and driving the stage as usual; he released the handbrake and let in the clutch as carefully as though no personal disaster had overtaken him.

"It's all right, doc. I know ya done all ya could. But it's good that both of us has got work to do now. I'm glad of that."

CHAPTER VI

I

It was early New Year's morning. Mallory was shaving in his bathroom before the wavy mirror that hung above the washbowl. The glow of an electric bulb suspended from the ceiling feebly augmented the light that came through the window at his left, but the surface of the glass reflected his face in distorted planes. Suddenly a misdirected stroke of the razor drew blood.

"Damn it!" muttered the doctor as he fumbled in the medicine cabinet for a styptic pencil. "Safety razor indeed! Safe for the man who lets it alone, they mean."

When he had finished, he looked out the window. The rain was pouring dismally down as it had been doing for weeks. Sometimes Mallory wondered if he would ever see the sun again. The warm bright days of summer seemed sheer illusion. He counted back; since the seventh of November there had been not a glimpse of blue sky or sunshine. Every time he came in from a trip on the river he was drenched: nothing could shed the rain that fell in the Silticoos valley.

Moodily he glanced down at his leather puttees and drab breeches spotted and stained with mud. Nothing went right any more. Nothing had gone right in all the eight months Katherine had been away. A week before, Alice and Henry had invited him to share New Year's dinner with them, but five hours ago he had received a relayed telephone call to go to see a family at Westlake, fifteen miles north of Glenwood along the railroad. As he usually made such trips on a speeder, he had called the section foreman in Southport only to be told that the speeder was dismantled for repairs. So it was that he was getting ready to catch the northbound morning train, knowing perfectly well that he could not get back before late afternoon.

He snatched a shirt off the nail beside the bathroom door, but it proved to have two buttons missing, and he flung it into the laundry hamper. Then he went back into the unheated bedroom with its twin beds and its pink rag rugs to rummage in his chest for another shirt.

"I declare," lamented Sairy as she served him poached eggs and hot cakes, "I think it's terrible, you havin' to go off like this on New Year's. Seems like people pick out the worst times they is to get sick, don't it?" Having put a fresh griddleful of batter on to fry, Sairy resumed her monologue. "It's lonesome to-day, ain't it, with nary a patient in the house and Mrs. Hathaway gone off to Baypoint? My, but that Painter kid was glad you let him go last night. Yistiddy mornin' he says to me, 'Sairy,' he says, 'I just gotta get outa here to-day. Ma's havin' two geese tomorra'.... Not that I can see how the Painters can afford two geese, but..."

Having now arrived by circumlocution at the point she was interested in, Sairy continued with an elaborate pretense of indifference, "I kinda thought mebbe Mrs. Mallory'd be down to visit you for a while, bein' as it's Christmas and New Year's and everything."

Mallory flung out savagely at this.

"Oh, shut up, Sairy. If you'd pay more attention to your griddle and less to my private affairs, your cakes might be fit to eat. . . . I want some hot coffee."

"Good gracious!" said Sairy to herself as she watched him gulp down the last of the scalding coffee and clump off down the hall in his hobnailed shoes, "that man's just like a bear with a sore head! He's gettin' crosser every minute. I reckon it's that woman of his never comin' back that makes him so cranky. She's a fool, she is—leavin' him. . . . Oh, you shut your mouth, Juanita! I wisht I'd never learned you to talk. I'm sick of you yellin' at me all the time. Shut up, now! I'll be back in a minute."

Disregarding the wails of "Hank oo, Hairy! Hank oo, Hairy!" Sairy ran to the surgery windows in the front of the building and watched the doctor climb into Hansen's Ford. The light that came into her pale eyes as she stared after the little car bouncing off down the corduroy road died slowly away when she returned to the shrieking Juanita and a litter of dirty dishes.

On the train Mallory dropped into the corner of a seat in the smoker, lit his bent-stem pipe, pulled his hat down over his forehead, and gazed out with blind eyes at the rain-soaked landscape. When the conductor stopped at his section, he held up his railroad pass between two fingers and returned only monosyllables to that official's pleasant attempts at conversation. Presently the conductor returned to the other car.

Alone again, Mallory pulled from his pocket a soiled envelope with a London postmark. This letter from Norman Reilly had arrived last night—the first word of him in six months. Mallory held the sheets of flimsy paper in his hands. There was really no use reading them again; he had gone over the letter three times last night and knew it almost by heart.

Reilly had been in the British Medical Corps for over a year. He had been in France and had been wounded. Now he was in London, convalescent and scheming to get out to Mesopotamia. Gerty, he said, had been in London, too; she was a great success in the music halls. After Reilly was invalided back to England they had had a great time together. The letter was full of brilliant comments on the war and its conduct by the Allies and of witty cracks about the reaction of English officers to his Irish name. But there was not a word about Katherine, not even an intimation that Reilly knew she had married Mallory.

With this letter open in his hands, Robert Mallory sat staring out into the drizzling perpetual rain. Two years ago he and Reilly had still been in the Pacific City Hospital and on New Year's Eve they had worked together in the police emergency station. Last New Year's Katherine and he had spent in the Grand Hotel at Baypoint, so engrossed in each other that they had no need for other company. And to-day Reilly was in Europe, completely gone out of the old life, and Katherine was in New York with her father and mother on the eve of starting to South America, and he was on the Silticoos in the rain, alone.

When he stopped to think, it seemed impossible that Katherine had gone away in April, eight months ago. At first she had written almost every day—short, hurried notes, full of anxiety for her mother. Then, as Mrs. Harper improved, the letters turned into ardent pleas for him to leave Glenwood at once and join her in Pacific City.

"Dearest," she wrote, "you can see the broker here and arrange to sell the hospital through him. If you still feel that you can't let Bentley have it, you can sell to some one else. It won't matter if you do lose what you've put into it; we'll be well rid of it.

"Father plans for us to go to Honolulu as soon as mother's able to travel. You must come with us. Think what a grand time we could have in Hawaii, dear. No night calls, nothing to worry us, just the joy of being together every day. And then, in the autumn, we'll go east and both of us can begin studying. Boston or Philadelphia or Baltimore, whichever you choose. I'm sure I can find something I need in any of those places.

"I'm sorry we can't go to Europe, darling, but I've been talking to some of the doctors we've had for mother, and they tell me you can get as good graduate work in the United States now as in Berlin or Vienna before the war. Germany, they say, will probably never get back her old prestige in medicine. So I'm sure it would be wiser not to wait, hoping to go abroad, but just to get to work at home. And I'll be so happy to have you out of that wretched valley, dear!"

In July, unable to endure separation longer, Mallory went to Pacific City, where he was received with moderate enthusiasm by the elder Harpers. Katherine's accounts of him and her obvious affection for him predisposed them in his favor, and soon John Harper found himself genuinely fond of this sturdy, well-set-up, independent son-in-law of his. He gave them his yacht, and on it Katherine and Mallory spent two weeks alone. During those days the girl was her loveliest and most charming self. Happily her husband watched the strain of her mother's long illness disappear from her face, saw her ivory skin take on a delicate tan under the mild Oregon sunshine. He begrudged every instant she was out of his sight and thrust from him the sense of impending trouble that had taken root in his mind on the last day she was in Glenwood.

But when, at the end of the fortnight, Katherine insisted on discussing their plans for the autumn, she found him adamant.

"When I first came out from Glenwood, before we had the yacht, I went around and looked things over and talked to a lot of the fellows I know, and I didn't like what I saw and heard. I'll never be any good at playing medical politics and bootlicking, Katherine, and that's what a man's got to do here to get ahead. I'd have to wangle a clinic appointment, and then try to inveigle patients to my office; I'd have to solicit opportunities to speak to medical societies in small towns around the city, and ooze articles I'd written into medical journals. I'd have to play churches and lodges for business.

"You see, my dear, it's not that there isn't plenty of work to be done, but there's only part of the population that have the money to pay a doctor. That means that we have to compete for paying patients just like ten-cent stores do for trade, if we're to make a living. And I don't want to spend my time scheming to get enough patients to pay the office rent. It would take me years to make enough for us to live the way your friends do.

"And I'm not going to pull up stakes and trail after you to

Honolulu like a playboy. I'm not going to use your money to go and study, and then come back here to be set up in practice as John Harper's son-in-law. Your father means well, I know; he hinted that he might be able to put me into the medical department of his insurance company. But I can't do that sort of thing, Katherine. I want to stand on my own feet or not stand at all. I want to be where I'm needed, not here in the city where there are so many better trained men than I. Nobody in Pacific City needs me or my services. They can get better doctors for the asking.

"But in Glenwood, whether they realize it or not, they do need me. I'm a better doctor than they've ever had there before. I even think I'm as good or better than any of the men in Baypoint. That's why I'm going to stay on the Silticoos."

Passionately Katherine protested. She pointed out to him all the reasons why he ought not to be worried about money, all the opportunities he might have to do research after he had finished his post-graduate work. She asked why he should care whether he ever built up a large practice when her father was wealthy and she was his only child.

"And what's wrong about your going into the insurance company if father wants you to? I'm sure Dr. Tompkins is an old fogey and years behind the times. He's been there for ages, and I know he hasn't learned anything new since he graduated from medical school thirty years ago. If you loved me, Bob, you wouldn't be so stubborn and mulish."

But Mallory's determination held fast, and Katherine sailed to Honolulu without him.

It was when he came back to Glenwood alone that pain began to look out from his level blue eyes and etch furrows in his smooth tanned cheeks. He acquired a way of looking through people without seeing them. Doggedly he ate his meals, saw his patients, read his professional journals; but only in the hours when he read Katherine's letters and wrote his blundering answers to them did he live.

On his desk, watching him as he toiled over those letters, stood her photograph in a golden frame. He often talked to it in an undertone, trying to explain himself. He did not want Katherine's pity, so he wrote her that he loved her, would always love her, that he longed to make her happy. He told her what the Blakes and Mrs. Hathaway were doing. But he did not tell her how he listened, when he came into the hospital, for her voice singing or how he had closed the little music room because he could not endure the sight of her piano. And so the stalemate between them persisted.

He flogged himself to endless work so that night might find him sufficiently exhausted to sleep. He went down to the mouth of the river and tramped miles on the beach in the wind and rain. Helplessly Mrs. Hathaway and the Blakes watched him. Mrs. Doan and her coterie looked knowingly at each other and fabricated salacious tales about his married life. Now and then Sairy's witless tongue lashed raw memories until he flung angry words at her.

Then there were always money troubles to prick at his patience. For all his care to send out monthly statements promptly, collections continued small. The notes at the bank, though reduced, were never paid in full. And there was always new apparatus he needed and new books to be bought and better beds for the hospital patients.

But, in the face of all this, Mallory knew that he was winning his way, bit by bit, in the valley. Slowly both the volume of his work and his income, inadequate though it always was, were growing. Long before, he had chosen these people as his, and now—hardly knowing that they did so—they were making him theirs. Gradually they were coming to accept him, constantly it became harder for Burton to send people to Baypoint to his commission-paying patrons.

In the autumn, when Katherine returned from Honolulu, Mallory planned to go to Pacific City to see her, but when the time came there was a miniature epidemic of septic sore throat in Glenwood and Southport and he dared not leave. Then she wrote him that her father had decided to go to South America in January and wanted her to go also. He determined he would see her at Thanksgiving, but gave that up, too, when she sent word that an aunt and three cousins were to spend the holiday and week-end with the Harpers.

Early in December Katherine left for New York to prepare for the cruise. She and Reilly and himself, thought Mallory, dotted around the world—New York, England, Oregon.

II

At Westlake Mallory got off the train in a drizzling rain. There was no shelter, not even a shed, only a sign post with 'Westlake' in tall back letters. The doctor accosted an old man who was walking down the track with a mail sack, and asked for directions.

"Oh, yeah. You're the doc from Glenwood, eh? I heerd the Sapps had sent for you. Yeah, I kin show you where they live. It's right clost to here."

Mallory went with him to the lake shore where a small cabin launch was moored. To the west was the railroad trestle cutting across a narrow neck of water at a curve in the lake; beyond the track the main body of water widened and spread off toward the green hills in the distance. To the east an arm of shallower water bent northward not over fifty feet from the trestle. On all sides towered the dripping, fir-clothed mountains, green but forbidding.

The old man motioned Mallory into his boat.

"I'll drap you on the Sapps' landin'. It's just 'round this here curve, on 'tother side of the lake. I live two mile furder around the bend myself."

When Mallory got out on the teetering wharf at his destination, the old man gave him advice for the immediate future. "If I ain't mistaken you won't want to stay at the Sapps' till time for the afternoon train, and it'd be a cold wait out there under the sign along the track. Now that there trail along the edge of the lake goes back to Glenwood over the mountains, if you ain't feerd of walkin'. Turn to the right at the first fork and after that you can't get offn it nohow." The boatman took a large bite off a plug of tobacco and lifted a hand in farewell as he chugged away.

Some twenty-five yards back from the landing, close to the edge of the forest, stood an unpainted board shack. A muddy path led up to it through a tangle of dead weeds. From the chimney Mallory saw a thin ribbon of smoke curling upward. The atmosphere was so depressing that he found himself thinking of 'the house of Usher.'

When he knocked on the door a barely audible "Come in" came to his ears, and when he opened the door he was immediately engulfed in an outrush of stale malodorous air. The interior was so dimly lit by two small dirty windows that his eyes were slow in adjusting themselves to the gloom, but presently he made out two wooden bedsteads, three decrepit rocking chairs, and a baker's dozen of human beings. The beds, it was plain, had not been made or the floor swept for many days. The wraith of a fire flickered wanly in a cracked iron heater. Through an open door the doctor could see a littered kitchen with a fireless cook stove balanced on three legs. Fetid breath and the odor of feverish unwashed bodies filled the room.

Beside the heating stove crouched one young man who seemed less ill than the others. Rapid-fire questioning brought out the fact that all these persons except the youngest of the five children were sick, that the eldest son had been taken ill first after returning from a trip to Baypoint, and that all the rest had fallen ill within the next four or five days. They had had no warm food for three days and no medicine or treatment of any sort. Mallory knew at once that the infection was influenza and soon determined that one of the sons was developing pneumonia.

The wood box was empty; the tiny fire in the heater had been started with a few rungs out of one of the chairs. Back of the kitchen, in a lean-to, Mallory found a pile of slab wood and swiftly he split and carried into the house enough to last for a day or two. Then searching the kitchen shelves he came upon some tinned soup and, having built a roaring fire, he brewed a kettle of hot thick broth which he poured down the throats of his patients.

From his big black bag he produced fever powders and cough medicine which he arranged on the kitchen table with sheets of paper underneath covered with written directions. True to type, the disease was not so severe in the grandparents or in the children as in the middle generation.

"Haven't you got any neighbors or any relatives that can look after you?" Mallory inquired of the least sick daughter-in-law. "Your husband will need more care than any of you can give him." He nodded toward the bed nearest the stove,

"We gotta sister over to the end of the lake, but we all got sick so sudden that we ain't had no chanct to go after her. She ain't got no 'phone, either."

Mallory pulled on his rubber coat.

"Where's her house? What's her name? I'll go after her now if you'll let me use your boat."

In an hour he returned with the sister, a fat middle-aged woman who cheerfully agreed to care for the sick and to administer the medicine as Mallory instructed her. After promising to return without fail in the next forty-eight hours, the doctor turned his attention to getting back to Glenwood himself.

If he took the launch across the arm of the lake to the railroad flag station and left it at the mooring there, he would be depriving the Sapp family of their one means of communication with the outside world. He did not want to sit in the unventilated shack with twelve cases of influenza until half- past three in the afternoon, and the prospect of sitting along the railroad track without shelter was equally uninviting. So he went in search of the trail the old man had described to him.

He found it overgrown with brush and slippery underfoot, but otherwise easy to follow. The rain was pouring steadily down and the wind blew branches into Mallory's face and switched their load of moisture down his neck. Wherever there was a comparatively open space the muddy water ran down the little depressions underfoot in rivulets or stood in yellow puddles deep enough to reach the eyelets of his boots. The trail was old and evidently little traveled since the railroad's advent. It did not lie along a ridge, but climbed hillsides and dipped into the canyons between.

Soon Mallory was steaming inside his slicker and was forced to take off his coat and vest and put the rubber coat on over his shirt sleeves. In one hand he carried the extra garments and in the other his heavy calling bag. This bag contained everything he was likely to need in an emergency and its weight before long was an annoying burden.

After walking for an hour he began to get hungry. Along the trail were a few late thimble berries and salal still clinging to the dripping bushes, but there was little sustenance in them. Always the muddy path grew more and more slippery; for every foot ahead he seemed to slide back two. The steep switch-backs made his legs ache and the bits of descent meant nothing but breath-taking scrambling beyond. The fifteen miles by train, he decided, must be nearer twenty by trail.

Little creeks of cold soft water crossed his path at intervals and at them he stopped to drink. He began timing himself by the watch: twenty minutes' steady climbing, then five minutes' rest. When he emerged from the timber on top of the ridge that overlooked Glenwood in the late afternoon he was profoundly tired.

Down the last steep slope he dragged himself wearily, past the little white cottages in which lights were beginning to glimmer. He knew the hospital would be empty: even Sairy had gone home for dinner. Craving the presence of another human being, he tried the door of the drug store, but found it locked; the dime-chasing Burton was at home eating roast goose. Then he remembered that he was to have dinner with the Blakes at six o'clock and hurriedly stumbled upstairs to wash and change to dry clothes.

III

When the doctor came down the precipitous trail from the hills and passed her mother's house, Sairy saw him from the kitchen window where she was standing wiping dishes. As soon as she had finished her task, she snatched a shawl and umbrella and ran out of the house. Through the rain she trotted—an ungainly figure—to Henry Blake's house and knocked loudly at the front door.

Alice looked a surprised query at the bedraggled woman.

"Have you et yet?" panted Sairy clutching the shawl under her protruding chin.

"Why no, we haven't, Sairy. I've been waiting for Dr. Mallory. Henry went down to the train with Olaf and they haven't come back yet. I suppose the train is late again."

"I dunno about the train, but the doctor's home. He walked. I see him come down the trail outa the hills just a bit ago. He come right past ma's place. He's went to the hospital; I seen a light there as I come by just now. And if you don't go after him, I reckon he'll just set there alone. He's all broke up, Mrs. Blake, over that there wife of his that went off and ain't never come back. I'd go up where he is, but I'm worse 'n nothin' to him, I guess. You folks…" She stopped.

"All right, Sairy. Don't you worry. Henry will go and fetch him the minute he gets back from the train. I appreciate your coming to tell me about it." Then, moved by a sudden impulse, Mrs. Blake went on, "Won't you stop for a little while, Sairy?"

The ill-favored cook looked wistfully past Alice Blake at the warm, comfortable, well-lighted room with its open fire, then she shook her head, and clutched the shawl still more tightly around her head.

"Oh, no, ma'am. Thank you just the same. But I got to get right on back."

She departed as breathlessly as she had come.

IV

Before the stove in the waiting room Mallory knelt down, piling kindling on crumbled paper. Not only was he wet and tired and hungry but, more than all, heart-sick. At the recollection of the old words "It is not good for man to be alone," he smiled sardonically. Only the warmth of the leaping flames recalled him to the present.

Deciding to make some hot coffee while he heated water for a bath before going to the Blakes, he trudged down the hall to the kitchen in search of the percolator. Innumerable small greasy finger prints made by Juanita glistened on the window panes in the rays of the electric light, and over them, on the outside of the glass, slid a film of rain. Behind a curtain concealing a row of shelves he found the coffee pot and in it a grimy little chunk of pie-dough, another relic of the deplorable Juanita.

In the waiting room once more, he put the pot on the stove beside a large tea kettle in which water was heating, and sat down to take off his sodden boots. Then, out of the corner of his eye, he caught sight of a little pile of mail lying on his desk. Leaving one shoe on the floor, he hopped into the office.

On the top of the pile was a thick white envelope addressed in Katherine's handwriting. Instantly his heart began to pound and a hard knot gathered in the pit of his stomach. His hands shook so that he could hardly tear open the envelope. Something in the feel of the paper brought Katherine back to him—her soft dark hair, her gold-flecked eyes, her slim white hands, the limp abandon of her body in his arms. The muscles in his thighs twitched and the skin of his legs tingled. He sank down into his desk chair and began to read the letter.

It took some time for his tired, excited brain to interpret the words he saw, but bit by bit the sentences etched themselves into his mind forever.

"…I can't come back to Glenwood, Bob. You must choose between me and the valley, and I know what your choice will be. You care more for the Silticoos than you ever did for me. … We shouldn't ever have married each other. Nature pulled us together when we weren't on our guard. But medicine has been pulling you away from me ever since; medicine is your mistress and I was only your wife. . . . And music draws me away from you. I can't give it up, Bob, not to vegetate in Glenwood. If you had left the valley and done as I wanted, we could have been happy, lived decently somewhere among civilized people. I would have been willing to keep music in the background and find my success in helping make you a great man. . . . But to be the wife of a nonentity, to degenerate into a villager—the sort of woman her husband calls 'mother' and regards as a machine for the production and feeding of children—that is beyond me. . . . I won't be a party to your burying yourself alive in Glenwood. It is your privilege to ruin your own life if you wish, but in the last eight months I've come to see that I can't let you ruin mine too…You'll probably think there is another man, but there isn't. I still love you enough that, if I were to go back to you, I couldn't get away again. You'd dominate me just as you always did, you'd sweep me off my feet. I didn't let you see me this fall because I was afraid of you, afraid you'd be able to keep me. And I didn't dare go back to Glenwood, for the same reason. . . . One other thing you don't know, I think I should tell you. Even if I had had a baby—and if something hadn't gone wrong last summer in Hawaii, I would have had one—I would not have gone back to Glenwood. Long ago I made up my mind not to bring any child into the world down there. . . . If you should change your mind and decide to be sensible, when I come back from South America in the spring, we can talk things over…"

So that was all! The end of that part of life! A sob rose in Mallory's throat, but he choked it back. Katherine had gone and he would never see her again. She had decided, and he must accept her decision. And there would have been a child if…

Thrusting his hands out blindly before him, he felt his fingers close on the pipe she had sent him only the week before, for Christmas. It was a beautiful brown briar, but he had not smoked it: he could not, with her not there. Now he twisted it around in his hands and the flickering light from the stove caught in tiny lance-like reflections on the yellow bowl. Life was a funny thing! He had loved Katherine, and married her, and been happy. But now she had gone and he was more alone than ever.

She sent him a pipe to remember her by! He lifted his head and laughed. A pipe! To remember her by! That was a joke. He laughed again and the pipe fell out of his hands and rolled over on the floor with a little clatter.

She was gone. She had been his glimpse of music and beauty, and she was gone. She would never come back.

Like a mechanical man, he walked down the hall, opened the door of her little music room, and went in. There was her piano. It wasn't all paid for yet. He must find out next week whether the store would take it back. The polished wood glistened in the light. He put his hand on it: it was smooth and lovely to look at, but it was hard.

Little trickles of water ran from his wet breeches and made tiny dirty puddles on the floor. Outside, daylight had fled under the mantle of a stormy night. To Mallory there seemed something inhuman about the monotonous dripping of rain from the eaves: it went on and on and on, like the years that were before him.

Years without Katherine. Years without love. Bleak, empty, terrible years! He felt them drawing out ahead of him endlessly. A decade and more, he saw them barren and lonely.

Suddenly it seemed to him that he could not breathe in that room. Katherine was still there, her presence stifled him. He rushed out and locked the door behind him, trying to escape the years he dreaded. But they danced down the corridor before him, mocking him—a procession of them, not to be escaped—stretching endlessly into time ahead of him.

PART THREE

CHAPTER I

I

From the rose arbor Henry had built for her on the bank of the river, Alice Blake watched Jean Stuart's shining copper-colored head disappear down Main Street. She knew that by all the canons of housewifery she should be in her kitchen helping the village handy-woman prepare refreshments for the Sunshine Club that afternoon, but instead of hastening to these duties she lingered in the arbor and enjoyed being alive. Twenty years on the Silticoos had made her hair gray instead of black but, in spite of being on the verge of her fifties, Mrs. Blake was still radiant with vitality and good cheer.

It was mid-morning of a June day—just such a day, Alice reflected, as the one on which she had come to Glenwood, a bride, in 1913—and over the great green hills and the broad river swept the dull soft blue of an Oregon summer sky. Her own consciousness of well-being made it seem all the more incredible that any young woman in her late twenties could have been as drawn and haggard as Jean Stuart when she arrived in Glenwood two weeks before.

Before she came west Alice had known Jean as a bright-eyed bubbling little girl with red hair and freckles and a zest for living. She had been in the only Sunday school class Alice had ever taught, and she had greatly admired the tall, black-haired, low-voiced young nurse. Long after Alice had gone to Pacific City Jean had continued to pour out in letters her problems and hopes and plans. Now she had come to Glenwood to visit the Blakes and recuperate from a breakdown brought on by the struggle to hold a job and make ends meet on a reduced salary.

This morning Alice was happy because Jean was already regaining her energy.

"I feel marvelous," the girl had said at breakfast. "My freckles are all popping out and my hair is coming to life again. I think I'd make a wonderful advertisement for the Silticoos valley as a health resort."

"You sure would," agreed Henry, buttering a stack of hot cakes. "And so would Alice." He grinned across the table at his wife.

"Oh, she would make a much better story than I," laughed Jean. "Twenty years in Glenwood and she still looks like a bride."

"Why not?" asked Blake. "There's lots worse places than Glenwood, and, for all you know, there may be worse fellows than me to be married to."

Mrs. Blake, her pale skin slightly flushed, said, "Brides don't have gray hair."

Jean looked intently at the older woman.

"Please don't point out your gray hair and crows' feet, Alice. You're ever so distinguished looking. If I'm ever half as handsome I'll be satisfied. But red hair fades into such a nondescript color, it never turns a beautiful dark iron gray like yours."

Mrs. Blake still blushed faintly.

"You are blarneying me shamelessly. As soon as I finish eating I'll escape to the kitchen."

"Well, I'm going to escape too. I'm tired of being an invalid. I feel childish and gay this morning and, since you won't let me help you, Alice, I'm going out on the river. Then I'll at least be out of the way. But I'll be back for the party if I have to swim all the way."

"If I was you," advised Henry, pushing back his chair, "I wouldn't swim far. Not to get to the Sunshine Club. Days it meets here I hide out till I see 'em all leave before I come home. Doc Mallory calls it 'a concatenation of disappointed females,' and he's about right."

Alice Blake, sitting among her roses thinking of the breakfast table conversation, looked up and saw Dr. Mallory's big white cabin launch coming rapidly upstream along the north shore. The stocky figure at the wheel raised an arm in salute and Alice waved back at him. She had planned to have him to dinner to meet Jean as soon as the girl felt equal to guests— perhaps to-morrow night, when the Sunshine Club was out of the way—and she hoped he was not off now on one of his forty-eight-hour trips into the back-country of the upper valley. Progress as exemplified in road building had not, even in 1933, invaded the upper Silticoos.

Swiftly Mrs. Blake's face sobered as she watched the doctor's launch swing out along the point of land above the village. It had always seemed unfair that she and Henry should have a life so full of happiness while the doctor's was so bleak and lonely. It was eighteen years since he came to Glenwood and more than seventeen since Katherine had left him. Sometimes Mrs. Blake wondered if she had ever regretted leaving Mallory. She knew that the girl had gone abroad after the War to study, married an English musician and composer, returned to the United States to go into concert work. She was now a well-known pianist, but Alice often wondered if she was happy. Would things have worked out if Katherine had stayed in Glenwood? Mrs. Blake was doubtful. Although she greatly admired Mallory, she thought he had never understood his wife. For her part, Alice had never shaken off the spell of Katherine's beauty and artistry; she could still close her eyes and hear the girl playing Chopin, singing the gay-sad war songs of 1915 and 1916. She could never hear "The Long Long Trail" without a catch in her throat.

A shrill voice broke in upon her thoughts.

"Miz Blake, Miz Blake," Hattie Smith, brawny official assistant to Glenwood hostesses, shrieked from the front door of the house. "You're wanted on the 'phone."

II

Jean Stuart, walking swiftly down Main Street toward the Mill Store dock, felt something inspiriting in the fresh cool air, swung her legs back and forth under her body with pleasure in her returning sense of health. She was full of illogical joy at being alive and so far from the hot Chicago office on this lovely June day.

On the wharf she encountered Burton. Upon him time had left less visible trace than upon Alice Blake. His hair was still black with only a few threads of white, and his dark eyes still skipped back and forth in search of nickels and dimes. A flat, telescope-crowned hat tilted far forward over his nose. Jean could dimly recall her eldest brother in a similar hat and peg-top trousers and an absurd coat with huge padded shoulders. 'Really,' she thought, 'it's a feat to balance that hat as he does. I'm sure he must have bought all the Mill Store had in stock twenty-five years ago.'

With a trace of malice she spoke to the druggist.

"Good morning, Mr. Burton. I'm so glad you came along just now. You can help me get the boat out."

Burton hesitated. "Well, I was in a kinda hurry to get over to Southport, but…"

To his own surprise the man found himself pushing Henry's outboard motor boat up alongside the landing. To the surprise was presently added annoyance when Jean, taking advantage of his preoccupation with the engine, stepped in without assistance. Mr. Burton was regarded by the community as a model husband but there was something covetous in his red face when he looked up at the girl. As he often remarked to his male cronies, he still knew "come hither" when he saw it.

Jean found the pudgy druggist, crouching on the floor of the boat, smirking up at her, an unpleasant sight.

"Thank you so much for helping me. I'm sorry I'm not going across the river or I'd take you over to Southport. Some other time perhaps. I think that's your boat over there now, isn't it?"

Burton scrambled out upon the landing and ran toward the passenger launch that was about to start up-river. With more than a hint of the gamin in her face Jean smiled after his retreating back.

Once out in the stream the girl stretched herself luxuriously in the sunlight. She could feel the wind's cool fingers ruffling her hair, slipping over her cheeks. Her eyes, weary of shop windows, rested gratefully on the broad river between lush green banks and on the ring of huge, sprawling hills that rimmed the valley. Against their summits brushed the soft white clouds of early summer.

Jean thrust her long slim legs out in front of her and ran careless bony fingers through her thick mop of short red-gold hair. Already she felt alert, as though she were absorbing energy from the sunshine. She was filled with that curious sense of well-being which accompanies convalescence in vigorous young people.

When she was some way above Glenwood, Jean looked back to see the little town in perspective and was surprised to realize how many elements of beauty it presented. Most of the houses were painted white and the unpainted ones had weathered to a soft gray. The flat next to the river and the densely wooded hill behind the village were both brilliantly green. Against this background the houses, gray and white, made a pattern that was pointed up by the occasional red and green roofs.

Above the last row of cottages on the mountainside was a large plot of ground enclosed within a white fence where a green lawn and bright flower beds surrounded a building of dark red brick with a dull green roof. Its windows reflected the sunshine in glittering radiance. Looking up at it from the river, Jean began to understand why the Blakes were so proud of the hospital. Because it was beautiful it was its own best advocate. Jean knew it was called "The Haven." She liked the name. It prejudiced her in favor of the hospital. Alice and Henry had told her much about it.

"Doc's got a great huge light on the porch," explained Blake, "that burns every night from sunset to daylight. You can see it all up and down the river, and it looks mighty good to a fellow comin' in cold and tired, or sick, I can tell you. Whenever you look up and see it, you know there's somebody there ready to take care of you if you need 'em."

About the doctor himself Alice and Henry had been less communicative. Although he was a great friend of theirs, they said little of his history. Jean gathered that he must have had what she in her early teens would have called a blighted past, and once or twice she had seen him on the village street—a stockily built, middle-aged man of medium height in a baggy gray suit. The only things about him that had impressed her were his mass of gray hair brushed straight back off a high forehead and very blue, deep-set eyes. Taking for granted that the man did not belong to her generation, Jean had paid him little heed.

Sudden silence startled the girl. Without any premonitory misfiring the engine stopped. Jean wound the cord about the wheel and spun it vigorously but there was no answering explosion. Then she unscrewed the cap of the gas tank and peered inside; the tank was empty. A hasty glance about the boat confirmed her suspicion that she had forgotten to bring a spare tin of gasoline.

"What an idiot I am! When Henry took such pains to show me where he kept the extra tins."

Jean sat back on her heels and eyed the oars with disfavor.

"Nice job rowing back against the tide, with the engine

dragging behind. And awfully good for a nervous wreck!" She laughed aloud.

Realizing that she was too near the north bank for her voice to reach the few passing boats in the middle of the stream, she settled down to drift with the current.

"I'll just wait like Micawber for something to turn up. I'm not keen on swimming all the way back to Glenwood in these clothes. Besides, who knows what may be around this next bend in the river?"

She rummaged in her jersey pocket for a pack of cigarettes. The past fortnight had been for Jean a repetition of the days when no decent woman dared smoke except in her bathroom with a window open. Alice had warned her that Glenwood still regarded cigarettes as the trademark of the "fallen woman." Inhaling deeply Jean discovered that her old pleasure in smoking had returned—a certain evidence, she had been told, of returning health.

Drifting slowly upstream, the motor boat soon rounded a point of land and came into sight of an unpainted floating house beside which lay a trim white launch. Jean's eyes brightened. Here was a source of gasoline. She steered in alongside and sprang out upon the platform that served as a porch.

Tossing her cigarette into the water she knocked at the door of the shack. Although she could hear voices inside, there was no answer. She knocked again. This time she heard the rumble of a male voice in what was unmistakably an order of some sort. Rather annoyed Jean pushed open the door. She saw at once that no one had heard her knock and that the order had not been an invitation for her to enter.

There was but one room in the shanty. Near the door was a cookstove with a roaring fire and in front of it stood a tall elderly woman in a faded cotton dress and a young girl in a dirty red calico frock. Both of them turned and stared at Jean with round, wide-open eyes. On a straight chair in the middle of the floor sat a man with his back to her; on his lap was a strip of stiff white canvas. In the far corner was an old-fashioned wooden bedstead surmounted by a curious frame-work of two-by-fours. On the bed lay a white-faced woman who groaned now and then; one of her legs was bare.

Without looking around the man said, "Shut the door, Minnie. Your mother'll feel the draft."

Hastily Jean stepped inside and closed the door behind her. "I beg your pardon," she said, "I just wanted to ask if I could borrow enough gas to get back to town. I ran out down the river and drifted this far. When I saw the boat here…"

The elderly woman whose gray hair was skewered to the back of her head with a single long hairpin interrupted.

"None of the men folks is to home."

Clearly, so far as the old lady was concerned, that settled the matter, for she crammed the firebox of the stove full of wood and went on about her work. But Dr. Mallory left off struggling with the canvas in his lap long enough to say, "I can't leave my patient now, but there's plenty of gas in my boat outside—if you can help yourself. Take what you need."

The man's eyes, Jean thought, were the brightest blue she had ever seen. They looked straight at her in completely impersonal fashion.

"Thank you. I will." Turning to go, she added, "I'm visiting the Blakes, Dr. Mallory. Henry will see that the gasoline is returned."

"Oh, that's all right," answered Mallory. In the same breath he said crisply, "Hand me that square box on the table, Minnie. Shake a leg now! I'm in a hurry."

Jean went out, closing the door in what she tried to make a dignified manner. The doctor had annoyed her a bit. He might at least have told the old woman to help her or asked her to wait until he was through. Jean Stuart was not accustomed to cursory treatment from men.

"I suppose he thinks I'm an eastern tenderfoot. Westerners are like that!"

She stepped down into the cabin of the doctor's launch. In a rack on the wall were several tins of oil and gasoline, but above this rack, level with her eyes, was a small shelf containing a half-dozen books. "The Education of Henry Adams," "Lord Jim," "The Nigger of the Narcissus," "Looking Backward," "Of Human Bondage," "Arrowsmith." At once the doctor became an interesting figure. 'At least he's interested in modern literature,' she thought.

But when she crossed the landing with the emergency tin of gasoline her boat was not there. Scanning the stream Jean at last saw it drifting slowly off, a few hundred feet away. She set down the can of gas and glared at the offending boat.

"Oh, damn! Why can't I learn to tie a painter so it won't come undone? Now I'll have to explain to the doctor and ask him to take me back to town when he goes. What a fool I am!"

And yet she laughed to herself when she approached the door of the shack and stole inside once more.

This time she saw Mallory balancing precariously on the footboard of the bed and the back of a straight chair, engaged in fastening to the framework above the bedstead a long sling of white canvas suspended from two pulleys.

"Minnie, hand me those staples. And be quick about it! D'you want me to fall down on top of your mother?" Twisting his body the doctor fished out of his hip pocket a hammer. "It's a good thing I learned how to build suspension frames out of 'what have you,' Mrs. Painter. If I hadn't, you'd 've been out of luck to-day. Now, Minnie, give me that white cord on the table. No, not that twine string. The stuff that looks like clothesline."

Fascinated, Jean watched the doctor—unconscious of her presence—driving in the staples. The old woman, her back to the door, was stirring something in a pan on the stove. Only the fourteen-year-old Minnie saw the intruder and made her eyes and mouth round with astonishment.

"Oh, doc," she cried out. "Here's that…"

"Keep still, Minnie. I can't talk to you now."

Jean, leaning against the door, watched Mallory working on the frame over the bed. His short legs made his straddled position hard to maintain; his shirt was half out of his trousers' band, his short gray hair stood up in wild disarray, and his necktie hung down over his left shoulder. But in spite of his awkward position and the thickness of his arms and body, Jean's impression was of deftness and precision in all his movements. She was sure, from that moment, that he was a man of far more than ordinary skill in his profession.

Finally he drove in the last staple. The canvas sling now hung limply from the overhead frame, ready to be raised or lowered on its pulleys.

"Well, that's done," grunted Mallory. "Now, Mrs. Painter, if I can get down from here without falling on you, I'll soon have you fixed up." Then he caught sight of Jean. "Huh! You back again! What's wrong now? Can't you find the gasoline?" His tone was peremptory.

Now that he faced her directly Jean noticed the deep perpendicular lines down his cheeks and a certain sternness in his face.

"I'm sorry," she began almost diffidently, "I'm sorry to bother you. But I've let my boat drift off. Would you mind my going back to Glenwood with you, doctor?"

His blue eyes swept over her in swift appraisal.

"No, certainly not. But I have to finish here first. Mrs. Painter broke her femur this morning. . . . You're not a nurse, by any chance, are you? . . . Well, then you'd better go outside. You'd be no use in here and you wouldn't enjoy the next few minutes."

Jean went out obediently, half-amused and half-angry. She had been put in her place, she said to herself, just as earlier in the day she had put Burton in his. It was true that she knew nothing about broken bones and that she probably would have been in the way, but the doctor had not sent Minnie out. Indeed she could hear him calling the girl by name frequently. Then, as groans and cries of pain came to her ears, Jean flinched.

"One more good pull, Mrs. Painter, and we'll have it. Minnie, you hold her hands. That's it. . . . There, now it's all over. Not too bad, was it, Mrs. Painter? Better than being sick from ether all afternoon, eh? Minnie, hand me that sack, the one full of stones. . . . Day after to-morrow I'll bring up the portable X-ray machine and make sure the bone's straight and not overlapping. . . . I wish all my fracture patients were as good scouts as you are.

... How's Tom these days? ... Well, don't you know husbands have to be watched? You ought to keep better track of him. ... What'd you say, Minnie? ... Why, the stones in the sack are a counterweight to pull the leg bones out straight again. And don't you let any of the kids go monkeying with it, or I'll skin them alive."

Presently Mallory appeared in the doorway, wiping his face with his handkerchief, and tucking in his shirt; he looked down at Jean where she sat in the sunshine with her back against a piling.

"What did you say about your boat, Miss...Miss...I'm afraid I don't know your name."

"Stuart," said the girl briefly. "There's my boat. Up there." She pointed upstream at a dark object close to a log-boom.

"Uh-huh, I see it." Mallory screwed up his face and stared at the distant boat. "It's Henry's outboard, isn't it? Well, I'll pick it up and tow it in. I'll be ready to go in a few minutes now."

Jean could hear him giving orders to the old woman and Minnie. She realized that his voice was low and sweet-toned and that, if she were his patient, it would make her feel safe in his care.

When he carried out his bags and packed them in the launch she studied his thick body and tanned face. He was weather beaten and his cheeks were deeply lined, but there was about him a self-possession and an air of quiet determination which appealed to her. His wide shoulders gave him a staunchness and solidity that she was sure must be reassuring to his patients. He was, she felt, the right sort of man to build a hospital and call it "The Haven." She glanced once more at the little book shelf in the cabin of the launch. This man was a doctor but he was interested in other things than medicine. She was sure he would be an interesting individual outside the sickroom.

III

The sight of children running over Alice's flower beds and climbing the balustrade of the front porch warned Jean that the Sunshine Club was in full swing. Slipping quickly among the staring youngsters she hurried along the side of the house and into the kitchen. Mrs. Blake's worried face, bent above a salad bowl, brightened when she looked up and saw her.

"My dear, where have you been? I made Henry promise to start hunting you the minute he got back from Southport. Everyone came early to see you and…"

"I wasn't here," laughed Jean. "I'm sorry, if missing inspection meant anything to you. And I hope I haven't spoiled your party. But you see I've had an adventure."

"Sh-sh, Jean. Mrs. Doan is reading a paper and she doesn't like any noise. Sit down, my dear, and get your breath. You're like an excited child."

"Getting excited is what makes things fun, Alice. . . . I don't suppose I can get to my room by any hook or crook without being seen. Well then, your lady friends must take me 'as is.' Do you mind awfully?"

The Sunshine Club was Glenwood's one organized attempt at feminine culture. When Alice Blake first came to the Silticoos valley it seemed to her that there was, now and then, in the careworn face of some woman struggling to stretch a meager income over the needs of a large family a glimmer of longing for something that concerned herself as an individual rather than a housekeeper, a mother, or a wife. Accordingly Alice had at last organized an informal club for the reading of books and their discussion, but before long Mrs. Doan and her clique of militant church women began to dictate the policy of the organization. Although the club finally came to embrace all comers because none could be left out without mortal offense, the bloc of church workers still maintained their dominance and set the tone of the meetings. Free discussion there was in abundance, but it concerned the absent members, the morals of the school teachers and Dr. Mallory, and any strangers or visitors in the valley.

When Jean slid stealthily into a chair beside the dining room door, Mrs. Doan's strident voice was enunciating certain facts which the girl was sure she must have cribbed bodily from an encyclopedia. "The southernmost part of the Dark Continent is known as the Cape Colony. Its chief port is Cape Town. Nearby rises that huge flat-topped rock called Table Mountain. Southward from this rocky plateau…"

As the shrill voice rasped on, Jean recalled what Henry had said Dr. Mallory called the Sunshine Club: "a concatenation of disappointed females." Her twinkling eyes rested on the speaker's fiery red hair. What a dismal classification for a red-haired woman! It was with difficulty that Jean repressed her amusement and assumed the air of seriousness befitting a visitor to Glenwood.

When at last Mrs. Doan finished her paper, the women relaxed and settled down to the real business of the afternoon. First of all, they inspected Jean sharply for evidences of what they called "toniness." Then they memorized the details of her rather too informal clothing and noted her middle western accent. After that they turned to a discussion of the weather—past, present, and future—and the projected activities of the Ladies' Aid Society.

The older children, brought to the meeting because their mothers had no one to leave them with, played noisily in the yard; the younger ones shrieked to go outside and join them. Then, having been knocked down or stepped on, they shrieked again to get back inside the house. Two or three girls in their early teens, assaulted by boys of ten or eleven who resented being dragged to a feminine party, bit and clawed their tormentors until a committee of mothers separated the combatants. The babies too young to walk crawled about the living room floor, bumping their heads and getting their fingers under rocking chairs. The babel of women and children seemed to Jean deafening, like the clangor of The Loop at home.

"There goes Dr. Mallory past," she heard Mrs. Doan's piercing voice announce. "Now I wonder who's sick up this way. Maybe the Jones baby's worse again." Mrs. Doan tossed the head that at fifty-five showed not one gray hair. "I declare that man gets more careless about his clothes every day. I notice it because Samuel is always so neat."

Someone near Jean sniggered. "Samuel! He can't get away from her long enough to get mussed up!"

A dumpy woman whose feet lacked three inches of reaching the floor looked out the window at the man walking up the street with a black bag.

"I heerd this mornin' that Lulu Paine was sick. He might be goin' there. She's expectin', you know."

"I declare that Paine family is the limit. Something oughta be done to 'em! Lulu's got six already. And Sairy always got into trouble regular. I wonder whatever became of her, anyhow?"

"I heerd onct that she was doin' housework down in California, but I don't recollect just where."

"I guess she went plumb to the bad," said another woman with manifest pleasure, "after Doc Mallory let her go."

"There's one thing I'd like to know for certain about Doc Mallory. Did his wife get a divorce from him or didn't she? Some says she did and some says she didn't. And you can't get a word about it outa *him*."

"Well, you remember that Mrs. Snyder that used to live over to Southport and moved away right after the War? She wrote me that she'd seen in a San Francisco paper that Mrs. Mallory got married again two, three years after she left here. Of course I don't know it of my own knowledge but…"

"And you recollect what that assistant of Mallory's told, don't you? What was his name? Duke or Hook or something like that, seems to me. Names is my weakest spot. Some day I'll forget my own. … Oh, yes. That's it—Cook. Well, Dr. Cook told us when we had him for Blanche the time she had the gathering in her ear—that must've been thirteen years ago—Blanche is twenty-three now and Ruth's a year younger—well, anyway, it was right soon after the War and Dr. Cook had been in one of them big cantonments back east—let me see was it Camp Grant or Camp Meade…"

By this time the speaker was so involved in dates and place names that she could not hold her own in the conversation.

"My land, how many young fellers has Doc Mallory had helpin' him anyhow? Seems to me there musta been four or five of them."

"It's been so long since they begun comin' I can't hardly remember all of them."

"You'd think he'd learn after while that he can't keep none of these young ones fresh outa school."

"I guess he has," observed the woman who had reported Sairy's final downfall with such relish. "Anyhow he ain't had none for two, three years now."

In a momentary pause a mousebrown woman who thus far had said nothing spoke in a soft disarming voice. "Ralph and I think Dr. Mallory is fine. Ralph says he likes him better every year. And certainly The Haven is far superior to either hospital in Baypoint."

Although she talked gently Mrs. Fenton looked about her with an air of challenge. As the wife of the only dentist in the valley her opinion carried a certain weight, but it was not long before the current of gossip that she had checked for an instant swept away whatever impression her words had made. All about her Jean heard phrases and fragments of sentences about the doctor.

"...Doc Mallory said it was all foolishness but when Dr. Kronheit operated...Doc Mallory said her stomach was all right but the X-ray pitchers she had made in Pacific City showed her insides was all outa place and everything...Her man told Burton and he told Mike...It makes a person feel better just to see Dr. Bentley comin' into the room...That Scott baby up-river when it died...Whoever heard of a baby havin' tuberculosis or consumption either one?"

In the midst of bedlam Almira Doan's loud voice reasserted her leadership of the herd.

"I could forgive Dr. Mallory everything else, as I've told Samuel a hundred times, except his refusal to line up with the powers for good. He might have been one of the big men in the church and found solace for his trouble there, but as it is his influence has always been for evil." The sonorous ring with which she pronounced the word "evil" reminded Jean of certain pompous preachers she had heard. Then her mind flashed back to the books she had seen in the doctor's launch; perhaps they offered a solace better than that of Mrs. Doan's church.

During the afternoon the red-haired zealot covertly studied Mrs. Blake's guest and finally she told the woman who sat beside her that, in her opinion, the girl was not ill and probably never had been. "The modern Babylon contaminates all who live in it. Samuel and I feel we can never be too thankful that Nellie is growing up far from all the wickedness of a great city." With her customary abruptness Mrs. Doan crossed the room and sitting down near Jean invited her to sing in the church choir. When Jean quietly but persistently refused, her expression changed to one of outrage and when she had returned to her own chair she informed her neighbor that Miss Stuart was "no better than she should be."

Sensing the disapproval in the air Jean fled to the kitchen where Mrs. Blake was superintending the making of a huge pot of coffee.

"Alice, why don't you get these women to play bridge or contract or rummy—anything to stop them tearing people to pieces this way?"

"The Silticoos is convinced that afternoon card parties for women are an instrument of Satan."

"How ridiculous!"

"Yes, isn't it? But how can I help it?"

Jean drew in a long breath. "And I thought this was an age of enlightenment! But evidently the light doesn't go far—either in Glenwood or Chicago."

"My dear, you mustn't be too harsh with these women. They live in a small world, of fish and lumber camps and husbands and children. They gossip horribly but, when real trouble comes to their neighbors, they're nearly all kind and helpful."

But Jean shivered a little and said, "I feel as though I'd been picked to pieces myself, and been at Dr. Mallory's post-mortem and seen him dissected."

Suddenly there came from the living room a loud crash followed by childish wailing. Alice hurried out but presently returned to the kitchen with fragments of glass in her hands.

"I should know better by this time than to put flowers around the room. Some child always upsets them and cuts himself on the vase." She looked at the table with a worried expression. "I do hope there will be food enough. The crowd is larger than usual to-day and so many of the women have brought their children."

Each in her own way, Alice and Jean and Hattie Smith marveled as the salad, sandwiches, cake, and coffee melted away. Mrs. Blake was horrified to see the children in her yard trading their refreshments to urchins on the sidewalk outside the fence for value in hand received.

"Really," she said, tasting a crumb of her own cake, "it's a terrible task to entertain the club now."

An instant later there came another louder crash from the living room. This time Alice found the large front window broken and bits of glass scattered over the floor. Mrs. Doan was peering sharply through the screen door.

"Mrs. Blake," she announced, "it was Willie Dean threw that stone."

Willie's mother bristled in defense of her offspring.

"You couldn't see who threw it from away back in that corner where you was sittin'. Like as not it was your Nellie."

Almira Doan did not bristle, she spoke with Olympian assurance.

"Nellie doesn't throw stones." In these words were compressed all her inordinate pride in this thirteen-year-old product of her middle-age and Samuel's.

Mrs. Dean rose gallantly to this challenge.

"Oh, is that so? That shows all you know about it. While you're in the bank Nellie's up to all kinds of things, let me tell you. Why, only last week the widow Morgan saw her..."

"The widow Morgan," interrupted Mrs. Doan loudly, "has always had it in for poor Nellie, for no reason whatever. Her say-so doesn't mean a thing. But with my own eyes I saw your Willie run around the corner of the house just as I went to the door. Why was he running if he didn't throw the stone?"

There was a murmur of assent from the other women and the briefly rebellious Mrs. Dean subsided. One or two ladies near her heard her mutter to herself, "Just the same Nellie…" But the revolt had been quelled and the shrill-voiced 'Almira Doan was once more firmly in control of the Sunshine Club.

Silently Alice Blake swept up the bits of window glass and carried them into the kitchen. Noticing Jean on the back porch, she called to her, "Did you see which child threw the stone?"

"Yes, I saw her, but I don't know who she is." Jean pointed straight to the spot where Nellie Doan was viciously shaking a cowering little boy much smaller than herself. "The one there in the pink dress and no stockings."

Looking at Nellie and Willie Dean, Mrs. Blake's eyes became as hard as she could make them.

"To-morrow," she said distinctly, "to-morrow I shall have business with Mrs. Doan."

CHAPTER II

I

"Go on with your dessert, Mrs. H., I'll answer the phone." The elderly woman noticed with concern the glint of pain in Dr. Mallory's face.

"It's for me," he added.

"Thank you, doctor." Mrs. Hathaway smiled up at Mallory. "I'm not energetic to-night. I suppose you'd say that I'm still being affected by the increased ultra-violet in the summer sunshine."

She listened to the man's retreating footsteps. Something warned her of danger, and when Mallory returned to the table she saw how slowly he walked and how he fumbled with his napkin. Holding his fork motionless above his plate, he was looking at the nurse without seeing her.

With deepening concern Mrs. Hathaway ventured an inquiry. "What's happened, doctor? That appendix case in Blackberg isn't worse, is she?"

Mallory started.

"No, that is, not that I know of." After taking two or three mouthfuls he rose, pushed back his chair, and said, "If you'll excuse me, Mrs. H. . . ." The nurse heard him go across the hall into his private office and close the door. Something about that sound made her more apprehensive than ever.

While the maid cleared the table, Mrs. Hathaway sat drinking a third cup of coffee, and pondering. After nineteen years of almost daily association, she knew Mallory. Ever since that summer when they had first worked in the old hospital over the drug store, she had shared all his struggles and defeats as well as his few triumphs. She had helped him save money, had watched him borrow over and over, had finally seen The Haven materialize. She loved that rambling, dark red brick building with its wide porch and outlook over river and mountains just as Mallory loved it; her life was in it just as his was.

But, proud as he was of the hospital, Mallory was never satisfied with it. There were always better beds to buy, or an improved hydraulic operating table, or shadowless lights for the surgery, or new X-ray equipment, or more apparatus for the shining wide-shelved laboratory. Although it had required dogged persistence to gather the money for interest and salaries, Mallory always paid his employees well and gave his nurses good quarters. He had once said to Mrs. Hathaway, "I wouldn't put the guinea pigs and rabbits in a dump like I lived in when I was an interne."

All these years the nurse had watched his professional skill growing. Occasionally she visited large hospitals in Pacific City or San Francisco or Chicago, and now and then some visiting doctor came to Glenwood in consultation or operated in The Haven. But, to her mind, Mallory lost nothing by these comparisons. She treasured the little list of articles he had published in medical journals since 1917, and whenever a new one appeared she mailed reprints of it to his professional acquaintances.

None of the four young men who had been Mallory's assistants had she thought of half his caliber. All of them, dismayed by the long hours and hard work of country practice and the meager collections, had moved away; whenever at long intervals Mrs. Hathaway heard of some one from the Silticoos going down to Candon Bay to consult either of the two who had located there, she sniffed. Undoubtedly there would always be people who were more impressed by sleekness and pretense than by honest ability, and probably Burton would always be able to divert certain patients to his commission-paying patrons, Bentley and Kronheit. But long ago the Candon Bay doctors had ceased to be a menace to Mallory's practice.

Now and then he read to her extracts from the occasional letters he received from Norman Reilly. Reilly had served in the British Medical Corps in France and Mesopotamia; he had had influenza in 1918 and dysentery and malaria before that, and he had stopped a rifle bullet and contracted a permanent limp. Since the War he had traveled about, dabbling with anilin dyes in Germany, studying miners' consumption and hunting elephants in Africa, and working in a leper hospital in the Malay peninsula. Recently he seemed to have a genuine interest in the new treatment of leprosy and had published several excellent articles about it. His letters, which Mallory seemed to enjoy hugely, were brilliant cynical commentaries on events and personages in medical research and public affairs.

To-night Mrs. Hathaway's mind kept reverting to Reilly. In his last letter he had said he might return to the United States "just to see what the place is like after being away for seventeen years." She wondered if he would come to Glenwood to visit Mallory and found herself hoping that he would. She was sure something had happened, she felt the nagging of a premonition of trouble.

When the clock struck seven she roused herself and went to her own small office, where every evening she spent an hour scrutinizing the patients' charts for significant changes. She had grown a little stouter and her hair was almost white, but her eyes still looked upon a world of foolish people with the tolerance bred of thirty years' nursing them.

II

Precisely at 7:15 a small man with smooth iron-gray hair and dark eyes stepped into the lobby of The Haven.

"Come in, Mr. Doan." Mallory's voice contained an overtone like the thin-drawn high notes of a violin. "Sit down," he went on, leading the way into his consultation room. He pushed a half-empty box of cigars toward the banker. "Won't you smoke?"

Doan glanced about uneasily, then thoughtfully selected a cigar.

"Thank you, doctor. I will smoke this evening, though I seldom use tobacco any more. It is so objectionable to my wife." He cast another furtive glance around the room, seeing which Mallory had an impulse to say that no one at The Haven would report him to Almira.

Even under the influence of the excellent cigar, Doan seemed uncomfortable; he cleared his throat and blew his nose on the neatly folded handkerchief he drew from his breast pocket. At last with manifest embarrassment he said, "Dr. Mallory, this whole thing is very distasteful to me, very distasteful."

Mallory's hand, brushing the ashes off his cigar, was perfectly steady.

"Don't apologize, Doan. It isn't your fault. I've seen this thing coming for four or five years, and in a way I'm glad to have the suspense over."

Doan was a gentle soul, genuinely distressed by many of the things he had to do as a banker. Now he twisted his cigar between his fingers and looked at it rather than at Mallory.

"But it is partly my fault, doctor. I was wrong to encourage you in building this new hospital. That meant more debt. But, of course," he coughed nervously, "I didn't foresee the depression."

Mallory smiled wearily. "Nobody did, that is nobody whose business was finance." He paused a moment. "But hard times aren't at the bottom of my difficulties, Doan. There was a day not so many years ago when a man could practice medicine with a handful of drugs and a horse and buggy. Calomel and quinine and digitalis and opium were his stock in trade, and there was practically no surgery done. The doctor didn't collect much, but he didn't have many expenses. Now things are vastly different. A modern doctor must have a hospital with a surgery and a laboratory and an X-ray department, and he must have experts to run them. Otherwise he can't find out what's wrong with his patients or treat them properly. If he did his work as his predecessors did, he wouldn't have any practice at all. Well, I built The Haven because I needed it, and then I had to equip it. I've always had good nurses and good food for my patients. All these things cost money."

Mallory leaned forward and laid one hand on a stack of papers on his desk. His voice grew rough with feeling.

"I had to have these things, Doan. But nobody except you and me knows how much I'm in debt for them. The total staggers me. But I was just going over the figures before you came in and I can't find a dollar wasted or spent for a useless thing."

"Burton," began Doan.

"Oh, Burton." There was contempt in Mallory's words. "He's small potatoes. He's sent patients down to Bentley and Kronheit on a commission basis ever since I've been here. But he's done me little harm." The doctor, seeing signs of disagreement on Doan's face, spoke more earnestly. "I do plenty of work. I always have ever since the first two or three years down here. I put eighteen or twenty thousand dollars on my books every year, and it stays there. Even when times were good I couldn't collect it. I've done more than a hundred thousand dollars' worth of free work in this valley. Think of it, Doan. Over a hundred thousand dollars! People spent their money when they had it for things they wanted; they all knew I'd come when they sent for me whether they ever paid me or not. The human being dislikes being ill, and he hates to pay a doctor bill."

Mallory threw away his dead cigar and lighted a fresh one.

"You know the story of the last three years as well as I do. I haven't been collecting over ten per cent of my accounts. No one can get money out of a man who hasn't got any. But all the time I've had the hospital to maintain and supplies and apparatus to buy, and a cook and a maid and a laundress and two or three nurses to pay."

The doctor tilted back his desk chair and stared at the wall above the caller's head.

"Everything that's wrong with the practice of medicine is boiled down in that speech, Doan. It's nobody's fault personally that I'm bankrupt. It's the fault of this cock-eyed economic system we haven't got sense enough to change. Business is in the saddle and it's riding the professions. But when we try to conduct a profession as though it were a business, we make a fearful mess of things. If you read 'Arrowsmith' you'll conclude that the doctors are to blame—the ordinary fellows like me who practice medicine. Lewis believes the laboratory men are different, far superior to us, and that if all the doctors were only like Martin Arrowsmith things would be lovely.

"That's where Lewis shows his ignorance. He knows just about as much about it as the social workers who are always denouncing the mercenary medical profession; they put in their time setting up clinics and bossing the doctors whom they argue into working there for nothing. The whole trouble, Doan, is that there are some things that are not business enterprises and can't be run that way. I tell you it's damn near impossible these days to practice any profession, with the world throttled by finance."

He scratched a match noisily on the sole of his shoe. After a pause Doan looked at his stern face and spoke hesitantly.

"A year or so ago you said something to me about an estate in the middle west in which you had a share. Why don't you take that and go somewhere else?"

"No. When I make a mess of things I stay with it. Besides, all I got out of that is gone long ago."

"You mean you put it in here?"

Mallory nodded. "What else could I do? I used it for interest payments last February and hospital expenses—every cent of it."

Doan shook his head and fell into a sober silence. The corners of the room were dark, but here and there a bright book cover along the open shelves was still touched with a faint radiance. The consulting room has a pleasant informality that had opened many a burdened heart. Doan himself had often sat in its friendly atmosphere before, talking with Mallory, had often come to borrow books or listen to music. He had to force himself to pursue the disagreeable subject they were discussing.

"Last week I thought there was a possibility of extending the time on your notes, but now I find that this is impossible. Your creditors will give you ninety days to make whatever arrangement you can, but no more."

"Arrangement! What arrangement? I haven't a dollar outside The Haven. Perhaps my…creditors would like my underwear. It's all I've got that isn't plastered with notes and mortgages." Mallory laughed bitterly. "My God, Doan," he cried, springing up, "I hate money! All my life I've been struggling for just enough of it to live decently and do my work. And now the lack of it is ruining the thing I've sunk my whole life into! Suppose these people take over the hospital, what then? What can they do with it—a bunch of ignorant financiers who probably think a chiropractor can cure diphtheria by twisting the patient's neck! They'll hire some one to run it, put a commercial outfit, a hospital association racket in here. Here—in The Haven that I've tried to make what a hospital ought to be!"

Mallory's outburst stopped as abruptly as it began, but it touched the neat gray banker with the same emotion. Forgetting himself, he said in a trembling voice, "Dr. Mallory, I've got a little money of my own lying idle that might tide you over until…things pick up."

Then caution overtook him. "Of course, I wouldn't want anyone to know about it…It would have to be a…private affair between you and me. In my position, I couldn't…" His words tailed out lamely.

For one moment, Mallory's blue eyes shone, but only for a moment. Too vivid in his memory was the endless series of borrowings behind him. He shook his head.

"No. I couldn't let you do that, Doan. Neither as a gift nor as a loan."

In spite of himself Doan's face displayed relief. It would have been awkward: his wife always found out everything he did.

Engulfed by his own timidity and conservatism, he made a few inane remarks about local affairs and took his leave rubbing the small hand that still ached from Mallory's grip.

Alone once more Mallory sat with his arms stretched out on the desk before him, hands spread as though clinging to the smooth wood. He did not move, he did not smoke, he did not think. It was the most he could do to endure the passing minutes.

Those things that had so often comforted him in the past were useless now. The colorfully bound books—science, biography, economics, fiction—beckoned in vain; even Conrad had nothing that would avail in this moment. The orthophonic Victrola in the corner, flanked by its library of great recorded symphonies, had nothing to offer him: Beethoven and Bach and Greig and Sibelius seemed aliens now.

With his old mannerism he lifted his hands and stared at them. They were still thick and strong and skillful. Why had they failed him? Why had they long ago let Katherine slip away from him? Why had they led him into failure and bankruptcy? He dropped them back on the desk. Why?

He heard Mrs. Hathaway's firm step outside his room, but he did not speak and she walked on. At last quiet settled over The Haven, but for the man alone in his consulting room there was no peace.

Slowly his hands doubled into clenched fists with hard white knuckles. Before him he could see a savage prospect: no work to do, no money to live on, no place to go. All the labor of eighteen years wiped out as though he had never done it. All his plans and hopes for The Haven gone. He remembered the sunny day when had first brought Katherine to the old hospital, and the horror of the first winter he had spent there without her. He felt once more the burden of debt heaping itself higher and higher; he felt solitariness creeping over him—the solitariness that grows into hopelessness.

Doan had said ninety days. Ninety days. And after that—a blank. Youth was gone. He was only an atom of sensitive protoplasm caught between the millstones of chance and misfortune. There was no hope for him who had defied the impersonal inevitable, and no hope for a world full of selfish stupid human creatures.

"All is vanity and vexation of spirit." Suddenly Mallory was tired. Day and night for years he had driven himself mercilessly. Now he nust scourge his mind toward tomorrow and the ninety days of grace. But he was tired, desperately tired, in body and in heart. His head sagged down upon his arms.

Then without warning, something seized him and squeezed his breast pitilessly. Sharp pains stabbed through his chest. He could not breathe. His face turned ash-gray, drops of sweat gathered on his forehead and upper lip. He crouched motionless against his desk, afraid to move lest the hideous pain increase.

Somewhere in his brain he could hear a still, small voice. "As for man, his days are as grass; as a flower of the field so he flourisheth. . . . And the place thereof shall know it no more."

When at last the paroxysm passed he fell limply forward with his face in the hollow of his arms. "His days are as grass; as a flower of the field..."

III

At midnight the entry bell at The Haven rang violently. After its second summons Mallory groped his way out of the unlit office, but by the time he reached the waiting room he could see the night nurse hurrying to the door. Queerly dissociated from his surroundings he stood where he was. Distantly he heard a torrent of words in a vaguely familiar voice.

"I tell you I gotta see Dr. Mallory. He knows me, and he'll see me even if it is midnight and after. I gotta talk to him, right away. You go and tell him."

But the nurse insisted on taking the visitor to a room before she called the doctor.

Grateful for this respite, Mallory went back into his office and snapped on the lights. He took a monograph on "Vascular Diseases" from a shelf and sat down to read sections of it. For six months he had ignored the occasional sticking pains under his breast bone, but there was no mistaking the attack he had that evening. He was only a little past forty-six, but the coronary arteries that supplied blood to his heart muscle were older. A man really was as old as his coronaries. Behind him, as he had known for years, was a bad heredity of circulatory disease. The words on the pages of the book danced and blurred before his eyes, mocking him. No one, he whispered to himself, must know: no one must know.

Here Mrs. Hathaway presently found him. She looked at Mallory in his rumpled gray suit, then at the trays of ashes and cigar butts and the heaps of disorderly papers on the desk.

"You haven't been in bed to-night," she said sharply. "What's the matter?"

Mallory forced his stiff lips to smile.

"Oh, Mr. Doan was here…on business. And after that I went over a lot of old papers and things. That's all…But what about Sairy? When did she get back to Glenwood?"

The nurse's face became nearly as grim as was possible in so kindly a woman.

"Sairy is pregnant. Six months along, she says. She came home on the afternoon train and, when they found out what was wrong with her, her mother and sister-in-law kicked her out of the house. She's been up in the brush on the hill ever since. I put her in Room 17 for the time being."

"So there's another Juanita on the way."

"Yes, and not the first time either. From what she tells me, Sairy must have had several abortions before this, but this time she couldn't afford one. She's tried to do something to herself, I think, but hasn't succeeded yet."

"Well, we'll just have to do what we can to stave off the next Juanita, don't you think, Mrs. H?"

"If you ask me what I think, it's a crime to let that woman bring children into the world. But what does she care when she can come here knowing that you will take care of her when no one else will—and the baby too? To tell the truth, I came near showing her the door to-night. What right has she to impose on you? And of course she hasn't a cent."

Mallory laughed without making a sound.

"Certainly not. Sairy never has any money. We're alike that way, Sairy and I."

Then, seeing the nurse stare at him, he straightened his contorted mouth and said, "Leave her in 17, Mrs. H. I'll have to look after her."

Mrs. Hathaway's face filled with consternation. What had happened to him? What had Doan said? Was it something about The Haven? Here, this hard-bitten man who laughed soundlessly; down the hall, the cowering babbling Sairy. Hearing a shriek from Room 17, she ran out of the office.

Mallory followed her more slowly. He knew what he must do. He had always been a rebel against rules. He grinned savagely, thinking how Bentley and Kronheit would handle this situation. He could picture them in grave consultation, with a vast concern for Sairy's health, while they probed her for the information that would settle the matter. No money, no help; plenty of money, a fat fee split with McIntyre, their abortionist friend.

In the surgery door Mallory stopped to catch his breath. The heart attack had left him weak. He looked at the tiled floor and soft green walls. Green, that was the color for modern operating rooms. No more of the old stark white surgeries he had known as a student. Green—the color of new grass. "His days are as grass." It was an effort to drag his mind back into the present.

When approaching sunrise shone upon the mountain and scattered patches of translucent silver on the green roof of The Haven, Dr. Mallory and Mrs. Hathaway were in the small dressing room off the surgery, pulling off their rubber gloves and blood-spotted operating gowns.

"I look at it this way, Mrs. H. Sairy's not responsible for having been born what she is. But society is constantly pushing her into situations that demand a degree of self-control she's not capable of, and then it punishes her because she doesn't protect herself. I used to see the same thing when I was a student in the Rescue Home. Our whole sex code is shot through with injustice and stupidity. Compared to human beings, animals are gentle-folk."

Mallory thrust an arm into his shirt sleeve.

"And this isn't the end of Sairy's troubles. She's tough and she'll make an uneventful recovery, and probably be in the same fix again next summer. That's why I object to abortionists: they do a lot of good, but they never cut off the source of their business."

A few minutes later Mallory stood besides Sairy's bed, studying the thin sallow face. Pop-eyes, goiter, and all, it looked very like the face of the girl in the Rescue Home at Mannewaque, the girl whom Brantner—poor devil—had been so proud of saving for the sake of his record. The old burning sense of unfairness, the old pity swept into him. He could not allow Sairy to bring more illegitimate children into the world: he might not be there to take care of them. Juanita, for years in an institution for the feeble-minded, was still a living burden.

Sairy, restless, gagging, opened her eyes and saw him standing there.

"Oh, doc, don't let 'em run me outa here!" she shrieked. "Oh, don't let 'em git me! They'd kill me, and they said they would. It wasn't my fault this time, honest it wasn't. And I had to come back here because nobody else's ever been good to me like you, doc. Ma and Lulu ran me outa the house, they said I couldn't never come back again. Oh, you won't let anybody at me, will you, doc? Not now! Please! Not now!" The wail ended in a crescendo of abject terror.

Mallory bent down and seized her thrashing hands.

"Hush, Sairy. You'll wake the whole place. Nobody can get you here. We'll keep you, Mrs. H, and I, until you're well again—and longer, if you want to stay. Now be still. And try to go to sleep."

Sairy closed her hard, bony hand on Mallory's. He made no effort to loosen her hold until he saw on her thin unlovely face the softening brought alike by sleep and death.

CHAPTER III

I

Jean Stuart, in tweed skirt and brushed-wool sweater, watched with interest the clambake sponsored by the Glenwood Commercial Club. This was her first opportunity to see the Silticoos valley at play. The crowd on the beach was democracy at its best—or worst. Dirty urchins in torn shirts stood besides little girls in immaculate frocks; a handful of angry little boys wandered about in unaccustomed short trousers and clean blouses. The women were dressed in light silk or boucle costumes, the half-grown lads in dirty corduroys and open-necked shirts, and the men in overalls or rough second-best suits.

In the immediate foreground, near Jean and Alice, was a thin woman with a fat baby in her arms.

"How do you do, Mrs. Simmons, I'm glad to see you here."

"Oh, how'd do, Mrs. Blake. . . . I'm pleased to meet you, Miss Stuart. . . . Yes'm, it is nice to get away from home once in a while. Seems like it gets harder'n it used to be, what with them kids and all. Rob, you quit throwin' stones at them Brown kids! Come back here, Opal Birdie. You stay right here, both you, where I can see what you're doin'." Mrs. Simmons seized the dirty-faced, under-sized lad in front of her by the shoulder. "Speak to Mrs. Blake and the other lady. Opal Birdie, come here and shake hands with the ladies. You see," she explained to Jean, "they're twins and the boy is named for Dr. Mallory. They was one of his first pairs of twins on the river." Mrs. Simmons shifted the heavy baby from one arm to the other. "Kids are awful hard to manage as they get older," she sighed.

Jean looked at the twins who stood digging their bare feet into the warm sand. They were thin and pale, and their skins were soggy like the fish and boiled potatoes that formed their diet. Seeing them, she begain to realize how refractory is the raw material with which the new and better world we dream of must be built.

A plump, well-dressed girl whom Jean recognized as Nellie Doan went past. In spite of the simplicity of her frock, there was a sort of pink-and-white sensuousness about her. At a discreet distance a gangling boy whose trousers did not reach his ankles followed Nellie in the direction of the driftwood at the foot of the sandhills.

"Considerin' who she is and how she's been raised, her technique's pretty good," observed Henry Blanke, drily.

He and Dr. Mallory had just come up from mooring their launch on the waterfront. Blake was taller and thinner than Mallory and more darkly tanned. Jean thought he looked very handsome in the brown flannel suit Alice had persuaded him to wear. The girl smiled to herself. Alice and Henry, in Glenwood of all places, exhibited the married comradeship which she had begun to think a myth.

Mallory, rather to Jean's surprise, had appeared in striped gray trousers and a blue double-breasted coat with brass buttons. For the first time she realized that in his rugged fashion he was attractive looking; and it seemed to her that he held himself more erect than usual and talked with unusual animation to Alice.

Looking anxiously about her, Mrs. Doan hurried up to the little group.

"Have any of you seen Nellie? I can't find her anywhere." There was genuine anxiety in the termagant's face.

Blake drew down one side of his mouth and winked at Mallory.

"Why, now I seem to recollect seein' Nellie just a minute or two ago, goin' over into the driftwood."

"Was there…was there a boy…with her?"

"Well, there was a ganglin' kid following along behind her, if that's what you mean."

The banker's wife flushed and bit her lip.

"Junior Brown. I'll soon settle him!" Every red hair bristling, Almira Doan rushed away.

"That woman's a wonder," said Henry with conviction. "Proud as punch of Nellie's come-hither and scared stiff of what's goin' to happen one of these days."

A moment later Jean noticed a group of young people about a woman who limped slowly on up the beach with a cane.

"Why, there are the Painters," she exclaimed.

Mallory looked up and scowled.

"That woman's got no business here. If she were to fall down, that femur of hers would snap like a dead stick. I've had nothing but trouble with it from the start. Confound the woman!" He strode off to meet his patient.

"How many of them are here, Henry?" asked Alice.

"Seven with her to-day. Too bad Mussolini wasn't offerin' prizes when she and Tom were goin' good, a few years back. They had fourteen kids all told," Blake explained to Jean, "and twelve of 'em lived, believe it or not."

Watching, they saw an awkward girl rush up and clutch Mallory's arm.

"That's Minnie—the one you saw in the floatin' house the day you ran out of gas," said Henry.

More than a little surprised, Jean saw Mallory throw up his head in laughter, then settle Mrs. Painter on a log so that her lame leg was supported, and walk away down the beach with Minnie hanging to his arm, looking up into his face.

"Minnie," explained Alice," is a favorite with the doctor. Three or four years ago when she was still quite a child, she had appendicitis and had to be operated on. She liked The Haven so well she wouldn't go home: whenever her family came for her, she'd suddenly get ill again. Mrs. Hathaway curled her hair and gave her a dressing gown, and Minnie sat up in bed with a mirror, admiring herself for hours at a time. The girl really would be rather pretty if she were only fixed up."

This statement was accurate, but it did not convey half what Mrs. Hathaway and Dr. Mallory meant to Minnie Painter. Reared in such squalor that, at eleven, she had never had a pair of shoes or been farther from home than Southport, she had been brought to the hospital a forlorn wisp of girlhood, sick and in terror. She had expected harshness and torture; she met kindness and solicitude. After her operation she lay in bed, asking innumerable questions, reading the simple children's books Mrs. Hathaway found for her, looking at old files of the pictorial section of New York *Times*. She pored over Mrs. Hathaway's copies of "Alice in Wonderland" and "Through the Looking Glass," and laughed at the illustrations of a quaint British Alice. During the weeks she spent in The Haven, a smothered sense of beauty awoke in the child and thenceforth Mallory and Mrs. Hathaway were her gods.

"It's too bad Minnie can't be taken away from her family and sent to school somewhere," continued Mrs. Blake. "Dr. Mallory says she has a real talent for drawing."

Thoughtfully Jean looked after Minnie and the doctor.

"Perhaps I could give her a few drawing lessons," she began, but broke off when a tall, thin man with a narrow tongue of fair hair between high bare temples came up to them.

"How do you do, Mr. Blake. And Mrs. Blake. It is certainly a pleasure to see you both again."

"Well, well, Kronheit. I haven't seen you on the river for quite a while." Henry's observation was correct: since the depression Kronheit's business in the valley had fallen off badly. His terms—cash on the nail—were hard to meet.

"It's a wonderful day for the bake, isn't it?...Very pleased to meet you, Mrs. Stuart. I hope you're enjoying the West...I wonder if you good people could tell me where Dr. Mallory is. I wanted to speak to him a moment before I go, and I must leave in time to catch the afternoon train to Baypoint."

"Well, Dr. Mallory's down the beach a ways, Kronheit. But I don't reckon he cares whether you see him or not, to-day or any other time."

Jean had never seen Henry so angry or heard him speak so curtly.

"Now, Alice, don't you go begin scoldin' me for sawin' old Kronheit off at the pockets. He makes me madder'n hell, comin' up here to try and fix up his fences. He's always tryin' to hand Doc some kind of raw deal. I'd like to kick the seat of his pants up through the roof of his mouth!"

Mrs. Blake put a hand on her angry husband's arm.

"Henry, dear, I don't blame you a bit, and I'm glad you said it to him. But don't you think we'd better go and bring Dr. Mallory back? They're going to serve very soon now. I can hear Otto Schmidt bellowing over there by the trench."

"Yeah, I guess we'd better. When Minnie gets hold of a fellow she fair talks the arm off him. Besides, if I stay around here where I can see that bird, Kronheit, I might say something nasty in his hearing."

As they walked after Mallory and his companion they came upon Sairy Paine, clad in a red and white striped dress, in the midst of a knot of laughing boys and girls, all much younger than she. To one side of her head clung an absurd pancake hat, and her hair straggled over her face in mousy wisps. She was talking loudly to her audience, and they were plainly making sport of her. A chorus of shouts came to Jean's ears.

"Go on, Sairy! Go on and tell us some more. Gee, this is swell!"

"Sairy's makin' a fool of herself again," said Blake, and strode off toward the group.

He seized the pimply youth who was the ring-leader by the arm.

"Clear out, all of you! Don't let me catch you, any of you, pesterin' Sairy any more. Scram!"

Before Henry's angry face the group melted away. Blake looked down sternly at Sairy.

"What do you want to mix up with these kids for? They just torment you and make a fool out of you."

"Aw, lemme alone, can't you?" cried the woman sullenly, and flounced away down the beach.

II

On the previous day a trench, six feet long and four deep, had been dug on the lee side of a sandhill and in it a fire of hardwood built among large stones. On the morning of the bake the trench was opened, the coals raked out, and great sacks of razor back clams and potatoes dumped in on the hot rocks and covered with sand. On three sides of this pit was a wide, board counter; at intervals on it were huge stacks of sandwiches, enormous pots of coffee, great piles of enamel-ware cups, big bowls of sugar, brimming pitchers of thick cream, and bottles of catsup and Worcestershire.

In the center of the area thus enclosed Jean could see a great mound of sand with a sheet-iron door in one side of it. Behind the counter were Burton and Otto Schmidt in large dirty aprons. The cheerful German was yelling at the crowd.

"All ready, folks. Come and get it! Everybody come. Help yourselves to sandwiches and coffee. The plates is at the far end there. Pass 'em along the line down! ... Hey there, you kids! You don't got to crowd like that. Scatter out there. There's plenty grub for everybody. You don't got to act like pigs! Take it easy."

The red-faced Otto teetered on his creaking wood leg and brandished a huge towel.

"I open the pit now!" he shouted and threw back the sheet-iron door.

Out rushed a blast of hot air laden with savory odors. Schmidt grabbed a long pole with a hook on one end and began to rake out sacks of clams and potatoes. With a swiftness developed at his own soda fountain Burton ladled both on the plates thrust toward him from every foot of the counter. Then there fell upon the gathering the comparative silence of the feeding herd. Not until they had devoured the last mealy potato and succulent clam would the Silticoos folk have time to consider anything but food.

Unostentatiously Jean and Mallory strolled with their plates and cups toward the driftwood piled along the foot of the sandhills.

"This is such fun!" cried the girl, gesturing toward the crowd with a hand that held a sandwich. "I get a lot of fun from seeing things like that. The mob, the beach, the surf—it's all so picturesque.

Mallory's blue eyes met her gray ones thoughtfully. He thought he had never seen more interesting eyes. And her hair was beautiful—a nimbus of red-gold above her face,

"Yes, I suppose it is," he answered. "But of course we're so used to it that it doesn't strike us as it does you. It's always the newcomer who finds the romantic."

"But all life is romantic. Not sentimental, I don't mean that. But what is romance, if it isn't being born and living and dying?"

"I wonder. I see a lot of being born and living and dying, Miss Stuart. It isn't often romantic. It's much more likely to be sordid or stupid or just meaningless."

In the man's eyes flickered an interest that belied his quiet manner. It had been a long time since he had talked about such things with a young woman. But he had felt surprisingly well and strong to-day. For six weeks he had not had a single stabbing pain in his chest. "It was probably a false angina brought on by worry," he decided. At any rate there was relief in knowing that the worst had happened; having touched financial bottom, he need struggle no longer.

He knew that it was a pleasure to be near Jean. When he was with her some of his forty-six years seemed to slip away. He was even grateful that he was gray and not bald. Since it was impossible to be young again, it was nice to talk to a young woman.

"I'm sure, Dr. Mallory, that it isn't only on the Silticoos that life is often sordid and stupid. Stupidity was still common in Chicago when I left there, in spite of the Century of Progress. When I went to the Fair I wondered which way the progress had been. But still, even though we grant that most people are ignorant and stupid, human life has a meaning, is worth something, isn't it?"

"That's what I don't know, Miss Stuart. I used to assume that life in itself had a certain dignity and desirability. But I'm beginning to doubt it. How can you prove that my doubts aren't right?"

Jean glanced at Mallory's profile as he sat facing the ocean, and half turned away from her. She got an impression of sensitiveness and capacity for suffering which she had missed before. When she looked down at his brown hands she felt again a sense of sureness and skill.

"I can't prove anything about life. I just know it, 'with my knower,' as the little girl said. But if I wasn't sure that human life has a meaning I couldn't go on living. You see, Dr. Mallory, I have faith in humanity—not for what it is or ever has been, but for what it may be some day." Jean smiled straight in the man's grave face. "And whether you admit it or not, you live by the same code. You wouldn't be a doctor if you didn't think human life worth saving. You'd never have built The Haven."

Mallory felt the glow of companionship between them. He leaned toward her, his eyes searching hers.

"That used to be my code too. But I've lost it. I just practice medicine now because I don't know how to do anything else."

"You may think you do, but you don't. I know that isn't true."

"Then tell me what you would do if you'd lost everything you'd worked for, if you lost it all when you were middle-aged because of something you couldn't help any more than you can help the color of your hair. If someone took away everything you'd lived for and smashed it before your eyes, left you barehanded in a world full of selfish people like those over there."

Jean felt his eyes boring into hers, demanding an honest answer, and she looked straight back at him.

"Dr. Mallory, I'd do—or at least I'd try to do—the very thing you'll do. I'd try again. I'd start over, go on. And I'd keep on trying as long as I lived. That's all there is to life—trying. If there is a God, he'll admire you for that. And if there is no God... well, you haven't squealed...That's what you'll do. You're too big a man to lose faith in life or go back on your creed."

Her voice rang out triumphantly, her cheeks flushed, her eyes shone with eagerness. And Mallory, staring hungrily at her vivid face, suddenly knew that Katherine's long dominance was over. He loved this girl beside him.

But square across the way stood his forty-six years, his bankruptcy, his failure. He had no right to love her, to love any woman now. Since he could not help caring for her, he must keep it to himself, say nothing. He shut his eyes lest they betray him. He had no right, no right. He must be fair to her. With a supreme effort he closed the long unused door in his heart that had been for a few moments half open, and deliberately shattered the spell that both felt hovering between them.

"You've entirely too high an opinion of me, Miss Stuart. I'm afraid that you have a complex about the noble country doctor. But...I've enjoyed talking with you. More than you know... Now if you'll let me have your dishes I'll return them. You see the crowd is scattering and Alice and Henry will think I've run off with you."

III

At half-past four when the tug of war, the sack races, and the horseshoe pitching contests were over, the gathering began to break up into small groups. Among the drift logs Sairy Paine talked volubly to a little knot of girls. Presently Nellie Doan worked her way to the edge of this cluster and called to her mother.

Mrs. Doan's fiery hand cleaved straight through the chattering gesticulating group. She hurled incisive questions at Sairy and demanded precise and definite answers. Under this cross-examination Sairy's face gradually became overspread with fear and before long she fled in tears from her inquisitor.

Immediately the group dispersed and militant Almira bore down upon her husband.

"Samuel, what have I always told you about that man Mallory? Haven't I always said he was dangerous? Perhaps you'll learn some day to respect my intuition. You've always stood up for him."

"But, my dear, I don't know what you're talking about," expostulated the banker with a worried frown.

"Well, I know, Samuel. And that's enough. Don't ever let me hear you say again that Mallory is a gentleman. I don't intend that any of our family shall ever go near him again. Nellie is too attractive to be thrown with unprincipled men."

"But, Almira, what in the world…"

Mrs. Doan disregarded her husband as though he had a fly.

"Sairy let it all out just now. She was in the family way when she came home this summer, but she went to The Haven and the doctor took the baby. Then afterwards he operated on her so she can't ever get that way again. Sairy says now she can do just as she wants without ever getting into trouble again. Why, Samuel, I'll be bound that Dr. Mallory's been doing this sort of thing for years. I can think of more than a few women on the river that I'm pretty sure he's done something like that for. And I never knew it!"

Samuel Doan coughed deprecatingly, he loathed this type of talk, but he feared his wife more.

"Perhaps," he said diffidently, "perhaps you misunderstood Sairy."

"Misunderstood!" snorted Mrs. Doan. "The kind of language she uses anybody would know what she meant—except maybe you. And now I understand a lot of things. I always wondered why he was good to Sairy and why he looked after Juanita and got her into the Home and everything. It was because Sairy had something on him, Samuel, don't you see? He was afraid she'd talk, tell what sort of things he did in that hospital of his.

Well, now she has talked. And at last we know what kind of a doctor he is."

Having thus rationalized her own frame of mind, Almira Doan hastened to spread this exciting bit of news among all the respectable women at the clambake who would listen to her.

CHAPTER IV

I

The hotel clerk looked admiringly at the gray-green tweeds of his guest. It was not often that he saw clothes like that in Baypoint.

"Room with bath, Mr. Reilly?"

"Shower," was the laconic answer.

"I'll take you up. The bell boy's gone out on an errand." The clerk picked up respectfully the two huge kitbags with their half-worn-off labels. "Probably I'd better put down a call for you in the morning, too. The train leaves at 8:20. . . . To your left, sir." Deftly, the young man unlocked a door and stood aside for his guest to precede him. "Will there be anything else? . . . Good night, sir."

Norman Reilly surveyed the room with interest. He had not expected to find in a lumber and fishing town like Baypoint, Oregon, a new Hotel Grande eight stories tall, with a lobby in black and silver, nor yet in his room an art modern bed without a footboard.

"I wish they'd furnish elastics with clips on the ends to put around a man's neck and hold up the covers. They're all the while sliding off, in these beds with no dashboards." He limped over to peep into the bathroom. "Nothing wrong in here but the poisonous lavender. The United States has certainly gone mad on colors."

He threw himself into an armchair and pulled from his pocket a thick letter written on the letterhead of The Haven and signed "Rachel Hathaway." A fortnite earlier, that letter had reached him in New York at the very moment when the superiority of American plumbing was beginning to pall on him and memories of the Malaysian leper colony were invading his consciousness. Reilly's eyes rested on those two words, "The Haven." He had always thought that a characteristic name for Bob to give his hospital. Then his face grew serious: only ninety days to start with, and part of that was gone. The problem of how to help his friend had occupied his mind all the way from New York to Baypoint.

Driving into town from California that evening he had soon learned that the "improved road" shown on his map between Candon Bay and the Silticoos was still in the stage of dreams. "Hell," said the garage attendant, "everybody got stung so bad on the big hotel that there ain't enough money on the Bay nowadays to build a cinder path to the backhouse, let alone a road to Glenwood."

"Well, I'm here," thought Reilly. "And now my job is to save that hospital of Bob's. But that won't be easy."

He got up to unpack his bags. It was over eighteen years since he had seen Mallory. It didn't seem that long, but in between were all Bob's years on the Silticoos and his own War service and post-war wanderings. It was a different world to-day than it had been when they were internes together. Balancing awkwardly while he removed his trousers, Reilly swore softly: that damned stiff knee of his would always remind him of the blasted War.

He wondered if Bob would be fat and gray. Mallory's dark brown hair would turn gray earlier than his own blonde head.

In their forties Reilly thought he would still have the advantage of a more youthful appearance. He admitted to himself that he was somewhat vain of his smooth brown face, his flat stomach, and the skin that was still taut under his chin.

Reilly stopped in the lobby on his way out, to ask the clerk where he could find a good restaurant.

"You don't happen to have any one here from Glenwood, do you?" he inquired as an after-thought. Baypoint was, after all, the metropolis of this section and Bob or Mrs. Hathaway might easily be in town for the evening.

"Nobody but Dr. Mallory. I guess he's down for the medical meeting to-night. D'you know him?"

All Reilly's nonchalance left him. "Is he in the house now?" he asked sharply.

"No, he went out quite a while ago. Do you want me to locate him? Or get a message to him?" The clerk had been trained to "serve with a smile."

"Oh, no. Don't bother. But if he should come back before I do…" Reilly hesitated. "Oh, let it go, old man. I'll be in before he is."

The clerk's respectful eyes followed Reilly's erect flat back to the entrance. "That fellow's a big shot from somewhere. I wonder how he happens to know Dr. Mallory."

After eating a club sandwich in leisurely fashion and having a glass of beer—it was nice to have American food again—Reilly strolled down Main Street, looking with surprise at the sophisticated shop windows. He reflected that he must have forgotten how successfully small towns can ape the city. Wandering on out of the business district, he came to the Outer Drive along the waterfront. He could see the dark water in the harbor, the vague bulk of mountains rising back of the bay, the lighted buoys that marked the ship channel. Here and there were lights on rapidly moving motor boats.

In spite of the snapping outboard motors and the automobiles that rushed past him on the Drive, he had a sense of underlying quiet. Even the sawmills along the wharves were dark and silent. He leaned on a railing above the sidewalk and let the soft cool sea breeze blow against his cheeks and hair. Reilly's whole existence had been cluttered with movement and adventure. No family, no relatives, no dependents, no sense of belonging anywhere. He sniffed the damp salty air. Over his head, dimly seen in the zone of light from a street lamp, a seagull wheeled and screamed in the autumn light.

"Poor old Gerty! She'd have liked seeing this. She was like me, always going some place, never staying there. Hell of a way for a woman to live! Maybe if I'd been different..."

Even Reilly was not immune to the melancholy of what might have been.

II

Dr. N. B. Warren, president of the Candon Bay County Medical Society, shuffled a stack of papers on the table before him and peered uneasily over his glasses at the members present.

"Is there any other new business before we proceed with the scientific program?"

In the rear of the room Robert Mallory coughed and a small group in front of the platform stirred slightly and glanced significantly at each other. But no one rose. Warren looked anxiously at a large man in the front row of chairs whose pompous air was enhanced by the broad black ribbon that dangled from his eyeglasses.

"Dr. Bentley, did you have something to bring before the society?"

Very slowly Bentley rose to his feet, addressed the chair, and turned toward the audience. Secure in his position as the leading surgeon of the Candon Bay district, he usually spoke fluently, but tonight he was less voluble than Mallory had expected.

"Mr. President, members of the society," Bentley brushed back his flowing gray forelock and began ponderously. "Some time ago the board of censors asked me to investigate certain rumors that had come to their ears and make a preliminary report at this meeting. I need hardly say to you gentlemen that I would gladly have avoided this disagreeable task"—he coughed genteelly to emphasize the next point—"but I am accustomed to do my duty toward my profession."

Mallory's blue eyes hardened and he muttered audibly, "Oh, yeah!"

"Order!" President Warren rapped the table with his gavel.

Bentley resumed.

"It has been rumored that one of our members has recently performed an illegal operation on a woman who is mentally unsound and that he, somewhat later, sterilized this patient without consultation or legal advice. Corroboration is difficult because the patient's testimony must be discounted by reason of her mental status and because there were no eyewitnesses to these operations except the physician and certain nurses in his employ."

Bentley pulled a large white handkerchief from his breast pocket and wiped his eye glasses carefully. "No one," he went on, "can over-estimate the problems that confront a practicing physician and it may be that, if this case had been brought to our attention before these operations were done, all of us would have seen eye-to-eye with our fellow member. But unfortunately this was not done. The physician in question has jeopardized his own standing in his community and the good name of our profession as well. In these dark days of widespread criticism by the lay public, it is very ill advised to arouse further antagonism toward medical men. It seems to me that, under the circumstances, this society dare not condone any member who brings down public disapproval upon himself and us."

Bentley's pale gray eyes swept the room and came to rest on Mallory, who was sitting motionless, staring straight at the speaker with silent contempt. The other thirty-five men in the audience watched Bentley closely. After a moment the ponderous surgeon sat down again with impressive dignity.

President Warren surveyed the rows of faces uneasily. The silence began to be oppressive. One man leaned over and whispered to Bentley, but that worthy shook his mane of gray hair decisively. The chairman gazed imploringly at the great man, but he did not stir. His attitude said plainly that it was someone else's turn to take up the attack. A small knot of Baypoint physicians put their heads together self-consciously, but none of them took the floor.

Finally Warren himself was forced to speak.

"I'm sure we all understand the delicate position Dr. Bentley is in," he said nervously. "It does his scruples credit to feel that he cannot carry the discussion farther at this time. But I am sure there are others here who have something to say about this matter."

Warren's eyes were restless and his voice shook a little. Mallory smiled grimly: the chairman knew he was the tool of stronger men who were using him for their own purposes and he was manifestly in terror lest they leave him holding the bag. In the thick silence that followed Warren's timid words, the noise of the match that Mallory scratched on the sole of his shoe was a startling sound.

Dr. Bentley turned an exasperated look at his junior partner and the tall, lanky Kronheit rose reluctantly.

"I feel that we all must agree heartily with what Dr. Bentley has said in his usual forceful way. Certainly procedures of the sort the doctor mentioned should be discussed by the society before action is taken." The smooth sanctimonious voice seemed to seek for words that would placate Bentley. "For myself, I can only say that abortion and sterilization have always seemed immoral: they help people escape the just consequences of their sins." Not for nothing had Kronheit been a Sunday school superintendent. He sat down among approving nods, and almost at once a short dark young man got up.

"Dr. Tucker," Warren acknowledged more cheerfully.

"Gentlemen, may I first express my full agreement with all that Dr. Bentley and Dr. Kronheit have said? But I wish to emphasize the fact that we have no personal animosity in this matter, only the deepest concern for the dignity of our profession and the public welfare. No doubt our colleague thought he was doing right, but the individual conscience, gentlemen, is a notoriously poor guide. It even appears that some Socialists and advocates of state medicine believe they are in the right.

Mr. President, I move that a committee of three be appointed to make a complete investigation of this matter and submit a written report to the society at its next regular meeting."

Bentley wagged his head at Tucker in approval. Warren looked expectantly for a second to the motion. But the doctors from the outlying communities looked blankly at each other wondering what all the to-do was about, and the self-conscious group of Baypoint physicians still hesitated.

Then came the thud of a chair pushed over and Mallory with the bitten-off stem of his pipe sticking out between his teeth strode toward the platform.

"Discussion is not yet in order. There is a motion before the house. Do I hear a second?"

Mallory pulled the stub of amber stem from his mouth and flung it on the floor.

"Dr. Mallory, you are out of order." Desperately Warren rapped with his gavel. "I must ask you to take your seat until the motion is opened for discussion."

But Mallory looked down contemptuously at the soft hand that held the gavel.

"Shut up, Warren! And put down that stick! I've got something to say and I don't care whether it's in order or not." He faced the audience. "And I don't care whether you like it or not," he went on.

Most of the Baypoint physicians looked at their feet, but the country doctors watched Mallory with excited approval. They always felt that they were too little regarded in the medical society, but here was a country doctor who was going to speak his mind.

"What these wind-bags didn't have the guts to tell you," said Mallory, thrusting his hands deep into his pockets, "I'll say in words that every one can understand. Some of you, I can see, don't know what the fuss is about."

He ran a hand over his shock of thick gray hair and turned his bitter blue eyes on Bentley and Kronheit.

"These fellows are talking about me. I'm the guilty man. A few weeks ago I did a prophylactic abortion in my hospital in

Glenwood, and a little later I sterilized this woman. Under the same circumstances I would do both operations again to-night. And furthermore I deny your right to condemn my action."

There was a rustle as men turned to look at one another.

"The patient is a feeble-minded individual whom I have known and attended professionally off and on for the last eighteen years. Her mother is an epileptic with marked mental deterioration. Her father drank himself to death in his late thirties. One brother who also had epilepsy died of tuberculosis in his teens, another half-witted brother supports his mother and wife, after a fashion, by fishing. The only living sister has six children, two of them already in the school for the feeble-minded.

"When I first met my patient she had an illegitimate child who was a hydrocephalic imbecile, and she did housework to support herself and the child. She was dirty and inefficient, but I employed her as a servant for over three years. During that time I managed to get her child into an institution. But eventually the mother became restless and insisted on leaving Glenwood.

"For the last fourteen years she has worked as a maid in various towns up and down the coast. From what she tells me she must have had four or five abortions during that period. Don't ask me how she escaped sterilization through venereal disease: I don't know. But this summer she was pregnant again and had no money to pay for another abortion."

The silence in the room was by this time almost palpable.

"One night last July she showed up at my hospital; I hadn't seen her for some fourteen years, mind you. But she had come home and her mother and sister-in-law had put her out of their house. She came to The Haven because she knew no other place to go. I aborted her that night. She had already started things herself, but I finished the job.

"If she had been sterilized when she was a girl none of these dangerous illegal operations would have been necessary. Since she still has some seven or eight years in the childbearing period, I decided to sterilize her as soon as her condition would permit. This I did. She cannot again inflict upon herself and society another illegitimate child who might easily be an imbecile like the first. Of course it wasn't legal, but when has legality had anything to do with justice? This woman is now and always has been incapable of protecting herself, and society has hitherto made no provision to help her."

Mallory wiped his flushed face with his handkerchief. Every eye in the room except Bentley's was fastened upon him.

"I knew this so-called investigation was going on. I knew Bentley had been snooping around Glenwood, and I knew my patient had talked. But I didn't care about those things, and I'll tell you why.

"I came to the Silticoos eighteen years ago last summer. It was my first practice. I'd studied medicine because I loved it. I was full of enthusiasm and ideals. I wanted to mean something in the life of that community. Of course I soon found out how ignorant and careless people are about everything relating to health, and how hard it was going to be to maintain a decent hospital and make a living. But, after all, what could a man justly expect of ignorant, uneducated people in an isolated valley like the Silticoos?

"The thing I found out that hurt was something else. I found that my profession had been turned into a business engaged in for hope of profit. I found that I must sell my services as a merchant sells boots and shoes. I found that I must give more attention to my collections than to my medical journals. I found that the most prominent doctors in this section of Oregon were not the ones who did the best work but those who blew their own horns the loudest. And that was not all I found out. Fee splitting…"

A ripple of excitement passed through the audience.

"Fee splitting, for instance. Dr. Bentley was the first to approach me. His framed oath as a member of the American College of Surgeons not to engage in this practice hung then and still hangs on his office wall. But that oath means nothing to him.

"Your president, Warren, who holds himself to be an orthopedic surgeon on the strength of a few weeks in a base hospital in France, also offered to split surgical fees with me. He is an excellent advertiser: his cousin who owns the Baypoint *Gazette* keeps up a steady ballyhoo about his great deeds for crippled children until you'd think the county was full of his ex-patients.

"Kronheit is another who offered to split fees with me. Then he and his partner went one better than that: they began paying a layman in Glenwood commissions to solicit patients for them."

Trembling with rage, Bentley struggled to his feet.

"Mr. President, I protest against these gratuitous insults! I demand…"

"Be still, Bentley," ordered Mallory roughly. "Sit down and keep quiet! For eighteen years I've been listening to you blathering about professional ethics. Now you're going to listen to me to-night. Sit down!"

Bentley collapsed into his chair.

"Twice Dr. Hamil has been president of this society. He didn't believe in germs when I first came down to this country and he never has been known to count his sponges. Once I had occasion to tell him privately that I had found one of these sponges in a patient when I re-operated her, and he said I was a liar and ordered me out of his office. His technique is so poor that his surgical cases all have a long tedious convalescence, but who has ever done anything about it?"

A fat old man with white side-whiskers jumped up.

"Don't go, Hamil. Wait and hear the rest get theirs. You're no worse than most of them." Mallory counted off on his fingers. "Cole and Tucker and Black and Moran have all cut figures I'd already quoted to patients simply to steal the work from me; they slashed their fees far below what they charged their Baypoint patients, and it must have hurt to do that. All this when I've always held my fees well below the society's adopted schedule.

"McIntyre over there in the corner has been your official abortionist for years. He has a fine house and he's a member of this society in good standing. I wouldn't care if he had ended those pregnancies that should have been ended, but his business has been murdering unborn children for good fees. His patients come mostly from the wealthier circles in Baypoint, and you men send them to him.

"Years ago, I had a patient who had undergone three major operations here, two by Bentley and Kronheit and the other by Hamil. Five minutes doing a white blood count told me that he had leukemia. Why, in God's name, didn't these surgeons take the trouble to do a blood count instead of operating blind? But they haven't learned their lesson yet, they still do the same sort of thing.

"Most of you have in your offices vibrators and ultra-violet lamps and X-ray machines and other gadgets you don't know anything about. A lot of them are useless and the rest you don't know how to use. No man has any business with apparatus he doesn't understand. All of us are pestered by the detail men sent out by the manufacturing drug firms to sell us their stuff and tell us how to treat our patients. These fellows recite a spiel they've learned by heart at the home office, and then we swallow it whole and use their nostrums on our cases. I call that quackery. There are as many quacks, gentlemen, inside the profession as there are outside."

All the pent-up bitterness of years rushed out in Mallory's words and flung itself at the listeners; not a man protested or moved to go.

"The trouble is that we've degraded medicine—all of us. We studied a profession and then we turned it into a business. We're motivated by the hope of profit; we all want to be rich, we all try to make money. Few of us get rich, that's true; but it's because we aren't shrewd enough—not because we don't try.

"It's all but impossible to practice a profession decently in a world dominated by money and the lovers of money. When a decent young chap, like Belknap over there, does come along, you scare him into line. The future of every doctor who locates in Baypoint is in the hands of a half dozen members of this society: they make him or break him. The young man with a wife and perhaps a family can't afford to defy them; his lack of income is the club that they use to beat him into line. I don't blame the young men for being what they are; they would have to be supermen to defy organized medicine to-day.

"Of course, there are men in Baypoint, in this room to-night, who are honest and fine, who love medicine and not the money they may get out of it. They take the curse off our profession and make it still the finest on earth. But they are in the minority and so they can't set the tone for doctors as a whole."

Mallory leaned forward with his hands on the desk against which President Warren was cowering.

"All this uproar about me is 'sound and fury, signifying nothing.' The big shots down here have never liked me: I wouldn't split fees with them; I did my own surgery; I built my own hospital. I wouldn't play the game their way. But now I'm bankrupt, I'm about to lose The Haven, I'll soon be leaving the Silticoos for good. So, with the true instinct of the sportsman, they jump on me now it's safer to kick a man when he's down!

"I think I did the right thing for that poor simple woman last summer. I'll always think so. Whether this society approves or does not approve means not a God damn thing to me!

"I brought to this meeting a letter addressed to your president and I request that its contents be incorporated in the minutes of this meeting." Mallory stuffed an envelope into the flaccid hands of the trembling chairman. "This letter is my resignation from the Candon Bay County Medical Society. For fear the secretary won't read it to you at the next meeting I'll tell you now why I am resigning. I resign because I'm ashamed of the policies of this society and of the standards of medical practice in this part of the state. The men who control medicine have defiled it by turning it into a business, and even a banker would be ashamed of their methods of conducting it as a business."

The man's eyes blazed with fresh blue fire.

"I shall never practice medicine again unless I can do it the way I was trained, unless I can give my time and energy to my work and not to squeezing a living out of my patients. I want the standards of our profession so high that few men can get into it, and then I want those few assured by society of food and housing and clothes and the apparatus for their work. Then and never until then can doctors practice medicine! If that be heresy or state medicine or communism, make the most of it!

"But I tell you there are thousands of men who feel as I do. There are men in this room who agree with me. To them I say—don't be afraid. Go on! You're—most of you—young and things may change during your lifetime. If you love your profession, clean it up! Throw out the stuffed shirts, like Bentley and Hamil and Tucker and Kronheit and their crowd! Stop the fee splitting and the hum-buggery and the commission paying. Run the incompetents out of medicine. You can do it—if you're willing to pay the price. But make no mistake, the price will be a big one!

"As for me, I defy you. I'm not afraid of any of you, or of all of you put together. If you want to do anything to me, go ahead. But here and now I charge again that the Candon Bay Medical Society of which I have been a member for nearly eighteen years has been betrayed by its leaders and turned into a charnel house full of dead men's bones!"

Mallory stared down with hard, fearless, blue eyes into the upturned faces of thirty-five men. Some were sullen, many were angry, a few were ashamed, and a handful were eager and inspired with hope. When he had looked at them all one by one, he stepped heavily down from the platform and went out.

He was like Samson, he told himself: he had pulled the temple down upon himself; he had denounced his profession—his mistress, medicine, whom he loved. But presently this depression gave place to exaltation. He had flung down a challenge, announced a purpose. Defiance lingered in his heart.

In the lobby of the Hotel Grande he threw himself down into a deep leather chair to smoke and think. Vaguely he was aware that a man came in and sat down near him, but he was too absorbed in his thoughts to change his position or look up. Only when his cigar had gone out and he heard a voice saying, "Have a fresh one instead of that stale butt? Are you ever going to learn to smoke a cigar properly, Bob?" did he raise his eyes and see that Norman Reilly was leaning toward him.

CHAPTER V

I

On a bright September Sunday, twelve days after Reilly's arrival, he and Mallory climbed the trail back of The Haven to a little clearing on the crest of the ridge where Mallory often went when he wished to be alone and out of reach of the telephone. Midway Norman called a halt and the two men sat down on a fallen log to rest.

Mallory had been up most of the night with two confinements. He was tired and climbing made him short of breath. Suddenly he felt that Reilly's shrewd diagnostic sense might fathom the cause of his breathlessness, and looked sharply at him; but Norman was apparently engrossed in shaking the dirt out of his oxfords. Reassured, Mallory relaxed again.

"Two confinements in one night even though they are in the hospital keep a fellow jumping. Obstetrics is hard work—almost as hard as having the babies—but I've always liked it. When I'm through with a case, I have something to show for it."

Reilly grunted.

"I don't know a damn thing about obstetrics, Bob. Soldiers and hard rock miners don't have babies, and the Malays had theirs without any help from me. . . . Shall we mosey on, old boy?"

Climbing slowly up the last switch-back, Mallory's memory harked back to the girl who had so nearly died of eclampsia years ago in the Rescue Home when he was still a student. He wondered if she were still alive. She would be thirty-five or six years old now, and her son about twenty. Old enough to be a soldier. Looking at Reilly limping ahead of him, Mallory winced: Norman had always carried himself so well before his knee was smashed. War. Ten million men wiped out between 1914 and 1918; it would take an army of mothers and doctors to get ready another ten million soldiers to be killed in the next war.

Breathing heavily, the two of them came out in the little clearing on the summit of the ridge. They could not see The Haven, but the houses at the foot of the hill, the river front, the stream itself, and the mountains beyond were spread before them like the pattern of a gameboard. The sea breeze tipped the tops of the firs toward the east. The autumn sun stood in a pale cloudless sky. Wind, earth, water, sun, and sky—all the elementals.

Mallory threw himself down on the warm ground. He liked to lie thus, face down, on the earth or stretched on his back on a log staring up into the emptiness of the sky, because everything irrelevant was swept out of him then. Once more he was the guardian of life against death. But he felt he had been a poor defender of life. He had tried to stand between his people and death, but he fought a losing battle: the youth who escaped the infections and accidents of early life met disaster in middle and later age. Perhaps the whole struggle was futile.

But Mallory would not admit that. He loved his people, he loved his valley, ugly and crude as it was. And he coveted an adequate protection of life in that valley. Man lived a puny creature—in an indifferent universe. The spark of life in him must be protected. What was that life? For the first time it seemed to Mallory he had an answer to that question.

He saw a great sea of primal energy and on its surface waves that were a part of it. Those waves were human beings, living things. Always running up on the beach and breaking, they were not destroyed, for the water that made them ran back across the sand into the great sea of which it had been a part and from which it had never been truly separated. The individual waves "as such" ended, but there was no end to life. No end. The important thing was not that some one had died, but that life marched on.

Bit by bit a sense of the oneness of life had come to Mallory. He and the earth and the sun and the wind were all one. The spark that was his individual existence glowed hotly to-day. From the ground into his heart came the conviction that he could not die, that after he had gone and his friends could see him no more, he would still be there—in the earth beneath them, in the wind and in the sunlight. The flame of life might flicker very low, but it could never perish.

For a long while Mallory lay there very still in the sunshine with closed eyes. He was thinking of the valley. The people in it were commonplace, dirty, ignorant, fickle. Probably they always would be. But, in spite of that, Glenwood was one of man's outposts in the universe and the life that was there must be sheltered until one day, grown to a mighty flame, it would burn away all pettiness and meanness. He was warm with a happiness he had not known for years because he was not going to be driven away from the valley.

When he opened his eyes, Reilly smiled at him.

"Been asleep, Bob?"

"No. Have you?"

Reilly shook his head.

"No. I've been sitting here thinking, believe it or not." He swung about and stretched his stiff leg out along the log on which he sat. "Thinking—about Gerty and me. I haven't told you, Bob, but…she was killed two years ago. In southern France. I'd got a bit fed up on the lepers and then my Mesopotamian dysentery flared up again, so I spent the autumn with her on the Mediterranean coast. The night I was to leave to go back to Asia, we had a motor accident and Gerty was killed."

The man fell silent for a little.

"It was queer about Gerty and me. We never thought we cared seriously for each other, but we couldn't stay apart. I've followed her thousands of miles and spent hundreds of hours standing off-stage waiting for her. And two years ago things seemed different. Age will tell in a dancer in spite of exercises and make-up. Gerty was a little older than I, though I never knew exactly how much. But there we were: she getting so she didn't draw her old audiences and me with my game leg and my dysentery. One day on the beach I seemed to realize that we belonged together.

"So I asked her to marry me. I expected her to laugh at me, but…she cried, Bob. I believe that, in our own fashion, we'd always loved each other. And so we agreed to get married after her next season. In the spring she'd retire from the stage and we'd find a villa somewhere along the Mediterranean and settle down. It was the next night that she was killed." Reilly cleared his throat hoarsely. "It's queer, but nothin's ever been quite the same since."

There was a long pause. Then Mallory said, "I know, Norman. I understand things like that." He felt for his bill fold and from it took a scrap of paper which he handed to his friend.

When Reilly had unfolded the worn bit of newsprint, he saw on it Katherine's face. Beside her in the picture stood a sturdy-looking boy about five years old. Underneath was a long caption.

"Mrs. Gerald Ellsworth Ramsay of San Francisco and New York, who with her husband and small son is visiting her parents, Mr. and Mrs. John Harper of 2267 Edgecliffe Terrace. Mrs. Ramsay is a well-known pianist and will be guest soloist at the symphony concert next Wednesday evening, when she will play the famous Brahms' Concerto in D minor with the orchestra. Mrs. Ramsay's friends will recall that she appeared here two years ago in concert with her husband, who is a composer and violinist of note. Many former acquaintances are entertaining for Mr. and Mrs. Ramsay during their stay in Pacific City."

Reilly looked long at the picture. It seemed to him that Katherine was unchanged; he contrasted her unmarred beauty with Robert Mallory's worn, tired face. He had always disliked Katherine and, now, suddenly, he hated her. But before he could utter the bitter words that came into his mind, Mallory began to talk.

"You lost the woman you loved, Norman. So did I. That's why I understand how you feel about Gerty. Nothing was ever quite the same after Katherine left me, either. For a long time she dominated my emotions, and when I first found that picture in the *Chronicle* I felt that she'd cheated me out of that boy. But since then I've come to understand that she could never have lived here as I've done: it was too crude, too primitive, and she was too civilized."

Mallory's hands, which had been clenched about one knee, relaxed; the color came back into the knuckles.

"The tragic part of it all, Norman, was that we loved each other. Don't shake your head. Katherine did love me, she still loved me when she went away. I was the first man to stir passion in her. She was the first woman I'd really loved. Instinct brought us together, we couldn't help ourselves.

"But I was a blind young fool. I took it for granted that she was an ordinary girl who'd be contented in a country town with a house and a man and a family. Even when she tried to tell me she wasn't like that, I still didn't understand that she was being torn in two between her love for me and her love for music. I wanted the conventional thing—a home and children. She wasn't the sort of woman I should have married. And, having married her, I should never have brought her to Glenwood. But I didn't know that then. I was a fool. I was passionately in love with her, and I expected her to give up everything she was used to and be absorbed in my life. I didn't see that her passion for music and her ambition were as irresistible as my passion for medicine.

"When she came down here she was alone a good deal of

the time while I was out on the river, and her love of music and ambition began to pull her away from me. She honestly meant to give up her own career when we were married, but she couldn't do it…not to be a country doctor's wife on the Silticoos. The break-up was inevitable…just as you'd told me it would be, Norman."

Mallory held out his hand for the clipping and put it away again in his bill fold.

"Katherine has had her career. She's made a success, not I. Once…when I was going through Chicago, I went to hear her. She played with the symphony there, too. . . . It was just as it used to be: the moment she put her hands on the piano she came alive with passion. I realized then that husbands and children weren't the big things in her life, and never could be. After that, even if I could have had her back, I wouldn't have wanted her; she never belonged here. And lately I've been more glad than ever. The sort of thing I've had to face about the hospital is better met alone."

He stood up and, pushing his hands deep into his coat pockets, looked out over the valley below them.

"I know—just as well as Katherine did—that these people are uncouth and selfish and fickle. I know their lives are sordid. I know that fishing and logging and rather primitive sexual experience are about all they see of life. I know the place is peppered with syphilis and illegitimate children. But there's one thing about these folks that has always appealed to me, Norman. Their courage. The men know that sooner or later they'll be crippled or killed in the woods or on the river, and the women know it too. But they don't squeal. When something happens, the ones that are left get up and go on. They're like Walt Whitman's animals.

They do not sweat and whine about their condition,
They do not lie awake in the dark and weep for their sins.

And I admire them for it."

Reilly was beginning to see how much Mallory had changed.

As medical student and interne, he had stood out from his fellows by reason of his ability, his obstinate determination to master his profession, and his stubborn pursuit of his own ends. Reilly smiled a bit wistfully at the memory of Mallory's disdain for social life and the niceties of existence, his pity for the defeated and dispossessed, his attempts to appreciate Bach. There had been in him then the making of a great man, but only the making. Crude, unformed, he had been driven by emotions he made little effort to understand or control.

But he had changed. Suffering and hard work and loneliness had done their work—they and something else. Passion Mallory still had, but now he was master of it. Reilly saw that, without that passion, without the egoism and disregard of the cost to himself and every one else, Mallory could never have withstood the valley or built The Haven. He himself could not have done it, for he was too much dominated by reason and his judgment would have overcome his emotional drive. Only to Mallory had the valley seemed worth sacrificing everything. And yet, in that sacrifice, he had made of himself a tolerant, cultured, understanding man.

His library was proof that he had well used his sleepless nights and scanty leisure. Literature and philosophy had kept him out of a professional rut; his critical appraisal of medical practice had led him to social science and economics. On his book shelves in the consultation room at The Haven, Conrad and Samuel Butler and Joyce stood beside Sinclair Lewis and Stuart Chase and Veblen and Briffault, Hemingway and Selma Lagerlöf and Mann and Nexø and Wassermann and Remarque and Hamsun; Carl Sandburg and the Imagists jostled Walt Whitman and Edna St. Vincent Millay.

Reilly had looked with approval at Mallory's collection of orthophonic records and listened to many of them: Beethoven's "Eroica," "Finlandia," Grieg, Bach, Brahms, Chopin, César Franck. "I've learned to listen for the instruments I like best," explained Mallory. "Of course I've always loved the strings, but there are the French horns too. When I hear them, I feel like an old hunting dog who sees his master getting out the guns.

And the oboes. It always seems to me when they pipe up that they must have a joke on the whole world that they can't keep to themselves any longer."

The more he watched Mallory the surer Reilly was that he belonged in the valley, that something beautiful would be destroyed if he were forced to leave. Reilly had not expected The Haven to be what it was; he had had a mental picture of small town hospitals as they had been when he was a student, of the Rescue Home, and the police Emergency. All the more remarkable, therefore, seemed The Haven with its broad halls, its laboratory, its X-ray department, its modern surgery, its excellent beds, its expert nurses, and its good food. It was a projection of the man who had conceived it, and Reilly smiled triumphantly at the thought that he had saved it for Mallory.

"I tell you, Bob," he had said with all the persuasiveness he could muster, "it would be a crime to let this place fall into the hands of a commercial outfit. I'm sick of jazzing around anyhow, and I'd like nothing better than to settle down here in Glenwood with you and use part of the fortune my grandfather made in an experiment with community medicine. What good has my money ever been to any one? Except for my leprosy work I've never done anything to justify my existence. You've got a fine plant to start with and, since the medical society decided not to accept your resignation, you've still got an established professional reputation. Surely you can't object to my furnishing the capital we need to get started."

Characteristically Mallory had asked for a week to think, and at the end of that time had said he would do as Reilly suggested.

"Only you'll have to go slow, let me figure things out before I jump. I see plenty of things that are wrong, but I'm not always sure that the obvious remedy is the best one. I guess I'm a conservative radical. Anyhow I want to hang on to the old ideals of our profession, use them for guides. I'm not afraid of state medicine, but I'm not sure it's the solution for our troubles either. I'd like to see how a community hospital would work in the country and I'm willing to try it out. But let's keep our feet on the ground, Norman. Let's not throw away our old galluses until we see how dependable the new-fangled 'braces' are going to be."

Following which sensible decision the two men had drunk to the new firm of Mallory and Reilly in some excellent pre-war whisky that Mrs. Hathaway had produced from a linen closet.

II

At five o'clock these three went down to the Blakes for Sunday evening supper and, when the meal was over, settled in front of the fireplace in Alice's pleasant living room.

Jean sat in the corner of the settee opposite Reilly, smoking a cigarette. He found something that charmed him in her red-gold hair, her wide gray eyes and chiseled features. She was not beautiful, not even pretty, but she attracted him. Norman smiled wryly as he recalled once overhearing an acquaintance say, "Oh, Reilly always likes 'em long and snaky." He admitted to himself that he was on the verge of falling in love with this tall, copper-haired, husky-voiced young woman, but the irony of the situation was not lost on him. As young men, he and Mallory had quarreled over Katherine, and now in middle age they both loved Jean. Not that Reilly intended anything to come of his emotions; on the contrary he intended to do what he could to fan into love the admiration for Mallory he saw in Jean's face. For himself he could not complain. There had always been women in his life, no doubt there always would be. Not like Jean Stuart of course, but as good as he deserved. Then he smiled briefly, sardonically, to himself, for it had just occurred to him that Gerty, looking from her niche in the world beyond, must be amused at his dilemma.

Mallory stood on the hearth, rocking back and forth on his heels and toes, smoking a pipe, and watching Jean. As well as though he had spoken, Reilly knew he loved the girl. Suddenly Norman shook himself and leaned forward.

"Why don't you tell the folks what we're planning about The Haven, Bob?"

Reilly saw the expectancy that flashed into Mrs. Hathaway's

eyes, the quick interest in Mrs. Blake's face, the swift turning of Jean's gaze toward Mallory; and his own pulse quickened as though he had once more embarked upon adventure.

Puffing his pipe alight, Mallory began, "We're going to experiment with community medicine. Going to turn The Haven into a community hospital and operate it on the insurance principle. Every one pays so much a year, depending on the size of his family and his age, and that entitles him to all the hospital care and medical attention he needs without further payment. We'll get our living and small salaries out of it, and any surplus will be kept for times of need in the future."

Alice laid down her sewing, Mrs. Hathaway hitched her chair forward into the circle of light from the floor lamp, Jean sat bolt upright, and Henry leaned forward in his chair until the firelight caught his profile with its bold forehead and jutting nose. They were all silent and watchful.

While Mallory talked Reilly kept his eyes on Mrs. Hathaway. He saw her straighten up. He knew she was thinking of the young Mallory, shock-headed, wide-shouldered, in a crumbled, stained white uniform, working in the police Emergency; of the scarcely older Mallory plunging his youth and enthusiasm into the Glenwood Hospital as he had found it eighteen years before. Clearly she meant to be a part of the new "Haven." Reilly smiled; after all she was only about fifty-five and had a good fifteen years ahead of her still.

Then he heard Mallory saying something he had not heard from him before.

"It seems to me that science has broken down these last years because it hasn't been a focus for modern life. Back in the Middle Ages the world centered around the good life and heaven after death. Then, as time went on, that order broke down.

"Some people focused their lives on imperialism and nationalism and they finally got us into the World War and its aftermath—economic war. And some people centered their lives on business and they eventually got us into the rotten social system that we're always trying to patch up for another generation or two. There are a few who live for art, and there've been men whose great ideal was political freedom. But there can't be any freedom when ninety-five per cent of the people in the world are slaves to the five per cent that own the world.

"And then somebody pointed to science as the great hope. Scientific books came to be popular; the air was full of 'popularizing' knowledge. Everybody began to talk about relativity and Jeans' theories of the universe. But most men saw in science nothing but a way to put nitrogen into the soil or make it into ammunition, or to grow two potatoes instead of one with the same amount of human labor. The machine began to crowd out the man.

"Only a handful of people ever saw science as a way of life— just a handful, like the Curies and Rutherford and Einstein and a few doctors. And that was what we needed: not more ways to make a living, but a way to live, a pattern of life that would be something more than interwoven sex and greed."

Listening, Reilly felt that Mallory was a dreamer, a crusader, who had seen life realistically and seen it whole, and therefore revolted with all the emotional strength of his character against the stupidity of modern civilization.

"You see," Mallory went on, "my patients are part of me and more important than the rest of me. Something of them comes into me, and something goes from me into them. That's why I fight for them. And that's why medicine will always be the finest profession in the world!"

Reilly looked at the group around the fireplace: Alice Blake with her sewing neglected in her lap; Rachel Hathaway looking as though she had just heard a call to arms; Henry, a plug of tobacco forgotten in one hand; and Jean perched in a corner of the settee, her eyes damp and shining. He was long to remember that picture.

CHAPTER VI

I

Around the bend in the river above Glenwood came Mallory's big white launch at top speed. In the cabin on a cot lay Tom Painter, his big chest heaving spasmodically and the breath bubbling in his lungs. The lobes of his ears were purple. His wife was whimpering beside him.

The doctor stepped out and closed the cabin door behind him. That woman sniffling in there would convince her husband, if he had a lucid moment, that he was going to die. But what could be done about it? Mallory had never found a way to keep a frightened woman quiet.

He pulled out his pipe and automatically packed the bowl with tobacco. He was worried. Early in October people had begun to fall ill with aching backs and fever, the symptoms of an ordinary grippe. But when rainy weather set in, there was a change for the worse, and ten days ago there were two deaths twenty-four hours apart. Now The Haven was nearly full and no less than twenty others scattered up and down the river were ill. Tom Painter had pneumonia and, the way things looked, he wouldn't last long. His account with The Haven, eighteen years old and including few credit items, would soon be closed.

All day Mallory had been rushing about in the launch, taking temperatures, peering down people's throats, listening to their breathing, doing white blood cell counts, ordering them to bed. He did not like what he had seen: these patients were prostrated. And he wished that Reilly were in Glenwood to help him instead of being in Chicago studying health insurance systems.

It was forty miles to Baypoint to another doctor. The Haven was the only hospital in a territory seventy miles long from north to south and sixty miles wide from east to west. Mrs. Hathaway vowed she could squeeze fifty people into it, and she had already put beds in the corridors and turned the larger rooms into small wards. Two more nurses had come from Pacific City to help her.

"Tom Painter's coming up the hill," Mallory told his head nurse when he reached The Haven. "He's got pneumonia and he's a damned sick man. Put him on influenza routine and keep an eye on him yourself. And muzzle his wife! . . . No, she's not sick; just a little crazier than usual."

Struggling out of his dripping slicker, the doctor inquired, "How's everybody here? Any of them worse?"

"No." Mrs. Hathaway shook her head. "But the cook ran off. She left on the afternoon train, afraid she'd get the flu. It's lucky the patients are all on liquid diets." The sound of heavy feet on the porch interrupted her. "That must be the men with Mr. Painter."

Mallory looked after her, frowning, as she hurried away. It was one thing to be afraid, but to be craven and run away as the cook had done was another.

At the nurses' desk in the main corridor he leafed rapidly through the patients' charts. Pulse rates climbing, blood pressure falling, respiration faster and shallower. Nothing seemed to do any good—coal-tar products, cough mixtures, serum, pituitrin, adrenalin, caffein-sodium-benzoate. Even the cases he found early took the same course.

A nurse pushed Tom Painter past on a cart. The big man was fighting for his life and every breath he took was a triumph of the will to live. Mallory propped his elbows on the desk and closed his eyes. There were four nurses and himself—five of them in all—as a barrier between this disease and eighteen hundred people. Four women and himself.

II

It was just when he had finished the rounds of the house that Mallory heard in the lobby a jumble of words poured out in a familiar strident voice and, putting his head in the door, saw Sairy confronting Mrs. Hathaway.

"How are you, Sairy? Did you want to see me? . . . Let me take care of her, Mrs. H. I want you to get an oxygen tent over Painter as soon as you can."

Mrs. Hathaway looked from him to the puddle on the floor where Sairy had stood.

'That woman,' she thought, 'is an evil omen. She brings bad luck with her. I wish I'd got her out before the doctor saw her. Why couldn't she have died last summer like any normal woman would?' Then, horrified at the sincerity of that wish, she hurried toward Painter's room.

Mallory closed the door of his office so that Sairy's shrill voice might not disturb the patients. The woman sat far forward on a chair with water trickling from her straggling hair and dripping from her skirt in dirty rivulets. She fixed imploring eyes on the only person who had ever been uniformly kind to her. Illogically enough, at that moment there floated into Mallory's mind a picture of the night at the Fishermen's Ball when he had danced with her.

"Doc," she began hurriedly, "I come back up here. . . to stay. I been livin' down in that shack by the old skid-road and it's so far to walk that I'm kinda late gettin' here. But I heard this afternoon that the cook had run off. . . . So I come back. I ain't scared of the flu, not when you're here, doc. And I learnt a lot about cookin' since you et after me before. You'll leave me stay, won't you?"

Looking at the untidy figure before him, Mallory hesitated. He too thought of Sairy as a herald of misfortune. The woman grew panicky.

"Won't you leave me stay, doc? Down town they been tellin' me you'd never have anything more to do with me. They 'lowed you was sore at me for tellin' at the clambake what you done to me last summer. That ain't so, is it, doc?" Her voice rose on the last words. "Is it, doc?"

A sudden smile crossed Mallory's face.

"No, of course not, Sairy. Why should I be sore at you? Certainly you can stay here. I'm glad you've come. Got your things with you? . . . Well, I expect Mrs. H. can fix you up for the night."

Something in the way he said these commonplace words stirred the emotions that were always on the verge of turbulence in Sairy. Motionless and tense, she sat waiting on the edge of her chair until Mrs. Hathaway came for her.

After swallowing a pick-up supper in the diet-kitchen, Mallory went to his consulting room and sat down for the first rest he had had since morning. He tilted back his chair and picked up a copy of *The Living Age*. His hand hovered uncertainly over a box of cigars—the more he read the less sure he was whether smoking did one's arteries harm or not—but finally, with a little flattening of his lips, he dismissed the question and selected a panatella that was neither too firm nor too dry.

But he could not relax and presently threw down the magazine. His patients haunted him. He knew the history of the recurrent influenza epidemics that sweep over a state, a continent, the world. He felt that he was worse than useless, that neither drugs nor vaccines would prove of value. Only rest in bed and good nursing and a strong constitution did any good.

By this time it was dark, the rain was pouring down, and the wind was beginning to howl about the building. Suddenly he jerked up his head. What was that sound? With an incredible despondency surging through him Mallory strode to the window and listened. Was it death outside, riding the wind? The sound—wailing—came again. Then Mallory laughed harshly. It was only the creaking of the tree at the corner of the porch, rubbing against a post. He shrugged his shoulders. He had spared that tree because Mrs. Hathaway thought it beautiful, but if he were to have the jitters over the sounds it made—

Mrs. Hathaway tapped at the door and came in.

"Are you busy?" she asked. "I wanted to speak to you a moment. I understood you to say you were going to write new orders for Rob Simmons, but I can't find them on the chart. And we should order more oxygen. I thought it might be better to phone for it. It takes so much for these cases."

"How's Painter look since you got him under the tent?"

"His color's a little better, but…" the nurse hesitated.

"I know," nodded the doctor. "Not one chance in a hundred."

"Alice came up this afternoon," continued Mrs. Hathaway. "She and Miss Stuart want to help."

Mallory started. "Miss Stuart isn't a nurse," he exclaimed. "We don't want her up here."

"That's what I told her. But Alice is splendid in the sickroom, doctor, and if things get worse I'd like…"

She was interrupted by a distant crash. Mallory listened a moment.

"It's only Sairy." A half-smile flickered over his mouth. "She hasn't been here an hour but she's busy already. You'll have to add new china to the hospital budget, Mrs. H."

The office door was pushed suddenly open and a white-faced nurse cried, "Doctor, can you come? Mr. Painter…"

Both Mrs. Hathaway and Mallory ran out after her.

From Tom Painter's room came the sounds of hurried footsteps, rapid movements, low-voiced orders, and clinking instruments; then a smothered, choking cry, then silence. In the corridor outside the door Mrs. Painter began to sob hysterically. When Mallory looked at her he remembered the shriek in the wind.

III

Under the lowering autumn clouds on the Silticoos a battle began in which five white-clad, pale-faced women and one tired man stood as the only defense against disease. Compared with this, ordinary life faded into insignificance.

Rachel Hathaway and Alice Blake and the three other nurses worked harder and harder. Every day their faces seemed thinner and bluer under the eyes. With an aching throat Mallory one evening watched two of them sponging a delirious fever-ridden lad. They were disheveled and their uniforms were wrinkled and stained, but to him they represented the eternal mother defending the life she had brought into the world. They stood at the gates of the future as some woman has once stood for every man at the gates of the present, to bestow the gift of life.

Long before, Mrs. Blake had come to The Haven to stay. "My technique may be old-fashioned," she said, "but I know how to take care of sick people," and Mallory knew that she was right.

The same day Henry also came up the hill.

"Give me the keys to your boat, doc. I'll take care of your transportation from now on. I'll pull a man off the passenger run up-river and one or the other of us'll be on the job day and night. You're beginnin' already to look like something the wind's flattened out. And just forget about the money, doc. I want to do my share and there's nothin' else I know anything about."

But on one point Mallory was adamant.

"I won't have Miss Stuart up here, Henry. You tell her so, for me. She's not a nurse, she'd just be in the way. And we can't be bothered training her in the midst of this epidemic."

Fear had thus wrapped itself protectingly about Jean: her crinkly smile, her husky voice, her red-gold hair were precious to Mallory.

At these emphatic words Blake cocked a wise brown eye at the doctor.

'I guess I know what ails you,' he thought. 'And I ain't goin' to try to stop it. You might go a long way and do worse. In fact, you've already done worse—a damn sight worse—before. This

time you'll have better luck.' Something very like a chuckle
rumbled in Henry's throat, but abashed at levity in such serious
times he hastily turned it into a cough.

With a rush like a forest fire the epidemic swept over the
valley. There were new cases every day. Soon nearly half the
population was ill and panic seized those who were still well.
People who had always gone unquestioningly to their neighbors'
aid now shut themselves up in their houses and refused to stir
from them. The bachelor lumberjacks and fishermen tossed in
their tumbled bunks untended.

In the morning Mallory crept out of bed before daybreak,
made hasty rounds in the hospital, gulped down breakfast beside
Sairy's range in the kitchen, and went out on the river at six
o'clock. He made it a point of honor not to come in until he
had seen every patient, but he knew that his hurried calls and
the medicines he left behind were of small use.

"Good Lord, Henry," he burst out as they clumped down
the slippery plank from the floating house where Olaf Hansen
lay alone, "it's nursing these men need. But The Haven's full.
Somebody will have to die before there's room for Olaf, and
that'll be too late. He's lying there now in the same underwear
he wore the last day he met the train and he hasn't even had
his face washed. And nothing to eat but these cursed bouillon
cubes we fix for him. But when there are so many others sick
we can't stop to do more for Olaf."

"Have you tried to get more nurses again, doc?" asked Blake.

"Hell, yes." Mallory buttoned up his slicker and hunched
down in the cabin of the launch. "In Pacific City and every
other town on the coast. But the epidemic's everywhere and all
the nurses are working eighteen hours a day already."

Henry glanced now and then at the doctor's wet, shapeless
hat and finally he could contain himself no longer.

"God damn this flu to hell, anyhow!" he cried. "I used to
think anything that'd kill off some of the old-timers would be
a good thing for the Silticoos, but some of these folks that are
goin' out we can't spare. Like Olaf. Pretty soon it'll be dark in

that shack of his. And it's cold and damp. I hate like hell for Olaf to die all alone like this."

Blake spat a huge mouthful of tobacco juice through the open window beside him, the very vehemence of the mannerism proving the depth of his distress.

Mallory's face was drawn, his eyes were feverish with fatigue, they seemed to have receded far into his head; but there was still the old rock-like staunchness in his voice.

"I know how you feel, Henry. It's hell to go into these shacks and find the fellows stiff in their bunks. But we all have to go out alone—when the time comes. Into something we don't understand. Everybody's born alone, and everybody has to die alone."

Blake shivered a little.

"We're almost to Sidney's floatin' house, doc," he said after a few minutes.

Wearily Mallory picked up his bag.

When they pushed open the door of the shack, chill stale air that had in it a terrifying effluvium rushed out upon them. Slowly they approached the bunk. There, under a soiled gray blanket, lay Clifford Sidney with his head drawn back and his lips curled off his teeth as though to catch the last possible breath. His face was grayer than the blanket and his body was stiff. Mallory felt his own skin break into gooseflesh.

"Yesterday," he said slowly, "I promised Sidney to send what money he had to his family instead of burying him with it. There wasn't much. Only fifty dollars, he said."

"That's just as well, I guess," answered Henry. "They told me on the dock yesterday that old man Simpson wasn't goin' to handle any more bodies except for cash. The old man may be an amateur undertaker, but he ain't an amateur at collectin'." Blake's tone was grim. "Sidney was a friend of mine, doc, and I don't aim for him to be stuck in the ground improper. I'll make him a box myself—a good one. Give me that money and I'll put a little with it and see to sendin' it off."

Together he and Mallory unbent the dead man's stiff knees

and unwound the rigid fingers that clutched strands of sandy hair; then they wrapped Sidney's body in a blanket and carried it out to the launch.

All day whenever he looked back at the long gray mound in the stern of the boat, Henry prickled with horror. "Of course I know, doc, that it's more sensible to take him along than to have to go back after him, but damned if I like haulin' my friends around like this, dead."

When they docked in Glenwood that evening they first of all bore the body into Henry's workshop on the waterfront. It was one o'clock in the morning when Blake closed the lid of Sidney's home-made coffin upon him.

Day and night became almost indistinguishable for Mallory. Both were filled with people who rattled horribly when they strove to suck air into their water-logged lungs, who turned ash-blue and clutched in terror for some human presence as death drew near. Many of them he found with sardonic grins on their twisted lips as though they were mocking their finished lives. Even when he was in bed he could still hear their last hissing breaths, feel their last feeble heart beats, watch the twitching muscles that tried to carry on after the brain was dead.

Dead man after dead man he and Blake discovered who left neither money nor family address, whom no one could tell where to send. These they sewed into their blankets with twine and sack needle and, on the ebb tide, slipped into the river.

For all his precautions Simpson sickened and died and no one would take his place. It became impossible to get caskets from the supply houses and the dead went to their graves in rough fir boxes past the closed doors of the church. Fog and rain dripped down on scores of fresh-made mounds along the Silticoos.

In November Burton was taken ill and a week later his wife took to her bed. After that Mallory taught Jean Stuart to fill capsules, fold powder papers, and bottle and label medicines. When he came off the river at night he went to the drug store to tell her what he would need for the next day. One night the girl saw him stumble across the floor mumbling, "Right foot, left foot, right foot, left," so weary that his walking reflexes were gone.

At The Haven Sairy did astonishing work. Up every morning before five, she cooked breakfast for Mallory and the nurses. All day she cleaned, and prepared liquid diets, and washed linen. At night when the doctor came in, she always had hot food waiting for him and, while he ate, she wrung out his soaked clothing and hung it behind the stove to dry. After that she prepared fruit and stirred up hot cake batter for his breakfast while he studied the patients' charts and wrote his new orders. Finally she carried a thermos bottle of hot chocolate into his room before he went to bed.

Life resolved itself into a grim routine. Wind and rain were incessant. Daily Mallory and Blake brought patients into town and found people dead in their beds; nightly they went on calls to the dying. The doctor's mind was a kaleidoscope of livid faces and river burials. Now and then he felt little stabbing pains in his chest, but when they passed he went on about his work without apprehension for himself.

IV

Late in November on a wild evening when a gale from the southwest blew rain through the air in blinding sheets, Mallory came in from a prolonged call at Doan's. Mrs. Hathaway met him in the lobby and took him into the dining room for hot coffee.

From his pocket the man pulled a bottle and poured whisky into the cup.

"I've taken to drink, Mrs. H." He propped an elbow on the table and gulped the mixture of whisky and hot coffee. "But somehow I've got to keep awake tonight. . . . What in the world would we do, you and I, without Sairy to feed us and make coffee?"

Mrs. Hathaway refilled his cup.

"I've changed my mind about Sairy. All day she cooks and cleans and washes. And half the night. I never saw anyone do so much work before. We couldn't manage without her."

Mallory drank his second cup before he answered the question in the nurse's eyes.

"Yes, Nellie's gone. I'm sorry for Doan, poor devil. That wife of his acts like a mad woman. I don't think she realizes that the girl is really dead." He pushed back his chair. "But the other village treasure is better, Mrs. H. I mean Wellington D. Burton."

It was the first time Mrs. Hathaway had heard a bitter note in his voice since the epidemic began. She looked closely at him and felt that his face was thinner and grayer than it had ever been before.

"Must you go down to the jetty to-night?" she asked. "Wouldn't it be safe to wait until morning? You're worn out yourself, doctor."

"Boloney, Mrs. H! Why, I'm not even tired this evening. Only one death to-day. It's you that needs a rest. You haven't been outside The Haven for weeks."

"But there are five of us here, and we can sleep a little at least every other night, while you…"

"Save your tears for them as wants 'em." Mallory grinned crookedly at the nurse. "No, I've got to go. Jake Whitney would never have sent for me if there hadn't been something wrong. Besides, I've been expecting his wife to go bad. She's pregnant, you know." Slowly the man pulled himself up off the chair. "Will you call Henry for me while I put on dry socks. And tell Miss Moore to put another box of pituitrin ampoules and some adrenalin in my bag."

That night the river was covered with whitecaps. Against the cabin windows of the launch the wind hurled the rain in shattering gusts and the water slid over the glass in blinding sheets. The staunch little boat pitched and rolled. Mallory sat with a lantern under the tails of his coat and when the warmth penetrated his chilled body he nodded drowsily.

"Doc," yelled Blake above the roar of the wind, "I can't make the far landin'. I can't get anywhere near it."

Instantly Mallory was awake and alert.

"Don't take any chances, Henry. We mustn't smash up down here to-night. Go back to the east end. I'll walk from there."

For a little longer the launch rolled wildly in the swells, but Blake soon brought it into comparative shelter beside a small float at the landward extremity of the jetty.

Mallory buttoned up his slicker and tightened the chin strap of his hat.

"You better anchor around here, in the lee, and take a nap, Henry. I probably won't get away from Jake's before morning, and a few hours' sleep would do you good."

"Oh, yeah! Well, no more damn good than it would do you."

Mallory jumped out on the bobbing float and made for the ladder. Blake caught a glimpse of him on the plank runway overhead, bending into the wind, with the light from his electric torch moving slowly in front of him along the wet plank.

"Watch your step, doc," he yelled and then went back to the launch.

It was five hours later when the door of a weather-beaten shack on the trestle between the jetty and the sandhills opened and two men stood silhouetted in the doorway against the lamplight within.

"I won't argue with you, Dr. Mallory. But I know she'd never have made it if you hadn't been here."

"Nonsense, Jake! I didn't do it. You're either strong enough to pull through or you're not. When the flu strikes to kill, I can't stop it. Why, man, I've had over three hundred deaths in this epidemic." Mallory laughed shortly.

The other man tried to laugh too, but the sound he made was more like a sob.

"Have it your own way, doctor. But when you stepped in here last night I felt something that had been hanging over us all day go out. I knew then she wouldn't die."

Mallory struck his chest and took a long breath.

"Well, I must be on my way, Jake. The Haven's still full. I'll send down a refill of that one prescription tomorrow." He screwed up his face and looked at the sky. "Storm's quieted down, but it might blow up again. Good-by, Jake."

"Good-by, doctor. Be careful now. It's easy to go off the jetty before it's full daylight."

The wind had died down and the rain had ceased, but everything swam together in the dim light of early morning. Mallory tried to recall how long it was since he had been in bed. Was it twenty-four hours or forty-eight or longer? He gave up the effort.

It was queer how his legs acted. The instant he took his mind off them, they stopped. Aloud he chanted, "Right foot, left foot, right foot, left," but the old jingle had lost its potency. Nothing would do but to watch them. Mallory fastened a stern gaze on his unreliable feet, picking them up and setting them down in turn.

It was a long way back to the landing, much farther than it had been last night in the storm. But that was ridiculous. The fault of his legs, of course. Mallory plodded doggedly on.

Through the framework of the jetty he could see the water splashing over jagged rocks. It wasn't far down there. The rocks looked almost inviting. He would like to lie down and go to sleep. He didn't want to go anywhere to see any one who was ill or look at any one dying. He wanted to go to bed and sleep. Sleep, not watch a pair of silly feet that went on and on and never got anywhere.

Once, he seemed to remember vaguely, he had come in tired and gone to bed with his head on a pillow beside Katherine's. Her hair had touched his face; it was soft and it smelled sweet. But—queerly—it was not dark; it was ruddy red-gold and firelight flickered on it and on wide gray eyes. Not Katherine's hair. Not Katherine's eyes. Jean's!

At the edge of the walkway above the float he stopped and looked down. Then he heard a shout and, glancing up, saw Henry waving to him from the anchored launch. He raised an arm in answer.

"I'm ready," he called out.

Then a vise closed on his chest. He could feel it squeezing the life out of him. He tried to cry out, but before he could utter a sound emptiness engulfed him. For an instant longer his figure was etched against the gray sky, then it plunged downward and thudded wetly on the landing below.

CHAPTER VII

I

Over The Haven brooded stillness spawned of fear.

In a room that looked down over the village Dr. Mallory lay battered and unconscious. Under a week's growth of beard his face was pale and haggard, and one arm was in a metal splint. His head rolled back and forth upon the pillow and from his mouth came an intermittent, incoherent mumbling.

Softly Norman Reilly stole into the room. He took Mallory's blood pressure and temperature, counted his pulse, listened to his heart sounds, and adjusted the splints on his broken arm. Now and then Mallory's eyes would light up with a gleam of half-rationality. Once he licked his dry crusted lips and Reilly winced when he put a drinking tube in his mouth and saw how hard it was for him to swallow.

"I think," said Norman to Mrs. Hathaway, "that it's one of the small branches of the coronary that's involved. Otherwise Bob wouldn't be alive. If he can only pull through the next ten days or two weeks he may come out in pretty fair shape after all. He's young for coronary disease."

"He wouldn't stop, Dr. Reilly. He'd been going on coffee and whisky for a week before this happened and he hadn't been to bed for four nights when he went down to the jetty." The nurse's voice suddenly became harsh. "The engineer's wife a silly little flibbergibbet! She wasn't worth it. . . . What about Dr. Mallory's health if he does come out of this attack? Will he be an invalid?"

"No, I think not. He'll never be able to work as he always has, of course." Reilly's face was very grave. "But that won't matter, Mrs. H. I'll be here and you and I can carry on and let Bob take it easy, can't we?"

Mrs. Hathaway's eyes filled with tears.

"Oh, it's been terrible here this fall, Dr. Reilly. Death going up and down the house, striking first one and then another. Just as though he marked those that were to go from the beginning. If the doctor should die, I couldn't bear it."

In the flabbiness of her lips and the quavering of her voice, Reilly saw how near collapse the woman was. He took her by the arm and led her away.

"Listen to me, Mrs. H. He isn't going to die. And now you're going to bed, if I have to undress you and tuck you in myself. Bob didn't have any sleep for four days before he blew up and you haven't had any for the week since Blake brought him home. Come on. I'm giving the orders in this hospital now."

After Mrs. Hathaway had gone to her room Reilly went out to stand on the porch alone and look at the forbidding wet green mountains which all about him lifted their crests against a leaden sky. The grayness of rain shrouded them and the wind moaned among the firs. Reilly stared up at the low clouds scudding before the gale, and flung defiance at fate.

"He isn't going to die! I won't let him! He still has something to do in the world!"

In the mornings after an anxious question about Mallory, Sairy fled to the kitchen to bury her dread for him in broth and custards. Reilly, thin and pale from his own bout with influenza in Chicago before his return to Glenwood, grew less and less debonair, but still carried his flat back defiantly erect. Mrs. Hathaway seemed to have turned into an old woman in a week and Alice Blake's pale skin became waxen with worry. Jean's cheeks faded and even her freckles seemed less conspicuous.

"My God, Reilly," burst out Henry Blake one day as he left The Haven, "how long can this thing last? Doc'll have to get well or die pretty soon, won't he?"

"I know it seems an age to all of us but on the calendar it is just ten days now since his attack, and it's this second week that is the most dangerous. The heart muscle may rupture or a blood clot may be swept up into the brain now. It's this stupor persisting so long that worries me most. That's a bad sign, but don't tell the women I said so."

Striding away in the rain to the post office where each morning a group waited for news, Henry swore loudly and profusely.

"This God damn flu! A man's as helpless with it as he is in one of these cock-eyed southwest gales. Why couldn't that bastard Burton's heart've gone haywire instead of doc's? But no, he gets well, damn his soul!" Blake put his thumbs and middle fingers tip-to-tip in a circle. "He ain't so fat since he was sick. I could choke the son of a bitch—easy!"

II

Lying in his bed Mallory sometimes opened vacant blue eyes and stared up at the ceiling. But the fitful gleams of reason that crossed his face always faded rapidly again into the lacklustre of coma. Now and then his mouth twisted as if in pain. Days and nights dragged past with dull monotony.

Through Mallory's disordered brain there flitted swarms of fantasies and shadowy figures, dreams of other days and fragments of the present. An angular woman with stringy mouse-brown hair wept unendingly over a room full of imbecile children all of whom looked exactly like Juanita. Another woman, sometimes young and sometimes old, carried about a glass tube and tried to force it down their throats. A broad brown man blew his nose resoundingly and then it turned out that it was a trumpet and not his nose at all. Then there was a company of big brown men who lined up on the stairs of the old hospital and blew trumpets in unison.

A vaguely familiar figure in golden brown with a flaring collar behind her head walked up and down. Sometimes she sang and sometimes there came with her the sound of a piano. She often spoke to him but so softly he could not catch the words. Her hair changed from black to gold, her eyes from brown to gray; her voice became husky and choked with laughter. Over and over she changed; sometimes she drifted slowly downstairs between the trumpeters, dark, and reached the sidewalk fair.

There was a small boy who sat on a horse block in front of a huge refrigerator full of bodies. And there came a muffled putt-putting which the small boy knew the preacher would tell him was the morning stars singing together. That was it. The music of the stars. But somehow the small boy knew it was an engine, an engine in a boat—on the river—on the Silticoos.

The boy was going somewhere—in a boat. On a long journey among the stars that sang together. At great speed he flashed past the planets, sped beyond the sun, and circled the universe. It was curved after all, just as the professors had said. It was like an empty orange and he was running round and round on the inside of it. He was always upside down. The middle was always below him. He never got anywhere, not even back to the place he started from. It was his feet. They wouldn't go unless he watched them. The damned feet, always tired. "Right foot, left foot, right foot, left," he chanted.

And besides the feet, there was a body too. Sometimes it was near and sometimes far away, but he couldn't get rid of it. It was fastened to him like one of those iron weights they used to tie to the bridles of the horses on ice wagons. Tied to him somehow, and always slow and always tired.

He could see it lying below him at an infinite distance. It was ugly and bruised and thick around the middle; its face was vacant and covered with whiskers; its lips flapped weakly in and out. He had had enough of that body. It was worn out. Why not cut it loose, leave it behind? It was only a burden. But the body clung to the bond that bound him to it. It remembered things, it clung fast.

He heard music again. Chopin, Etude.... The stars sang and the big brown men blew their trumpets and an orchestra played "There's a long, long trail." He danced with the girl who was first dark and then fair. He stooped to look into her eyes. When they were brown they were beautiful, and when they were gray they were kind and full of fun.

Then he saw creeping up behind her a bloated loathsome beast. It was coming from the darkness between the worlds. It meant to take the girl from him. It fell upon him, bore him down, crushed him. It cast a band about him, pulled it tighter and tighter, squeezed out his breath. The open spaces between the stars were suddenly filled with rocks and planks and foaming surf. He was falling, falling, and the monster was clinging to him, falling with him.

He clutched at its hideous hairy throat, sank his desperate fingers into it. The beast arched its enormous body over him and dropped down on him. The weight was too great, his strength was failing. The brute raised itself again, twisted away from his clawing fingers, then wrapped itself around him, smothering him, choking him. He screamed in agony.

There was crackling, roaring in his ears. The music died away. Darkness came. Then a crackling noise. God—broadcasting over the cosmic wave length!

From around a corner the beast grinned at him. It had a wave of dark hair over its forehead and its teeth were yellow. There was a bottle in its hand. Something went stinging and burning down his throat. "Burton," he gasped. The beast slunk away, but as it went it flicked its tail once more over his heart. His muscles cramped and twitched.

Haunting music again. The trumpeters of elfland blew softly in his ears. Elfland. But these men were too big for elves. Their voices told him to sleep, to think no more, to try no longer. But the bond that had been slowly loosening suddenly tautened.

It pulled him back. There was a blinding rush through space. Time-space. Space-time.

He flew down toward the body in bed. He spiraled over the smooth inner surface of the empty orange. Now he was in the stratosphere. Why was it empty? Where had the girl gone? A door in another hollow orange flew open and a curly-haired man looked out. A professor of physics? No, it had turned into Norman Reilly. He said, "You're all right, Bob. I'm here."

Then he was back in Henry's boat on the river. It was dark and the water was rough. A storm was blowing. "Doc, I can't make the far landin'." The trumpet was in the way of the steering wheel. What was Henry doing, chewing tobacco and spitting in a trumpet?

Gray eyes again, red-gold hair, silvery tears on his face. Tears! Straining with all his strength Mallory lifted his eyelids. The stars were gone and the monster and the music and the trumpeters. But the girl was there; her gray eyes full of tears were above him.

He wanted to speak, to tell her not to cry, but his throat was too stiff. His lips wavered into a tiny smile. He tried again to tell her he had come back, but only a squeak issued from his mouth. He let his eyelids close and clasped his fingers on the thin freckled hand that lay beside his. Then he slept.

III

That day for the first time in weeks, the sun rose clear. Its golden light splashed into the room where Jean Stuart sat by Mallory's bed, afraid to withdraw her hand from his white fingers lest she wake him. Reilly looked down soberly at the pale, thin face on the pillow, then smiled across the bed at Jean and nodded.

Other people too slept that day. The crest of the epidemic was past, half the beds in The Haven were empty, and the remaining patients were convalescent. The tension over Mallory broken, Mrs. Hathaway and Alice Blake and Reilly all slept behind drawn blinds.

Down in the village Henry Blake rushed about with the

good news. Everyone seemed glad. Even Burton said, "Gee, Henry, that's the best thing I heard since doc told me I wasn't goin' to die."

Since his illness the druggist was no longer pudgy, but although his face was thin it had gained no spirituality. Blake scowled at him, thinking 'Damn it, man, don't you ever say anything without puttin' a stinger in it?'

He hurried on to the post office, the telephone exchange, the barber shop, and the pool hall. Otto Schmidt looked up anxiously from dusting the shelves back of his cigar counter when Blake came in.

"Doc's outa the woods this mornin', Otto."

Schmidt beamed with his whole good-natured red face. "Gosh, Henry, and ain't I glad to hear you say that? I thought sure he was goin' to die."

"So did all the rest of us too," said Blake soberly.

"Did I hear you sayin' Doc Mallory's better?" drawled a tall, thin man in the ring of idlers around Schmidt's heating stove. Nate Simmons' voice had lost none of its whine since the night, eighteen years before, when Mallory had operated on his father in the shack up-river. Both Henry and Otto turned their backs and went on talking to each other as Simmons approached them.

"Don't you think we'd oughta get up a celebration for when Doc gets up and around again, Henry?"

"Just what I been thinkin' about, Otto. You kinda sound out the boys comin' in here and I'll do the same at my end of town."

"I'll just do that. Mallory pulled a lot of people through this flu." Schmidt resumed his dusting. "And he deserves a real celebration for it. I guess there ain't a better doctor in Oregon than he is."

"Oh, I don't know about that, Otto." The tall man with the whining voice put a greasy elbow on the cigar case. "There was a lot of folks died on the river too. I guess some of the docs down in Baypoint could show Mallory a thing or two. As I look at it, this man Mallory's not so hot. I ain't forgot him bullyin' me into lettin' him operate on pap when he first come here. He's never satisfied with anything, he's always wantin' everything different than what it is. And look at that big place of his'n up on the hill. Where'd he get the money to build it and buy all them fancy gadgets that's no mortal use? Why, he's been takin' that money outa the people in this valley for nearly twenty years. That's where he got it."

"I bet it ain't much he got out of you, Nate Simmons," retorted Schmidt, all the geniality gone from his face. "I don't know how much you owe Doc Mallory but I bet it's plenty. And so long's you're talkin' so big, just fork over for that last box of stogies you got off me."

A shout of laughter went up from the loafers. Nate Simmons, discomfited, began going through his pockets with a show of surprise.

"Why, I don't know if I got the change with me right now," he said.

Schmidt leaned across the counter, his face red and threatening.

"Then get out and get it and don't come back here no more without it! I'm sick of you bellyachin' and raisin' hell in my place. I don't want you around here no more."

"Better you run, Nate," advised a man in the circle of idlers. "Otto'll take off his wooden leg and lam you in the head with it pretty quick."

Simmons departed with more haste than dignity. Schmidt glared after him.

"That guy makes me sick!" he declared. "Spongin' on everybody all his life and always kickin' them that give him the most. I bet you he goes straight down to Burton's to tell him what was said in here just now."

"Oh, sure. He and Burton are good pals," said the man who had advised Simmons to leave. "Two of a kind. Did you hear what Burton's up to now? . . . Well, he's raising the bills for medicine put up while he and his wife were out of the store sick, so that the folks that got well will have to pay for them that died."

"Why, that dirty low-life!" cried Blake. "Jean Stuart and Doc fixed all the drugs and stuff for a month while he was sick. And he thinks he can pull a stunt like that!"

"My friend, he doesn't think so, he's already done so," rejoined the other.

Otto Schmidt looked at Henry's furious face.

"Now, now! Don't you pay that guy Burton no attention, Henry. He ain't worth it. And Simmons is worse'n Burton. But there's a lot of the rest of us that is for Doc, don't you forget that."

Blake paused when he reached his own front gate and looked up at The Haven on the hill. Its windows were glittering in the winter sunlight. Slowly the anger died out of the man's eyes and the old waggish look took its place. He threw out his chest and drew in a deep breath of sweet clean air.

"By gum, I ain't felt so fine since last summer." Ruminatively he bit off a bite of plug tobacco and began to chew. "Guess I'd better get busy and clean up the house some. Alice will maybe be comin' down home to-night. That won't be so bad either. I had about enough of bein' a bachelor."

On his way across the lawn he stopped to deposit a mouthful of tobacco juice on a low-lying weed, then smacked his lips. It was the first time tobacco had tasted better than sawdust for a month.

He opened his front door and went into the deserted living room. 'Might as well be a flop-house when Alice ain't here.' While he gathered together broom and mop and dustpan he was thinking of Otto Schmidt's suggestion for celebrating Mallory's recovery. This was the time to start such a project, while people were still chastened by the deaths of relatives and friends and their recent fears for their own lives. Once let them forget and they would be as ungrateful as Simmons and Burton.

'I'll just talk it over with Reilly and Jean and Otto some more and see what Alice thinks. Maybe between us we can stampede these folks into doin' something decent for doc and The Haven.'

CHAPTER VIII

I

On a winter day when there were but three patients left in The Haven and Mallory was sitting up in his bed reading *The Modern Hospital*, Mrs. Hathaway found Sairy flushed and feverish.

"You should have let me know as soon as you felt ill," she rebuked the cook gently.

Sairy's red face became distressed.

"Aw, now, Mrs. H. I just kinda thought I'd lay down this afternoon. I'll be okay by evenin'. It's just my back that aches so bad."

"You're to go straight to bed, Sairy. Here, slip this under your tongue and close your lips on it. I want to see how much fever you have. Then I'll ask Dr. Reilly to examine you."

"Aw, now, Mrs. H.," mumbled Sairy in protest, out of the corner of her mouth. "Don't you go to bother him. I ain't really sick; just my back aches and I'm tired all over and my head feels funny." A fit of shivering stopped her talk.

Later in the day Mrs. Hathaway discussed with Reilly the advisability of concealing Sairy's illness from Mallory.

"If he gets on his feet now, Mrs. H., he's simply inviting disaster. It takes seven or eight weeks at least for the heart muscle to build a strong fibrous scar that will hold."

"But if anything happens to Sairy, he'll never forgive me."

"I'll assume all responsibility. Bob is worth more than a dozen Sairys."

Preoccupied with cost sheets and hospital reports Mallory did not miss Sairy's usual evening visit, but the next day when he requested a special omelet she had often prepared for him during his convalescence and it came in an utter failure he asked, "What's wrong? Sairy lost the art?" Mrs. Hathaway's floundering answer aroused his suspicion.

"What's the matter? Has Sairy gone away, or is she sick?"

At this moment Reilly put his head in the door. "Phone, Mrs. H." Then he went on airily, "What are you two fussing about?"

As she left the room the nurse shot him a warning glance which Mallory noticed. He pulled himself up straighter in bed and looked sharply at Reilly.

"What are you trying to put over on me, Norman? Where is Sairy? Is she sick?"

"What put that notion in your head, Bob?" parried Reilly. "Surely Sairy can have a day off if she likes. Don't you think she rates a holiday?"

"Sairy is sick. I know it," said Mallory quickly. "She's got the flu."

"Now, listen, Bob. Keep your shirt on." In his own mind Reilly could see the woman tossing in the nightmare of fever but he stuck to his story. "She had a little temperature yesterday and Mrs. H. had her go to bed. That's all. It's nothing serious, old boy."

Mallory turned an accusing pair of blue eyes upon Mrs. Hathaway as she reëntered the room.

"When did she take sick?" he asked.

"Yesterday." The nurse made no further attempt at evasion.

"I found her with a backache and fever early in the afternoon."

"And you two were going to keep quiet about it so I wouldn't know? . . . I suppose you've got a chart for her. . . . Well, bring it to me right away. I want to find out the truth about this."

"Bob," cried Reilly, "this is all my fault. Mrs. H. wanted to tell you in the first place and I wouldn't let her. But I've examined Sairy carefully, gone over her chest and X-rayed her. It's ordinary flu. She's toxic but she hasn't got pneumonia. Can't you trust me to handle one case for you?" There was desperate urgency in the man's voice and a trace of bitterness. "Don't you think I know enough? You mustn't get out of bed now."

Mallory put a hand on his arm.

"I'd trust you, Norman, with my own life or Sairy's. It isn't that. But Sairy needs me now, not as a doctor but as a friend. We've gone through things together and I can make her fight better than you can."

Mrs. Hathaway came in with the clinical chart.

"Temperature 103.6. Pulse 132. Toxic is right, Norman. Did you say you X-rayed her chest last night or this morning? . . . Well, we'd better do it again this afternoon. It's astonishing how fast these people develop lung lesions." Mallory overruled all objections. "Bring me my stethoscope, Mrs. H. I won't dress— just slip on my bathrobe. And I'll ride in a wheel chair if you like. But I must go and see Sairy."

When they reëxamined her chest that afternoon and compared the new X-ray film with the earlier one, Mallory looked very serious.

"I'm afraid, Norman. She's blue already and her lungs are water-logged. And here on the right there's beginning consolidation. Besides, I've had a hunch—from the start."

Mrs. Hathaway nodded sadly.

"I know, doctor. I've had one too. Poor Sairy."

Mallory pushed his wheel chair over to the big south window in the waiting room and looked down over the huddled houses of the village.

"Mrs. H. and Sairy and I started out here together over

eighteen years ago. And now, when it looks as though our troubles were over, this has to happen! But I'm not going to let her go without a fight."

This last outcropping of the influenza was deadly. On the third day, forty-eight hours after Mrs. Hathaway put her to bed, Sairy was comatose. Her lips were dusky blue and her eyes were glazed and shiny. The breath bubbled through her water-filled lungs. Sometimes in a choked voice she babbled of Juanita but oftener she mumbled only disconnected and unintelligible words. Slowly her blood pressure fell and the fluid crept higher in her lungs, filling the air cells with watery exudate.

At her bedside Mallory and Mrs. Hathaway and Reilly watched by turns, giving stimulants, injecting sugar solution into her veins, manipulating the oxygen tent. Her body responded, it seemed to clamor for life; every cell clung tenaciously to existence and every fiber of heart muscle beat stubbornly on.

All the while Reilly followed Mallory with anxious eyes. Over and over he explained to Jean Stuart and the Blakes how the softened muscle in the wall of the heart, now in the midst of a repair process, must assume the load Mallory was putting on it by his physical exertion and anxiety over Sairy. That thin layer of fibrous tissue, he told them, was their only hope. Would it hold? They looked at each other with dread-filled eyes.

On the fourth day of the malignant disease Sairy's relatives, summoned at Mallory's orders, came and stood stupidly in a row staring now at the unconscious woman in the bed and now at the stern-faced man in the wheel chair beside her. When they had spread the news that death was but a matter of hours, the people of Glenwood once more found Sairy an engrossing topic of conversation.

Completely unconscious of their own fickleness, they told each other that she was the real heroine of the epidemic. Forgetting Mrs. Hathaway and Alice Blake and the other nurses, they said that Sairy had played the noblest because the obscurest part. Now she was about to pay for her heroism with her life. There were some who suggested that kindness had been long overdue her. Otto Schmidt said boldly that Mallory was the only person in the valley who had always treated the woman decently. Approaching death having thus cast a mantle of glamor over her, Sairy Paine was for the first time in her life discussed by her fellow townsmen with neither obscenity nor ill temper.

II

"The hospital meetin' tonight'll seem kinda flat if Sairy dies, won't it?" asked the kindly Schmidt, leaning across his cigar case to speak to the small group of loafers smoking about his stove.

"It sure will," agreed a man who seemed to be spokesman for the idlers. "But I guess Henry couldn't put it off after she got sick, when he'd sent out all the notices and everything."

"No, the cards went up-river Tuesday mornin' and Sairy wasn't taken with the flu till afternoon, the way I heard it," said Schmidt.

The door opened and Burton bustled in.

"Say, Otto, can you let me have a box of them Juan de Fuca secundos? I'll return 'em just as soon's my next order gets here. It's due day after tomorrow. Not often I get caught short like this but I sure miscalculated the trade this time."

"Why, yes, I guess I can accommodate you," answered Schmidt, but his voice had none of its usual genial quality. He creaked off on his peg-leg toward his stock room.

The spokesman of the group about the stove winked at his companions and called out, "How are you making out on your collections for the flu, Burton? Having a hard time, doctoring up the books so you can make up your losses out of them that got well?"

The druggist flushed and bristled with anger.

"That'll be enough outa you, Jake Whitney," he said in a trembling voice. "You got no kick comin'."

Whitney grinned broadly at the men around him.

"No, I know that. But it's because I kept a record of all the medicine Dr. Mallory sent down to me and gave you a check for the exact amount. I know you of old, Burton. And don't forget you gave me a receipt marked 'paid in full.' You know you ought to tear up all those phoney sheets in your ledger if you want to keep out of trouble." Whitney's voice took on a dangerous smoothness. "And I want to tell you something else. If you don't come through with a decent subscription to the hospital fund at the meeting to-night, I'll get up and tell the audience what you're trying to put over on them with these accounts. Figure out for yourself how much you'll collect after that."

Burton turned pale and ran an uneasy finger around the inside of his shirt collar. From the group beside the stove, eleven pairs of hard level eyes watched him.

"Now, boys, I don't want you to get me wrong. I was only jokin' about them accounts for medicine that Doc Mallory and Miss Stuart sent out." But the twenty-two eyes did not waver or show any amusement. "Jake, you wouldn't take advantage of me, would you? I'm not well yet myself and I lost a lot of business bein' away from the store like I was. I'm willin' to do anything reasonable but…"

"Well, the only reasonable subscription you can make to the hospital fund in my opinion," said Whitney, enjoying the perturbation on Burton's face, "is five hundred dollars." Burton gasped but Whitney did not pause. "Or more. I might change my mind in the next few hours and raise the ante, of course." The druggist, white as his shirt collar, scuttled toward the door but his tormentor called after him, "If you don't show up at the meeting I'll spill the works just the same."

The men about the stove shouted with laughter as Burton slammed the door behind him.

"Well, I never!" exclaimed Otto Schmidt coming out of the stockroom with the box of cigars he had gone after. "What's eatin' him not to wait for this? Something must've happened to him."

"Something did," said Whitney. "And the rest of it will happen to-night in the Odd Fellows' Hall, Otto, about half-past-eight. You want to be there."

III

It was nearly nine o'clock when Alice Blake and Jean slipped into the Odd Fellows' Hall and sat down in extra chairs placed along the side wall of the room. Norman Reilly quietly joined them.

"There's no change," whispered Jean to him. "Dr. Mallory said to tell you not to hurry back."

Reilly nodded and settled himself beside her.

Mrs. Blake watched his handsome blond head turn bit by bit until he could keep his eyes on Jean while apparently watching the platform at the end of the room. The girl's high fur collar stood up about her throat so that only the crown of her red-gold hair appeared above it in the back. Reilly's emotions were betrayed by his face because he thought he was unobserved. Alice found herself wondering whether Jean might prefer him to Mallory. He was, after all, a very attractive man and a very intelligent and companionable one.

Then she tore her eyes off Reilly and looked about the crowded hall. Except for two Sunday services in the church, this was the first large public gathering since early October. There were many gaps in the familiar ranks: Olaf Hansen, Tom Painter, Rob Simmons, Nellie Doan, Mrs. Spaulding, Clifford Sidney, and many others were gone. Alice searched the rows of faces for the softening she hoped to see and saw Almira Doan's bright red head only a half-dozen places away. The woman's face seemed as arrogant and self-righteous as ever. Alice sighed. Henry said Nellie was better off dead and to-night she was inclined to agree with him.

"You aren't paying any attention to the speeches," whispered Reilly in her ear under cover of a scattered applause. "They're clapping because Doan stopped talking. He is, beyond all doubt, the most dried-up man on earth."

Alice reflected that this was the very argument Henry had always advanced as a reason for doubting Nellie's paternity. Then, with difficulty, she reclaimed her errant thoughts, for Jacob Whitney, the jetty engineer, was getting up.

"I'm no orator," he began. "But I've got something to say to you people. I want to talk about Dr. Mallory. If he hadn't come down to the jetty after I sent for him he might never have been sick. He hadn't slept for four nights, hadn't laid down or had his clothes off for ninety-six hours. I sent for him because my wife had been desperately sick all day. I was there alone with her—you know we couldn't get help during the epidemic—and I watched her hour after hour, choking, barely able to breathe, turning that awful purple the flu patients got. I was terrified. I was sure she was going to die. All day I could feel something in the room with us, something awful, horrifying.

"Then about midnight, Dr. Mallory got there. And that thing that had been there all day went out, beaten, when he came in. It was death!"

Over the crowd there passed the sound of many quick-drawn breaths.

"I'd always liked Mallory, always thought he was honest and capable. But I'd never realized, before, all he could do. I owe him my wife's life and my own. Most of the rest of you owe him the same sort of thing—your own lives or the lives of some of your family. We can't pay debts like those. But we can pay Mallory the money we owe him, and we can raise a fund that will let him know we appreciate what he's done for us.

"I've heard people around here calling him a failure because he went bankrupt a few weeks ago. But I want to tell you that, if he's a failure, then the thing that's wrong with Glenwood is that it's not full of failures. I wish to God I was that kind of a failure!

"You people can't pay Dr. Mallory for what he's done for you any more than I can. He's worked for you winter and summer, ridden the river in storms and at night, walked and gone horseback into the hills and the upper valley. He's brought your children into the world and he's stood by when people died. He's listened to your troubles and given you advice and told you not to worry about his bills. He's fought death and disease for eighteen years on the Silticoos and with mighty little help from any of us.

"And to-night he's up in The Haven with Sairy Paine. Nobody else in Glenwood was ever kind to Sairy, nobody else ever cared what became of her. But Mallory cares. He's still fighting for her. He's taken his life in his hands to get up out of bed and look after her. But I guess he's used to that; he's risked his life so many times he don't think much about it.

"I tell you he's a great man, a great doctor! We've never realized it before, but now that we do let's prove it to him. Let's make up for all the nasty things we've said about him, and done to him. Let's make up for the times we went away from home to other doctors we had to pay in spot cash while Mallory waited for his money, the times we wouldn't believe him or do what he told us to. Now that his partner, Dr. Reilly, has cleared The Haven of all debts and promised to finance this health insurance plan and the community hospital until it's on its feet, let's us all get behind Mallory and him. Let's say what's on our minds in cash, so they'll both know we mean it. Are you with me?"

There was an outburst of clapping, and voices called out, "Sure we are!" "Atta boy!" "Go to it, Jake!"

Whitney turned toward the platform where Samuel Doan, somewhat embarrassed by this show of sentiment, stood uncertainly behind his desk.

"Mr. Chairman, I would like nothing better than to head the subscription list myself." There was a subtle change in the engineer's voice. "But only this forenoon Mr. Burton said to me that he insisted on being the first subscriber."

Alice Blake was puzzled both by the queer note that replaced the passionate sincerity of Whitney's earlier words and by this announcement. Could the druggist really have had a change of heart? But Whitney was hurrying on.

"Not only do Mr. and Mrs. Burton owe their lives to Dr. Mallory, but during their illness the doctor and Miss Jean Stuart carried on the prescription business. Mr. Burton assures me that they kept such accurate accounts of all medicine dispensed that he will have very little loss from the prescription work while he was ill and out of his store."

Hearing a commotion behind her, Alice Blake turned and saw Burton, white-faced and thin, struggling to attract the attention of the chairman. A man beside Whitney whispered something to the engineer and he sat down.

"Mr. Doan," cried Burton in a trembling voice, "Mr. Chairman, I mean. I want to subscribe five"…he swallowed hard…"five hundred dollars to the hospital fund for the comin' year." The silence of utter astonishment seized the crowd. Burton gulped and went on. "Doc Mallory done a lot for me this fall. Like Jake Whitney just said, he saved me and my wife from dyin' with the flu. And then he and Miss Stuart tended to the prescriptions while I was outa the store. Of course, there ain't hardly any profit any more in prescriptions, but they gotta be tended to." The druggist paused and seemed to gather himself for a supreme effort. "And I want to announce that I'm goin' to cancel every account for medicine they put up for flu patients in my store. That includes refunds to them that have already paid their bills."

When Burton sank into his chair, no one made a sound. The audience was stunned. Burton's avarice had been a byword for twenty-seven years, and this sudden reversal of attitude overwhelmed his fellow citizens.

But after a few seconds of dead stillness, Jacob Whitney sprang up and shouted, "Atta boy, Burton. And I'll put two hundred with that. Now come on, everybody. Let's go."

There was a roar of hand clapping and whistling. Lean little Mr. Doan pounded his table with the gavel, but to no purpose. Bedlam was upon him.

Henry Blake slid quietly among the excited, gesticulating, shouting crowd and sat down beside his wife.

"It was the only way we could put it over," he whispered. "They're a mob, and you got to handle 'em accordingly. But what we can get out of 'em here to-night will do 'em more good than all the other money they ever saw in their lives put together."

IV

While the mass meeting at the Odd Fellows' Hall, swept by mob spirit, was pledging support to The Haven as a community project, Mallory and Mrs. Hathaway sat watching at Sairy's bedside. Once more death hovered close at hand.

Sairy clung to Mallory's fingers. She had come to the last adventure, she would soon find the answer to that riddle which puzzles every man. There was no reason to be sad: here life had nothing to give her, but on the other side there might be hope even for Sairy.

As night drew on she slipped slowly away and when her last tortured breath hissed through her purple lips they were already stiffening. Gently Mallory slid his hand out of the one that only a minute before had still clutched it feebly.

He wheeled himself from the room and paused before the broad front window in the lobby. Wind had broken up the clouds. Fugitive moonlight came and went upon the water. Below him lights twinkled from many windows. Glenwood, he knew, was unchanged; to-morrow it would be as dirty and cruel and intolerant as ever. But yet to-night it seemed different.

Clouds were scudding across the winter sky, now concealing and now revealing the stars between them. Moonlight was kind to the village, turned it into a brightly lighted outpost of human life in the universe, and made the river a broad lambent band of quicksilver.

With a new lucidity Mallory looked back over his years in Glenwood and saw that behind men and the something they call God there are two great immortalities—truth and beauty. To serve them and keep them always before one's eyes was all that was worth doing. The man who did this could not be lost even though he died. Sairy was dead, but she was not lost. In the last weeks of her existence she had found all she had missed before—loyalty, faith, devotion to a cause. And these—the best part of her—could never die.

Mallory found himself ready to go back to life. He was poor

and obscure, he knew he was likely always to be so. But he was not alone: there was Reilly to help him, to carry on if anything happened to him. Reilly and Rachel Hathaway and Jean Stuart and the Blakes. Back of them he saw the third eternal thing he must add to the other two—love.

The sudden disappearance of the lights in the Odd Fellows' Hall downtown attracted his attention. The meeting to call for public support for The Haven which had once seemed so important shrank into insignificance compared with what had happened that night in the hospital. But he remembered that Jean and Alice and Henry and Norman would be coming up to inquire after Sairy, and then he noticed that the floodlight on the porch was not on. Both he and Mrs. Hathaway had forgotten it.

Deliberately he rose from his chair and walked outside. It was good to be on his feet again, and smell the clean damp night, to feel cool air on his flushed cheeks and draw it deep into his lungs. Life was suddenly good again.

He straightened his wide shoulders, turned toward the light switch and put out his hand. In that instant something inside his chest seemed to burst and a great iron fist closed about his heart. His hand dropped. A moment longer and he toppled against the wall. His shoulder, falling, struck the switch and pushed it down, then slid slowly to the floor.

Above this somber dead thing the beacon of The Haven flashed on.

THE END

NORTHWEST COLLECTION TITLES

*The Northwest Collection is an ongoing series of titles that represent the
rich literary history of the Pacific Northwest, published in editions featuring
introductions and insights from contemporary writers. All Northwest Collection
titles can be purchased at www.propellerbooks.com*

Sheila Evans The Northport Stories
Alan Hart The Undaunted
Evan P. Schneider A Simple Machine, Like the Lever
Mary Rechner Nine Simple Patterns for Complicated Women
Ticasuk The Roots of Ticasuk
Alan Hart Doctor Mallory

www.ingramcontent.com/pod-product-compliance
Lightning Source LLC
Chambersburg PA
CBHW061631190726
48289CB00006B/1563